D. HALE RAMBO

FRAYED EDGES

THE PLANAR PAGES

Contents

To my dog Griffin: Oof you were really distracting for this one buddy. I will miss your hatred of my laptop. And, I'll try to remember to take breaks and chase bunnies as often as I can. No one knew how to get me to step away from work like you did, boo. Thank you.

FIONA COULDN'T REMEMBER WHEN she had been more surprised in all of her life. There was, of course, the time that she learned about the endless ocean beneath the floating islands in Rise and the fact that *no one* had traveled to them. She was also surprised when she learned that her long-time mother figure, Mac, was the vanished Summer Monarch of *all* faekin and the entire Court of Copper page. That truly seemed the news that would take her breath away this year. But Richard's answer to what nonsense he had been doing instead of continuing to kiss her truly took the cake.

She had followed him from the Forlorn Tower fireplace to his bedchamber at the palace using the book he had left behind. Him in the midst of frantic activity and her in the midst of resolute frustration. To believe that he was trying to get back to work after leaving her so abruptly! But then he had kissed her again, and she was preparing to make amends when the world had gone gray and wobbly. Now, sitting on a wooden stool in the Thorn Palace archives, she wondered if even the kiss had been real. Or any of the feelings he had mentioned before he so rudely extracted himself from her. But his answer still rattled in her mind.

Fiona focused her gaze on him. "Your brother? You said he died."

Richard winced. "I didn't say that."

"You certainly implied it!" She crossed her arms and took a step toward him. "Why in Larrakane's name would you be guarding against your brother?"

"Let's focus on the real question. How do you keep remembering what I say and do?" Richard countered. He ran a hand through his golden-red hair, leaving it in disarray.

She hadn't the faintest idea, but she never let not knowing a thing stop her when she was intent on getting answers. She pursed her lips and took another step toward him, closing the distance. Warmth radiated off him, but his expression was that of a guilty suspect.

"That's beside the point," she said. "How does making books guard anything?" She shook her head, the edges of fuzziness ebbing away. He had seemed so surprised when she recognized him. "Were you trying to do something with my memory?"

"Yes!" Richard threw up his hands. "And your stubbornness about it is starting to worry me. First you, then Hawkport. You two are shielded against me in a way I can't begin to understand. I've not run into anyone who remembers what I don't want them to." He slid around her.

Fiona grabbed his arm, gently stopping his retreat. "Richard."

He sighed, shoulders slumped, but remained silent.

She wanted to give him a moment, but if she did, he would close up. She was sure of it. Fiona ran her fingers down his arm softly. "You can make people remember specific things?"

"Or forget. When what they remember is dangerous." He glanced back at her over his shoulder, seemingly unable to meet her eyes. "But you never forget. Blessed by Larrakane herself. Must be."

Fiona snorted at the unlikely assertation. "If it doesn't work on me and Hawkport, there must be a connection." Her brain started ticking. She was a page turner, lived on Spine, and was among the most diverse group of people in the Book. He was a noble who, for all she knew, never left the page except perhaps on a holiday. She'd have to figure out exactly why Richard's power didn't work on them both. Besides being human, they were very unalike. That is, if Hawkport was completely human. He had been "cousins" with Stella, and while Fiona thought that was simply a trick on Stella's part, one couldn't be too sure. "What about nonhumans?"

Richard shook his head, golden-red locks tussling. "Works on them too." He added under his breath, "Thankfully." He withdrew from Fiona slowly and walked back to the printing press. He began tampering with it as if that was the end of the conversation.

For Fiona it was not. There was so much here, so much to unpack. And after the daring rescue, traumatic page turn, and chase after Richard, she felt she more than deserved answers. "Can you at least tell me about this power? Since you're clearly avoiding my questions about your family."

"Can't." He turned back to her. "Can't go into details on the family history. Would take an approval from Larrakane herself, and you don't need to be in the middle of things."

It was almost exactly what Nicolosia, the Elder druid, had told her when they refused to answer her questions about the Guardians. Fiona stood taller. "I am *already* in the middle, and quite frankly I'm sick of people trying to protect me. I'm intelligent—"

"Of course you are," Richard said, waving off the notion, "but once you're in this tangle, you're in it forever. And that's not for me to decide." He sighed and took her hands in his rough ones. He squeezed them once but kept hold. "But some things are, I suppose. My abilities I can tell you a little of." He rubbed his thumb across the back of her hand and then dropped them. "That shouldn't topple the whole card stack."

Fiona raised an eyebrow but held her tongue, feeling on the brink of finally getting information. Like seeing your coffee just about to be done after being tired all day. She promised herself she didn't have to be quiet forever.

Richard ushered her into the small archival room. Was it truly only a tenday ago she was here and trying to get him to work with her on finding the Guardian of Rise? It all felt a little ridiculous now that she knew it was him. He had truly been trying to throw her off the scent from the moment they met. She made a conscious decision to withhold her ire. There was more here than Richard lying to get his way. After seeing Rise fall apart, would she have done differently in his shoes?

Richard left the door open and leaned against the drafting table to watch over her shoulder. "My abilities allow me to give rise to what people *think* is happening and to rewrite their immediate memories. Through a variety of ways, I'm able to control what they remember about me, my...relations, and events involving this page."

Fiona was thunderstruck. Rewrite memories? It seemed so...specific. So delicate and grossly overpowered. What about people's free will? It was their memories after all. "How could you do something like that?"

Richard tugged on his beard. "I didn't set out to do it. It's my responsibility. To ensure that this...that we're all safe."

He struggled with that, Fiona noticed. Why?

"How?" she asked. "Surely if you told people what they were up against, even people who could help like myself, we could fix it."

Richard scoffed. "Even Larrakane couldn't fix it. And it was her failing."

This wasn't the first time he had mentioned that things were the goddess's fault. But he seemed so sure.

"You're being cryptic on purpose," she accused. "I know you feel you have to hide things, but please, you can trust me."

Richard stared at her, inscrutable golden eyes wavering, and then nodded. "When you've spent two hundred years lying to everyone you meet, pretending you don't exist, trying *not* to exist, you become used to relying on yourself."

"Not anymore." Fiona reached out tentatively and rubbed her thumb across his rough-bearded jaw. She had been wanting to do that for ages. It was the right amount of prickly. A reflection of him.

He sighed and patted her hand. Pulling a scroll from the rack above them, he unfolded it to reveal a sketch of an open book, its pages blank. "When Larrakane created these realms—the pages, as we call them—they were completely separate. I believe she thought herself an architect of sorts. And we the structures. I've studied all the mortal pages, and I do believe she was simply recreating the same world over and over again with small changes. Some sort of vision, you see. And then watched to see what would happen."

Fiona dropped her hand, warmth and awkwardness making her movements jerky. She ran it over the scroll, but it was smooth, devoid of ink. "Like an isolated experiment. I've seen Gaili do that before, trying to get the best outcome."

Richard nodded. "When I was—that is to say, over two hundred years ago Larrakane revealed herself to us. To humans." He shook his head. "It did not go well. We had our own way of seeing the world, you have to understand. A very concentrated idea of what was right and wrong and who created us. Of course, there were billions of us, and we conflicted on these ideas."

Fiona held up her hands. "I'm sorry, you said there were billions of people in the Book?"

"Humans. Billions of humans."

Unbelievable. There were only a few million humans at best spread throughout the page of Rise. And even then, the floating islands were stuffed with people. Where could they possibly fit ten times that number of humans? Where had they been living? "What happened?"

He huffed. "Larrakane happened. Oh, she told us she was our creator. Nearly half of the religious sects in our world went to war overnight. But her power was unimaginable and inarguable. It was clear that she was the one. And then she gave us a gift." Richard pulled out a small book. Fiona hadn't even seen where he had gotten it from. It was leather-bound and wrinkled with use. He cracked it open. On the page was a portrait of Larrakane, but not as Fiona had ever seen her before. Instead of being immensely tall and unapproachable, she was a small human woman with deep-brown skin and jet-black hair, but the cloak of starry night about her shoulders was the same that it was in all of the pictures and depictions of the goddess.

Richard tapped the picture. "Larrakane gave humans the true words. A sort of magic if you will, like the faekin have, but instead of being able to use it for alchemy or inventions, we were able to learn it to shape our world specifically into our happiness. Up until then magic had been a fairy tale, something no human ever thought truly existed, but the goddess made it real for us. Unfortunately, not equally." He turned to Fiona and implored her with his eyes. "You understand about ambition, it's one thing I think that all the mortal pages share and what truly makes us equal. That spark of desire and hope within each one of us that makes us strive for the things we want. Back in my day, humans were inundated with it, and I'm sad to say we took the Word, as we called it, and we twisted it. I—" He stopped, his voice becoming thick.

Fiona stroked his arm gently, watching the myriad of emotions play on his face. Regret. Anger. Guilt. No matter what she said, she would not be able to fix this for him, though she wanted to.

"It was my responsibility to make sure the people under my care, in my kingdom, were safe. I used the Word to protect them. And in that struggle of protection, to keep my throne and the power to push back my—someone who could usurp me and rule worse than myself, I made a choice. And the reaction to that choice was deadly. Our world was destroyed. My role as Guardian is to make sure that can never happen again." Richard closed the book. "My use of the Word is limited now, thanks to Larrakane. It can only affect myself, this page, and the people in the Book who would do it harm. I can't change who you are or who anyone is, and I can't change what's already been done. Just their perception of it. That's everything."

Fiona held on to Richard's arm, trying to push through the waves of information. There had been more humans, and they had destroyed themselves with what Larrakane had given them. Well, not all of them. King Richard and his brother had destroyed them. What was Richard's choice? He wouldn't voice it, which meant he probably couldn't. It must have had to do more with his family. She shook her head as if trying to jumble her thoughts into alignment. If the fae had been given magic and used it to make their world glorious, why had humans used it to destroy themselves? "What about Kerus? What were the beastfolk given?"

"I think Larrakane was looking for something, or someone, special. And unfortunately, she found it with us before then." He rubbed his face. "But as I said before, I can say no more on that particular subject. Doing so is more than keeping a secret, I assure you. It is dangerous to all of us." Richard swallowed and tugged on his beard. "Simply know I do what I have to do. I take no pleasure in rewriting the memories of all these people."

"But what are you doing to stop *having* to do it?" Fiona said, raising her chin. "Richard, you're telling me that you sit here, and you protect the page against possible danger, but danger came right to your door! Clearly the Painted Edge knows who you are, and according to Stella, they got what they wanted." She placed her hand on his chest with trembling energy. "I can help. People can help turn this around so that you don't have to make all these decisions on your own."

Richard clasped her hand. "I have to do this on my own. It's the only way to keep everyone safe, including you."

"I don't need your protection. Haven't you figured that out yet? I may not be a Guardian, but we are equals as far as I'm concerned." Fiona took a step back. "Or are you trying to say there's nothing here between us and it's merely a king guarding a helpless princess."

Richard snorted. "I'm not a king anymore."

"That was not the point, and you know it." She wanted him to tell her of course it was different. Of course he saw them as equals and was attracted to her. He had kissed her again. He had said he cared about her. Well, dark edge swallow him whole because *he* was the one making it so difficult. Fiona took a breath. "Richard, I like you. And even though you're stubborn, proud, and a bit arrogant, you're also thoughtful, clever, and quite charming when you want to be. When we were working together you even approached treating me as a partner. Why can't that continue? We're going to have to work together as we fight against the Painted Edge."

"Blasted woman, because I can't help you! Hell, I can't even leave the page. I'm stuck here. And that's a good thing, too, because if I can leave it means I've failed," Richard said in a strained voice. "You want to be out there investigating and making this frayed Book safe."

"So?" Fiona shrugged as if unconcerned. "I'm not saying we run off, get married, and become inseparable—though Larrakane knows it would make my mother happy. But I'm simply saying we could try to see what this is. Or are you always attracted to every woman who argues with you?"

Richard shook his head. "Please don't tempt me with things I don't deserve." He took a step back from her. "And I cannot have."

Fiona's anger flared up again, but before she could tell him how foolish he was being, there was a loud clang on the archive doors.

Richard jumped at the unexpected noise. He glanced at her and said, "Please don't tell *anyone* what I have said. I trust you know how dangerous it could be to the wrong person." He reached toward her but pulled back sharply and walked out of the room.

She didn't follow, instead rolling up the scroll on the desk roughly as if it was Richard's neck. How dare he act like such a blotter! He was the one with all the knowledge, all the power, and yet was consistently punishing himself. And for what? Oh, he couldn't tell her. He didn't want her to get involved in the tangle. Well, that wasn't his choice. She *was* involved. Up to her neck in it honestly. Oh, liking him made things all the more complicated. She stopped balling up the scroll and dropped it to the table. Fiona took a deep, steadying breath. He was the first person in a long time who had truly sparked something within her. In more than simply a curious way. She enjoyed being with him, talking to him, and yes, well, kissing him. But she wouldn't sit around and be rejected forever. She had chased him once. She wouldn't do so again. She wouldn't tell anyone his secrets, of course, but that didn't mean she wouldn't investigate them for herself.

Footsteps echoed in the archive toward her position. She put on her best glowering face, ready to give Richard another volley if he had so boldly chosen to come back to her at this moment. But Fiona stilled seeing a royal court messenger tentatively step into the room.

"You're wanted in Queen Brilliance's private chambers, mistress," the messenger said quickly. He bowed, a little wobbly, and then got back up. "I'm happy to escort you."

Fiona frowned. She had already told the private secretary outside the stolen ship exactly what she thought about fulfilling the Queen's request. She really had nothing more to say, but perhaps she had to say it to Brilliance's face to get her to understand. Regardless of how she felt about the man currently avoiding her in the next room, she would not give him up to a power like the Queen. Fiona followed the messenger out of the room and through the archives. Richard sat at his desk tidying papers as if completely engrossed in his work.

Fiona was tempted to barge right past him but said, "It seems the Queen has questions for me. But don't think our conversation is finished."

Richard tilted his head and eyed the messenger coolly before replying, "I wouldn't dream of it."

Fiona nodded curtly and exited the room after the servant. *Proud, arrogant man. Lionheart. More like Lion's Stubbornness.*

She fumed quietly as they made their way through the winding stone passages. The messenger kept glancing at her, and the fifth time he snuck a peek it broke through Fiona's thoughts. Why on earth was he watching her? Perhaps he was to report any suspicious activity to the Queen. Fiona straightened up. She was missing a valuable opportunity here. She shouldn't let Richard distract her so.

"How fair things with the Queen? Is she well?" she asked nonchalantly.

The youth jumped. "Yes, mistress. She's very well. Thanks to you of course." He ducked his head. "Begging your pardon, mistress, but please know my hearty thanks at all you've done for us."

Fiona pursed her lips. Richard said he had rewritten memories. Shouldn't people not remember a thing? What had she done for them that even a messenger would know about it? Oh bother, she hadn't gotten a chance to learn what exactly Richard did. How could she ask the messenger what he meant without appearing daft? "That's very kind of you. I suppose if you know, then more people know who I am?" She winced. Not the best question, but perhaps he would be too awestruck to notice it.

He nodded eagerly. "The royal court is singing your praises, mistress. Lord Hawkport thwarted and the Queen returned all in one fell swoop." He warmed up to his subject, grinning. "Why, what they wrote about you in the last *Card* is more than true."

Ah, Hawkport. Well, it was true that he was planning something dastardly for the Queen so he could take over. But surely the Travel Guild had dealt with him. How did Fiona's name come up in connection? And returning the Queen? Where had she gone?

There was no more time for questions as they approached the private chambers of the royal court. Unlike Fiona's first introduction to this quarter of the palace, falling through a secret door—another thing Richard had gotten her into—this time she was escorted into the small audience chamber.

Queen Brilliance sat upon her makeshift throne, a decorative wooden chair at a large dressing table. Her frizzed red curls encircled her face, and the golden brocade of her gown twinkled in the many smokeless candles bordering the room. A few scattered nobles surrounded her, the principal secretary in large neck ruffs to her side. And peeking from the other side of the throne, not even a hair out of place, was Richard. How in the world had he gotten here before her? Tunnels must abound in the palace. He seemed much calmer than he had ten minutes ago. Her eyes met his and then fell to the floor. Fiona's chest tightened and she kept her gaze roving around the room again so as not to draw attention to their connection.

Several nobles in the chamber gave Richard a curious glance. It was as if they'd seen him before but were puzzled as to his seat beside the Queen. The Queen leaned over and whispered to him. He nodded and gazed back at Fiona. What she wouldn't give for some form of enhanced hearing. But the look they gave her was the opposite. All eyes on her, all watching and somewhat intrigued by her every move. She patted herself conspicuously, remembering that she was no longer in Rise-appropriate attire and instead in her everyday altered plum doublet, verdant wool stockings, and bright multi-pocketed scarf. Well, there could be nothing for the right fashion after solving an important case.

The Queen acknowledged Fiona with a wide smile. Evidently whatever she had done had not only pacified the Queen but delighted her with Fiona. By Larrakane's grace, what had Richard written?

"Mistress of the Page. It is with appreciation that I call you here today to thank you formally and officially for what you've done for Rise," Queen Brilliance stated.

Fiona swallowed, the heat of many stares making her confusion more frustrating. She bowed and simply said, "It is what any Schiflan would do for their world."

"Be that as it may, you have gone above and beyond, and I would be remiss in my duties if I didn't thank you personally for saving me from those painted ruffians." The Queen teared up, somewhat dramatically. She dabbed at her eyes with a gold-thread-embroidered cloth. "To be stolen away to such an unimaginable place as that cursed jungle, bound with rope—" She stopped speaking and covered her face with her hand, seemingly overcome.

The principal secretary, ruffs quivering, stepped forward and handed the Queen his handkerchief. "Her Brilliance underwent quite the ordeal by this Painted Edge. That you found her and brought her back home to safety when no other could is most appreciated. In honor of your—"

The Queen cut him off with a sharp raise of her hand. She threw her shoulders back and smiled, all traces of tears gone. Loudly she said, "I proclaim you no longer simply Mistress of the Page but Baroness Thornbeard, lady of Forlorn Tower and protector of the court. You may thank me."

Scattered gasps, murmuring, and exclamations burst within the small chamber. Some nobles looked outraged while others were amused. Fiona pressed her lips together trying to hide her surprise but couldn't help glancing at Richard. He surreptitiously nodded and looked at the Queen with a wry smile and an arched eyebrow. Fiona warmed, for a brief moment not from anger at him, but to delight. He had given her and her family quite the boon.

Fiona quickly bowed low to the floor to hide her delay at answering and said loudly, "Thank you, Your Majesty."

The Queen nodded. "As for Lord Henry Hawkport and his family, I renounce all title and lands from them. Lands will be dispersed by hand of the principal secretary on the morrow and titles revised." The Queen raised her voice over another burst of chatter. "Come, Lady Thornbeard. You will attend me."

The principal secretary swanned into the group of nobles who clamored toward him. Richard held out his hand for the Queen, who took it, rising from her seat. A guard opened the door, and Richard escorted the Queen into the hallway alone. What else could the Queen possibly have to say that she wouldn't dare say in front of the royal court? Fiona hesitated for a moment before following.

Richard walked slowly down the hallway with the Queen at his side. A few guards flanked them, but as the Queen approached, they disappeared into the shadows swiftly. Fiona walked behind Richard and below the Queen as manners dictated.

"I have given you and your mother an advantage," the Queen said. The swish of her skirt against the lush carpet on the floor underscored her words. "While Forlorn Tower is not much, there is space for a home, I believe."

"Did Baron Lionheart suggest I be given the lands?" Fiona said with a practiced light voice. How far did Richard's rewriting power work? She couldn't pass up this chance to test the boundaries. To see just how much he balanced free will and his power.

The Queen paused but didn't turn around. "Baron Lionheart? Who is Baron Lionheart?"

"I believe Lady Thornbeard is thinking of one of Your Majesty's privy members, Griffintail." Richard interjected smoothly.

So Richard had erased his true name altogether then? That was in conjunction with what he said he kept his powers to. Fiona gripped her hands behind her back as the Queen addressed her sternly.

"It is I, of course, who rewarded you with land for your deeds. Our charming historian here provided information about the overlooked land, and I cleverly deduced it would benefit you."

"Of course, Your Majesty," Fiona said quickly. It seemed that Richard only adjusted what made sense. He could've made the Queen do much more. Putting Forlorn Tower into the hands of Fiona was wise, yet so at odds with his rejection of her help and the need to protect everything himself. Perhaps he could not say in words what he could do with action. Fiona realized there was no more conversation flowing from the Queen and quickly pulled her thoughts to the leader, saying what was expected: "We are very grateful to be in your thoughts."

"Yes, yes," the Queen said somewhat impatiently. Perhaps the needs of others were beginning to take up too much of her time. "But to more important matters. I am relieving you of your need to find a Guardian of Rise."

"Oh?" So no one remembered her speech at the airship then? Pity, she had quite liked rejecting the Queen's request.

The Queen smiled. "I am to be named Guardian of Rise soon. And the Travel Guild will be putting more jackets in place to support me."

Richard spluttered. He tried to turn it into a cough, but Fiona watched as his tawny face grew red. This most certainly had not been part of his plans. Then whose were they?

Brilliance gave a tinkly laugh. "I see I've surprised even you, my good friend. Well, all in a day's work, as the pulp say." She laughed again. "Please see the principal secretary for your deed and decree." She waved her hand dismissively and began ordering one of the invisible guards to retrieve her maids.

Fiona bowed and turned down the first corridor she approached away from the Queen. She had so many plans to make and not a wink of sleep before then. What to do about the Forlorn Tower now that it was hers? Fiona stumbled as a thought occurred to her: How would she protect its secrets, and Richard's, from her mother once she knew about the island?

"Mistress Thorne," Richard said behind her.

She was proud of herself for not jumping, as engrossed as she was in her own thoughts. She raised her head high and turned slowly to him. "Yes, Sir..." She faltered. All of his names were made up, were they not?

Richard blushed and he lowered his head. "Lionheart. But they should know me as Mourninghide again."

She nodded, not wanting to let her voice betray her feelings about his topsy-turviness. Nor the way he looked when pink tinged his cheeks. Yes, she could see how he looked as a man of four-and-thirty years so long ago.

"I know I have very little right to ask you for a favor, but I must. This Travel Guild business. Do you know about it?"

"No, it was just as surprising to me."

Richard bit his lip. "It's probably for the best. Perhaps the Guardian in Spine is making it harder for the Painted Edge. The devil only knows how many ruffians remember what actually happened versus what I wrote."

Fiona's brows furrowed. "The devil? And what Guardian in Spine?"

"I've never talked to them, but I... Well, I know there's a Guardian for every page. I assume Spine is no different."

"Have you talked to any of these Guardians?"

"None that I know of." He dipped his chin down. "But then I suppose I don't know as much as I thought I did."

Fiona hesitated, but affection took over and she placed a hand gently on his arm. "None of us ever do."

Richard glanced at her. He took a small breath and said in a rush, "Should you ever want to toss ideas with a frustrating old man, this is for you." He produced a small bound journal from his doublet and thrust it at her. "Don't feel you have to, of course." With a quick glance at her face, strode off.

Fiona had no time to recover, barely saying, "Richard," before he was gone from sight. She sighed, frustrated. Topsy-turvy of a man. He was always saying things that didn't make sense, words that she had no definition for in her vast vocabulary, and making her hot and cold all at once. She turned the journal over. It was warm from him. A small quill was tucked into the spine, but other than that it looked very nondescript. Her curiosity was piqued, but she tucked it into her multi-pocketed scarf, putting it in the lace pocket where she liked to keep her dearest items. She would look at it in detail after getting home. For now, there were more pressing matters: the possibility of a Guardian of Spine, the Painted Edge's dangerous plan, and an unknown leader whom Stella worked for. Trouble was piling up, and although it had already been a truly long day, she felt it would be longer indeed. She had a date with a druid and would need to meet Nicolosia before something else untoward could occur. Eager determination was sometimes the only way to get to the bottom of anything at all.

THE DRUIDS SEEMED TO be waiting for Fiona at Forest's Edge. Before she could raise her hand to knock on the wooden door, it opened and a young woman waved her in. With a quickened step they walked through the druid grove along the looping path toward Nicolosia's home. The symbol the path made on the ground stirred memories of how eventfully repetitious life had become. Here yesterday, it felt like. And the Elder's hut almost six months ago.

Sparks of excitement shot through Fiona as they got closer to the hut and clearing. Having never seen the grove in the middle of the night, it was quite a change. The empty inky sky hung above, no moon bathing light through the trees. Frogs and grasshoppers croaked loudly around her, or was it her heightened senses in the dark that made it seem so? The perpetually vibrant trees of the forest that surrounded the area stood still in the darkness, shapes Fiona could barely make out in the dim light of the young druid's torch. Without their rustling leaves they reminded her of fortress walls. The kind in ruins on Rise but very prominent in Kerus to this day. But what sort of fortress truly had one like Nicolosia as its commander? The Elder druid had always been gentle with Fiona, even when rebuffing her curious questions. Fiona could not think them dangerous enough for anyone to go to war with.

She shivered. It had been so cold and rainy in Rise the entire time she had been there. Of course, that had been the fault of the page turners of the Painted Edge and Stella. But also Stella's leader, no doubt. She hoped that she would get everything she wanted to know about the Guardians and what was going on in the Book from Nicolosia without a debate. They had said as much before she left, but with the many, many hours between then and now, changes could be afoot.

Fiona was warmed that the Elder had told her their real name, and she wouldn't take it for granted. When the guide stopped near the crackling fire in the midst of the clearing, she addressed the warm golden-brown-skinned fae kneeling outside their door properly: "Good evening, Elder."

"Good evening, my dear Fiona," Nicolosia said with a quirk of an eyebrow barely seen in the flickering light. "Or early morning, depending on whether one is an optimist or a pessimist." Nicolosia thanked the guide with a wide smile and rose from the ground in one swift motion.

Always sprightly they were. If Fiona hadn't known they had lived in Spine so long and were so prominent, she would've thought they weren't much older than she was.

"I'm glad you didn't dawdle. Only the vines of the forest can hold them together, and even those are starting to recede. The coffee is done, and we can start off." Nicolosia hefted a satchel onto their back and waved Fiona after them toward the trees.

Fiona frowned. What were they talking about? And be off where? "What's going on?" She walked quickly to catch up—the druid had taken off like a spooked doe.

"Let's make haste and you'll soon know more than you ever wished you could," Nicolosia called over their shoulder.

Fiona snorted and shook her head. "I'm not sure that's possible."

The druid stopped abruptly and tilted their head, assessing her. "Are you sure you want to know everything? I have promised to explain and will keep to that promise, of course, but—"

"But once I'm in, I'm in," Fiona said wearily, pulling up Richard's words. "Yes, I *am* sure."

Nicolosia nodded, lips pressed tightly. "While we can talk somewhat safely here, there's a better place in Spine for this discussion and a few people you have a right to hear from as well." Nicolosia strode to the tallest, widest tree on the edge of the small clearing and placed their hand on it. In less than a blink a wide doorway opened in the tree. "Follow me." They took a step and were gone.

Sweet smells of sticky tree sap overwhelmed her senses, but she walked after the druid, curiosity always leading. As she stepped over the threshold, the scent grew stronger.

Warm.

Tired.

Waking.

Fiona stumbled out onto the cobblestone streets on the back side of the turner district. Though the houses could be mistaken by an unread turner as somewhere else, Fiona recognized the tower of the Thread, its robin's-egg blue exterior and white lace roof not too far in the distance. An emblem of tranquility in the dark. She'd recognize it anywhere truly. A journey that should've taken over an hour took less than a minute. Could she convince Nicolosia to teach her to walk through the trees as well? She supposed not unless she became a druid. That much green would never suit her though.

Nicolosia walked out beside her, and with a resounding snap the tree behind them closed. "I'm sure you know your way, but if you'll let me lead for a moment more." The Elder druid began to walk quickly, practically running across the stones.

Fiona had no time to pepper them with questions if she wanted to keep up. She ran after them in the dim, deserted streets. Light bloomed from the trees and puffed out onto the stones ahead. Not simply any light but bright flowers of various sizes like lily pads on a pond. They muffled their steps as they continued on. Many more blossoms, like a quickened wave, flew with the wind and blanketed the travelers.

She marveled at the cloak of flowers and plants that concealed them as they ran. Was this the trees' doing or Nicolosia's? Just before she burst from withholding her comments on what was happening, they were at the door of the Thread. Fiona tugged on her scarf, her tired brain working furiously to tie all the pieces together.

Vines wrapped around the door and the nearby windows. Nicolosia tapped them and they receded, leaving the wooden exterior bare. Opening the door revealed an empty and shadowy bar room.

Fiona shivered following behind the druid. She had never seen the tavern like this before. All of Mac's warmth was gone, as if it had been sucked out of the room by a cold wind.

Nicolosia sprang into the center of the room and called out in a frustrated voice, "I should've expected you wouldn't let me handle this as I saw fit."

"And why should *you* be the determining factor in letting some unread turner know my business?" a deep voice said from the dark.

"Our business," Nicolosia said simply. "Where are the others?"

"We're up here, Nic," the familiar bubbly voice of Mac came from the stairwell. Golden bursts of sunshine flowed on from one lamp to another. She sauntered down the steps and clasped her arms around the druid. "He thought he could slip past me to greet you without me noticing. He forgets that this is *my* domain." She jerked her head to the only corner to remain somewhat darkened even with the light.

Fiona focused on the shady area and found she could now see a tall fae glowering in the corner. His skin was bright and white like untrodden snow. Swirling patterns of silver and rose ink very visibly covered his nose, cheeks, eyes, and hands. His long silvery hair was curled and parted so that it flowed over the shoulders of his gray doublet, blending into the waves of scalloped cream lace that covered his throat. Long, downy cotton furred ears lay flat on either side of his head, half hidden by his hair. He raised his pert, slim nose in the air but did not smile. If he had, she may have been able to tell how young or old he was. For now, he seemed a balance between Mac and Nicolosia. He didn't move from his position, instead watching them as if waiting, hands resting on an adorned silver walking stick.

Nicolosia hugged Mac tightly. "I am glad to see your spirits aren't dampened yet."

While surprised at the familiarity, small thoughts of past events began rapidly clicking together in Fiona's mind. She burst out, unable to contain herself, "Mac? Elder?" She pressed her lips together. How could she not have seen the obvious connection before?

"Oh, Fi," Mac said and hugged her tight. Her warm embrace melted the cold from Fiona and put the Thread back to right, as if something settled into place. "I didn't expect you to get involved this soon, but I guess that's my own fault."

"She will not be involved," the snowy fae man in the back said.

"She has every right. After all Fiona has done for the Book, for everyone. Think of how much easier it would be if she knew what she was up against," Nicolosia said.

He waved his walking stick in the air and pointed at her. "She can continue doing the work she does without knowing what concerns me."

Fiona was sick of everyone talking about her as if she wasn't here. "I have a right to know what is going on, and I can be spoken to directly." She pulled away from Mac and toward the center of the empty bar facing the fae man. "Whether you like it or not, I am already very involved in whatever these troubles are. Who are you to deem how I may act and what I may do?"

The tall fae rose and strode toward her like a sudden storm. He towered over Fiona. "I am the Binder of this Book. The leader of the Travel Guild, and the first fae of the Circle of Seasons. That gives me the right."

Though she was momentarily awestruck by the Binder's declaration, it soon spurred fire within Fiona. She leaned toward him pointedly, not breaking eye contact. "Perhaps over someone else, but not over me." If this truly was the Binder, then possibly there was some part of him that could be pressed upon to be amicable to Nicolosia sharing information with her. The part that Dodger so reverently looked up to. "I know you have those whom you see as family now but distrusted in the beginning. Surely you know an ally when you see one."

The Binder's face hardened, and he took an imposing step forward, completely closing the gap between them. "You don't know the first thing about me, unread. Don't think simply because you know them that their regards of you extends to me." He pointed toward Mac and Nicolosia. "You may have fared well so far uncovering the Painted Edge, but we don't need to compromise ourselves further by allowing you into our business. We'll soon have what we need on the Painted Edge to stop them once and for all."

"Calm down, Arc," a voice sang from the stairwell. A fae woman hopped to the floor, dusting off her hands. Small in stature with ochre skin like earthen clay and downy ears Fiona recognized her as the guest to Nicolosia on her last visit to the druid camp. Though her clothing was plainer than before, she was still a striking contrast in pale cornflower bodice and skirt with golden patterned stripes across her midsection. She flipped her deep-copper-colored hair over her shoulder casually. "We all know you're the one whose voice matters most. But you also know if she asks to be bound to Larrakane under Nic, you can't prevent it."

The Binder sucked in a quick breath.

Mac looked uneasy.

Nicolosia sputtered, "Dani!" wide eyes giving the fae a warning look.

Bound? Fiona grimaced internally. She had already been bound once to Mac. While it had come with a host of good things it had almost drained her ability to turn the page, and her strength along with it. Could she really do that again?

As if reading her mind, Mac said quietly, "It's not like that, Fi. Not a promise. It's much bigger."

The Binder looked between Mac and Fiona. He glowered. So he hadn't known that Mac and Fiona had already been bonded before? Interesting. Even Mac hid things from this so-called leader.

"What does it entail?" Fiona said. If she was going to be somehow bound even more to the deity, she'd like to know what she was in for. She didn't have a choice when it came to being inked, but she understood Mac's warning. This was more than an oath to a friend.

"What I can tell you," Nicolosia said, glancing at the Binder, "is that you would be more connected to Larrakane than you are now. And more protected against certain…forces. You would answer to me, on occasion, for your actions in regard to people and the pages. And in turn I would be in charge of making sure you, as my protégé, were prepared to one day take my place as one of the Book's leaders."

Fiona's eyes widened. She had always wanted the power to do more for people, make life easier for page turners (versus what the Travel Guild had done, in her eyes), and support the city of Spine. Through connections and cases, she was intent on clawing her way up into a position that could have true impact. But a leader among the hidden players…was this how it always worked? "Are all leaders bound to Larrakane?"

"No," the Binder said curtly.

"So just the ones in Spine then?" An invisible pathway she never would've stumbled on if it hadn't been for persistence and a pushy nature. It didn't seem a fair shake to anyone else who wanted a chance.

No one answered her. The ochre fae, Dani, started to break the silence, but the Binder thrust out his hand and said, "No. You've interfered enough. Why don't you go back to your fields? We have decisions to make."

"She has a right to be here and you know it," Nicolosia said, grabbing Dani's hand and squeezing it gently. Old friends indeed.

Mac, unfettered, placed her warm hand on Fiona's shoulder. "You can have faith to be bound to Larrakane or not. Don't be hasty. I know it sounds like your cup of coffee but—"

"There's not a lot we can tell you about what's going on without getting on with it. There's plenty I'm sure you can infer though." Dani smiled wide. "I've heard you're quick. Your brain must already be ticking ahead. And protégés are only the best and the brightest the Book has to offer."

Fiona had already begun to guess some things as they all interacted with each other, and she leapt at the diversion Dani offered. "Mac is Summer, Nic is Spring," She tilted her head, assessing Dani and the Binder—or Arc, as she had called him. They certainly seemed complete opposites but how much were they really? "You're Autumn and the Binder is Winter." The Circle of Seasons were all still very much alive. And running Spine apparently.

"Enough," the Binder said, pushing past the women. "We need to be planning our next course of action. Not this." He waved toward Fiona.

"Which we should do with Fiona," Nicolosia said. "She's interacted with Guardians directly. She's talked to the Painted Edge leader more than once."

Fiona tried quickly to hide her surprise at the latter assertation. Stella had been clear she wasn't the leader and there was another. Had Marcia, Gilded leader in the Travel Guild, not mentioned this to the Binder yet? She glanced at him, but all she got was a disapproving glare. It infuriated her. She refused to let another dictate the course of her actions, Binder or not. She had been far too reactive to everyone else. Well, now they were in *her* home base, and she wouldn't continue to be off-kilter. She wanted answers, real answers, and if she had to ask them of Larrakane herself, she would. "I'll be bound." She took a breath and said loudly, as if commandeering the attention of a dozen nobles, "I request to be bound under Nicolosia."

Dani clapped her hands, her young enthusiasm startling Fiona. She seemed so unlike the poised woman she had met a few days ago.

The Binder stamped his walking stick and looked at Fiona. He sighed deeply. "So be it. As Binder of the Book, I grant you the right to be bound." He raised an eyebrow and said wryly, "May you be accepted by Larrakane and undertake all the conditions she avails to you." He stomped to a chair and sat down. "And may you survive not to regret it."

"Let's use my temple, okay?" Mac said, threading her arm through Fiona's. "I'd like to say it's more your style than the stuffy one in the center of the city, but Larrakane knows I haven't been there since Arc—I mean, the Binder built it." She pulled Fiona smoothly from the room and up the familiar stairs. The light and springy steps of Nicolosia followed closely behind them.

Fiona sucked in a breath, glad to have Mac's reassuring form beside her. "Can you not leave the Thread, Mac?"

"Can, but don't." Mac tilted her head. With a lowered voice she said, "We decided long ago it was best to have our areas of control, like we did in Copper." Mac sighed. "Sometimes we go along to get along. We're much better off in our corners."

"Clearly that doesn't stop you from fighting when you're all together," Fiona muttered.

"There's a reason seasons come one after each other and not all together," Mac said grinning. "Like a small cataclysm, we are."

Nicolosia coughed. "Mac," they said in a cautious tone.

"Though much less in Spine," Mac added hurriedly. She patted Fiona's arm. "Format says we've disappeared and that's the dry."

Fiona nodded, taking Mac's meaning. Her sudden descent into turner slang meant she was sure Nicolosia wouldn't understand. Fiona supposed the druid didn't travel outside of the forest much and wasn't around normal page turners like Mac was. There were several people who knew Mac's true nature. How much trouble would she get into? Fiona said loudly enough for Nicolosia to hear, "I'll keep it in the Thread. No one else will know."

They got to the third-floor landing of Mac's private quarters. She placed her hand on the door and after a moment it opened up. Fiona had hoped to see the fae magic at work again but knew it was a small chance after her bond to Mac had been broken. She swallowed her disappointment and followed Mac inside with Nicolosia.

The room was as it ever was: formal yet soft like its owner with a pillow-stuffed settee, papers and contraptions overflowing on the desk. Mac strode through to a closed door, ethereal azure robes trailing behind on the wooden floor. Popping it open, she motioned them to follow her into what was clearly her bedroom and to a small circular metal staircase. Fiona tried to take it all in quickly, having never seen the room in person. A large, sumptuous bed took up most of the space, but even here were bits of metal, stacks of books, and blueprints tacked to the walls. Nicolosia cleared their throat, and she squashed her remaining curiosity and stepped quickly up the spiral staircase.

A small attic, the pointed roof denoting it was one of the tower rooms that made the exterior of the Thread so unique, sat at the top of the stairs. Lavender, a smell not infrequent in Mac's bar area, permeated the room. A soft amber glow lit the space, adding an odd warmth, as it was cozier here than it had been below. The wooden walls held sketches of the various seasons beautifully illustrated and painted. But summer reigned supreme on the northern wall. A sunburst in vivid oranges near the roof was raised against a bright-blue backdrop of sky. Large shade trees formed a semicircle behind a bursting sculpture fountain. Fiona could almost smell the tall green grass that edged the floor in the painting. As she stepped closer, she noticed small pops of purple flowers mixed in with the grass and inhaled deeply. Fiona grinned, enamored at the tower room. It comforted her, along with the knowledge that Mac knew it would.

"You can kneel here, or sit, however you prefer. When you're ready to reach out to Larrakane, light these candles in a circle, starting from the west." Mac squeezed Fiona's arm reassuringly. "It's really up to you and her if the connection happens. Try to get her attention. I know you're great at that." Mac smiled, her warmth encompassing Fiona once again. She nodded to one candle, and its small wick sprouted a flame. Without another word she headed back down the stairs.

Fiona glanced at the pillows, the table, and the candle. She clasped her hands. "Well, Elder, do you have any words for me then?"

Nicolosia shook their head. "Nothing so great or lauded as Arc would have or comforting as Mac." They sighed. They seemed so much younger as the night went on. Younger and unsure. It was as if out of their domain they felt less control.

Fiona relaxed her shoulders and raised an impish eyebrow. "Give me what you always give me: wise words."

Nicolosia chuckled softly. "Well, this may be difficult for you. But it will be for her as well. Have some patience, my dear, but not too much." Nicolosia lifted up their chin. "Make your own choices. In yourself you can always be sure."

"Perfect." Fiona smiled. It was one of the best things to hear.

Nicolosia left, soft steps disappearing down the stairs. The door below opened and then closed. Fiona was all alone in the small temple.

FIONA KNELT ON THE pillows but immediately changed positions to sit with her legs crossed. If she was going to be here for a while, she was going to get comfortable. She sighed, wishing she had a chance to confer with Gaili or pester Richard more about Larrakane. It would just delay things truly, but it would make her feel less alone. She thought about the journal but pushed the thought quickly aside. She was procrastinating. A thing she almost never did. But it was reasonable, wasn't it? All of a sudden she had a moment to connect with Larrakane, an almost impossible moment, and she wasn't quite sure she wanted to.

She had often thought about what she would say if the deity ever appeared again as she had done at the beginning of the Inking. Why give power to people to travel through the pages? Why not simply create doors anyone could walk through or whole areas that merged together? Why show herself at all if she was going to go away for hundreds of years?

But like with many of her curious questions, she had worked out the answers to these over time on her own, or with the help of her friends. She understood more now than she ever had before. She didn't think this one moment would be enough for all the new questions she had. But more importantly she didn't trust that Larrakane wouldn't lie to her regardless of what she asked. If the deity had given Guardians such slim information, what hope had she to get honesty?

Fiona shook her head and refocused. She pushed an errant curl out of her face, picked up the candle Mac had ignited, and quickly lit the other candles in a westward circle. She would treat this as she treated all meetings with people who had more power than her: as a chance to get information, voice her suggestions for the betterment of everyone, and uncover the truth.

She quieted down, closed her eyes, and thought of all she knew of Larrakane. The different pictures and paintings of her across the pages. Her portrait painted on the ceiling of the Hinge was the most immediate one that came to mind. Her skin was dark and blue as a night sky with stars for eyes and tears that flowed like shining beacons of light. Her wavy black hair fanned out behind her and faded into the sky as pinpoints of light in sparkling colors. Though the artist had stopped just below her throat, you could see the high neckline of a frosty white gown. It was the only thing slightly odd about the mural, as many historical records said she had worn blue. And her eyes followed everywhere.

The room grew warmer. Fiona loosened her scarf around her neck and fanned herself. The candles shouldn't have given off any heat, Copper Court made and all. She opened her eyes nervously, her chest tightening at the scene around her. The room was darker, the candles far in the distance now. Tiny dots of light. Fiona scrambled to her feet, the sound echoing around her. She was no longer in the temple. But where was she? She began walking into the darkness toward the candles. Her steps took forever, but as she got closer, candlelight blazed into sunlight shining into the dead chamber from a doorway. Fiona ran for the door, leaping over the threshold and bursting outside.

The landscape around her shifted. She was in a hedge, a small path before her. It seemed to take a turn where more hedge was in sight. Her slow walk became a curious canter. Going left, right, and ever around, she found quite quickly that she was in a maze with more dead ends than there had any right to be. It reminded her a bit too much of the maze where she and Gaili fought Clara, and she called out a hello. No response nor echo of her voice. Fiona took another turn but stopped at another long, winding path behind her. She drew a breath slowly and released it before saying, "I won't be moving from this spot until you tell me how I get to you."

"A logical solution, though the world can continue moving without you. Therefore, does it make sense?" a deep reverberating voice echoed out of the greenery around her.

Fiona whirled around, dust flying up from the ground, looking for the source. "Are you playing games with me?"

"Enlightenment is not a game," the voice said, closer. Its timbre deepened as it commanded, "Speak."

Fiona wet her lips but thrust her chin up toward the hedge. "I have asked to be bound to you under Nicolosia."

"Have you?" The voice sounded surprised but then wavered. "I did not expect that from you."

"Pardon me?"

"One who struggles with the barest of rules requests to be bound by a deity who governs everything? Yes, most unexpected." The hedges rustled as if amused.

"Have you not been paying attention to what's going on?" Fiona shouted, straining her voice. "I no more have a choice to be bound to you so that I can help the people who really need helping than I had to be inked. Which I do believe was also of your desire."

The hedges rustled again but shifted to melding from outdoor barriers to wooden walls. The sunlight that had suffused the bright sky softened and shrank till it was pouring through a small window next to a short table with two chairs. Fiona recognized the interior. A long wooden bar anchored the room, and Mac's drink-pouring contraptions stood at attention on the back wall, silvery and shining as if new. This Thread was not her own. It had the same qualities but there was no warmth, no lavender, no Mac.

On the table appeared two mugs, steam rising from them. Within almost a blink a woman sat in one of the chairs, her smooth oval face turned toward the sun. The amber light danced twinkling across her darkened skin. The midnight-blue gown she wore spoke of an older time, cinched in at the waist and flowing till it faded from sight. Larrakane smiled into the sun, then turned to Fiona and gestured to the chair across from her. "There's always a choice. You of all people know that."

Fiona narrowed her eyes at the deity and the chair. Though Larrakane looked as if she had walked out of the drawings Fiona had always seen of her human form, there was a small flicker, a fading moment as if Larrakane was not only breathing but somewhat erratically. She strode to the chair and sat down slowly. The scent of fresh-brewed coffee engulfed her, and she wrapped her hands around her favorite brew. "Are you saying if I didn't want to be a page turner, if I didn't want to be inked, you would change that?"

Larrakane tilted her head. "Are you saying that you want it changed?"

Richard's words of Fiona being bound echoed in her ears. But she shook her head. "No. I wouldn't change that for anyone or anything in the Book."

Larrakane nodded as if already aware of her answer. "Then what would you change?"

Fiona raised the warm mug and took a slow, tentative sip as she thought. It was delightful but not perfect. While it tasted like Rise coffee, there was a hint of sweetness that was more than she liked her own to be. But that was because it wasn't her own. None of this was anyone's own but Larrakane. And none of it would change if she didn't speak up. If she was truly being asked for her opinion, she would certainly give it—on everything. "I would change the way the Inking is handled."

Intelligent eyes appraised her. "And if I said everything was managed in my carefully planned way for a reason?"

Frustration threatened to bubble over at her evasive answers, but Fiona gripped the mug tighter to control her reaction. "I would say that you owe us all an explanation, then, for it is our lives you are manipulating."

"You have an interesting way of addressing a power that is beyond your knowledge and capabilities," Larrakane said in a clipped tone and did not look away from Fiona.

"Beyond my knowledge? My knowledge of you is scant, but whose fault is that? Where were you when Blaze was dying and Rise was sinking?"

Larrakane's fingers curled tightly around her mug. "I was there. I am always there. Have you no understanding? I am the air that fills your lungs. The fire that petered out. I am the darkness that holds back the void. The light that brings forth a new day." She jerked from the table, pushing away from it, and flung her arms toward Fiona. "I am the turn from one page to another. The people who watch your back and protect these realms from cover to cover. And you would question my dedication? What right have you?" The windows of the tavern darkened like the day fading into night. Larrakane's form faded as she took in another breath, but still her wide eyes searched Fiona's.

Fiona tensed watching the overwrought deity. That she considered herself everything wasn't unreasonable. That she considered herself the very people she created was something new. Nicolosia told her to have patience. Why the deity would need patience from one she clearly thought beneath her, however, Fiona didn't know. But an angry power was not a useful fount of information. She bowed her head, breaking eye contact first. "What are the Guardians for?"

The goddess wrinkled her pert brown nose, sliding back into the chair seamlessly. She brought her own mug to her mouth and sipped it slowly, seemingly human again. Ensconced candles on the walls flickered on when they weren't there before and gave the place a brightened look. She set her mug down. "What aren't they for? Come, do not waste my limited time with questions that Nicolosia will answer when you return."

Did she not know about the Seasons in the Thread? Or that the Binder approved her being here? "Are you all-knowing?"

"One cannot be everything and all-knowing." Larrakane pursed her lips and muttered, "I cannot be, at least."

The Thread's scenery rippled. Fiona found herself at the threshold of the Thread door, no longer at the table. Larrakane was already outside in a version of the cobblestone streets surrounding the tavern, though in the distance there was nothing but darkness. No buildings or forest in the view. Was the deity impatient for the conversation to be over? Fiona took a step outside the tavern to stand at her side. "What is your criteria for the page turning ability? Why do you choose who you choose?"

Larrakane shrugged. "I choose those among you who ask to be chosen."

Fiona thought of those among them who hated being a page turner. Of Stella's words before she disappeared into the dark edge. "You have an interesting way of knowing what is asking and what is pondering a question."

"A question? One that mortals want answering only when convenient for them." Larrakane clasped her hands together in front of her, back upright. "I suppose nothing I do could ever be good enough for you all."

"From a mortal's perspective, we have been asked to endure, to survive with little instruction and guidance only from the hands of an overarching Guild one can only trust so much."

"*You* can only trust so much. There are many others who are very confident in the Guild and its thoughtful leader." The deity's eyes brightened.

That Larrakane gave praise of the Binder directly surprised her. "You chose him?"

Larrakane turned away from her and strode down the street deeper into the darkness.

"You cannot give us power beyond comprehension and expect some to not think of it as a punishment for having the desire to change," Fiona called after her. She pinched the bridge of her nose, pushing away the frustration welling up inside of her, and hurried after the deity.

"Do not speak to me of punishment." Larrakane's voice emanated outside the human body again. "I was here while one of my sisters shattered and the other fell to her creations. I cannot undo any of that while I remain. All so that you can live." Her voice thickened. "So that together we can stave off our enemies as they appear. If the freedom of wandering the pages as you please is a punishment, then you know nothing of the word you speak."

For the first time Fiona looked at Larrakane and truly understood she was being honest. She was not all-knowing, nor unfeeling. What, who was this creature really before her? Words died on her lips, but she thought of what Gaili would say in response. "I am sorry for your sisters."

Larrakane turned, assessing Fiona. She seemed surprised. "Do not be sorry. Be clear. I have given up everything to these realms. Do not think I would not give the very essence of my being to rid it of enemies, of their betrayal, of—" She stumbled forward as if tripping on stone.

Fiona reached out to grab her instinctively, her hands passing through the deity. If she could not grab on to her, was the stumble for show or more? The world changed once again, and they were completely surrounded in the inky black void. Fading black chains trailed behind the deity, attached to her ankles and arms, the midnight-blue gown ethereal among the dark.

Larrakane spoke quietly. "To be bound to me is to answer to me. To give your bonded word that you'll do everything in your power, regardless of the cost, to aid me and fight against those who mean the realms harm. Is this something you can agree to?"

Fiona had already told herself she would do everything in her power to protect those she loved and make sure the Painted Edge couldn't succeed in their plans. But regardless of the cost? And to support Larrakane? Answering to a power like this went against everything she held herself to. But if Larrakane gave her more than just answers, perhaps she would have the means to be on an equal playing field with at least the Circle of Seasons and helpful to those who needed it most. "Did Richard agree?"

The deity's eyes widened. "You are very familiar with him. *Richard* volunteered, though at the time it was of little consequence." The vision of Larrakane faded for a moment. With it a tremor washed over Fiona. It was as if the world around her was shaking, but what was there to move? She saw nothing else. As Larrakane solidified again, she waved her hand dismissively. "You cannot follow in his footsteps. This choice must be made for your own."

"Will you give me the Word?"

Larrakane took a step back. "My word, yes."

"The Word. Magic." Fiona let the gap linger between them and dropped her hands. "I could be helpful to our people if I had something more than my wits to tackle the Painted Edge. I've seen what it can do—"

"No."

"But—"

"I will never give another human the Word again." Larrakane spoke with finality. "You will not have it. You cannot control it." There it was again, that sliver of something that quaked the entire place. Larrakane looked hastily around. "Our time is done. You do not truly want this. And without that desire I cannot trust you enough to give a larger piece of myself to you."

Fiona didn't know if this was a trick of Larrakane or something else. But if she left here without being bound, then she wouldn't know more than she knew now. Couldn't help more than she was already doing. She licked her lips. She needed to separate her emotions from this situation. Had she not been so caught up in giving Larrakane her thoughts, she may have had a chance to actually connect with the deity. Perhaps if she was honest with her instead of evasive, she still could. "You're right. I don't want this. I have never wanted to be aligned with powers I have not vetted. And I'm wary of your reasons for everything you've done." She stared at Larrakane's fading form. "But I do want to be the voice of those in the cracks. A champion of the people who have no power of their own and must accept what is forced on them by everyone else. I will do everything in my ability to aid and fight against those who would do them harm." She took a step toward Larrakane. "Trust me to follow through on that."

The fading visage of Larrakane stood still, watching Fiona. With a tilt of her head, she nodded once. "I do believe you'd give your very essence for them, if not for me. Perhaps that is how it should be." She opened her arms and embraced Fiona.

Warmth encompassed her. Not too hot nor too cold. Perfectly balanced. Fiona felt rather than heard Larrakane's blessing before she was shunted out of the darkness.

"Endeavor."

She fell into a heap on her back, eyes staring up into the welcoming bright eyes of Mac and the cold, hard stare of the Binder.

The Binder stamped his stick on the floor. "What have you done?"

"I've done what I said. I've made an agreement with Larrakane."

He appraised her with narrowed eyes then stalked out of the room, stick tapping loudly on the floor as if saying what he would not.

How did he know what went on? Was he simply guessing or intuitive? Fiona wiped her sweaty palms on the edge of her doublet. "What happened?"

"We were talking with the others when he came running up here. It was all I could do to get him to stop from shaking you."

"Why though?"

Mac swept aside her ethereal azure robe to kneel next to Fiona and help her up. "I'm not quite sure, but I've only seen Arc like this a few times. It takes a lot to break his icy wall." She let out a sigh. "If anyone can crack someone, it's you, Fi. But try to be careful with him, okay?"

"You sound like you care for him quite a bit," Fiona said, grasping Mac's hand. She did feel a smidge weaker than expected.

"I do, of course. He's family. They all are. Though I don't always approve of the way he handles his duties, it is simple to judge for we don't have the burden." She stopped, her golden face flushing. "That's always been the case though. Come on. Let's get you downstairs so you can hear it straight from Ice King's mouth."

Fiona patted Mac's hand but stilled her movements. "But how do you know I've bound myself to Larrakane and I'm not just saying so?"

"Well, beyond the matter of knowing when you're lying and when you're not"—Mac grinned and rolled her eyes—"you've got her mark." Mac pressed her warm fingers against Fiona's chest. "Look for yourself." She gestured to the mirror in her room.

Fiona rubbed where she pressed but felt nothing. She strode to the mirror and opened her doublet. A small black circle within a larger ring marked her there, as if it was tattooed on her chest. It felt like nothing beneath her fingers, and as she pulled her hand away it faded. She sighed. Had she done the right thing? Would being further in this situation truly give her the power to do right by others she thought needed someone watching out for them? Or had she simply jumped headfirst into satisfying her own needs of meeting her goal? Her reflection's frown increased and she turned away from the mirror. There were more trusted individuals to ask these questions of. As soon as she could get back to her house of course.

Pulling away from the mirror Mac ushered her downstairs slowly in companiable silence. Everyone turned to look at Fiona when she arrived. She stopped, surprised to see additional familiar faces. Priestess Raina, the temple leader of the Followers of Larrakane, nodded her head in cool greeting, and Fali sat beside her. Fiona hadn't seen Priestess Raina in some months. Not since she had gone in search of Fali to trade information on the smugglers of the fire creatures. Though she had always wanted to meet her in a more professional capacity, she hadn't expected this moment to be the place. But she should've known that the most beloved religious leader in the Book would be well connected.

Fali, being the elephas he was, grinned and strode to meet her, oblivious to the tension in the room. He wrapped his elephantine arm around Fiona's shoulder. "I knew you'd find your way in somehow. Welcome."

Fiona gave him a wide welcoming smile. "What are you doing here?"

"His duty," the Binder said in a loud voice that carried throughout the tavern. "If you're so inclined to dawdle less, then let's not tarry with chatter and get to it." The Binder stamped his walking stick. "Investigator Thorne has been bound. Though it took longer than it should." There was a distinct hush over them all as they looked at her.

Fiona warmed with the attention. It wasn't exactly the sort she craved. She raised her chin and took a step forward. "We came to an agreement."

"Yes," the Binder said, his words growing harsher. The air chilled.

"Well, I'm glad to have a protégé like you." Nicolosia swept their pine-green hair behind their ear. "I took a long while to decide."

"If I am a protégé, what are you?" Fiona said.

"We are the Leaves of Spine," Nicolosia said, pulling her hand toward a seat. "We are bound to Spine and each do our part to safeguard the Book and the people in it."

"How is that different than any other Guardian?" Fiona asked. The Leaves of Spine. Another wordplay. She was beginning to think that the Binder's faeness was certainly showing in these titles.

As if he could read her thoughts, the Binder said somewhat defensively, "Things connected create harmony." The Binder pinched the bridge of his nose, an almost humanlike gesture. "Priestess, if you'll please share your memory with her, we can skip the questions and get to planning. I have much more business to attend to before the evening is out."

Priestess Raina inclined her head, though she did not soften her look of annoyance at the Binder. It seemed he got on everyone's nerves. She moved gracefully to Fiona, sable hair swinging, and stood beside her. "So that a protégé can have the full knowledge of a Leaf, we're able to impart our memories to each other." She smiled and held out her hands. "It only works if you're from the same page however. A sort of tending to one's own garden. May I?"

Fiona nodded, her shoulders tensing. However much she wished it could be Mac or Nicolosia's memory, she knew complaining wouldn't change anything. It seemed she was going to have to continue letting others past her walls today.

Cool fingertips pressed against her forehead and she heard the Priestess whisper, "Once upon a time, there was a queen."

Shoulders tense, Fiona waited patiently but the Priestess said nothing else. She opened her eyes but found that she was no longer sitting in the Thread. Instead, she was standing in the middle of a small green staring up into a bright-blue sky and surrounded by forest as far as she could see. Was this Spine?

Fiona turned around, the rustling of her silken skirts catching her attention. Looking down, she saw she was indeed richly dressed in finer silk than she had ever worn before.

Though it seemed incredibly outdated in its cut and shape. Her head continued to dip down, weighed unusually. She reached toward her curls to find a very solid crown perched there. What in the good name of Larrakane was this?

Steps echoed on the soft grass as if made deliberate. Fiona turned in the body that was not hers to find Mac blinking at her. But this wasn't her Mac of the Thread and bar tabs. No, her golden face was bright and the tattoos rich cream, indigo, and olive stood out predominantly as if freshly done. There were countless tattoo swirls on her face, more than Fiona had ever seen before. Her long sunglow-gold hair was curled to perfection and framed her face and wilting ears. Her flowing azure robes were not as ethereal as they were now. Indeed, they were solid and billowing. No, this was Marcela Aurica Caragiale before Fiona knew her.

"Who are you? Why have you brought me here?" Mac said.

"Queen Eleanor Pompania. And *I* have brought you nowhere," Fiona said in reply. Or at least the memory did. Fiona said nothing but the sound came from her, nonetheless. She waved her hand, but Mac didn't notice the gesture. Odd, perhaps she couldn't do much but watch in the memory of the Queen.

Giddiness rushed through Fiona. However she thought becoming a protégé would go, getting a firsthand view of the Inking from the seat of Queen Pompania the Good was not even in consideration. What would Gaili and Mistress Humbledraft say when she told them! *If* she could tell them, that was. She wasn't sure of all the rules yet and she feared there would be many.

Fiona broke away from her thoughts, hearing other voices, other words being spoken by herself. A thought intruded into her head. *Perchance this is what Larrakane spoke of when she said a gathering was at hand.* So she could hear Queen Eleanor's thoughts as well? Fiona strove to pay attention and take in everything she could as more people arrived as if out of thin air.

Two more fae had appeared and were conversing with Mac. One was easily Nicolosia with their warm golden-brown skin and pine-green hair. Like Mac they dressed more regally and with greater excess than Fiona had ever seen the Elder druid possess. The youngest of the fae, shorter in comparison to them both, had ochre skin and was dressed in robes of subtle bronze and gold with light tattoos across her face. This had to be Dani, the fae that could be both poised and disordered.

Queen Eleanor took a step back. Fiona sensed she was worried about the temperature and sudden wind coming off of the trio. It was chaotic, at best, and Eleanor had no desire to be swept up in whatever they were. *I've had enough interaction with magic for a lifetime.*

Fiona started. Eleanor had already dealt with magic before the Inking? She supposed that made sense based on the little history Richard had given her. But that she remembered it was interesting. Perhaps the Leaves of Spine at this time were warded from Richard's power or he didn't have them yet?

It seemed the fae noticed Queen Eleanor's movement. Nicolosia smiled and broke apart from the three. Mac looked over and nodded, moving away as well to stand apart. The temperature leveled out and the wind died down just as a smilodon appeared. His lion mane swirled around him, brushing stately against his draped cream robes as he stalked onto the green.

He stopped, eyes roving over all that he saw. "Greetings. Enemies? Allies?"

"I hope the latter," Queen Eleanor said quietly. "You are well met, Sir—?"

"I am Julius Sebastius, consul of Roma."

This surprised Queen Eleanor. Her thoughts were too quick for Fiona to understand anything more than passing familiarity and confusion. Why would that of all things be the most confusing part to the Queen?

Before Fiona could dwell on it further, the view in front of them changed and the world peeled away as if turning a page in a book. From within a landscape of snowcapped mountains stepped a neat fae man with bright ivory skin. The Binder. His silken robes were swaths of frosty snow, sky, and sleet. Extending his hand, he pulled a young human woman with deep-brown skin and jet-black afro hair through the vignette. It closed behind them without a whisper. The page had been turned.

Queen Eleanor bowed to the woman, immediately recognizing her. It took Fiona a moment more to understand that this was Larrakane. This small human woman in a dress as black and blue as the night sky. Lights dotted her shoulders, and she shifted this way and that. She was human? *No,* Fiona's own thoughts bubbled up, *she was as one wanted to see her.* What did the smilodon Julius, or even the fae see?

"Greetings, venerable leaders. I come to you as I said, seeking your aid." Larrakane glanced at them each in kind.

Eleanor seemed to stiffen at the words. *Seeking is soft playing it, Larrakane.*

Fiona focused, trying to read deeper into Eleanor's mind. She couldn't get more than surface thoughts. This was a memory, after all. It's likely Eleanor didn't give more than she needed to her protégé. Interesting that she had passed on these though. To Fiona it was clear that Eleanor was already aware of what Larrakane was about to say.

"Your worlds and those within them are in danger. You have all seen the images of her world." Larrakane pointed to Eleanor. "We must act quickly to ensure that no further damage is done."

"You must show yourself to be more than you are," Julius said. He gathered his robe on his arm and moved closer to her, narrowing his eyes. "I admit I was curious when you reached out to me in my dream, but how do I know you are not some plot by my enemy?"

"I believe an effect is in order," the Binder murmured, scowling at Julius. The other fae moved to stand behind him as if in support. "For you have little time to waste."

Larrakane frowned at the Binder and at Julius. She barely moved as a ripple of duplicated Juliuses burst forth across the land beside her. They moved separately but all looked exactly like the smilodon. Confusion, surprise, and more raced across their faces and his. They all began to speak at once but here the similarities ended. Anger, frustration, joy, and eagerness were the tones of each copy. Singular-minded, they began to act in their fashion.

Julius stumbled back, dropping the edges of his robe. He grabbed his head. "No, give them back."

She shifted a step and the Juliuses disappeared one after another.

Julius straightened up, eyes wide. He bowed low. "Forgive me. I did not know."

"The only harmony there can be is through symmetry within," Larrakane said quietly. "I do not need to prove myself again."

Julius nodded and quickly fell back with the others. "What are we to do?"

"I *am* the ruling force of these realms. You must ensure that I am known and known well. Place me on the lips and in the hearts of all that you lead," Larrakane said.

"And this will keep the danger back?" Dani asked. "How can that be all that is needed?"

"How sure are you that this will not bleed into our realms?" Mac added.

"I am no more certain than I am omniscient. But it has worked for my kind before and still does. As long as I am the ruling force of these realms, the danger can grow no larger. Even now, bound away, the world it broke is healing." She threw up her hand and turned the page of the world once more.

Smoke rose on the horizon from bright fires in the distance. Roiling dark clouds covered the sky. Larrakane strode through the portal and the others came after her, stumbling as if yanked by some unseen force. They stood on the edge of a precipice of jagged, scorched rock. Far below, the land was cracked and broken, as if it had been impacted time and time again. Colossal craters dotted the view and the acrid stench of burnt earth stung Fiona's nostrils. This was ruined far beyond anything she had ever seen before. Where were they? Even as she had the thought she knew, in her heart, that this was her home. She felt herself, Queen Eleanor's body, tremble. Fiona heard the voice of the renowned Queen whisper, "I will not let this happen to anyone else."

"What remains?" Mac said, grasping Nicolosia's arm.

"Enough to have hope," Eleanor said. She looked out into the broken landscape. "But not enough to have certainty."

"You must not allow tears—" Larrakane gasped and stumbled back as if she had been hit. Fiona and Queen Eleanor as one reached out to catch her shivering form. She weighed almost nothing. Larrakane stood and patted Eleanor's hands before glancing once more back at the ruined landscape. She strode through the open portal, pulling them back with her. With a swift movement of her hand, she wiped away the door, closing off the broken world.

Julius said, "What will you give us to do this?"

Mac strode forward, her gown billowing as she pointed at Julius. "You would ask for something in return after what we've just witnessed?"

He stood taller and faced her down. "I have not gotten where I am by being anything less than a negotiator. Our people will need help if we are to keep something that could rip a whole realm apart at bay." He turned imploringly to Larrakane. "We need an army."

"An army you shall have." Larrakane nodded. "But you must never name the danger. For a name would give it credence."

"How could my people ever forget what happened to us? We will never," Queen Eleanor said.

Fiona pushed to read Eleanor's thoughts. Sadness overcame her but along with it was anger. At herself, at Larrakane? She couldn't decipher it.

"You will never forget." A pained look crossed Larrakane's face, but she swallowed hard and said, "They *must* forget their names, their heritage, and their destruction. He will see to it."

Fiona didn't need to read Eleanor's thoughts to understand who Larrakane meant. Richard truly had no choice, did he?

Where had he been in that ruined landscape? And was this danger, this unnamed force of destruction, his brother? Why would Larrakane not acknowledge that a person had done these deeds if that was the case?

"You must all remain here in order to succeed. I have cobbled this place from my own. The danger cannot survive here, and as long as you remain, you will keep me strong against...it."

There was hesitation there. Fiona couldn't tell if it was her or Eleanor noticing, but it was there. *You do not trust them enough to tell the whole truth,* Eleanor's thoughts intruded again. She knew more than Larrakane was letting on. But she didn't seem inclined to uncover the deity. Why?

"Are there more of us? More realms?" Dani asked in a hopeful tone.

"Your realms are the most in danger," Larrakane said quietly. Her eyes met Eleanor's.

Don't. Don't tell them about the Word or its abstracts.

Larrakane looked away toward the Binder. "Each of you have a task in hand. You have your own powers. Use them, together." Larrakane's head dipped and she jerked herself upright. "I must retire if I am to set things to rights before the day is done. What say you?"

"And if we refuse to do as you ask?" the Binder said with an arched tone.

"Then you will be forgotten as well. And very much alone," Larrakane said. She arched her shoulders back, staring into his eyes unmoving.

Was this how Eleanor saw her or how she was?

"It seems we have no choice then." Dani glanced at the Binder. He nodded to her once, as if commanding. She bowed her head.

"There is always a choice," Larrakane interjected. "Whether the options are pleasing is another matter altogether. But would you wish what happened to Earth happen to your worlds?"

In turn they each shook their head no. Eleanor breathed a small sigh of relief, her shoulders lowering. Fiona got the sense that she knew this would come down to them all making the choice. A choice the Queen had already made.

"Very well. May your stay in this place be successful. You will each name your successor when needed, but I hope it does not come to that." Larrakane's person began to fade into the surroundings of the green grass and bright-blue sky. "I will be back before long. Gather yourselves for one last visit to your homes." She faded away.

The group stood and watched her go. Fiona's mind raced as the visage of the deity disappeared. How long would she still remain here? Fiona quickly began looking at the other leaders. The fae stood apart, but the rest of the Seasons looked toward the Binder as if waiting for him to speak.

Julius paced, clearly thinking. He had requested an army. Had that been granted? Of course, yes. Fiona winced as she realized with alarm that's what page turners were certainly made for. An army. Larrakane had said as much to herself moments before. To be conscripted into a fight one didn't even know was happening. This was why Fiona wanted to bind herself for people and not Larrakane. Power used. Regardless of the cost.

Fiona wished she could look outside of this body to see Queen Eleanor's face. As far as she could tell, no thoughts were flitting in the Queen's head. That seemed unlikely. Why couldn't she hear everything?

Queen Eleanor spoke, addressing the others. "We will need places to sleep for the time being and to converse for the hours ahead so we can work together."

The Binder nodded. "I have seen to that. If you'll all follow me."

How could the Binder have already seen to their comfort? Did he know before they did? Fiona sucked in a breath, the blue sky and green grass melting abruptly from her view. Cold darkness pervaded her space. Was she moving to another memory or being pulled away? Faint lights flashed on and off in the distance. Stars? No, it was the dark edge. Its familiarity washed over her and she steadied herself. Larrakane had given them almost nothing, but the show of total collapse of Queen Eleanor's home was real. Earth? Not just a word but a title. And all humans made to forget their names, their heritage. There were so many odd things about this memory, but the questions she could put to others. She would need time to dwell on all she learned but feared that time wouldn't soon be at hand.

SHE OPENED HER EYES to see intent faces watching her. Blinking, she said, "How long was I in her memories?"

"A minute or so." Priestess Raina took a step back. "It is a lot to take in. Some can't handle it."

"I wonder—"

"At another time," the Binder interrupted. "If you cannot run, you can be left behind."

Resisting the urge to say something cutting, Fiona nodded. She didn't want any more special attention. This was the time to watch and learn as much as she could. How different were the Circle of Seasons now versus the beginning of the Inking? Though they may not have realized, they had just given Fiona a boon of information. There was so much to unpack. It was doubtful she'd sleep for weeks at this rate.

The Binder seemed satisfied with her agreeance and carried on. "The Painted Edge's attack on Rise has to be the last attack to take us by surprise."

"Surprise?" Fiona interrupted. "You all had no inkling of it?"

"We know them to be smugglers, even skips, but taking an island? That has no value that any normal thief would know,"

Fali interjected. "So the question has quickly become, What is the value to the Painted Edge?"

So they remember the island. Well, that proved that the Leaves could hold their own memories against Richard.

"I don't need to know its value to know they should be stopped at all cost," the Binder said. "We should do a full blockade. Take the jackets to all pagemarks, known and unknown, and setup rotations."

"We can't keep the other pages under siege," Priestess Raina said. "They will undoubtedly push back against that. They do have independence."

"This Emperor would use it to start another war. And then we'll be fighting on two fronts instead of one," Fali said.

"We should allow the Guardians to do their jobs," Nicolosia said. "If we could find the others in the mortal pages, alert them, perhaps combined—"

The Binder snorted. "It's taken you years to uncover their whereabouts, and we're no closer to reaching them all. The Guardians becoming more prominent is simply making it harder to keep the Book under control." He turned to Raina and Fali. "And your strategies are too slow. I have seen my share of war. A blockade in the pages would stop such notions, not entertain them."

"We don't even know what pages are still untapped," Mac said, moving behind the bar. "This new one Fi found, does it have a Guardian? Are there page turners from it yet?"

"That remains to be seen," the Binder said.

"So you don't know about any other pages?" Fiona said.

"If there are others, we've yet to uncover them," Mac said.

"Well, what does Larrakane have to say about it?" Fiona said.

"She can't say anything." The Binder stood up. "Every time we visit, it takes her energy. And she needs every ounce of it against…the situation. The ask of other pages are questions too small to bring to her."

"Not if it means having information your enemy clearly already knows. They got to the plant page first!" Fiona said. It was obvious they were not working together as well as Larrakane had hoped they would. For what reasons, she didn't know, but of all the people in the Book Fiona wasn't one to politely stay quiet for long. "You're all talking about what you should do instead of working to come up with a suitable plan together. You're used to working separately." She looked at Nicolosia and Mac, thinking of Eleanor's memory. "Perhaps it's even important you be physically parted across Spine. But if we don't all pull together what we know and concoct a plan together, then we'll never get anywhere. The Painted Edge wants chaos. They need it so everyone is too busy solving the problems they create instead of getting in front of them. We need to stop putting bandages on the wound and find the bow that's being drawn."

"And what would you have us do?" the Binder said, arms crossed. "What could you possibly know that we don't?"

"Well, for one thing, no one has even mentioned that both Rise and Blaze were considerably weakened by the Painted Edge's attacks. Who knows what would've happened to Copper if Clara hadn't been stopped? It's a pattern though. Weakening the pages seems to be at least part of their plan."

"If that's true, then for what purpose?" Raina said.

"Could it be to undermine you all?" Fiona tilted her head, taking the Leaves of Spine in as a group. "They tried to wrest control from the Travel Guild earlier this year by blaming the dying Blaze on you."

"I had nothing to do with that," the Binder said, straightening his shoulders.

"Of course not. But by not putting out any statements and working in the shadows with the jackets, it didn't help the cause. Follow the line. If that *had* worked, they would've flooded the markets with stolen alchemical goods, made profits, and had money to then overthrow the Travel Guild. Even if it took time to make the money, all they had to do was be better than the Guild to the rest of the Book to undermine you."

The Binder scoffed. "Fanciful notions. As if anyone could do that."

"All it takes is for people to feel you've overstepped your duties for them to become defensive," Fiona said quietly. "People want to feel like they have control over their own lives."

"The people of the Book don't know what we do here," Fali said. "They don't understand. It *was* working, Binder. People everywhere believed the Guild to be the enemy."

"What does this mean then?" Dani asked with a confused look.

"The Painted Edge is trying for power. Take Rise: the Queen was almost undone by the chaos they caused. If Lord Henry Hawkport had been able to get rid of her and taken the throne, they would've had a powerful ally in Rise. And their leader—"

The Binder interrupted, "Yes? This *human* woman, Stella, I believe. I've read full reports on her."

Fiona glanced at the Binder. He had stressed *human* when speaking of Stella. Did he not tell the others about her being a hag? Or did Marcia not tell him herself? Fiona looked toward the others, assessing her next steps. She didn't think continuing to keep secrets was the right thing to do here, but what would it do to Marcia if the Circle of Seasons knew she was a hag? The Binder had to know. Perhaps he was even the fae she was bound to. The one who gave her abilities to use when they were trying to find the plant page.

"She's under custody now, yes?" Dani asked, traipsing closer to Fiona. "I assume she was captured along with the other Painted Edge members in Rise?"

"Actually no." Fiona swallowed. "She tried to overtake the turn back to Rise and pulled herself into the dark edge."

The flutter of reactions was no surprise to Fiona. The dark edge was a warning given to all page turners as an end to life and the Book. But Stella wasn't a page turner. And Fiona wasn't sure anymore if it truly was simply an end. It could clearly be traveled through if needed. She had done so twice.

Out of all in the room, though, the Binder, Dani, and Nicolosia looked the most distraught. The Binder quickly smoothed out his face and nodded.

Mac said softly, "At least with the leader gone the Painted Edge should begin to fracture."

Fiona shook her head. It was clear now she was making her report before Marcia. "There is another. Stella was quite clear that there was a leader over the Painted Edge who was not her."

"How could that be?" Dani said. "She was the one who had her hand in everything."

"Perhaps she was simply trying to mislead you." The Binder smirked at Fiona.

"No. Stella misled for games. This was not sport for her. She was trying to convince me to join her."

The Binder raised an eyebrow. "And?"

"Arc!" Mac said, throwing her rag at him. "Don't you dare question Fiona's loyalties. She has given more to our cause than many of your jackets have."

He shrugged. "I ask because I have to."

"You don't," Mac said.

Fiona held up her hands. "It doesn't matter. Of course I declined. But who hasn't? Who else like Hawkport and the salamanders and Clara are waiting in the wings to help the Painted Edge and this leader? Even if unintentionally. We must get in front of them. They used the Spring Crown to control the page turn from Rise with an airship. What can they do with the others?"

"Spring Crown?" Priestess Raina asked. She looked at Nicolosia. "Is that your doing?"

Nicolosia grimaced, golden-brown face darkening. "Of course not."

The Binder turned to Fiona and said in clipped tones, "Not everything is open for discussion."

"Well, it should be. Work together. Perhaps then we can get somewhere quickly."

"You are not Queen Eleanor," the Binder said. "Having her memories does not mean you can tell us what to do."

"She's not trying to lead us, Binder," Fali interjected. "She's simply trying to make us useful to ourselves."

"There's too much space built between us," Nicolosia said. "Fiona is right. We must let down some walls if we're to tackle this threat. The Painted Edge are greater than anything we've come up against."

Mac stepped from around the bar and placed her hand on the Binder's shoulder. She glanced at Raina. "The crowns are creations of mine. From our time before the Inking. In Copper, Stella made off with three crowns. And I've given Dani the fourth."

"Why?" the Binder said, rounding on Dani. "What need could you possibly have for it?"

"It's mine," Dani said, balling her fists. "Why shouldn't I have what's mine?"

"It's better she keeps it, even in the fretful state it's in. She may need it in the days to come." Mac sighed.

"They were a terrible idea then, Marcela, and they're a terrible idea now. You should've given it to me. I could've put it in safe storage."

Fiona tried to dampen her interest so it didn't show. What was this? A storage that could contain powerful items like the crowns?

Mac interrupted her thoughts. "That's in the past now, Arc. Do you have the Spring Crown, Fi?"

Fiona shook her head. "I can get it, but it's in a safe place for now."

"I can't imagine how they used it to move an airship," Nicolosia said, "I suppose with the wind...and to a plant page, you said? It would be attracted to that." They sighed and muttered, "I would be attracted to that."

Fiona rose and took Nicolosia's hand, squeezing it. They could never leave Spine. The only source of their power that seemed to be able to move about the Book were the Seasonal Crowns. And by that logic, what even were the crowns? The crowns weren't Guardians, weren't part of other pages to be used as bookmarks. So why did the Painted Edge seek them?

Simply for the power they may wield? "We should narrow down what they could do with the other two crowns," Fiona said to Mac, "and then use that knowledge to run interference on what pages they might be attracted to and what they could affect. It stands to reason they stole them to weaken other pages as well. Known or unknown."

Mac nodded. "I'll get on it now."

"Anything else of considerable power they may have taken that we aren't aware of?" Fiona said to the group.

"Do other powerful items like the crowns even exist?" Fali asked the Binder. "Or magic in general we could use against the Painted Edge?"

Fiona glanced at Priestess Raina, who blinked at her wide eyed. It was a blink that Fiona knew how to read all too well. A feigned innocence. They shared the same memory now. There must be a reason for not telling the others about the Word. Perhaps she shouldn't either, since she'd have to explain Richard's secrets in the process. "It's possible," Fiona said. "The Book is thin. While Copper inventions are marvelous, who knows what else may be out there?" Glancing around the room, she was surprised that all the attention was on her. She supposed she had always wanted the leaders of Spine to listen to her. Simply with a little less argument about her capabilities. She turned to the Binder and crossed her arms. "And we should look at who else may be their ally." He was a hard one who wouldn't tolerate being told what to do. "Is this something the Travel Guild would look in to?"

The Binder snorted, the first crack of his icy demeanor. "You know that it is. By Larrakane's grace, Marcius was right about you."

Fiona crossed her arms. "That I'm a boon to any case?"

"That you're as stubborn as a smilodon and manipulative as a fae." The Binder arched an eyebrow.

It was hard to know if it was genuine or meant to intimidate her. Interesting that he called Dodger by his first name. That showed closeness, indeed, to someone who didn't report directly to him. But the inclusion of Dodger made her tilt her head and assess the Binder again. Had he been testing her? Fiona stood up taller and dropped her arms. She wasn't the one who should be tested. She had proven herself time and time again. He had yet to do so for her. "I suppose we should get on with it."

The Binder nodded. "I agree." He stretched his hand to the door of the Thread, throwing a frigid blast of wind to open it. "You can join us now."

Marcia strode into the Thread, keeping her eyes somewhat lowered as if she couldn't remember what she couldn't see. She stopped and stood at attention beside the Binder. Her human appearance, bunned hair and understated dress, were back to being neat and tidy as a pin. Fiona could barely notice a difference between her now and her before going to the page of plants. The hag's illusion was always maintained, it seemed.

Bouncing in after Marcia, much to Fiona's surprise, was Dodger. He looked just as shocked to see her and almost halted before coming to stand on the other side of the Binder. He, too, stood at attention but not before raising an eyebrow at her.

How long had they been outside? Had they heard anything?

"As we were taking our time here, I thought it best to bring reports to us. Though I much prefer the sanctity of the Hinge."

Mac closed the Thread door and locked it. "You know just as well as I that this has the same wards."

"And comfier chairs," Fali said in his wide seat.

The Binder ignored them. "Report."

Marcia stated, "Of all the Painted Edge members acting within Rise, only a few weren't captured. Our thanks for that go to our new allies, the plantians. The Painted Edge are awaiting trial at the Hinge. The others are being pursued by jackets."

"And the leader?" The Binder stood still as a statue, each part of his symmetrical fae face unmoving.

Was he trying to corroborate Fiona's story or see if she was lying? Or was it more that he wanted to see if Marcia knew what happened to her sister?

There was a brief hesitation on Marcia's part before she said, "She seems to have jumped into the dark edge as we made the trip back to Rise. We haven't seen or heard from her."

Something shifted in her tone even though her face didn't move. What was she hiding? Fiona took a step closer, watching her carefully.

"However, she has reported that there is someone else above her. Whether a manipulation tactic or truth, it is hard to determine." Marcia looked at the Binder and said, "She also said quite clearly that Spine was a prison and page turners aren't the only ones cursed from the Inking."

"So it would seem we continue running into the same problem," Mac said with a sigh. "Without a unified goal, some page turners just won't see being inked as anything other than a trap."

"We have a unified goal. Some people will make any excuse," the Binder said, throwing glares at both Nicolosia and Dani.

A much-trotted-out argument was evidently had between the Seasons. For how long, Fiona didn't know, but it was clear this wasn't the first time they had disagreed on this matter.

Would Mac or Nicolosia tell her more? Perhaps she could spend some time with them after a brief rest.

"How could they possibly change being bound to Spine, or how could non-page turners possibly change the fact that only page turners could do the traveling? Assuming that's why non-page turners feel cursed," Fali said.

"That is just the kind of information we are close to finding out." The Binder rocked back on his heels "Though you all may think the Travel Guild is *overextended*, we've had several spies infiltrate the ranks of the Painted Edge successfully. While it's a long game of waiting for information, we recently received a hasty report that indicates one has gotten closer than any of our other operatives. They had been tasked by the Painted Edge as part of a small group on an unknown mission. They are supposed to give a full report as soon as they return." He strode toward the center of the group and tapped his cane on the floor. "We had assumed the leader to be Stella and this mission to be simple like all the others, but now it may prove otherwise. We can't wait for our operative to come back home to us."

"Well, who is this operative?" Dani said, drumming her fingers against the table. "How can we contact them?"

"That information isn't needed here." He waved his hand dismissively, then nodded toward Dodger. "But Marbled Jacket Cervidus has been briefed and will lead the mission to retrieve the information from our spy or our spy themself. He will not interrupt the spy's undercover operation unless it is beneficial to these questions. Who is the actual leader of the Painted Edge? And how can we get in front of their next plan?" The Binder looked at Fiona with a smirk. "Since you are clearly of the mind that we should be pulling together, Investigator

Thorne, perhaps you will work with Marbled Jacket Cervidus on this one."

Fiona worked to keep her outward reaction from mirroring her inner one. He was offering something she would absolutely do, and he knew that. But why in this manipulative manner? She had no reason to lie to them all, and his games were beginning to wear on her. If she said no, what would that tell him about her? Instead of trying to read his expressions, it would be quicker simply to get that information straight from Dodger. "Of course. Anything to get ahead for once."

The Binder nodded. "I believe we are adjourned then. Dismissed."

Marcia relaxed her stiff posture beside the Binder and hurried toward the door. She glanced back at Dodger before she walked out, chin up and head high.

Dodger waited a beat before saying to Fiona, "Whiskey meeting?"

Fiona smirked at Dodgers' clear inference. He may be stuffy to some, but she knew how to read him well. "Of course. Keep it neat."

He inclined his head before heading out into the night, stopping only to help Priestess Raina on with her cloak and escort her out.

Fiona watched quite tiredly from her corner as Nicolosia and Fali spoke to the Binder. It was clear that despite the arguments and loyalty lines, the Binder commanded much more than the Travel Guild. No one had rejected this dismissal or the ending of their gathering. Almost everyone was making sure to connect with him before they left. Plans were set in motion by the Binder, and that was that. How often did it end this way?

"He can't stop taking control. I do believe if he tried, he'd perish like a melting snowflake," Dani whispered to Fiona, appearing beside her.

Startled at the quickness of the fae, Fiona smiled to hide her surprise. She hadn't expected a direct address without initiating it herself. Fiona glanced at the Binder and then back at Dani's carefully arched eyebrow and composed face. "He's quite sure of himself isn't he?"

"That he is, but why wouldn't he be? Chosen by Larrakane to command her army and lead the Circle of Seasons. Arc has been around longer than any of us. In Copper at least. If he doesn't get his way, he simply finds another route." Dani tilted her head, eyes wide with amusement "Then again, I can't say I don't either. There are always solutions if one just looks hard enough."

The Binder frowned at her as if having heard their conversation, then turned his back and marched out the door of the Thread. All warmth returned to the room at once. His Seasonal spirit was overwhelming, to say the least.

Fiona glanced at Dani, assessing her. She looked as young as she had in Queen Eleanor's memory. There was no power that Fiona could notice coming from her, but then what would it be like? She thought of Gaili's aged hand and swallowed hard.

The young fae waved her terra-cotta-colored fingers as if dismissing herself, seeming to see Fiona's unease. "Oh, don't mind what I say. So you are bound to Larrakane now. How do you feel?"

"Like I've gone several days without coffee and sleep." She started, realizing she had. But it was more than that, a sort of deep ache within her. "Do you ever get used to it?"

"Not really," Dani said, rubbing her chest, "but from what I've heard of you, you'll get over it in no time, I'm sure."

"Nicolosia says much to you about me?" she said.

"You would be surprised what people who like you say," Dani said, winking at Fiona. The corner of her eyes crinkled. "Not least of all Nic. Mac is also always singing your praises."

It did seem that those three had a closer relationship with each other than with the Binder. The Binder and Dani hadn't spoken at all after the meeting, though she clearly still took cues from him. Tired and on edge, Fiona didn't hold back her customary bluntness: "You and the Binder don't like each other much. Why?"

"Arc would have the Book always running to the time of his Guild and under his cold hand. I don't disagree that his role is an important one, but, well, it wasn't quite like that where we came from."

"You had more in Copper?"

Dani shrugged. "No more than any of the other Seasons."

Fiona heard a hint of resentfulness in Dani's voice. Was she thankful like Mac to be free from the responsibility of ruling so many? She'd seemed so young in the memory, but that meant she was over two hundred years old currently.

"How did Stella seem? This Painted Edge woman who thrust her way into the dark edge?" Dani said, glancing back toward the door.

Caught off guard by the change in topic, Fiona stumbled over her words before saying, "Resolute, really. She was a challenging woman. Clever." She grimaced remembering the split-second look on Marcia's face when she heard where her sister had gone. "I wish she hadn't done it," Fiona said softly.

"Would you have made another choice if you knew she was going to do that?" Dani shook her head slowly. "How could you have known, right?"

"I don't know if I would have made another choice, honestly. If I had known. Rise was dying and—" She tugged on her scarf as her chest tightened. There had been precious few seconds to make decisions. She hadn't considered she made the wrong one. Or that Stella had even given her much of a choice. "I would've tried to stop her if it hadn't endangered so many lives."

Dani cleared her throat and nodded. "I should get back to the Bluff. The aqueducts aren't going to keep themselves moving."

"You oversee the Rocky Bluff?" The cliffs were the northernmost area in Spine and encompassed the farming district and the massive lake, Depth's Door, which fed the aqueducts that ran throughout the city. Fiona had always thought Travel Guild jackets ran the area, for the lake was a pagemark to the water page. That it was the domain of the Autumn Monarch seemed natural, however.

"I would be happy to show you, if it interests you?" Dani said with a wide smile.

"I always love seeing Spine from another's eyes. I would like that, after this is all over."

Dani tilted her head. "Of course. Don't wait too long though. The rose of opportunity blooms but once and you've never seen a sight like the Bluff." She waved to Fiona. "Stay safe. The Painted Edge seems quite determined. No one is secure while they continue to work in the shadows." She strode toward the door, giving a long look to Nicolosia before departing.

Fiona rubbed her neck and sighed. It had been more than a long day and she supposed it would continue on without a stop. She needed to meet up with Dodger and hear his briefing. Even after her speech, she hated that the Binder had given the rest of the group no more information. But he hadn't put any restrictions on her. Rules never made could never be broken. As the investigation progressed, she had every intention of telling all the Leaves what her and Dodger discovered. Let him try to keep her quiet then.

"Dear Fiona, would you mind walking with me back to the forest?" Nicolosia said. They looped their arm in hers and tugged her toward the door.

Though she had wanted to poke Mac when everyone left, it seemed Nicolosia wanted Fiona's ears only. "Of course." She waved to Mac as they left, calling over her shoulder, "I'll report back soon."

Into the waxing early morning hours they trotted over the vined cobblestone streets. It was as if the road needed much maintenance. How much was this Nicolosia's doing?

"Are you controlling the vines?" Fiona asked.

"Hmm? Oh yes, quite. I stay better connected if I can feel the forest at all times," Nicolosia said distractedly. They said it so easily. As if days ago it wouldn't have taken Fiona much needling to get the depth of their true power admitted. Which piece of new information was distracting them?

"Where are your thoughts?"

They patted her arm. "Everywhere and here all at once. I hope that what you've done and what you've learned have answered your questions?"

"While giving me many more, yes, of course." Fiona stopped for a moment and watched her friend's scrunched face. "I don't regret you bringing me here, if that's what you're worried about."

Relief at being understood seemed to smooth their features. "It's so much to put on a person." Nicolosia sighed. "When we were told—well, it wasn't a unanimous decision all at once. We Seasons are particular."

Fiona laughed. "You don't say."

Nicolosia smiled. "I suppose you learned more by watching us than listening to what we said. You are quick, dear Fiona. I am hoping you'll be quick enough to help us all."

"I shall try."

"I know." Nicolosia sighed again. "It's just, I feel something is off and I can't put my finger on what. It all seems too easy for the Painted Edge."

"What do you mean? The chaos they've created?" The organization did seem to create quite a bit in a short time, but who knew how long they had been quietly working before they started?

Nicolosia nodded. "As you saw in Queen Eleanor's memory, Larrakane gave us each a specific task."

Fiona frowned. She hadn't seen that at all. While Larrakane had said they each had their task, there was no memory of the Queen ever being given one or the others being taken away to be given theirs. Had Priestess Raina hidden that from her? Why?

The druid carried on, too distracted to notice Fiona's pause. "While I've figured out some of the others over the years, I can be clear with you as my protégé and say that mine is to care for the Guardians."

"I had gathered as much from my conversation with Soots," Fiona said, "but I am glad to hear it straight from you. It is a large task."

"And a hard one. The reason there are no elemental Leaves in Spine is their chaotic nature. I've always known of the elemental Guardians in their pages, waiting for the day they would emerge. It took quite a few more decades than I imagined. But the mortal Guardians...I have been waiting too long. I suppose Arc is right. I shall have to be more proactive with the druids to uncover the others and get them ready if the Painted Edge should endanger them."

"I believe I can help you with at least one."

Nicolosia patted her hand. "Yes, I was somewhat surprised when you said the Rise Guardian was a man. I assumed it would be something more consequential to the page."

So Nicolosia didn't know or at least understand human history. Didn't know who Richard truly was. Fiona resolved to connect them and make Richard explain. He needed help, whether he would admit it or not. And perhaps it would show him he truly wasn't alone. But what had this to do with the druid's worry on the Painted Edge's easy time of it? "How is this connected to your concern?"

"No one knew, or should've known, about the Guardians until the first one. And yet the Painted Edge not only tracked down but got access to Blaze's Guardian so easily. I don't believe it was an accident or coincidence. How did they know? I've never told a soul. Not even Dani. And they've orchestrated such a large organization, right under Arc's nose. An impossible feat, I would've said years ago."

Fiona tilted her head. "You said you had guessed at the other Leaves of Spine's tasks from Larrakane. What are they?"

Nicolosia pursed their lips. "It is not my place to break oaths to Larrakane. I worry that it endangers her, to be honest."

Fiona sighed, though she could've guessed the druid wouldn't do anything that might go against the goddess. "Well, could someone else have figured them all out as well?"

"Only if they were *part* of the Leaves of Spine." They stood on the edge of the forest near the tree they had entered from. Nicolosia put their hand on the bark, their face softening as if comforted. But their voice trembled. "The Leaves have had five protégé's enter our group since the Inking. We Seasons have had none until you."

Fiona wet her lips, thinking hard. If that was the case, then what Nicolosia was afraid to voice was that someone within the group had the means to support the Painted Edge. Or lead them. "I see."

Nicolosia nodded. "I thought you would. It is hard to separate loyalty and love from reason. Certainly, for me. I can't see Mac or Daniele being involved that way at all. But the others, perhaps? But you, well, dear Fiona, I do believe you can separate loyalty and love from reason if needed."

Besides Nicolosia the only other person she felt she couldn't bear to be involved was Mac. She was sure of it. But where did that leave the others? It was clear Nicolosia was close with Dani. They had even slipped into using her full name without seeming to notice. Fiona didn't correct them or call attention to it.

The druid grasped her shoulder. "I share this only with you as my successor. Do not tell anyone what I have said, because if it *is* one of us, then we are all in danger. And if it isn't, then we'll continue to fracture while the Painted Edge wins. If you need me or have news for me, tell it to Spine."

"To Spine?"

Nicolosia patted the tree. "We all have our duties, Fiona. For better or worse." Nicolosia ran their hands down the trunk of the tree, and it split open willingly. "Take very serious care, my dear. I'll reach out to this stubborn man of yours in Rise and continue my duties. Once you've recovered the information, come to me. Together we can work out how to proceed with the others." They stepped into the tree and then was gone.

Fiona took a step back and wrapped her arms around herself, shivering in the left-behind cold of the druid's departure. So many secrets between them all. So many lies. If the leader of the Painted Edge was among them, they would not be easy to find. And they had just been told there may be a spy who could identify them. They needed to find the spy soon. Before a traitor found them first.

FIONA HURRIED THROUGH THE streets of the turner district to get home before the dawn brightened on Spine. She yawned involuntarily and rubbed her eyes, feeling the hours she had been away in every movement. Her Kerus slippers skirted across the ground without the energy to be stealthy on the uncovered stone streets. She wasn't the only one around at this time of day. Spine often saw travelers and page turners from all over the Book at any time. With so many other shifts of day and night, and in the elemental chapter no shift at all, the city was always open for business in one part or another.

The city. Spine was a part of Larrakane's own place. What did that mean? Was it part of where she lived? Or had lived? She seemed very much contained in her own space now, whatever she was before the Inking. The Binder said Larrakane needed all her energy to fight the situation. Was that situation the same as Richard's brother? Or an unrelated danger that destroyed the world she witnessed in Queen Eleanor's dream? It seemed impossible that that was the beautiful, thriving Restless Rise of today.

Larrakane had made keeping the danger at bay seem so simple to the leaders in Eleanor's memory. Keeping Larrakane in the hearts and minds of all people in the Book couldn't possibly be all that was needed. But Queen Eleanor Pompania hadn't argued against Larrakane's assertion, though she had clearly thought negatively about other things the deity said. Was she a queen before the Inking? How so if Richard was king? Were they—Fiona's tired mind struggled around the implication of Richard and Eleanor possibly being a ruling couple. She didn't have the composure to chew on that right now. So many questions. Would Priestess Raina know?

What had Priestess Raina kept from her and why? What specific task did Raina have? Foolish. If they each had a task at hand, how did they not know they were conflicting? What had the goddess been thinking, keeping them locked away like that so they couldn't transparently work with each other?

Heavy footfalls padded on the stones directly behind her, interrupting her groggy racing thoughts. She turned around to see Fali hurrying toward her. Remembering Nicolosia's fear, she tightened a grip on her scarf.

He stopped. "I didn't mean to startle you. Nicolosia whisked you away so quickly and I wanted to chat before you scampered off on the case."

"Ah, well, you have found me." She gave him a small smile.

Fali stood a moment catching his breath. "As I tried to say before the Binder interrupted, I'm glad you're here. I knew you'd make your way into this group in no time."

"I can't believe you're apart of all this. I never would've guessed." She shook her head "Not that you aren't caring about the Book and Larrakane, I mean," Fiona hastily added.

"But that someone so young could be in an institution so old?" Fali raised his trunk high and gave her a wide grin around it.

"Someone so down to earth could be with all these stubborn, evasive people," Fiona said, relaxing with a chuckle.

"Well, no one takes me seriously much."

"I do. And I appreciate your warm welcome." She sighed, glancing around the quiet street. The full daylight of Spine was just an hour or so off. But as sleepy as she was, she knew that Fali hadn't sought her out simply to say congratulations. "Tell me, what do you know about the rest of the Leaves? Any secrets?"

Fali laughed. "Eh, I'm not an ear for secrets, if you can believe it. The Binder was right in that I mainly do my duty to the teaching and words of Larrakane. Keeping her in the memories and minds of all I can with the Followers. From my time with this lot, I can tell you that no one is an open book. The fae have their own struggles with each other. Certainly goes back beyond my time."

Fiona nodded. They undoubtedly had a lot of time to squabble with each other. Having to live in the same city, no matter how large, for the rest of their lives probably didn't help matters. "But what about Priestess Raina? You two must be close as Followers."

"We have a common goal," Fali said slowly, "but *close* isn't what I would call it. Our working relationship is fine, and we see eye to eye on most things."

"But there are other things you two also disagree about?"

"Comes from the upbringing," Fali said. He shrugged his mountainous shoulders and patted her heavily on the back with his trunk. "While the others may be preoccupied, I'm here to tell you I'm happy to answer any questions you may have or support you in any way. This is not an easy role, and while you aren't submerged in it quite yet…well, just know I'm an ear if you need one. Or a trunk."

She watched the elephas with a studied eye. So far, he hadn't said anything that made hurrying after her a need. Could he be trusted? She had doubted him once before but had been wrong. Perhaps Fali still held true. "Thank you. And how long have you been a Leaf?"

"A little less than a year. I took over for Novia, who took over from Titus, who took over from Julius. It's been all smilodons until me."

That was quite a few generations. But that meant he hadn't been privy to Leaves information until recently. It would be quite a feat to start a secret organization like the Painted Edge in less than a year. "You were all from Kerus?"

He nodded. "It is the way. Or it was until you."

"I hope I'm not breaking anything by being bound under Nicolosia."

"I won't say Raina wasn't somewhat upset about it. But she seemed relieved when you came downstairs to the group."

That was interesting. Perhaps Raina was worried she'd take her protégé spot. Who did she have it in mind for? There was something odd about the way the older woman acted around her in this meeting, but perhaps it was simply the surprise of it all.

"I think you should be careful of Raina," Fali said with a lowered voice. "I am not advanced in the ways of human, but the more your name comes up, the more she glowers."

Fiona tugged her scarf. She couldn't think of what she had done to gain Raina's attention in that fashion. She didn't want the Priestess to dislike her. Could it be that she was orchestrating things and Fiona was a fly in the ointment?

"Thank you, Fali. I will keep that to heart." She relaxed and beamed at the elephas. Fali was continually a bright spot she hadn't expected. "Would you mind telling me if she says or does anything that would seem against me or the Leaves? I know I shouldn't ask you to spy on one of your own, but I won't be around for the next few days, I assume. I feel like this is a critical time."

He nodded. "I trust your instincts. I'll be on watch."

"I'll let you know when I'm back home from…" She trailed off and waved her hand.

"I understand. Till then. Hope you get some rest. This group will take it out of you." He waved off before heading back toward the center of town.

Fiona hastily moved through the streets and rounded the corner toward the side door of her home, eager to get inside. If Dodger wasn't already there, he would be soon enough, bottle in hand and glasses on the table. She pressed her hand on the door, and it swung open easily. She raised an eyebrow as she entered pleased that he had made himself at home.

The kitchen smelled lightly of lemon. Gaili must've cleaned up before she went to bed. Nothing bubbled or moved within the darkened interior. Fiona stopped for a moment to let her eyes adjust to the darkness before heading quietly through the gallery and into the office. She didn't want to wake Gaili or whoever else might be asleep. It had been long days for them all and they deserved this bit of rest. She was quite sure they would be losing sleep increasingly until the Painted Edge were taken care of. Fiona sighed, mentally preparing the list of things she would need to gather so she and Dodger could begin their mission as soon as he had briefed her.

Dodger lounged back against the wall. His fit furry cheetah body almost swallowed by his Travel Guild assigned cloak and always present bandolier. Ready for any occurrence. He had a whiskey bottle and two glasses on the table but also a piping cup of coffee beside it. "Why did I know as soon as I received word to be at the Thread in the middle of the night that you would be involved?"

Fiona scoffed and sat down. She snaked her hand over to the mug but wrinkled her nose. It was not coffee but a dark-green liquid with a terribly unpleasant odor. "What in the pages is that?"

"Tea," Dodger said and picked it up to sip. He grimaced and wiped his whiskers. "It's new, from the farming district. Well, new to me at least. Half the Hinge has been gulping through this stuff on the daily."

"I thought it was coffee." Fiona frowned.

He chuckled. "I'm worried what so much coffee is doing to your body."

"Nothing worse than the whiskey. Please take that rubbish with you when you go. I'm worried Gaili will take a liking to it and then I'll be stuck with it forever." She grabbed the bottle of whiskey and poured a small amount in a glass. "Well, read me in. I have...things to tell you as well, but I'd rather update you and Gaili all at once."

Dodger raised an eyebrow but inclined his head in agreeance. He pulled out a small metal contraption and placed it on the table. With a swift motion he opened the top and a small translucent covering shot up and into the air around them.

It smelled faintly of oranges and mint. An odd combination. "What in the crinkled pages of the Book is this thing?"

"A sound-blocking device. Copper made, of course. Marcia—that is, Gilded Evenhall loaned it to me." He bit back a smile. "Faekin may be chaos, but what they lack in some areas they make up for in imagination." He rubbed his whiskers, looking uncomfortable. Before Fiona could ask another question particular to Marcia he rushed on, "Nevertheless, our spy, a smilodon named Vinicia, started out joining a small band of thieves on Spine. Petty crooks and the like. She worked her way up quickly and was assigned to a unit that worked in and out of Kerus."

"Kerus," Fiona said, surprised. The mortal page housed the smilodons, elephas, and ursidon beastfolk. Humans had always seen them as humanlike animals and were quite vocal in this observation when the pages first interacted. That was until the smilodon Emperor tried to conquer parts of Rise. "I suppose I shouldn't be surprised. There seems to be a Painted Edge faction in each page."

"Our reports have said much of the same. But we're not sure if it's Kerus that the private Painted Edge mission is in. They could be anywhere. It could even be this plant page Marcia told me about, for all we know."

Fiona sat back. If the Painted Edge had more operatives in the plant page, it would be very hard to find them. It seemed a vast place and would take weeks, maybe even months, to canvass. Had the Travel Guild already made their introduction properly and sent spotters in? She stretched her neck, her head feeling heavy with the many questions piling up. "Have you an idea where to start?"

"In her home here in the Caseo district. It should give us some indication of her whereabouts. If not, we'll have to see about retracing her steps from her last logged entry, but she would've falsified that."

Most smilodons and elephas stayed in the Caseo district when rehoming in Spine. Dodger's home was in the turner district instead of Caseo. Much for the same reason Fiona's wasn't in New Rise—some turners wanted to be as far away from their original page as possible. "That's a muddle, isn't it?" Fiona rubbed her temple.

"You'd be surprised what a good operative can communicate that others would never notice."

"Hmm." Fiona fanned herself, feeling warm.

"Fi, you're almost dead on your feet. You need sleep. You're barely pestering me with questions."

"There's not time." She crossed her arms.

"There is. Even if only for a few hours. We just got the report today." Dodger glanced out the opaque windows at the risen light. "Well, yesterday. A few hours will make all the difference in your thinking."

Fiona opened her mouth to suggest otherwise, but a yawn betrayed her. "Alright, but no more than a few hours. I'll be ready to go by the time the others wake. I need to speak to you all."

Dodger got up swiftly and smiled. "I'll be back with supplies by then."

She waved toward his bandolier. "Procure me some of that shiny Travel Guild gear, why don't you?"

He laughed. "You got it." He swept back from the table, helped her up from her chair, and pushed her up the stairs.

Fiona trudged into her bedroom, not bothering to change before she laid in bed staring at the ceiling. She heard the door softly close downstairs. Dodger. Always looking out for her.

She hoped she could repay him in kind soon. Show she cared. She had given him a lot of words over the last few months, but besides their whiskey meets and the occasional dinner, she hadn't done anything demonstrative to really support him after their argument earlier this year. Not that he held it against her. But she knew friends like him were not a common staple. What would he think of all she had wanted to tell him? Of Richard?

She fumbled her fingers into the lace pocket of her scarf and thought of Richard's journal. It appeared within the scarf from some unknown place, and she pulled it out. Her head swirled with thoughts and questions. There was no one person she felt she could talk about everything to. The closest was Mac and perhaps Nicolosia. But she found her desire to talk to them wanting. In her heart she knew she wanted to talk to Richard. To hear his theories and answers. But he was so stubborn. Would this even get to him?

She opened the journal, the smell of fresh-cut paper lingering inside. She pressed inked quill to paper and stopped. How did she begin? She supposed the same way most letters started.

"Dear Richard." She stopped, looking at the ink. Would he know she was writing, or how would he see it? Frustration welled up inside of her and she wrote on. "You ridiculous man. You didn't give directions on how this works. And now I'm sitting here when I should be sleeping with the precious little hours I have scratching in a book and talking to myself."

As she dotted her writing, large sloping lines of text began scrawling beneath her words. She stopped, mouth open, but then her expression became a pressed line as he wrote.

"Mistress Thornbeard, it would appear you have figured it out, so what do you need of me to tell you how it works? The Word is mysterious and unknowable, at least by mortal standards. I am quite ridiculous, you are right. But no more ridiculous than any other fool bumbling alone in the dark."

"Have you hit your head, or do you normally spout nonsense in the wee hours of the morning?" Fiona wrote. She felt a touch more energetic to keep writing now that they had begun conversing.

"This is quite normal, thank you very much. I tend to say it to myself, is all." He wrote back. A line appeared as if Richard was dragging his quill. Perhaps he was trying to gather his thoughts? "It's rather pleasant to say it to you though. I imagine you're all frown and crossed arms."

Fiona huffed, erasing the frown from her face. He was incorrigible. "Are you going to converse with me in a fine manner, or is it going to be cross words every time I write to you?"

"Yes." was all Richard wrote back.

By Larrakane's grace she laughed. Her frustration dissipated some at such a typical Richard reply. "Good."

"Did something happen?"

"Yes," Fiona wrote back. She picked up her quill, trying to think of what to say that would break the dam on the many things that had happened. "I spoke with Larrakane." She wished she could see his face. Was he aghast? Mad? Did he tug his beard at her unspoken words?

"Of course you did. I am sorry." He drew a line again. "But also relieved."

"Why is that?" Fiona wrote. She could've asked a better question or even a more direct one, but there was something about not seeing his face that made it hard for her to assess what to do next. She felt vulnerable here in the candlelight of her bedroom. And with the need to keep quill to ink she could hide it. She never considered herself a coward before. But she could admit to herself that knowing when to run from a fight was a simple matter. Staying close to someone she worried would run from her was a bit harder.

"It's not every day I get to talk to someone who understands me like you do," Richard wrote back.

Her body tingled at his words, and she grinned, relaxing further into the bed. She scrawled back, "I'm taking that as a compliment and, since I have it in writing, proof. You can't take it back now."

"I have no intention of doing so."

"Good. Sharpen your quill, Lionheart."

"Sharpened it as soon as I gave you the notebook." He drew a line again and then hastily scrawled, "Blasted woman."

Fiona laughed, a freeing gesture she wouldn't have done if he was face to face. There was so much to unpack. Where to start? She dipped her quill back into the ink and begin scrawling her thoughts. "Though I still don't agree with taking away people's memories, I do understand a bit more about how it helps protects us. And what it seems to keep at bay. I suspect I understand more than anyone but you."

"She told you everything?"

Fiona could almost hear the bewilderment in his voice. He, who was bound to keep so many secrets. She quickly wrote back to ease his confusion, "No, but the people you think of as the Guardians of Spine did. After I saw Larrakane. It was all a condition of me getting more information and entering into their circle of trust." Before he could interrupt, she kept her pen scrawling recounting what she had said and done with Larrakane and with the Leaves of Spine. She kept to titles instead of names, now more understanding of Nicolosia's fears. None of the Leaves seemed to use their real or full names out loud much.

Though her hand began to cramp, it was a small release on the valve that she needed most of all. She finished and leaned back in bed waiting. What would he think of her conversation with Larrakane? Of the memory of the Queen. She hoped he would tell her if he was connected to Queen Eleanor.

The candle had dwindled down to a stub but the bright light of morning was coming in full force through her windows, allowing her to see without it. So much for her sleep. But there was a lightness and a burst of energy that hadn't been there before she put quill to paper.

"Only you would dive headfirst into an intrigue of epic proportions and come out with suspects and a case," Richard finally wrote back. He made a small flourish on the page. "But it is quite concerning what your Elder druid friend has said. Of course you will be investigating this invisible leader, but I implore you to keep yourself safe."

She shook her head, wishing to be able to roll her eyes at him in person. "I shall. And be kind to the druids. They will be visiting you soon." How to make it easy for him to accept them? She thought for a moment, then scribbled, "Though you don't need their help, they are bound to support the Guardians."

There was a pause, then Richard scrawled, "I will try."

Fiona yawned, stretching. Her eyes had grown dry and itchy. Perhaps she should pick up quill again after she and Dodger had set off. "I have more questions, but I can't keep my eyes open. Will you look into Priestess Raina for me in the page? You have access to archives that I don't. Who was she before she was inked? When did she last come back? Who does she communicate to?"

"Yes," he wrote back quickly.

She wished she could see his face and hear his voice. Was he being terse or simply concise? Sometimes it was hard to tell with him. She thought of letting it go and then wrote, "Do you enjoy working with me?"

A pause and then, "Yes."

Fiona pursed her lips. Was he teasing her on purpose? She tried to trap him: "Why do you enjoy working with me?"

Another pause. She saw ink dot the page as Richard tapped the quill. How could he possibly keep going with one word when she had asked such an open-ended question? She grinned to herself, waiting.

Finally, he wrote, "Challenging."

She laughed loudly. Yes, he was too. "Have a good morning," she wrote.

"Good night," he scrawled back.

* * *

Coffee was the first thing Fiona smelled that seemed to pull her from her swirling thoughts. She was in that dreamy half-asleep, half-awake state. The mind always played tricks, making one imagine terrible things or providing rare but inscrutable gifts of clarity. The Binder and Larrakane were sitting down to coffee and had just invited her to a card game of Triumph. Though the object of the game was to win three or more cards out of five, she noticed that they only gave her two cards total. The dream, however, popped and fizzled out as she fully awoke upon the realization that neither would be so cordial and polite to her in real life.

She rubbed her face and sighed, feeling lighter than she had in days. Sleep had done her good and coffee would do her one better. She picked up the cup and took a sip, its slightly bitter taste and velvety texture comforting and warming her. A thought intruded into her bliss: *Who is awake enough to have made coffee?*

Fiona bounded out of bed and threw open the closed curtains. She had most definitely not closed them when she lay down. The sky of Spine was bright and blue. People milled in the streets, moving to and fro from many places. *Curses.* She had slept for more than simply a few hours.

With less time than anyone who cared about their appearance might take, Fiona was dressed. She only stopped for a moment to glance at the new gray circle tattooed on her chest but rushed to complete her morning routine and gather her things. She picked up her journal with Richard and put it in the pocket that most reminded her of Rise, along with quill and ink. Regret over spending time writing to him was not on her list this morning. She could say with some measure of truth that she had wanted it more than other things, rest being one. But there was a deal of movement from below that told her there were a great many things going on downstairs, indeed, and she was loath to take any more time than was necessary to be among them.

Her boots thudded down the stairs, having opted for sturdier footwear than usual. The office was brimming with people, or at least more than Fiona ever had in at one time. Fiona stopped, surprised, as all eyes turned toward her. The only pair she recognized belonged to Gaili, who smiled wide and quickly strode to her.

"Fi, I'm so glad you're awake. Come on through to the *private office*." She clasped a hand on her back and pushed her forward.

"Investigator Thorne," one of the humans, a slight woman, in the office said. She pushed in front of the ladies. "If you would be so kind, Investigator Thorne, I'd like to engage your services. My family jewels have gone missing, and it is extremely important that they are found before the end of the week. Or I shall lose my home to a ruffian."

Before Fiona could answer, Gaili said, "Thorne Investigations is happy to talk about your case further, but please remain in queue. We will be with you in a moment." With a grace that only Gaili could present, she pushed Fiona forward and turned her back politely on the woman.

"Mistress Thorne!" another person called out as they were exiting the room.

Fiona, catching on to what was happening, took quicker steps toward the kitchen. Word had clearly reached others of Fiona's deeds, or at least written deeds. While a boon for business it seemed, it was a rather inconvenient time.

"Don't worry about it, Fi. I have it all in hand," Gaili said as she ushered Fiona into the kitchen. Henrietta and Matteo glanced up from their conversation.

"Bright mornings to you, mistress." Henrietta smiled. "And congratulations on a job well done. Knew allowing you in my boat would do me a world of good."

Now that she was in the kitchen, the light fruity scents mixed with fresh baked bread and glazed pastry reminded her that she hadn't eaten in some time. Famished, Fiona grabbed a cut of bread from the table. "What do you mean? The queen thing?" She hurriedly stuffed it in her mouth, waving for Henrietta to continue.

"The queen thing." Henrietta chuckled. "Modesty, eh? Well, don't expect any of that from me. I'm ready to tell the *Card* anything they like about my role in helping you recover her and her gracious gifts."

"Which is all well and good because I think half of the people waiting in the office are scribes of some sort," Gaili said, placing her hand on Henrietta's shoulder. She smiled at Matteo. "Would you be a dear and take their information? Get them to make an appointment for tomorrow or the like? I've gotten some of them to settle."

Matteo nodded, putting down his parchment. "Of course. Perhaps I can intrigue them with a deal of some kind." He winked and strode out of the kitchen.

"Why would you tell the *Card* anything?" Fiona sat, dropping her bag on the floor. "And what gracious gifts?"

"Well, they want to meet me to hear details about the rescue, and since you are disinclined to talk to the *Card*..." Henrietta grinned.

Fiona rubbed her temples, trying to understand. Richard had written that Fiona had rescued the Queen. She hadn't thought to ask who else he had involved. "Can you go over exactly what happened?"

Gaili frowned at her. "Are you alright?"

"Yes, just tired. A lot has happened in the last day or so. If you wouldn't mind, I would like to know exactly what you did."

"Okay," Henrietta said slowly, glancing at Gaili. "Which part? All of it?"

Fiona bit her lip. If she had Henrietta recount all of it, they would think something was truly wrong with her. Truly she just needed to know what Henrietta was referring to without somehow undoing what Richard had done. "The rescue will suffice."

"After we set that Marcia woman from the Guild free, we snuck through the Painted Edge's defenses to find the Queen on that stolen airship. There were more of them guarding her than coals in winter, but we went on the attack with those plant creatures. The plantians." She frowned watching Fiona. "Do you remember Caliope?"

Fiona nodded. She would not soon forget the leader of the vined plant people they had been rescued by in the jungle. They seemed formidable. What would their integration into the Book be like?

"Well, we rescued the Queen of course," Henrietta continued, searching Fiona for something. "On the ship? I flew it and you made the page turn to get us through?"

Richard had stitched the details together masterfully well. It spoke of too much experience having to do so for Fiona's taste. She sighed. "Of course."

Gaili placed a hand on her shoulder. "Are you sure you're alright? You haven't had much rest."

"Yes, yes, I'm fine. Simply trying to pull it all together after a rather eventful night." Fiona frowned, trying to decide what to do. Did she relay everything she learned to them so they could get it right? How long would it take to tell and how long to convince them? How much did they not remember? Perhaps if she could connect things to Richard that would be easier. "Do you remember what Richard said in the tower. About Larrakane?"

"Who is Richard?" Henrietta's eyebrows knotted in confusion.

Fiona steadied herself with a hand on the table. "The royal historian?"

Henrietta said, "Aye, doesn't ring any of my bells."

Gaili shook her head.

They didn't even remember Richard? He had said that was the point of it all, but she didn't realize it would be like this. No one knew him. How could she complain about him if she had to remind everyone who he was? Oh, this was beyond unfair. He had no right to tamper with the memory of her friends like this. He could at least have kept them intact as allies.

"Have I said something to upset you, mistress?" Henrietta said.

"No, absolutely not," Fiona said, reaching out to grasp her hand. "I find that my head is simply full of too much. And I've slept far longer than I meant to today."

"Sorry about that. You seemed so tired when I checked on you this morning. I thought you needed it," Gaili said, lowering her eyes to the ground.

It was sweet the way her friends cared about her. Fiona was thankful for that. "It's quite alright. You had my best interest in heart and I appreciate that." She patted Gaili on the shoulder and began piling a plate with food. "Has Dodger been by yet? There is much to discuss."

Henrietta swept graying strawberry curls from her face. "Not yet. Is he meant to come by? Gaili talks so highly of him I'm looking forward to meeting him."

Fiona nodded, distracted. "Before Dodger gets here, I wanted to ask for your help. I need to go on a new case, but I'd like you to do some extremely discreet digging on a couple of fae. A fae named Dani who manages the farms and other areas of the Rocky Bluff. And the Binder."

Gaili's eyes widened. "The Binder? Of the Book and Travel Guild fame? He's fae?"

"That's a lightning storm if I've ever seen one," Henrietta muttered. "What's he gone and done?"

"I have some suspicions about him that I need confirmed if I am to be working closer with him."

"You're working with the Binder? Have you taken up with the Travel Guild then?" Gaili's golden hand flew to her cheek. "Honestly, Fi, how much *did* you fit into one day?"

"Let's simply say I'm on the precipice of where I want to be, but one wrong move and I may fall down rather than fly up." She wrinkled her nose.

"I know it's important to you that you make connections with the leaders of the Book, but spying on the Binder..." Gaili glanced at Henrietta. "Those outside the leaders of the Guild haven't seen him since the Inking. I assumed he was fackin, but fae! That's surprising. I'm not even sure what he looks like."

"Aye, all orders seem to go through myriads of levels at the Travel Guild. But you've met him?" Henrietta asked.

"I have." Fiona tilted her head, trying to pull together her thoughts. How to assure her friends that this was necessary but keep them safe? "I can say confidently that in order to do what's best for the Book we should make sure these leaders are not harboring any large secrets. Or at the very least, none that would undermine the safety of the people." She took hold of Gaili's hand again. "I'm asking you specifically because you know more than most that others' secrets are occasionally good to keep when they harm no one." She made direct eye contact, willing Gaili to understand. "And allow legacies to rest."

Gaili's golden brow wrinkled in confusion, but she nodded. "I will take that into consideration, Fi."

Fiona sighed. "Good. And it's best not to talk about it in front of Dodger."

"My friend, he's here now," Matteo said, swinging back into the kitchen gracefully. He waved his hand prettily and Dodger strode through, looking slightly shamefaced at Fiona before shrugging and sitting down.

"You were supposed to be back to get me in a few hours," Fiona said, pushing a cup of coffee to him.

He pushed it back and twitched his whiskers. "Was I now? Fancy that. Must've lost track of time."

"You're all in a conspiracy together, you know that?" Fiona shook her head, smiling. "I've never been so rested, fed, or well spoken of in my life."

"I'm sure you'll find someone someday who will be able to go toe to toe with you, and then you'll be begging for your friends." Dodger chuckled. He pulled an empty plate toward himself and begin filling it with food. "But now that I am here, what say we get on with it?"

Fiona glanced at Matteo. "Are we all alone?"

"Yes, I've cleared out the stragglers, but many will be back tomorrow."

"Don't worry about that, Fi. I'm here. I've already sorted out a couple of small things in the last two weeks while you were gone," Gaili said gently.

Fiona beamed. She knew bringing Gaili in on the business was a stroke of genius. Not necessarily all hers, but she would take credit for a portion. She nodded and cleared her throat.

As briefly as she could, she recounted what happened on the airship with Marcia and Stella, flubbing some of the parts about Richard, and finishing with Stella's pronouncement of a leader who wanted Fiona to join them before throwing herself into the dark edge.

"That's what the lights were?" Matteo asked. His eyes widened. "When we were on that island and the sky opened up into Rise, it grew very dark, very chilly for a moment. But quite beautiful with more lights than one is used to seeing in the sky. For all that's troublesome about the dark edge, I dream of mapping those stars."

"And she's there now?" Gaili said.

"Presumably. But without any way to get to her, who knows? There's not a page turner in the Book who would risk their life to find out." Fiona stared into the dark liquid, thinking of Marcia. Perhaps that wasn't entirely true.

"So, this leader, do you have an inkling who they are?" Matteo said with a raised eyebrow.

"Too many suspects to knock a single one out," Fiona said. "But hopefully we will soon. There are good people trying to stop the Painted Edge."

Dodger cleared his throat.

She turned to him slowly with a look of annoyance. Of course she wasn't going to tell them the exact people. He was full of assumptions. Sure, she was going to hint and let them pick up the crumbs, but he didn't know that! "I wish I could tell you more."

Gaili tilted her head, assessing Fiona and Dodger. She smiled shyly and said, "Don't worry, Fi. I read between the lines better than most."

"It's why I treasure you, Gaili Pannete. Companiable and clever." She shook her head at Henrietta and Matteo. "You two better keep an eye on her."

"It never roams far," Matteo said and wiggled his eyebrows.

Fiona smiled, though there was a small drop in her stomach. She wished she could share this moment with someone who admired and respected her friends for their cunning. But they didn't even know Richard, and he hadn't gotten a chance to meet the lot of them. Of all the things he had done since they met, erasing their memories was the one she hated the most. Well, she would tell him so at the first opportunity.

Dodger popped the last crust of bread into his mouth and wiped his whiskers. "I've gotten the 'good supplies' as was requested. We should head out now before the residential parts of the city properly wake up."

Fiona stood and smoothed down her clothing. "I've got my pack ready." She pulled her scarf from under her doublet, never liking to get crumbs in it, and wrapped it loosely around her neck.

"People will know you from a mile away with that scarf, mistress," Henrietta admonished.

"Well, I'm not leaving home without it. It's my right arm. More valuable, actually, since it holds every good tool in the Book and whatever you give me from the Guild supply closet." She sighed. "I know it's common now but—"

"Actually," Gaili quietly broke in, "I've—well, with some help from Henrietta's storage items—"

"She means my loot." Henrietta laughed.

Gaili blushed but continued on, "I made a wash that should, temporarily, make your scarf one color. It's not harmful, I promise. And it shouldn't modify anything it does."

Eye's widened, Fiona said, "Oh? My, you *were* busy while I was in Rise."

"Bored silly is more like," Matteo said.

Gaili playfully slapped him on the shoulder. "If you give it to me, I'll test a corner first."

With some reluctance Fiona removed the scarf from her neck. It wasn't that she didn't trust Gaili, but it was her most prized possession. She was sure there wasn't another one in the Book like it. As she handed it over, she noticed something peculiar. There in a spot that usually held a lace pocket was a green one. Oh, the lace was still there beside it and the leather on the other side of that. It was as if the pocket had moved in to make room. "That's new."

"Hmm?" Gaili murmured, coming around the table to inspect. "It wasn't there before?"

"I know every inch of this scarf, and this wasn't there yesterday." Fiona ran her finger over it. Its smooth, supple texture felt like thin leather. Or a sturdy plant leaf.

"You know what? I believe this is from the plant page, Phyta," Gaili said, running her hands over it.

"Phyta?" Fiona said.

"Caliope told us that's what they call their world," Henrietta said.

"Well, how is a pocket there now possible? It's not as if a pocket could simply appear," Fiona said.

Gaili waved her hand dismissively. "Couldn't it? Think about it, Fi. If the pocket wasn't there, it's because it didn't need to be."

"Do things normally work like that around you?" Dodger said, moving closer to see.

"It does in Copper," Matteo said, running his finger over his mug. "Places, small and large, shift and move sometimes. It takes time to notice, of course, but time is often laughable to a faekin. I've had maps change over decades. Little by little."

"The essence of Copper and faekin is so very different than the other mortal pages," Dodger murmured.

"Aye, it's more like the elemental pages truly," Henrietta said. "Wind goes where it wants in Mistral and the clouds follow. The lightning people dance, and the clouds go back."

There was a reason for that, of course: Larrakane's magic. Fiona was very well aware now how much the other pages lost because humans had mucked things up. "Well, this is a lot to think about," Fiona said, rubbing her temple. "But Dodger and I should be getting on."

"Yes of course," Gaili said. She took the scarf. and after gathering pots and rather pungent ingredients that she assured Fiona would not make her scarf smell, she tested the dip. There was no disastrous effect on the pocket and it worked just the same. Fiona allowed the whole scarf to be dipped, and it became a dusty gray color. She frowned at the drab look.

"Best thing that's happened to it," Matteo said, stroking the embroidered vibrant cherry thread on his own fetching dress. He smiled and said softly, "I mean in the stylish way only, of course."

Fiona rolled her eyes but said nothing as she put it back on. Faekin were always so hard on everyone else's fashion sense. People couldn't go around looking like they were royalty all the time. Thinking of that reminded her. She pulled Gaili to the side and whispered, "Can you please take the Spring Crown to Mac for safekeeping?"

"Of course," Gaili said. "I'll get it over there this afternoon."

Fiona nodded, relieved she could count on her without more explanation. Louder, she called out, "Henrietta, if you don't mind, would you please tell my mother I'll be back soon? I hate that I haven't checked in on her yet but time, especially in Spine, waits for no one."

Henrietta laughed. "Aye, I will. She'll be very peeved."

"I don't think she'll be too peeved once she learns that she's now in charge of a whole island." Fiona smirked. That would give her plenty to do for a while. And a room at the palace to stay in for the foreseeable future. Safer in the same building as Richard than most places.

"What?" Henrietta said, startled.

Fiona opened her mouth, but Gaili waved her away. "Never you mind. We'll figure it out. Go."

Fiona nodded and looked to Dodger. "Shall we?"

He said goodbye to the others and thanked Gaili graciously for the meal. Fiona stepped out of her home into the calm, bright day. She glanced back once at the trio around the table, heart full at the sight of them. With friends such as these she truly felt more courageous than she ever had before. She smiled at Dodger as they trotted down the street toward the carriage stand. Family was what you made of it, Mac always said to her. Fiona understood now more than ever that she had been lucky to make something very great indeed.

THERE WAS SOMETHING ABOUT the Caseo district that howled *keep out*. Perhaps it was the stone wall that surrounded the area—high enough to keep all but birdfolk out and with unnecessary but thoroughly used watchtowers dotting its circumference. Large gray stone chiseled archways displayed battles and celebrations of Roma smilodon emperors of old. They comprised the entrance to the district, intimidating anyone who arrived by their height and shadows. Never mind that the district also housed smilodons from other cultures, elephas, and a few ursidon, cultures quite unlike the prevailing one that draped over Caseo like curtains muffling the brightness of day. But those first inked to the city of Spine had the pleasure of making it in their own fashion. Thus the beastfolk of Kerus had to follow the lead of the first inked from their page, Julius Sebastius of Roma.

Gleaming chariots of copper and ivory lined the entryway into the district, ready for immediate use. Though Fiona preferred the slow pace of the city carriages when she had something to work out in her mind on a case, she loved the ease of a chariot. She had ridden in one a few times and even chased a suspect down once—thrilling and exhilarating and a little death defying all in one. She stroked the edge of the wooden vehicle. *Let it not be said that all the best inventions came from Copper.*

The burbling water above snapped her out of her thoughts. She glanced up at the aqueducts that reached even this end of Spine. They had been reportedly constructed in the city by Julius when he was inked. Having watched a memory of the smilodon, she could see how that would be an advantageous introduction. Controlling the waterways that would supply all of a burgeoning new city guaranteed power indeed.

Dodger and Fiona made their way through the entrance and past the Roma guards posted. A helmet covered their heads—with room for their ears to sit through—and came down to a square over their forehead. They held lances in one hand and stared out into the distance almost like marble pillars. Though they were different types of smilodons (lion- and leopard-like, respectively), they were both clearly Roma with the bronze symbol of a laurel wreath on their equipment. The Roma were the most visible smilodons around. A culture of sackings, raids, and fighting for land meant that they had been first to arrive and support Julius. To try to hold some power within Spine, new as it was. But the non-inked Roma had also been the first to leave when it became clear Julius was not going to rule Spine alone. Though the Roma Empire had diminished somewhat in Kerus over the centuries, its influence was still felt in Spine thanks to their controlling the city that aligned with the pagemark in Caseo, Roma Nymar.

Dodger saluted as they passed through the arched entryway, walking with a stiff back and structured gait. The guards saluted back in the same manner, though eyes lingered on Fiona as they continued into the main street of the district.

Beastfolk carried on their daily lives in the streets, though not many lingered near toward the towering walls.

"I've never seen you so formal before," Fiona said as she glanced back at the guards. She smiled wide at them as if she was easy to read. It paid to present an easy-going personality that could be quickly dismissed in case they got into any trouble.

He waved her off. "It's good to be respectful when visiting the district."

Dodger had spoken of his time in Kerus as a rough upbringing, but he had never been one to talk at length about his time before being inked. Everything Fiona knew of it he had told her during their early years of turner training. It wasn't until recently she even knew that the Binder had a hand in raising him and getting him into the training in the first place. Though Dodger was clearly not Roma, she didn't know where he was actually born in Kerus or even if he aligned with any particular culture. She kept her eyes roving the people in the streets, noting more laurel wreaths than not. "And when being surrounded by the legion?"

"I have no love for the Romas and they have no love for me," Dodger said in a lowered voice. "My city may have been defeated by them but once I became inked…" He trailed off, tail twitching. "It makes no difference. I'm in the Travel Guild. The opposite of what they represent." He patted his black jacket insignia.

"You aren't simply *in* the Travel Guild, Dodger. You're a leader in one of their most important branches." Though there were quite a few offices of the Guild, regulation was the one that kept the Book turning swiftly.

He clasped his arms behind his back. "I'm simply a deputy."

Fiona nudged his shoulder with her own. "Words. You're very good at what you do and even better when you get to do what you want. You'll be Gilded in no time."

Dodger tilted his head, a small smile playing at the corners of his mouth. "Thank you, Fi."

"Of course," Fiona said and then winked. "Remember who your friends are when you're running things, eh?"

"I think you'll be running things long before I will. Seeing as how you were the one invited to the private meeting." He chuckled softly. "The Binder gave me leave to discuss all matters of the case and its surrounding information with you, but I suspect that's not a two-way street."

Fiona grimaced. Now that she wanted to open up to her friends and rely on their judgment, she felt she couldn't. She hated to lie to Dodger about something so important. Perhaps she'd simply leave the gaps there for him to fill himself. "The only matters that can't be discussed revolve around your Binder and his *friends*. Other than that, I'm happy to answer any questions *you* may come up with."

"I'll try to be as clever as you are then." Dodger nudged her shoulder with his in return as they continued down the quickly filling wide grid-like streets. Caseo had been structured after the famed empire capital, Roma Valar. Gleaming white marble buildings buffeted the glistening limestone paths in an orderly fashion. Light from the bright day bounced off the bright buildings beaming out from all directions Oh, there were pops of colors to be sure, but those came from the banners of rust and corn silk hung with a paw print in the shape of a legionnaire Roma helmet to represent the Kerus. Smaller, more colorful homes sat on the outskirts closest to the district walls for page turners who often had to come and go. The better areas, larger villas, and open spaces were in the center of the district. And in between them sat street vendor stalls filled with all manner of bread, meats, and imported fare to feed either side.

Fiona didn't visit Caseo much and certainly not its aligned pagemark in Kerus. It felt a stifling place, not least because there were miles of desert to get through if turning the page from Spine, but the current Roma Emperor was an unforgiving lout who barely saw the benefit in anything that wasn't more territory. It was a pity that Spine didn't align with either of the other two continents in Kerus. The cultures there were vastly less antagonistic, to Fiona at least. They had held out against Roma for centuries before the Inking. She had always wondered if there was a breath of relief when the pages opened up and the domineering empire had fixed their roaming eye on other pages instead of the continents.

Dodger led deeper into the avenues where the architecture and the patterns got simpler. The small apartments had minor mosaic decorations outside with hanging green plants in terra-cotta pots and vibrant colors to mark the different dwellings. Statues, mostly feline but Fiona spotted an errant elephas, dotted the street in oranges and grays. Dodger pointed to a building farther down the road. "Vinicia's home is in the bottom floor."

Fiona glanced around. Two smilodons were busy on the street moving crates, but other than that the only sounds came from where they had started near the entrance. "Ah, near the Travel Guild booth but far enough away as to not be circumspect."

Dodger nodded. "It's likely the Painted Edge knew she worked for the Travel Guild though. They tend to do a bit of research once someone starts becoming more involved, we've seen. It's why most of our operatives never got further than petty criminal activity. But defecting from the Travel Guild is how Vinicia would have sold it. And she must've sold it well. They must've seen it as a boon when she arrived."

"Well, the Guild does have a lot of secrets," Fiona said, raising an eyebrow, "like that your Binder is fae."

"And that one of our most prominent Gilded leaders is a hag," Dodger said, his tone neutral.

Fiona dropped her arms. "Wait, you knew!"

Dodger inclined his head, but his expression was hard to read. "She told me recently. And that you knew."

Surprise flooded through Fiona. Marcia was a truly buttoned-up and tight-lipped person. That she told Dodger her deepest secret must mean she trusted him completely. Fiona understood that sentiment, but she hadn't realized the two were so close. "I didn't think it was my place to tell you."

"You were right." Dodger relaxed and cuffed her on the shoulder. "I am glad you kept it to yourself. And for everything you did for Marcia. Thank you."

"Er, of course," Fiona said, thrown off. She tried again to understand his emotions, but Dodger's expression remained unchanged. He was being carefully guarded, but why?

He turned swiftly and continued up the street. "Vinicia will hopefully be easier to find than all the secrets of the Guild."

"From your lips to Larrakane's ears," Fiona said, striding to catch up. How truer it felt to say, having met the goddess herself.

Dodger and Fiona approached the stacked concrete apartments, stopping on the front steps. The buildings weren't as clean and gleaming here. Scuff marks, broken tile, and open windows said that little was done to keep up such a highly used area. Feeling entirely too visible, Fiona stood next door glancing into the window of a small shop while Dodger gained access to the apartment. Though she liked to say she would have been quicker with her tools than he, she didn't anticipate him bringing out a key.

"I didn't realize the Guild kept such things for their jackets." Fiona frowned as she skipped quickly into the door.

"Who do you think leases these buildings?" Dodger closed the door behind her.

They were in a small entryway, no bigger than a two-person chariot. He quickly lit the lamps in the room, casting light around the darkened interior. The dwelling was small and intimate with sparce furnishings. A main room held chairs, table, and hearth to cook. Another room could be seen through an opening that looked much the same with a plain bed. The living was clean and well put together, bringing to mind a person who perhaps spent less time at home than abroad. Two small statues were the only things of value within the room. Fiona bent to examine their feline forms—cheetah, or maybe jaguar-like—and their shape was identical in nature except for the coloring. One was silvery blue with darker spots, the other silvery gray. "Who are they?"

"Venus and Vixen. Two of our previous deities in our Oracle of Stars pantheon before Larrakane showed herself. Although she did show herself as Vixen in the beginning, it's said." He motioned to the silvery-gray figure.

Fiona removed her glove and ran her finger gently over the cold stone. Larrakane once again showing herself as others wanted to see her. For someone with so much power, she was quite conforming.

"Vinicia." Dodger pointed to a small fresco hung on the wall. A small cougar-like smilodon with reddish-brown fur stood in black robes holding a small fan. Beside her was another, slightly taller and older cougar. "Probably with her brother."

"Do you know where he is now?"

"Her file said he was still in Roma Mikar, where I'm from. But nothing specific reported on him."

She tempered her surprise at his direct mention and nodded. "Well, we better dig into what is around here. Direction isn't going to provide itself."

They began gingerly walking through the room, picking up blankets, clothing, furniture, and more, looking for some sign of where Vinicia was told to go. There was nothing from another page within the main room, which surprised Fiona. She had always thought page turners valued their prizes from other places and displayed them well enough. Even Dodger's place had a few tokens from his time during training when they were forced to go from page to page and get their bearings. Vinicia must've cleared her life here to show she was deeply rejecting of the page turning ability and the Travel Guild at once.

The bedroom bore no semblance of clues or even information, though it did have a lovely window that faced a communal garden and let in some daylight. Vinicia's clothes were neatly arranged in an easy-to-access chest. A wall shelf held a solid black feline statue. Dried flowers, small rolled parchments with simplistic prayers to the Oracles of Stars, and melted candles surrounded it like a shrine. An obvious alcove held personal tools and products like scented oils and brushes for grooming. They were all clean, as clean as the rest of the home.

Dodger looked perplexed. It was clear he had expected an easier trail to follow. He glanced back at the shrine, tail swishing, and rubbed his whiskers.

"What is it?" Fiona said gently. He was contemplating but she couldn't understand exactly what.

"Nothing. Well, no." He walked to the shrine and picked up the statue. "The other one is missing."

"Other what?" Fiona said inspecting the shelving. Though there were lots of little things surrounding the statue, there seemed to be no gap, nothing amiss.

"This is the sun oracle but she's usually always with another celestial oracle. Lore said they always followed each other, around and around in the sky. Each one getting to stop once a day and perform before they had to run off again, lest the other one catches them. They are never displayed alone. Usually they're one below another," he said, voice curious.

"Could it be a mistake?"

"No, not for someone deliberately trying to show themselves committed to Kerus like this. Notice there's nothing here even remotely connected to Larrakane or the other pages."

"I had thought that interesting as well, but it goes along with showing her commitment to the Painted Edge."

He nodded. "So to complete that picture, the other celestial oracle must be here somewhere."

"We've already combed through the front room inch by inch," Fiona said.

"It'll be here." Dodger took a few paces away from the feline statue and glanced to the opposite wall. "It has to be."

Fiona sat on the edge of the bed, focusing on each section of the room, looking for something that could be hiding a statue.

But everything was so open, so easy to see. It was as if this spy put everything on display, as if to say there was nothing to hide. She flopped backward on the bed but immediately jumped up again as a thought struck her. "You know, there is one place we haven't looked." She pointed to the bed.

"Fi, no one hides things under beds. That's the first place people look."

"Amateurs maybe. But trained agents don't normally bother. We didn't."

Dodger waved her off the bed before dropping below it. He crawled under the bed. "Nothing here."

"Look with your hands, Dodger. Not simply your eyes," Fi said, reciting her father's favorite adage.

There was rustling before he said, muffled, "Oof. Found her." He grunted, seeming to pull on something hard. The bed moved a few hands, scratching across the tile floor. He yanked again and crawled back out from under the bed, pulling out a large snowy-white feline statue, about half the height of Dodger himself. It was scratched in several places.

"Poor thing." Fiona rubbed the scratches with her hand. They were rougher than they seemed and pulled a thread on her glove. "Wherever it had been wedged, it was with purpose."

He ran his hands over the celestial oracle, scrutinizing every inch. "I thought there might be more information when I found it, but nothing." Dodger carefully placed the statue on the ground below the sun oracle.

There was a click. Fiona glanced at the floor beneath the statue. "Dodger, tell me that was a good sound."

Dodger tapped his foot gingerly on the tile beside the statue. It wobbled. He dove down and pried it up with his claws to find a small compartment with a few pieces of parchment. "Now this is more what I expected." Dodger unrolled the parchment gingerly.

Fiona recognized the look of it. "This is like the other slips of paper the Painted Edge used to communicate with their operatives in Rise. I worked to decipher those with Henrietta. Interesting that she would've kept it here rather than destroy it."

"What's destroyed can't be found by the Travel Guild if needed. Now that we've found something, I name you an honorary jacket of the Travel Guild for this mission." Dodger grinned. "Confidentially extended."

Fiona rolled her eyes. "Only if it comes with a lovely pass I can flash at people to gain my way again."

He raised an eyebrow as if to suggest that was unlikely and waved the parchment. "How's your Valerian?"

"Dreadful," Fiona said with a sigh. Her languages always were. One day she'd have to spend time on that failing.

"Well, I'll cover that portion of the text if you can help with the rest." He perched on the floor and held the parchment up to the daylight streaming in.

Working through the coded language, Fiona found the same pattern to Dodger's translated words that the Painted Edge's Rise team had used when planning their island heist. After less than an hour they had a simple message that made Dodger tense.

"*The hour of need draws near, amid the shifting sands and lapping waves. Venture forth to where the boundaries blur and the echoes of ancient pacts resonate.*" Dodger tapped the parchment with his claw. "Whoever this message giver is, they are fairly creative."

"Yes, their codes are almost an art form itself. But do you know what it means? Shifting sands and lapping waves? Isn't that simply a beach?"

"If so, it rules out too few places in the Kerus page and leaves open too many. There are miles of coast, even if we're just talking the continent of Siamor."

"Roma Nymar is a sea town, isn't it?" Fiona tugged at the edges of her scarf. It was already the pagemark from Caseo. Coded instructions seemed quite unnecessary simply to say, *Come to the pagemark.* But then there were the boundaries blurring and ancient pacts line. "There have been some agreements with the Val'ere romas from the other nations on Siamor, haven't there? I know your nation fought them, but did the Nyx'mir?"

Dodger's tail whisked from side to side as he clasped his hands behind his back. "Long enough to see us overcome. After that, they surrendered without fighting."

"Could it be that somewhere in Nymar is where she's supposed to meet fellow kin?"

"Or it could be on the edge," he murmured. He got up and begin pacing the small room. "When the Val'ere romas met with the Nyx'mir, they had overtaken the government and administration of my nation. In less than a month's time they had both nations at once. They made a treaty, formalizing Nyx'mir's defeat, on the western border of Mikar at our old trading site with Nymar."

"'Where the ancient pacts resonate. Shifting sands meet lapping waves.' This must be telling her to go to the trading site."

He clasped his hands behind his back. "Well, if messages must, we must." His tail twitched erratically.

Watching Dodger shut down so quickly had Fiona stepping into his pacing path with little thought. "What is it?"

Dodger glanced at her and then shrugged. "I had hoped for something less close to the empire. Not in the middle of it."

Fiona grasped his shoulder gently. "If it helps, I know a bit more now about the best way to handle having to go back home."

"Oh, yes? I suppose chin up and carry on?" He raised an eyebrow.

"Hmm, no, that's too vague. I was thinking more along the lines of 'Don't tell off the ruling power on the first day.' More of a third-day item really."

Dodger's tight face relaxed as he smiled. "I think I can handle that." He shook his head at Fiona and chuckled lightly. "Come on. If she had to make haste, it means we should too. It'll take a few days to reach that border. Let's go out through the garden, though, in case anyone is watching the front door."

Dodger removed the grate and climbed through the open window. With quickened steps they made their way back toward the Travel Guild booth. Once closer to it, Fiona relaxed and put on a bright smile as if nothing wily could possibly be going on.

They got to the wooden travel booth without incident. Banners depicting all the locations this booth could be safely traveled to hung from the top with the rust-and-corn silk Kerus one larger than the blue satin Shimmering Depths or verdant Court of Copper ones. Fiona wrinkled her nose, feeling for a moment the same as Dodger and wishing they were going for a swim instead of to the dry desert. But she pushed that thought away quickly. She had to be the optimistic, strong one for her friend. Though she wasn't sure exactly what played on Dodger's mind about his time in Kerus, she had never known any recounting to be positive.

They signed in, Fiona allowing Dodger to do the honors though she tutted when he began writing her real name instead of an alias. Requested by the Binder or not, she still didn't think the Guild needed to know all her movements.

Dodger walked toward the open square and grabbed Fiona's hand in his furry paw. "I'll lead."

"By all means," Fiona said with a smile. It saved her having to dig through her camouflaged scarf and reveal its nature to any hidden watchers.

He closed his eyes, one hand gripped around a dull buckle barely hanging to a bit of torn leather. Fiona watched the lines of her friend's face as he concentrated, his posture ridged and tail twitching back and forth. He was quite nervous to be going. She should try and help as much as possible by not being too pushy for details when they arrived.

Well, less pushy.

The stone wall of Caseo folded away, peeling back a corner to reveal bright-blue sky, an empty square save for a large statue of the Emperor as if welcoming them, and a mixture of voices cascading through the threshold. Sand drifted through on the wind along with the hot, sticky, salty air of Roma Nymar. They took a step into the sandy square on the other side of the page. A bell clanged loudly off in the short distance toward the docks as if signaling their arrival. The page closed behind them in a snap, the quiet of Spine gone. Dodger opened his eyes and dropped his hands. He quickly strode away from the pagemark, flashing his jacket badge at the Travel Guild booth attendant as he hurried by.

Fiona jogged to keep up the unexpected pace. "Wait, wait. Let me get my bearings."

"Let's get out of the public eye first," Dodger said over his shoulder.

"The pagemark is used all the time," Fiona said. "What makes you think someone is watching us?"

Dodger slowed and turned the corner, only stopping when they were between two narrow wooden buildings. "Youthful habits surface quickly. Apologies."

"If you're going to go *formal* every time something happens—" Fiona winced at her words and tried again: "It's fine. I simply wanted to know if you saw someone following us or if this is the nature of the area. I haven't come to Kerus from Spine since training."

Dodger leaned his back against the peeling red wall. "Fi, if we're going to be traveling through Roma territories, I need to know exactly how much you understand about the various areas and cultures here. Insults are easy to make depending on the citizen you're speaking to, and the social dynamics can be a bit much."

She sighed and crossed her arms. "More so than the Court of Copper?"

"More aggressive than the faekin, yes. They'll simply snub you if you don't fit in fashionably well or bar you from the page if you're an outsider who's been caught skulking without a guide. You can at least plead your case with them. Romas will imprison you or, worse, give you the option of your freedom tied to working for them if you step out of line. They don't appreciate rebels. Not at a time like this."

Fiona had made a study out of the different pages she had encountered over the years but from the perspective of someone wanting to travel through them or build up contacts within. She realized recently, after becoming friends with Gaili, that she had glossed over the intricate cultural aspects entirely. She blamed it somewhat on being human. They were all under one banner, one rule. Though they might look different, their society was very much alike through and through. An intrusive thought bubbled up as she remembered Richard saying there used to be millions of them. How different was it before the Inking?

"Fi?"

"Sorry," Fiona said, grimacing. She rubbed her chest. "Got distracted by how much I just don't understand about…well, it feels like anything."

Dodger seemed to take her comment as an admission and nodded. "There are two types of smilodon: big ones and small ones." He waved his hands, separating them. "Pardalis and jubatus. Now I'm jubatus and so is Vinicia, even though we don't look the same."

"Petronia, she was pardalis, right?" The tigress had been much bigger than other smilodon she had met before.

"Correct. Don't mistake a pardalis for being in command and a jubatus for being subservient in the Empire. This is a distinction I've seen a lot of humans make between smilodons, but it isn't the right one. It's not that easy."

Fiona pursed her lips. "Dodger, I would never think like that."

His tail swished. "I know, Fi, but I've encountered it so much…" He glanced away. "Look, the important thing is which nation a person is from and what they're displaying. You've seen the Val'ere romas in Spine, so I won't bother with them. But things are in flux at the moment in Roma. The Emperor is—" He stopped and looked around. Pushing himself from the wall, he got closer to Fiona and whispered, "He's new, which isn't rare these days, and he may be deposed at any time. What you've learned in your research is probably outdated by now."

"I didn't know you kept such a handle on current affairs in Kerus."

"Not Kerus. Just Roma." He stroked his whiskers. "The Travel Guild has used its power to push through many changes in exchange for trade agreements and the like, but the last year has been disastrous. We've been almost pushed out of the empire, despite our Spine pagemark and treaties. At this point we're lucky the pagemark is in Roma Nymar and not the capital itself. The distance from Roma Valar gives some breathing room. But it's a shallow breath." He paused his rushed sentences, his eyes shifting over her shoulder and around.

Fiona pinched the bridge of her nose for a moment. She had never seen Dodger anxious before. Usually he was so professional. So reserved. Sure, he had relaxed with her over time, but that was mostly due to the whiskey and the friendship. "Okay, I understand what you're saying. Things are unstable, and we should be judicious. I agree that we should take every precaution to make sure we get to where we're going in one piece."

Dodger let out a sigh of relief. "I'm glad you understand."

"Well, I am known to think before I act when needs must." Fiona smiled. "Let's lay out a plan to get to the eastern border and go from there perhaps. We'll have to figure out the next bit with the trading site afterward."

Dodger nodded, businesslike again. He cast an eye upward, watching the rooftops. "We can hire a two-wheeled carriage to take us through the province. Not an inconspicuous sight or sound, however fast it may be. Walking would be tiring, but we'd have the advantage then of being able to change our plans when needed and not having to involve another person."

"I agree, I don't think we should involve too many other people but walking for three days sounds deplorable. Perhaps we can hire a chariot? I do know how to handle one. But, Dodger, you're glossing over our most obvious problem."

His whiskers twitched. "How to follow the trail of a well-trained spy?"

Fiona shook her head. "I'm a human. There can't be too many roaming the streets of the empire."

He gave a small smile. "You would be surprised. There are quite a few humans who have been *introduced* into the empire. As long as no one thinks you're a complete outsider of Roma, you'll be fine." He assessed her clothing and wrinkled his nose. "You already seem to have a mishmash of clothes from the empire, but we'll need to trade out that wool doublet for linen. You'll thank me on the journey." He handed her a longer wine-dyed tunic and belt before pulling off his Travel Guild jacket and folding it carefully to store it in his satchel. Without it he was left with a cream linen tunic and a leathery rope tied around his waist, both of which hung past his knees. He rubbed his hands across the wall and, with a grimace, patted his bright clothes. "I look too clean, and I don't want to seem important." Pulling out a brown wool cloak, he wrapped it around himself and fastened it with a curious silver paw brooch.

Fiona quickly followed suit, removing her doublet and wrenching on the warm tunic. She opted to keep on her woolen tights as the new clothes covered them enough. While she had paper to purchase more suitable clothes, leave it to Dodger and the Travel Guild to have much more updated attire at hand for missions. She pulled her hair up and away from her neck, the humidity of the seaside city making her curls cling to her, and knotted it at the nape. Removing her scarf would be practical with the heat, but she didn't ever want it taken from her again. She tied it twice around her waist and made sure it was secured there.

Dodger nodded approvingly before handing her a small pouch. "Coins since Roma prefers the old currency. I think dropping too much money in the center of the city will cause questions of who we are. There's a person I know in the direction we're going who can sell us a chariot and horses."

"You mean to buy one?" Fiona exclaimed as they began making their way down the streets. Though there were a few glances their way they seemed to be nothing more than idle curiosity as people quickly minded their own business. They passed through the bustling visitors area before Dodger spoke again.

"The Binder said to spare no expense to find Vinicia." He pursed his furry lips, glancing around.

Fiona swallowed her question about the Binder and his notions on *sparing paper*. She would find a way to artfully question Dodger about the fae once they were on the road and he was more relaxed. She said lightly, "Lead the way."

The city center boasted buildings that seemed to take on the waves of the ocean and marry it with the rigid structures of the typical Roma architecture. Scalloped edges created fluid walls, like water rippling out from a shore. Was this Nymar before the Roma Empire conquered them or afterward? Brightly painted seashells provided sky blues and olive greens pleasing the eye at each residence they passed. Smilodons, paradalis and jubatas alike, strolled the streets, heading to the market or following the same road they did toward the edge of the city. The buildings grew smaller and less grand as the tall city walls began shadowing over them. Here were more apartments, modest housing with shops lining the street. The only outwardly ornate items were the bronze statues dotted here and there of a tall toga-wrapped smilodon panther with a diadem gracing his head. The Emperor. They were so prevalent it must have been done with purpose in a city that held an official pagemark with Spine.

As they approached what looked like stables Fiona caught a curious sight out the corner of her eye: a dark cloaked sleek jubatas cheetah was walking with haste toward the stables, darting past them and then gone. She might have blinked and missed the smilodon completely except for the fact that he looked almost identical to Dodger.

Fiona stopped short and tugged on Dodger's cloak. "Do you happen to have a secret brother?"

His eyes widened. "Why do you ask?"

Having expected a less reactive response, Fiona pressed closer, lowering her voice. "I would swear by Larrakane's hand I saw you run into those stables ahead of us. Cloak and all. But come, you look as if I've said something shocking. Do you know someone who could be your twin?"

Dodger swiveled his head quickly to the stables and muttered, "It can't be."

"What can't be?" She moved in front of him, breaking his stare at the stables. "Who was that?"

"It doesn't matter." He tilted his head and shrugged. "Your eyes are simply playing tricks on you. Human eyes are prone to mistakes, I've heard."

Fiona crossed her arms. "I may not have the senses of a faekin, but my eyes are not bad. I think I can tell the difference between one of my closest friends and some random smilodon."

"Let's hope not." Dodger started off again toward the stables and through the entrance of the smaller dwelling attached.

A young gray-furred cream-tunic-wearing smilodon at the counter eyed them cooly before straightening up. "Well met. What may I do for you?"

Dodger cleared his throat and said, "Is Domina Magunna here?"

The youth's furry eyebrows shot up at the name. She took a step back, looking at Dodger again, and then her eyes slid over to Fiona. "How can I serve you?" Her voice took on a more careful and respectful demeanor.

"To speak with Domina Magunna, if she still oversees this place," Dodger said again with more confidence.

"She does but she won't be able to help you." A short jubatas cheetah the spitting image of Dodger rounded the doorway behind the young smilodon. He patted the younger one on the back. "Go check the horses. I'll handle this." The youth stood taller and took a step toward Dodger, but the cheetah put a hand on her shoulder. He pushed aside his cloak displaying the symbol of a laurel wreath to everyone in the room. "This is Roma business." He pushed the youth away from the counter and took her place.

Fiona raised an eyebrow as thick tension filled the room. She glanced at Dodger, who had stilled as the cheetah entered.

Perhaps not a brother but something like it was clear to her. "We'd like to purchase a chariot and horses," she said, trying to break the silence.

"Unfortunately we can't allow that," the cheetah said without glancing her way. He kept his eyes on Dodger. "There's carriages you may hire that should work for your needs."

With a tagalong spy, no doubt. Fiona gently bumped Dodger to get him out of his stupor.

He snapped to like a stiff board and stuttered out, "Lucius."

The cheetah grinned wide. "Marcius. I was wondering when you'd say something."

"I was surprised, that's all."

Lucius crossed his arms. "I'd be surprised to see me too. But let's not spend time where it's not needed. No Guild jacket will have leave to go where they like anymore in the empire. Especially you."

FIONA STARTED, SURPRISED AT the tone of the smilodon. "Why especially him?"

"It doesn't matter," Dodger said, shaking his head. "Lucius, I'm sorry—"

"It doesn't matter," Lucius said in the same tone as Dodger. He raised his voice. "I give the orders here now."

"This is absurd," Fiona said. What Dodger said about the Guild being pushed out of the empire was farther along than she had thought. The shallow breath the Guild had in the Spine pagemark was clearly gone. Fiona took a step closer to Lucius. "You're going to deny the Guild access? I'm not their biggest fan, but surely that's going to deny the merchants quite a bit of coin."

"Coin from the likes of the Guild is worth nothing to the empire anymore."

There was a thump outside the archway behind Lucius. A shadow moved across the entrance. Was it the younger smilodon eavesdropping? Were the two smilodons related, or was it her business Lucius was so stubbornly interfering in? Perhaps she could speak to one through the other.

"I suppose quite a few travelers come through the pagemark in the city center," Fiona said. "How many of them get to this business with needs still? Not many, I suspect."

Lucius raised an eyebrow. "This family has no need to play favorites to outsiders for business. We are Roma. We don't worry ourselves with external matters."

"That's no longer the case," Dodger said, wiping at his whiskers. He rushed on, "The Book has changed quite a bit in the last twelve years, Lucius. You must know that. The empire is not alone."

"What do you care about the empire?" Lucius scoffed. "Now that you're a jacket, you're a saint as well? Jackets can't help the people here, and the small bit of money you hand over as you come through isn't worth giving the Guild any more footing." He waved toward the door. "I suggest you take your leave."

Dodger pulled on Fiona's arm toward the door. "We'll find another way." Dodger swallowed, then nodded to Lucius. "Glad you're doing well, at least."

Lucius snorted.

Fiona stopped and opened her mouth to reproach Lucius's apparent attitude, but Dodger tugged on her again.

"Fi," Dodger hissed, "we should go."

She followed him out but shot one more glance over her shoulder at Lucius. Expecting a glare, she was momentarily surprised to see a conflicted face. He turned quickly away from her and disappeared into the back room.

Fiona quickened her pace toward Dodger and asked, "Why didn't you say more? You have the means to negotiate here as a regulation Travel Guild leader. Regardless of what he said, I think the actual owners might have agreed."

"The domina wouldn't go against the tradition of the empire. I thought we'd even have an easier time there for a moment, but..." Dodger shaded his eyes looking up at the towering wall ahead of them. "I should've read the reports closer."

Lucius came into view leaving the building. He glanced momentarily in their direction before heading toward the wall and out of sight. Fiona eyed Dodger as he stiffened up again at the sight of the other cheetah.

"What is between you two?" she asked.

Dodger sighed. "We always competed, and I always won. Lucius never took it well. That's all." He rushed on, "We'll have to walk. We simply can't trust anyone else now. We'll try to find a hired carriage when we get closer to Roma Mikar, try again to disassociate from any Travel Guild appearance." He clasped her shoulder. "Thank you for attempting to make a deal, Fi."

Before she could speak, the young smilodon burst from the building, scanning around. As soon as she laid eyes on them, she leapt in front of them. "Follow me." Without waiting she leapt toward the stables.

Fiona followed as quickly with Dodger trailing behind her. They entered the stables, the smell of sweat and horses permeating the air.

Beside a short chestnut, the youth waved them over. "I'll give you a chariot and horses if you can agree to make our family the controlling source of horses for the Travel Guild."

Dodger assessed the young smilodon. "Why would you help us?"

She stood taller and smoothed down her cream tunic. "One day I will be the domina of this family. It would not do to ignore setting business in the other pages. My mother understands that, but reputation, and the empire, is more important to her than the future. It is not the best way forward."

Fiona was impressed with the young smilodon. She *had* been listening in on the conversation at hand. Fiona would've done the same if it was her home. Glad that the empire was not full of all Luciuses and Emperors, she said to Dodger, "It's your decision, of course."

He clasped his hands behind him. "Your reasoning is solid. But this is a big ask for a small return. The only source of horses for the Travel Guild would shift things considerably with our other agreements and impact the livelihoods of other families across the Book." Dodger watched the young smilodon for a moment as if looking for a reaction.

The young smilodon shifted away from Dodger, tail twitching. "Other pages sell horses to the Guild?" It was clear while she thought of selling to the other pages, she had not thought of competition from them. "What if instead we get first priority on filling contracts for the next season?"

"A reasonable counter." Dodger nodded. "If you can agree to favorable pricing and a set number of chariots to go along with them, I'll give you two seasons."

The smilodon grinned. "Agreed. Wait one moment."

After a short time, several scrolls of parchment, and a hasty seal, a servant prepared a brand-new chariot and two beautiful horses. Dodger helped Fiona into the chariot with their packs and then took the reins. The young smilodon directed them to a merchant entrance of the city wall and helped them pass through the guards. It was clear she had somewhat of a standing already in the city by the way they allowed the two to pass with little question.

"I believe you handled that negotiation with great care," Fiona said, patting the horse as they got onto the public road.

Dodger shrugged. "It was simply training." Dodger flicked the reins softly and the horses began to pick up speed.

Fiona held on tightly to the wooden sides of the chariot. Though she knew Dodger was less likely to career out of control than some, the quick speed was more than she expected. The dusty stone road was lined with borders of short stepping-stone pillars. While Fiona felt hearty thanks to emperors gone by for not having to drive on a dirt path or through shifting sands, it was not exactly a smooth ride. The wheels clacked loudly, drowning out even the hooves of the horses.

"Dodger." Fiona moved closer so he could hear. "Did the Binder teach you how to negotiate like that? I don't quite remember nuance being part of turner training." She grinned.

Dodger glanced at Fiona. "He did. He has had me study the various leaders of the Book. What was written about them and their own writings. Your Queen Eleanor Pompania was one."

"She was?" Fiona said, surprised. She hadn't imagined others outside of her page would find Queen Eleanor interesting to study. "And what did you learn from her?"

"That secrets make for tense friendships." Dodger smirked. "But also that she was a very dedicated ruler to her people. She seemed to have been picked specifically because she was a page turner."

Fiona murmured noncommittally. That Eleanor was much more than she seemed and even knew why page turners came about floated to the front of her mind. But she found herself distracted and turned the subject back to the Binder. "Why do you think he asked you to do that? Is that how he trains his Gilded?"

He shook his head. "At least Marcia wasn't required to study other leaders. But he simply has a way he thinks things should be done. He has reasons for everything."

"He does, does he? He seems quite inscrutable and quick to temper."

Dodger laughed. "He doesn't put up with a ton of nonsense, if that's what you mean. But he doesn't do much to hide who he is when he's around people who know him. He doesn't leave the Hinge often or travel outside of Spine. He didn't expect I would want to, either, when I was growing up. But once I helped him understand the things I could be learning traveling the pages versus all the reading he set before me, he understood. His versatility and ability to understand the changing times is tremendous."

Versatility was not a word she would've associated with the Binder. Or the Travel Guild. "Does he wish more people respected the Travel Guild?"

Dodger fumbled with the reins. "Fi, the entire Book respects the Travel Guild. Things wouldn't run smoothly, nor would people feel safe crossing page to page, if it wasn't for the Binder and the way he leads the Guild."

She tapped her lips and said slowly, "Yes, but it must've been unnerving to see how easily the public turned on the Guild when the Painted Edge was blaming them for the near death of Blaze."

"He was disappointed," Dodger said, staring out at the road.

"And not angry?"

"No, why would he be angry?"

Fiona snorted. "Isn't that what most people would be if their organization was attacked?"

"The Binder isn't most people." He glanced at her. "I know you, Fi. What are you trying to get at?"

"Nothing," Fiona said in the most innocent way she could. What could she say that wasn't actually a lie? "He has quite a lot of authority and power. He has access to many powerful people as well. But he also has taken the time to teach you, train you, and commands quite a bit of respect from almost everyone I've encountered who has worked for him. He's curious. And you do know how I love a curiosity."

Dodger laughed and relaxed. "Yes, I'm familiar with your nosiness. Okay, ask away. I have nothing to hide when it comes to the Binder, and in all frankness, I want you to give him a chance."

She frowned. "To do what?"

"Endear himself to you."

Fiona grinned. "Perhaps." She bit her lip, thinking quickly. "Well then, do *you* know his real name? Surely you don't go around calling him Binder even in private?"

"Actually..."

"Dodger! That's ridiculous. The man has a name." Though she knew it to be Archae, she hesitated to say it out loud. Did he let anyone say it? Perhaps it would mean that person knew his and the other Seasons' secret.

"It's a show of respect," Dodger said. "I know his name but that doesn't mean I have to use it."

Fiona rolled her eyes. "Do you think he already knows who the leader of the Painted Edge is?"

"I think he has a deep suspicion, yes. But the Binder isn't one to act without having all the materials in place."

That piqued Fiona's interest. If he was running two organizations, he would have to orchestrate things very well indeed around each other. Of course, having the Painted Edge accuse the Travel Guild and then letting that fail would make it less conspicuous that they may both be run by the same person. "What reason does he give you for why he doesn't travel the Book often?"

"He always says he's too busy. But I suspect he can't leave," he said softly.

Fiona's eyes widened. She didn't know why she was surprised. Dodger was a good investigator. She made another noncommittal noise.

Dodger winked at her. "Am I being clever yet?"

"You are," she said lightly, "and I am happy for it. Has the Binder taken you into one of his secret storage rooms or told you of any heists that he has yet to solve?"

A blank expression took over his face before he said, "That's the oddest question. I thought you were going to ask me where he lived or who he spent his time with. That's typically how I *investigate* a suspect."

Fiona glanced out at the stone border rushing by. "I never said he was a suspect of anything."

"And I never said I could drive a chariot, but here I am." Dodger cleared his throat. "Yes, I know about the storage rooms. All the Gilded and Marbled do, so whatever lead that is for you, it won't do much. And yes, there have been several missing items from them in the last year that even Marcia hasn't been able to track down. Until last night, that is."

"Which one?" Fiona said. She hated tiptoeing around subjects like this. Who would punish her if she spoke out loud? Larrakane, the Seasons, or the one that needed to be forgotten? "Metal or crowns?"

Dodger looked perplexed. "Metal actually. What is there to do with crowns?"

She waved her hand. "Never mind, that's a story for later then. So the metal *was* stolen from these secret holds?"

"Yes, along with a couple of other items. A few weapons, an ornamental dagger, those sort of things. But mostly the metal."

Fiona's attention snapped to the list. She narrowed her eyes. "Did he tell you what the dagger looked like?"

He shook his head. "Marcia knows about it. The only ones to have access to these barred items are the Gilded leaders and the Binder's *friends*, as you call them."

Fiona wondered if this was the dagger Stella had given her that Gaili had been studying. It seemed coincidental, but it would explain why Gaili couldn't deduce exactly what it was. Why did Stella leave it with her if it was valuable? It was a question she had been wondering for some time. Although maybe she didn't mean to leave it for long. She had said she'd be back to retrieve the fourth crown. Perhaps she would've scuttled the dagger as well. There was no telling what sort of chaos Stella had planned before she threw herself into the dark edge. Whomever she was working for had to have known how to handle her.

"Fi. Fi!" Dodger broke into her thoughts.

"Sorry, what?"

"I said, can you take the reins for a bit? You're chewing on your suspicions harder than usual. What is it?"

Fiona took the leather straps, holding them tightly. "Stella gave me a dagger as a parting gift when I first met her. I was wondering if it was the same and why."

Dodger stretched his arms. "You should tell Marcia."

She huffed. "Why, so she can be mad yet again that I didn't tell her everything?"

"She's not malicious. Simply thorough. If you shared more with her, she'd share more with you. I'm sure of it."

Fiona heard the earnestness in his voice and focused her attention on him again. He always sounded so confident of Marcia. And seemed to even spend time with her outside of the Hinge. They were a lot closer than she expected. But how close exactly? She turned her attention back to the road and said in a bright tone, "Are you and Marcia a couple, Dodger?"

He stiffened and his eyes widened. "What in the dark edge makes you think we'd be a couple?"

Fiona bit back a chuckle at his surprise. "It's clear you respect her, but lately you've been very talkative about her. You haven't called her Gilded in a while, except last night when you corrected yourself. She's on your mind, clearly, and I have to wonder if that's because you miss her." She knew what that part felt like at least.

Dodger glanced away out into the open yellow grassy plains beyond the road. He swiped his whiskers. "I was going to tell you, I promise. When we weren't running through the depths of Kerus. And when it was confirmed."

Fiona playfully swatted Dodger on the shoulder. "Well, you have my undivided attention. That's good and bad for you. But what do you mean, confirmed? Wait, no, start from the beginning." Fiona grinned. She had never, in all their years, seen Dodger with anyone. True, she hadn't been looking hard, but he had never even grumbled about there being a person he saw more than his paperwork and Travel Guild uniform.

Fascination mingled with care, and she said softly, "How long did it take you to notice her?"

"One day," he said brightly, "when I was assigned to the regulations department. She took all of us in hand and with some sharpness told us what she expected from us, what she wouldn't tolerate, and what we could expect from her in no uncertain terms. She was like a flower in the desert."

Though his voice quieted with embarrassment, Fiona understood his meaning. "So that's the sort of attitude that makes you interested?" Fiona said in a teasing manner to ease the awkwardness. "No wonder you never fancied any of the other trainees. We were all a bit moldable."

"She's strong," he said and ran his hands over the lip of the wooden chariot.

Fiona nodded in agreement. Say what you wanted about the hag, she had willpower. "Well, go on, how did it go from admiration to affection?"

Dodger tapped the chariot with a claw and shook his head. "Well, after some time working for her, I finally got to talk to her. Took the longest time too. She's not one to let someone get close. And I kept trying to do all these human customs to get her to notice me."

She laughed loudly. "Where in the Book did you take up human customs?"

"Well, you, Fi."

"Oh, well, there was one of your problems right there. I'm only a proper human when I have to be. That's never been with you."

"Well, it wouldn't have worked anyways, would it?" Dodger said. He leaned on the side of the chariot and crossed his arms. "She knew exactly what my mannerisms meant and skirted them all crisply and politely. After the first couple of tries I gave up and focused on my work. It took years to get a real opening toward a friendship with her."

"How did you do that?" While she wasn't vying for a friendship with Marcia, Fiona had noticed that the people Marcia seemed most comfortable with were all old hands by now: Mistress Humbledraft, Nicolosia, and the Binder. They had probably known her for longer than Fiona had been alive.

He grimaced. "I had been working on a report of activity in the mortal districts. Someone had been stealing jewelry from quite a few homes, and I had a breakthrough when compiling the report. I put a lot of hours into this and was excited to have a solid lead to act on. When I delivered the report to her, she barely glanced at it. I tried to speak up and she addressed me as if I was nothing more than a Guild messenger. The Binder had been saying I should be more persistent with people about what I wanted. Well, I wanted her to know I didn't appreciate not being heard when it was important." He sucked in a breath, then said quickly, "So I told her simply because she excelled in intimidation, it didn't mean I would continue to chase shadows with no response. That I expected her to review my work and, if she didn't think I was worth the effort, that I deserved an explanation so that I could be."

Fiona's jaw dropped. "You, Sir Professional, said that to your commanding leader?"

Dodger wiped a paw down his face. "Again, I was a bit upset. And you've seen her office! All those weapons and battle tapestries. It feels as if you're walking into a war when you're simply trying to file a report. But she did accept what I had to say." He smiled. "She even stiffly thanked me for my feedback. From then on, she started giving me real work to do. Letting me take lead on things around Spine. I mean, now I understand why she was so unfriendly, but—"

"Wait, why? Because she was a hag?"

Dodger shook his head. "Because she was the Binder's favored before I came along."

"Marcia was jealous of you!" Well, this recount was getting better by the moment.

He nodded. "I mean, how was I to know they even had a deep connection? I had never seen her at his home when I lived there. Though I caught moments with his other *friends*. And in the Hinge everyone is quite formal. The Binder meets with the Gilded. The Gilded meets with the Marbled. And down the chain of command goes. Either way. I didn't know."

It almost made her feel for Marcia, the only one of her kind, bound to Spine. That she would find her place with the Binder only to feel it threatened by a young smilodon who was polite to a fault. It must've irked her quite a bit. "And now you've both worked through all that and you're together," Fiona said excitedly. So much he had contained but with fair reasons.

"Not quite." Dodger pulled the reins back from Fiona and quickened the pace. He scanned the horizon, seeming to be looking for something.

Fiona didn't fall for it for a minute. She pulled the reins back. "Explain."

He sighed. "I want to make a proper go at it. We've had enough miscommunication and deception to bury any sort of relationship. But there's a lot there, Fi. We're good for each other. She reminds me of my value. I remind her to slow down. And Marcia sees it but I feel she's practically married to the Travel Guild."

Fiona shook her head. That said quite a bit coming from Dodger. "So because you two work together she doesn't think you should be together?"

"More than that. She says she must be focused on her work right now without distraction. I know the Painted Edge and the trouble they're bringing is truly important. But isn't that more of a reason to be with someone you care about than not?" He tugged on his whiskers. "I don't know what to say to her. And I don't want to lose her, but sometimes I feel as if I'm chasing the sun."

Fiona placed a hand on his shoulder, squeezing gently. She was in no position to give advice on matters of love. Larrakane knew that she had no idea how to bridge the gap between duty and wanting to be with someone. If she did, she'd shout it to Richard so he would bloody get on with it. That two people linked to fighting the Painted Edge and their leader felt so compelled to put everything aside to focus on it said a lot about the danger that lay before them. But like other dangers in the world, it would be there whether they took a moment to live for themselves or not. "Honestly, I'm not sure I'm in the best position to tell you what to do. Though I will regardless."

He leaned back against the chariot. "I would ask for no less than the Fiona Special."

"Try simply being there with her for all the times you can. You don't need something formal to make it real. And if we all survive this Painted Edge plot, why, then you have leave to take a page from my book and be as pushy as you like with her. Starting with, oh, I don't know, booking a holiday for you two. The Waterfall Palace in the Shimmering Depths is very romantic. Fantastic views and spacious rooms."

Dodger raised an eyebrow. "Since when do you go to romantic locations?"

"Since chasing a lead on a faekin case."

"Ah, for Marcia's sister."

She didn't know why, but Fiona still felt shocked by the ease in which he related well-kept secrets to her. "You two truly have come to terms, haven't you?"

Dodger patted her on the hand. "I'm glad I can talk to you about this. It's nice, not keeping it a secret. I wasn't really trying to before though."

"But when needs must," Fiona said quietly. She opened her mouth to say more but closed it just as quickly. She wanted to tell Dodger about Richard. About how she felt and who he was. But what if he forgot? She had no idea what Richard was even doing right now, but if something occurred, she didn't know if she could bear no one knowing he existed after everything again. As if he was a mirage or part of her imagination.

They stopped at an inn, more a farmer's roadside building rented for extra income than anything else. But it was a roof over their heads and, according to Dodger, not as dangerous as an actual public house on a road that saw many travelers, and those would rob them. Through some light questioning of the owners, they learned a smilodon matching Vinicia's description had passed through here as well less than a day ago. Celebration was short lived, however, hearing that she was with two other smilodon women. They would have to plan on their approach to make sure her cover was safe while they got their information.

After a short meal and a discussion about being up at first light, they went to their separate beds of the shared common room to sleep. Fiona lay for a bit, tossing and turning, before gathering up her stuff and going back out to the main room, where oil-filled lamps still glowed in the dimness. There was nothing of Copper ingenuity. Those in the Roma Empire were quite stubborn about using only what they had gained through their achievements, even if that achievement was taking it from someone else.

Fiona retrieved the leather-bound journal from the lace pocket of her scarf, making sure no one was watching her. After a brief waver of confidence, she put quill to paper. At this time he should have been either beginning to make rest or leaving from supper. How to start? It seemed a bit silly to write a greeting and then wait. She rubbed the edge of her scarf, her stomach fluttering. Realizing she was dallying, Fiona struck down with the quill forcibly and decided to just get on with it.

*"I'm in Kerus. Well, I'm in the Roma Empire, which is my **least** favorite part of the page. If you ever want to go somewhere I loathe, this would be it."* She sat back in the little wooden chair and glanced at the lamplight. How long till he noticed she had written and would respond? Did he simply know, or was conversation dependent on him looking at his journal?

Just as she decided to continue writing, Richard's fast, familiar sloping lines began scrawling across the page: "If I can ever leave the page again and the world is at peace, I hope you'll lead me somewhere calmer. A forest perhaps? Solid land beneath the feet."

She smiled in the dim light at his budding optimism. Did he realize what exactly he was saying? "I'll make sure of it," she wrote. She really would have to reintroduce him to the best parts of Mistral. Somehow.

There was a pause, then Richard's looping writing scrawled, "I made some progress about Priestess Raina today. When she was archbishop, she had the most communication with the royal court and the Queen, of course, giving her counsel. She spent a great deal of time on theology and taught students. So, in essence, she seemed to have done her job."

"Did she seem to love it? Were there any times she, say, overused her power?"

"From those I asked, no, but there seemed to be an anxiety there."

"A fear?" Could Priestess Raina make people too scared to speak out against her?

"Yes, as though if they said too much, someone would come down on them. I don't know who that would be, considering Priestess Raina hasn't been back to Spine since the day she was inked. Now I understand why, of course, being a Leaf of Spine and all. But the archbishop seat is still vacant, and the Queen is quite clear it won't be filled while Priestess Raina is alive. Perhaps they have an understanding between them. I don't know what she has said to the Queen, but it hasn't anything to do with me and I never prodded further."

Interesting. He was trying to make it clear that he didn't read Queen Brilliance's memory on this. Was Richard trying to prove to her he didn't use his powers lightly? "So then the Priestess seems to have a seat in the royal court while also living in Spine. Interesting. Much like Queen Eleanor."

"Yes, a bit like her."

"Did you know Queen Eleanor?" Fiona wrote slowly. While she certainly wanted to know more about Raina, she couldn't help but appease her curiosity. It didn't bother her to know Richard had been married, but knowing if it was the illustrious first human page turner would give her some information on the man he was before. Perhaps.

His quill tapped the page and dots of ink faded in. "I did, though I would suggest that be a conversation for another meeting. Perhaps in a dusty storage room?"

She tugged on an errant curl and sighed. Naturally there would be more than simply a yes or no. While she was pleased he promised to confide in her, she wondered why not in writing. "Of course." Was he smiling or pacing? If only she could see him while they conversed in this manner.

"As for her likeness, Priestess Raina certainly has her Followers of Larrakane spread throughout the page in a most blended fashion."

Fiona raised an eyebrow and scrawled quickly, "You mean they are hidden?"

"Perhaps not on purpose, but outside of the main churches there are Followers at every pagemark to Spine. Oh, I never noticed before that that's who they were, but the more common folks see them posted up almost as much as the Travel Guild brethren."

Fiona brushed the feather of the quill against her chin. Odd—why would they be at the pagemarks specifically to Spine? Did they also watch who came and went from Spine? Why not to any of the other pages? "Do you suppose they are keeping an eye out or poising to commandeer them?"

"I'm not sure yet, but I will be doing some more digging. I've also found that Henry Hawkport had taken rather an interest in Priestess Raina. They exchanged dozens of letters over the course of the last few years."

Hawkport! "Well, that's certainly incriminating. Do you know what they said?"

"No. The Queen still has them and I haven't been able to get close enough to get them. I didn't want to…" There was a pause and another scrawl, "I've refrained from making her give them to me. They'll be unattended soon enough. As soon as I get my hands on them, I'll bring them to the archives. I've had to put quite a few things in my storage room just to keep them away from the Queen and her nosy principal secretary."

She smiled as she could practically hear his indignation. "What about Henry himself?

"He hasn't been eager to talk since he's been arraigned. When I last saw him, he wouldn't stop smiling at me. It was unnerving."

Fiona tapped the tip of her quill against the journal. He thought he would be free soon enough, perhaps? He had more confidence in the Painted Edge's ability or desire to see him released than Stella had had. Or maybe someone within the family was poised to get him out. "And the rest of the family?"

"I've suggested to the Queen that only those directly involved be arraigned, and the Travel Guild has been tracking them down. The rest will have to find new places and new lives, but that's far better than the alternative."

It was more than they would've done for others under the hand of Henry. John himself had even been part of the airship cover-up. They were not equally guilty but guilty nonetheless. Richard had done those he could a great service in speaking on their behalf. Did he speak up out of guilt for foisting his responsibility on the family? Fiona hesitated to ask that directly, feeling it was more of an in-person conversation. What she could soften with tone of voice and touch would feel like salt in a wound read on paper. She wrote instead, "What about the airships?"

There was another pause and then Richard drew a flourish. It was clear to Fiona that when he was gathering his thoughts, he couldn't help but scribble on the paper. It was always the same sort of flourish or stroke, though, as if he was drawing something from memory. Finally, he stopped scrawling and wrote, "I've taken the oversight of the airships back from the Hawkports. I suppose it's time I got out of the archives and among the living after all."

Warmth flooded through Fiona and she couldn't help but feel a bit of satisfaction that perhaps this was partly due to her. "I think it will suit you well. The danger of someone else abusing the power won't be likely if you're at the helm. And Rise needs airships."

"Aye, but I wish it didn't. To use the Word in such a way brings back rough memories. Ones I don't wish to dwell on."

Surprised at his transparency of feelings, Fiona wrote, "I won't prod into your memories, but the Word? You're using this magic to make airships?" She could almost see him in his archives nodding at her so he didn't have to admit it out loud. She wrote quickly, "You made the Hawkports forget why they knew how to make them and what they said to do so."

"I wouldn't do it again."

"I didn't think you would," she scribbled.

"I was still overconfident in my ability to control the Word when I made the bargain with Lord—well, with Henry's great-great-grandfather. I vowed I wouldn't be anything like…"

Fiona watched the words appearing on the paper, waiting. It seemed so much easier for him to write his thoughts than it had in any of their conversations. He clearly journaled regularly. Who else could he talk to besides himself? He didn't finish his sentence, so Fiona wrote on the same line, "Your brother, I suppose. But truly you couldn't—"

There was a sickening lurch in her stomach that made Fiona drop her quill and gasp. Her chest ached, deep, as if she had been stabbed with the sharp end of a pen. She quickly pulled her doublet from her neck to peer down at what was attacking her. Larrakane's tattooed insignia glowed angrily, a gray ring bright against the blackening circle. A stinging cold as if she'd plunged into a frozen pool of water dripped from her chest and across her shoulders. Another pulse washed over her from it and then slowly the tingles of pain faded away. Warmth, her own body heat, took over and she shivered. What was that? Was it in reference to her words? Perhaps mentioning him connected in some way with Larrakane. Had she harmed Larrakane by doing it, or was Larrakane warding her from harm?

She picked up the fallen journal to find Richard's scribbled lines: "Don't mention. Don't write. Not in this manner. This too uses the same power, and it is vulnerable.

"Are you still there? I'm not trying to command you. Simply trying to give you all the information so you can know.

"If I could see through this journal!

"I will try to be patient but if needs must, I will."

She re-dipped the quill and wrote, "Larrakane's symbol pained me when I wrote that. Perhaps protected me?" She noticed the words she had written, *Your brother*, were no longer on the page. "And the words are gone. Was that you?"

"No." Richard's word was small and dark. Her stomach began sinking at Richard's terseness. But before she could address it or assure him, his writing continued, "Perhaps this was a mistake. I should leave you to your rest. Goodnight, Mistress Thornbeard."

"Richard," she wrote hastily, smearing ink on her hand. "Don't go simply because of one accident. How will we know what may work if we don't continue? I am a page turner literally inked by Larrakane and knowledgeable about your existence and past who *can* remember you. We, this connection and intelligence, have never happened before. Incidents may occur. Isn't it worth trying to understand what's going on in the Book, with the Painted Edge, all of this, together?" Fiona waited, her body feeling heavier by the moment, but there was no reply.

She dipped her quill back into the ink with force. Here she was at it again! Imploring him to give their back-and-forth a chance. Another chase. Well, she wasn't simply about to let him be saved by another interruption. She laid the journal flat on the table and began writing in earnest. "I know you have done things you regret, and you feel guilty about them. I can't fix that, but if you don't fight for your freedom and the lives of others, what was the point of giving up any of your honor in doing those things? You don't want to be romantically involved with me for fear of my safety—fine. Idiotic, but nevertheless it is your choice. But if you can't see we have the opportunity here to combine our knowledge in a way that may actually be helpful to not only the people in the Book but Larrakane herself, regardless of how you personally feel about her mistakes, then you are not as clever as I thought you were. Truly, you aren't the proud, stubborn man who stalled me at every turn. You're simply another idle power."

She leaned back in the chair, setting down the quill with trembling hands. Fiona bit her lips as tears welled up in her eyes. She quickly slid a piece of parchment in the journal so the ink wouldn't smear and closed it, binding it tightly. Let him acknowledge her or not. She had other issues at hand and would not be checking anytime soon. Fiona slipped the journal into her scarf and crept quietly back into the shared rooms. Lying down, she covered herself as best she could with blankets and tried desperately to forget about the tame golden-eyed lion. But her dreams were filled with the thought of him and her desire that he would fight for everything just a bit more.

# 9

AS FIONA AND DODGER prepared the chariot the next day, they heard a large commotion coming their way. A legion of Roma soldiers were riding heavily toward Nymar. Without conversation they both quickly stepped back inside the inn to watch their slow pass. If the Emperor was sending more soldiers toward the pagemark, then he indeed was staking his claim over the city. Anxiety took over Dodger's face, but Fiona didn't know how to reassure him. Her sleep had left her far from restful. They both decided they had little time to focus on the legion or the Emperor. The journey from the farmer's inn to Mikar would take the entire day and they needed to keep on Vinicia's tail.

Though Fiona felt she still stood out a tad, Dodger had been right that she wasn't the only human traveling through the regions. The inn had a couple of patrons who were clearly ingratiated with the empire. Where they may have been outsiders like Fiona before, they were Roma now—as much as they could be, denoted by their garments and bold laurel wreath symbol. What had made people from Rise assimilate into the empire? What was the Emperor offering them?

The gritty sand swirled across the road and covered them like crumbs on a tablecloth. Dry grass plains gave way to the signature Kerus desert as they drove the chariot and horses ever onward toward the city of Roma Mikar. There were few others on the trail besides them. Though they had barely stopped to rest the horses and themselves, Dodger felt they were in no way going to overtake Vinicia before she got to the coded meeting place of the Painted Edge. Over the loud clacking of their wheels, Fiona and Dodger discussed different avenues of approaching the situation. They were commanded not to interfere or break Vinicia's cover so that she could carry on with her spying. The easiest way to do that would be to bump into her strategically after the meeting but before she left Mikar. They would have to keep a careful eye out once inside the trading site so they could trail her as she left. Dodger said the building was once a temple to the Oracle of Stars but had quickly taken on a secondary life after Larrakane's arrival and the Inking. The massive structure featured a wide dome like a cap on the head but was otherwise open on every side for easy walking between stalls.

Finally they approached the sloping sandstone walls of the desert city. Deep, wide trenches encircled Mikar. The only safe places to travel in and out were the large, thick gates set on the walls. Shifting moats meant to slow or trap invaders were now unused. The invaders had won. But from the slits in the wall to the polished metal towers blinding approaching riders, if not riding for the gates, it was clear this city had known battle. It was unlike anything Fiona had seen before.

The guards asked them impertinent questions, which Fiona let Dodger handle. Though he felt just as weary as she, he knew how to put on a smoother supplicant role with the romas than Fiona could muster so deep into their territory. She simply glanced at the guards and then away again. Not too often but more than once to give the impression this was normal and expected and she was not in the least bit worried about their gaining entrance.

The guards let them cross in without further comment. Dodger took the reins back from Fiona and led them into Roma Mikar. The sandy walls of the desert city belied the beauty of the desert smilodons. Sun-dried russet bricks made up most of the tall buildings closest to the wall. Tall chimneylike structures topped each one, though Fiona couldn't guess why anyone would want a fireplace in the desert. But when she pointed them out to Dodger, she was surprised to find that they caught the wind and funneled it into the buildings, cooling them from the rising heat of the surrounding arid region. Arched doorways decorated with brown and green mosaic tiles made an inviting smile in to most of the dwellings as they made their way deeper into the city. Though they were surrounded by sand, painted frescos and mosaic tiles displayed art of dunes and the vibrant purples and pinks of wildflowers of remote places.

Dodger sighed, leading the horses around toward the way station.

"Miss it?" Fiona asked.

"Sometimes. Enough to be thankful it's still standing and looks as it ever was. But not enough to visit regularly." He handed the reins off to one of the attendants and then dropped a couple of coins in to pay for a night in the stables.

Fiona glanced out at the different clusters of people moving about toward the outer edges of a growing market. Though most were smilodons, she counted a few humans, elephas, and even an ursidon in the mix. More than she expected. What kind of people did Dodger associate with before he was inked?

Come to think of it, he hadn't said much about visiting anyone while they were here. Or avoiding them. He had seemed so surprised to see Lucius. "Your friends, before you were inked. Do you see them at all?"

Dodger shook his head. "I didn't have friends. Not like you and I. There were always other scamps around on the outside looking in. Running together. But those relationships always felt temporary. How could they not?" He grimaced. "There are some who clearly remember me, but I'm sure the others don't. It's for the best." Dodger glanced away into the crowds. His words sounded so final, but there was something there. Much he wasn't saying. It didn't sound like Dodger to let friendships go, however, and it was clear he was thinking of particular people.

"Well, you now know Lucius to be around. What about these others?"

"I suppose some are in the capital while others migrated to Disas as they could. There's always a welcome on that continent for those looking to try something different than all of this." He tugged on the edges of his cloak, not meeting her eyes. "It was difficult to understand my page turning abilities in the beginning. And by the time I... Well, I didn't want to interrupt their lives after years of silence. They didn't need that from me."

There it was: some form of guilt. Fiona recognized that tone, its familiar etching having run through her head a few times an hour in another's voice. She laid a hand on Dodger's shoulder. "Maybe after this you can reach out. No sense avoiding a whole page for unfinished business."

"Perhaps. Thank you," Dodger said, turning all formal. His shoulders rose and he clasped his hands behind his back, standing straighter. "Let's make haste to the trading site. The good thing about a public building is there's an expectation of people coming and going, so we shouldn't have any trouble. Follow me."

Reminding herself that forcefulness wasn't always the answer, Fiona silently agreed and they strode quickly through the streets. While Nymar had been all stone, salt, and remnants of sand, Mikar streets were compacted dirt after the thumping footsteps of thousands of people and horses since its foundation. Many mulled in the roads now, but the people began to thin out rapidly as they traveled farther toward the eastern wall.

"It's quite quiet all of a sudden," Fiona whispered.

Dodger's tail swished in the air. "Not sure why. This area should be heavy with—" He stopped, rounding the corner.

Fiona peered over his shoulder at the trading site. Its stacked pale-brown stones and open exterior was marked with rust-and-corn-silk banners. The stairs leading up to the market platform were swarming with more Roma soldiers than Fiona had ever seen in one place. "Why are there so bloody many?"

"I don't know," Dodger whispered. He took a step back and then pulled Fiona close. "Let's find a different vantage point." He scurried back into the streets, mixing with the throngs of other smilodons and around the corner into a thin alley. Dodger glanced around before beginning to scurry up the wall.

She caught up and shaded her eyes, watching him. "I hope you don't expect me to do that."

He grunted, shifting his weight as he climbed. "I know you're not scared of heights."

"Then you also know I'm not a natural climber. I always have my ornithopter to take to the sky."

"I'll be back." He continued up until he was on the roof. With a salute from above, Dodger disappeared quicker than she could catch a breath.

The bright sun made it hard to keep looking at the roof. She could see no part of him. Fiona dropped her hands and moved away from the building. It wouldn't do to be staring up and gathering attention on herself and possibly Dodger. She moved back to the edge of the crowd, running her hands down her tunic, and stepped lightly toward the fountain in the square. Getting closer, she surveyed who she might ask questions of without issue. Spying a short tawny-skinned young human woman in similar clothing, Fiona approached her in a confident manner and asked, "Is the trading site closed today?"

The young woman looked her up and down, assessing her. She pursed her lips. "To *outsiders*, yes." Then strode off without a backward glance.

Fiona pushed down the urge to mutter something confrontational and smiled as if it had been a congenial moment. She tried again with another person, smilodon this time, who told her in easy tones that the trading site had been closed for the last two days by the legion for inspection. And that no one besides approved people were allowed in or out. Fiona thanked her, grumbling about having made the visit to see the famous public building and saying she would have to stay overnight. She asked her for the best place in the city to stay and was directed to an upscale hospitable establishment that many travelers stayed in, the House of Falchus. Departing before her luck was pressed, Fiona meandered back toward where she had left Dodger to see him waiting for her, back against the wall.

"What did you see?" she said quietly.

"There are several guards on the roof as well as the top floor. The guards on the stairs rotated toward the back of the building. So they aren't there simply for show. They must've gotten wind about the Painted Edge meeting and decided to fortify the trading site."

Fiona frowned. "I've been told it's been closed for the last two days. One woman said specifically to outsiders, but that was with some prejudice, given her tone. Do you think this would have stopped them? Perhaps they've decided to reconvene somewhere else?"

"There could be any number of places in Mikar, but how would they communicate with each other so quickly? A backup must've been decided or alluded to in the note, but I don't know how."

"We can at least ask around about her likeness. See if we can find her that way."

He clasped his hands behind his back. "That's not exactly covert."

"But if we do it in a brazen way, it could work. We could ask the guards."

"You believe we should walk up to them and ask if they've seen a group of rippers with matching tattoos? And do they also conveniently have them locked up already?"

She waved away his words, well used to Dodger's pushback on her bolder ideas. "They would at least have an answer."

"And we would, too, though I'm not sure we'd have a way to use it, being shackled and all." He pushed off from the building and began walking in the direction of the trading site slowly.

"I won't let them shackle us. Promise." Fiona fell into place beside him. "Besides, even if they did, I doubt they'll use turn stoppers." It wasn't as if one could tell a page turner simply by looking at them.

Dodger inclined his head, giving no further argument. It was as much of an agreement as always when he knew she would continue to press and he had no real reason to keep denying. He stopped at the corner of the closest building to the trading site. "Make a scene if I need to jump in."

Without another word Fiona sauntered over to the nearest guards, a small jaguar and larger panther, at the bottom of the trading site stairs. With an exaggerated stance, she stopped at the bottom step. She tilted her head in a coy manner and directed her words at the jaguar smilodon. "I see the building is closed. Do you know when it will reopen?"

"No." He almost didn't move a muscle when speaking, his metal helmet barely rising.

"Not at all?" Fiona glanced away and then toward the larger smilodon. "Well, is there anyone who can tell me?"

"No," they both said, somewhat in unison.

If they thought one-word answers would put her off, they picked the wrong tactic. She was quite versed in them by now. "I heard the reason the building is closed is because *outsiders* were gathering in it. Rippers and the like. Terrible."

The jaguar stared at her openly. "*You* are from Mikar?"

She shook her head. "From Rise. Terrible place. The empire is exceptionally better." She grinned and leaned in.

"We will only grow in power." The jaguar stood a bit taller now. He waved off the other smilodon, who stepped back to his post a few feet away.

"Yes, I think my choice to relocate was a smart one. It's a pity outsiders ruin everything for Roma though," she said, waving toward the trading site. "I wish I could meet these ones. And show them what makes Roma superior."

The guard assessed her and then said quietly, "If you're looking for a true calling to service the empire, there is need. You can join others."

Confusion flooded Fiona, but she held a steady face. Perhaps if she could talk to others with a lower guard, then they could know if the Painted Edge had already come through or if anyone had seen Vinicia. "How?" she said brightly.

"The House of Falchus always has room," the jaguar said quietly. Then he nodded in her direction and said a little louder, "But until that time, please return to the public streets." He dismissed her, striding back to stand at attention.

Feeling she would get no more, she walked away without hurry. Were they asking her to join the militia? At a public house? An upscale one to boot. Fiona walked past Dodger, not acknowledging him, and melted into the crowd. She knew Dodger would keep up with her, but she didn't want anyone connecting them while they were so close to the trading site and guards.

Once they were toward the city center, the swell of people mingling and mixing created a heavy cover. Fiona stopped and waited for Dodger. He only took a few moments before bumping into her.

"Felicia?" he said with a practiced look of confusion and delight.

"Marcius?" Fiona said with fake surprise. She threw her arms around him. "It's been quite a while since I've seen you."

"So good to bump into you," Dodger said, smiling. He leaned in, whispering, "What did they say?"

Fiona pointed to a small bench, and they started walking toward it. She lowered her voice and recounted her conversation with the guard.

"The House of Falchus always has room, does it?" Dodger wiped his whiskers. "I've never been inside. Quite the out-of-reach place for an urchin like me, though I have heard of it. I wonder if the others mean the Painted Edge or simply a more questionable military group for the empire."

"I don't know. I expressly asked about rippers, but perhaps I leaned too hard on the outsider bit."

"We can at least check it out. It's all the lead we have. If it goes nowhere, we can fall back on asking after Vinicia's appearance with the guards."

Dodger led deeper into the central area of the city. There was a large sandstone wall backing multistory houses here with no shops or small stores to be seen. One of the grand homes had a painted wall with geometric carvings shaved out of the paint to create a pattern in the shape of a mountain peak. The sun radiated above it in bright-yellow mosaic tiles. The name *House of Falchus* stood prominently below the mountain.

They entered the stone-walled home to find it filled with people. Some were travelers with dirty hems but well-threaded cloaks or silver and gold clasps. Others wore cream or golden tunics with leather belts that seemed to have not seen much daily wear. There was a general murmur of voices quietly chattering, enjoying themselves and the atmosphere. Clinks of mugs on tables and string music from a shadowed player were the loudest noises within. Fiona and Dodger parted at the doorway after a few words of split duties. Dodger made his way to the large marble counter and the patrons sitting near it.

Fiona walked gently around the room, listening in on conversations. She stopped at the only statue in the room, a bust of the current Emperor, marveling at the detailed facial features of the panther. She kept her ears open as snippets of conversation caught her interest. Most were little more than gossip about Mikar residents or the Emperor's newly constructed forum across the sea in recently conquered land. But at the bottom of the grand staircase leading to private rooms, two women jubatas, one with cheetah appearances and the other cougar-like, whispered an unmistakable word that floated like a musical note to Fiona's trained ears: *Guardian.* Fiona kept moving, not wanting to seem as if she had heard, and took a table behind them near the stairs to listen further.

After a few moments there was little doubt that they knew something more than simply idle gossip. Hushed tones spoke of waiting for command to leave Mikar and of unnecessary attention gathered by the legion. It seemed that Dodger and Fiona's supposition that military had stopped the Painted Edge from gathering at the trading site was correct. Fiona had no doubt that these two were with the Painted Edge by their disgruntled conversation. But the cougar wasn't Vinicia. Much too tall in comparison to her picture. Perhaps she was here, though, upstairs in one of the rooms. Fiona needed to tell Dodger and then they could quickly make a plan to approach the spy.

Pretending to be impatient for her companion to bring back drinks, Fiona tutted, got up from the table, and swanned over to the bar. She stopped short at the sight of a familiar cheetah captivating Dodger's attention. Lucius. A complication she hadn't expected.

"Fancy seeing you in Mikar," Lucius said, widening his stance. "Tell me, what business does a jacket have this far from the pagemark?"

"I'm on my way to Roma Valar," Dodger said with some quickness.

Lucius tapped his claw against the bar. "Interesting. And what does the *Travel Guild* of all organizations have to do in the capital?"

Fiona quickly glanced around, noticing additional eyes were now turning toward the simmering pair. Not good. The two women were the only leads they had. They couldn't lose them. Fiona leaned in to whisper to Dodger, but Lucius barred his teeth at her quietly.

"That's uncalled for," Dodger said, darting in between them. "I would think after all these years you'd be happy to ignore me, Lucius."

The cheetah snapped his focus back to Dodger. "Who says I'm not? I'm doing much better than you, that's for sure."

"I never said you weren't." Dodger sighed and took a step back. He seemed to be trying to gain his composure.

Lucius took a step closer. "Tell me, Marcius, what's it like to work for an utterly failing institution?"

Dodger straightened up, clasping his hands behind his back. "The Travel Guild is not failing."

"Are you sure?" Lucius quieted his voice. "With the connections you have these days, I say it's trash in, trash out."

Fiona said furtively, "Is this really the place to be having this conversation? We're not here to fight you and I think you know that." Fiona narrowed her eyes. "I think if we could have a more *private* discussion, you might see us as allies to the Empire." If they could convince Lucius they, too, were against the Painted Edge, the real outsider threat, perhaps he would relent quicker.

Though he didn't show his teeth again, his tone was still threatening. "I don't need the likes of you or the Guild coming here to take care of Roma."

Dodger's tail twitched rapidly. "Come on, Lucius. We're long past childhood now. There are real matters at stake here."

"How would you know the stakes? You haven't been here." Lucius shook his head "You were a nuisance back then and you're a nuisance now." He glanced at Fiona. "Not surprised you're cavorting with a human. Probably less likely to do anything when you hang them out to dry."

Instead of taking a deep breath as Dodger normally did, he lunged at Lucius. Both Lucius and Fiona were taken by surprise, though Lucius not as long. He pushed Dodger off of him and jumped backward. Rearing back, he swung out at Dodger, who quickly moved out of the way. Lucius tried to wrap his arms around him, but Dodger ducked and came out from behind him. His look was one Fiona hadn't seen since training when he was first inked: a look of pure instinct and melted patience.

Dodger taunted, "You couldn't land a hit on me when we were cubs. Don't think you'll be able to do it now."

Lucius growled and whipped his tail around, grabbing a mug. Using his tail, he threw it at Dodger's head.

Dodger sidestepped, the mug missing, but Lucius seemed to have anticipated this and lunged for him.

People pressed in on Fiona, getting closer to the fight. She glanced around to see the two smilodon women were nowhere to be seen. Out through the open door she could see soldiers heading quickly down the street. So much for leads. She tugged on Dodger's cloak. "We need to go."

He dropped prone to the floor as Lucius swung back again to hit him. Lucius toppled with his forward momentum. Dodger jumped up and onto Lucius's back, not heeding Fiona at all.

"Dodger. Now," Fiona shouted. She jumped onto the counter away from the other patrons and grabbed him by the shoulders. "The rest of the soldiers are coming. We'll lose if we're shackled here."

His eyes snapped to hers and a grim expression took over. He nodded once, his reserve sliding back into place, and grabbed her hand. "Get on my back."

Feeling awkward, Fiona slung herself on his back, and Dodger jumped to the counter top. He glanced out the window at the approaching guards and vaulted onto the floor before running up the stairs.

"It's a good thing you're light."

"Yes, well, coffee doesn't have a lot of nutritional value," Fiona said.

They raced up the stairs and into a hallway. Footsteps echoed behind them. Fiona didn't turn around to see if they were from guards or excited patrons. Dodger ran through the corridor, taking the first turn they saw. Another set of stairs seemed to lead back down. To the commotion below or an exit out the back, Fiona didn't know, but they had little choice. Dodger headed toward the stairwell.

"Pages puzzle for sense and soul! Quickly." A tall black-rosetted leopard smilodon waved to them from an open doorway.

Dodger immediately turned into the room. The smilodon closed the door behind them and waved them toward the other archway that led away from the main chamber. Dodger wasted no time going into the adjoining room. He set Fiona down on the bed.

"Why on earth did you come in here? It could be a trap," Fiona hissed. She sprang up, glancing around the confined room.

Dodger shook his head. "Jackets have codes, Fi. At the very least if he isn't one, we need to know how he knew the symbology."

"Be quiet," the smilodon whispered. He closed the door on them.

There was a pounding of footsteps and shouts. Fiona counted her breaths, trying to slow her breathing and assess an escape route. There was a window here with a balcony. But it was fully viewable by the street the House of Falchus faced. Scores of people would see them leaving if they went that way.

Time trickled to a stop as the loud voices of searchers looking for them grew and faded into the hallway. She didn't dare look out the window to see if they had gotten into the streets. How long before someone started opening rooms? The bedroom was richly decorated with thick curtains, cushioned benches, and many bright blue and purple wildflowers painted on the wall. Perhaps in this sort of establishment, demanding open doors would take some time and cajoling of the patrons.

Dodger paced the room quietly, wearing a grim expression. He glanced at Fiona as if he wanted to say something but then shook his head and looked away.

The door opened and the tall black-rosetted leopard smilodon nodded to them bashfully. "You are from the Guild, correct? I heard the chatter."

"Perhaps." Fiona leaned in. "Are you?"

He shook his head. "No, but I help the Guild from time to time. From here."

"How did you know the phrase?" Dodger said, seeming to regain himself. He put himself between the smilodon and Fiona protectively.

The smilodon looked down at the ground. "Guild contact told me to use it with other jackets."

Dodger's shoulders relaxed. "You're an agent." He paced to the wall and pressed his back to it.

The smilodon held up his hands and looked from Dodger to Fiona. "Informant, more like. Want to change the empire for the better." He waved at Dodger. "You know what I mean."

She hadn't expected there would be people within the cities of the empire who would go against the Emperor like this. Outside, yes, but how many more were there working against the Romas while mingling with them? "Well, thank you for saving us," Fiona said.

"You're welcome. But you won't be able to leave anytime soon."

"Yes, I think you're right," Fiona said, pinching the bridge of her nose. She looked at Dodger, who stared tight-jawed at the door. What had gotten into him? Clearly what Lucius said made him lose his composure, but what had it meant? She sighed, irritated, and pushed that to the side. If Vinicia was in these rooms, Fiona wasn't sure how they'd find her without being spotted. She couldn't very well make herself look completely different without some supplies. Perhaps this agent might have seen her. "Have you seen a jubatas with reddish-brown fur, probably wearing traveling clothes? She was most likely with two other jubatas women, orange and spotted like our friend here." She pointed to Dodger.

The informant nodded quickly. "Another jacket. She didn't give me a name, but I spoke with her."

Dodger's head snapped up. "How did you know she was a jacket?"

"She said if other jackets come for her, to give them a message."

Fiona frowned. Why did Vinicia think anyone from the Guild would be following her? She couldn't have been made aware of their mission. Fiona held out her hand. "May we have the message?"

The smilodon looked at her hand and smiled. "No parchment. But she said to 'seek kin.'"

"She wants us to visit her brother," Dodger said quietly.

Of course. Her brother *was* in Mikar. But how were they possibly going to get out of here? They couldn't waste time hiding. "Do you know the way?" Fiona said.

Dodger nodded silently.

"Great. Then we need to go, now." She tugged the ends of her scarf around her waist reassuringly. The gray was starting to fade.

"Impossible," the smilodon said, glancing out the window.

Fiona sighed. "They'll continue to send guards, maybe even ask to see in rooms. If we go now, we have a chance before the net tightens."

Dodger heaved himself up off the wall. It was clear that Lucius had gotten a couple of hits on him, but he gritted his teeth. "You're right. Let me give myself up. That way you can go on."

"Don't be such a blotter," Fiona snapped. "It won't help anyone if you do that. Think about it. Then there will be a big scandal about a Travel Guild leader fighting in Mikar. More eyes will be drawn here. For now, it's just Lucius's word and a crowd of people who saw a fight. No one can say for sure you're a jacket or not, or even who you are."

"Fi—"

"No." She crossed her arms. "We can talk about what happened later, but for now we need to get out of here and to her brother's house. Think of a plan."

"So commanding," Dodger muttered, but he was already pacing the floor. "We could leave through a service entrance. There must be at least one."

"That would force us downstairs, and I suspect that's where everyone will be." Fiona wrapped her fingers around the edge of her scarf. No way to disguise themselves in a way that would pass inspection. It's possible the only other place was up. "Is there a way to access the roof?"

Tilting his head, Dodger said, "Most places have a ladder leading to the roof for clearing off sand or cleaning, yes."

"Then let's go. While they might expect you to take off that way, they'd never think it of me."

"How exactly are you going to climb down once we're up there?"

"Rope ladder?" Fiona shrugged. She was much better at planning one step at a time in situations like this. "We'll figure it out then."

They thanked the smilodon again and crept out of the room quietly. The floor was shockingly silent for the hubbub that was flowing downstairs. The crowd must've believed they had already gotten away out into the streets. If only they had been that fortunate.

Dodger led them to what looked like a small closet. Inside was a wooden ladder and bucket with a shovel. He closed the door behind them as Fiona took to the ladder, lightly moving from rung to rung. It reminded her of the ladder she and Richard used in the tower, and for a moment Fiona's chest grew heavy, her eyes wet. She brushed it off. No time for that. She emerged from the top to a flat sandy roof. Lying down on it, she rolled over, giving Dodger room to lie beside her.

So far so good. Night was slowly approaching, and the blue sky was bruised pink as the sun began to set. Sand was in her clothes, her mouth, and had even wound its way into her tunic, irritating her chest. What she wouldn't give for a hot bath. "Do you think you can find a way down?"

"Lower corner, over there." He crawled across the roof to the terra-cotta drain channel and quickly shimmied down it.

Fiona followed his lead, though with less grace. She placed her sandaled foot on the stone, but immediately it slipped. She gripped tight to regain her balance, but Fiona knew when she wasn't up to the task. She released her grip slightly and let herself slide down. She stumbled to the ground, Dodger catching her. They quickly lowered their heads and took off into an alleyway. Though her mind was brimming with things to say, she held her tongue. They needed to get to Vinicia's brother's house. If a larger search for them took place—and she hoped to Larrakane that it didn't—then being in a private home would make it easier to avoid any soldiers.

Through the rows of street they kept going, Dodger leading the way. Fiona had no idea where they were but followed after Dodger's sure feet. They came to a large sandstone wall blocking their path, but before Fiona could ask a question Dodger skittered to a section of the wall directly next to a drain. Here a grate was all that kept them from the other side. With quick familiarity Dodger removed the grate and pushed Fiona through before following.

They entered a part of the city Fiona had yet to see the likeness of: tall houses built around a central courtyard with a lush garden of date palms, citrus trees, and a bubbling fountain. Large arched windows shaded by the sort of stained glass one could only get in the Court of Copper created playful spectacles of light and color inside the homes. The same chimneylike wind towers graced the roofs to catch the breeze, though higher than the ones near the outskirts of the city. Few people milled the streets here. Dodger pressed his back to the wall, staring at Fiona, and said, "Her brother lives in the third house to the left."

"He's a bit higher up in society than I expected," Fiona said.

"I believe some of that is due to Vinicia. She used to send money home to him. He seemed to have done well with it. The kind of opportunities the Emperor doesn't want people to know about." He frowned and shook his head. "I'm sorry for the fight, Fi."

She crossed her arms and stared hard at him. She already had one irrational man in her life. Dodger usually was so sensible and mature. This page really brought out the child in him. She supposed because this is where he left it. "Why did you let Lucius get to you?"

"I didn't expect to see him again. I should've known better." Dodger rubbed his whiskers and said quietly, "I don't understand how Lucius, of all people, is working for the

Empire. But he must know something." Dodger sighed. "As soon as he saw me, I knew it wasn't a coincidence. He probably took a private road to beat me to Mikar."

"How could he have known that's where you were going?"

"It's directly on the way to the capital, and by trying to buy a chariot he could ascertain we were heading somewhere in a hurry. The real question is why he wants to thwart us."

Fiona snorted. "I'm not quite sure he's trying to thwart *us*, Dodger. It rather seems like he's focused on you." She dropped her arms and laid a gentle hand on his shoulder. "What did he mean, *less likely to do anything when you hang them out to dry*?"

Dodger glanced at Fiona and then into the darkening sky. "When we were cubs we ran together, a few of us. You know about that. Stealing to survive, living on the streets. But after I was inked Lucius disappeared. He was taken in by the Empire. I didn't find out till years later."

"You can't beat yourself up for things that were out of your control. It can take years to manage page turning. It's not your fault you weren't here."

"I know that. I do. Or I did, but seeing him again..." Dodger pushed off the wall and clenched his paws. "He's clearly still angry and I can't change that. You know the empire is littered with people who would rather not see me, or I'd rather not see. But when he just kept digging in...well, I got sick of taking it on the chin. I wanted to speak in the only way he would understand." Dodger rubbed his face hard with his hands. "I know you're disappointed. The Binder most definitely will be. And I messed up our lead at the hostelry."

Here was the heart of her strong, compassionate friend. She gripped his shoulder and tutted. "I am *not* disappointed in you. There have been plenty of times when I've been a blotter myself. And I think keeping everything bottled up as you do isn't good for you. You're not the Binder. You're your own person. If he's disappointed in you, then he doesn't understand you."

Dodger shook his head. "He does, Fi. He didn't just send me out here because I've worked with Vinicia and know her. He wanted me to deal with my past. Put it behind me. It's the only way, and I believe him. There's no way he could be the leader he is, handle so much, if he wasn't sure of himself."

Fiona pressed her lips into a thin line to hold back her thoughts. That the Binder was confident in his abilities was easy to see. But that he had put his past away, she wasn't so sure. He had to deal with the actions from the Inking every day. He had to struggle with that privately. Would it have driven him to forge a new path with the Painted Edge in order to cease that struggle? Daniele had said, *If he doesn't get his way, he simply finds another route.* But why put Dodger on the case? The Binder didn't seem foolish. He must've known Dodger would do anything to finish the case, and that might mean unmasking him.

Dodger slumped against the wall, staring off at the houses, deep in thought. Fiona removed her hand from his shoulder and blocked his view. "Listen to me. You're doing the best you can, and quite frankly that's all you can do. Instead of meeting people like Lucius head-on or seeking to prove you've changed, let them see it. You need to simply do your job. You've done enough work on yourself and grown so much from the temperamental urchin I met at turner training. Don't let others take away the person you've become."

Dodger clasped her hand in his paw and squeezed it. "When did you become so eloquent? Normally you'd be giving me a good verbal thrashing."

"Well, lucky for you I've used up all my verbal thrashings for today." She tried to say it lightly, though her throat closed on her. She cleared it. "And besides, Gaili would be quite upset at me if I didn't talk to you properly. She's very clear about her expectations and respecting one's friends."

He chuckled. "I like that she's rubbed off on you."

"Yes, well. One can't have a faekin friend without waxing poetic every now and again." Fiona smiled. Something tugged at her mind, like a flash of sunlight on metal, but before she could latch on to it Dodger diverted her.

"Alright, shall we?" He peeled away from the wall.

Fiona nodded distractedly, trying to remember where her brain had been heading. It was gone. She always hated it when that happened.

THE TWO OF THEM skirted around the courtyard, the bubbling fountain covering their footsteps. It was simple to avoid the few remaining people outside, though a couple she had thought were smilodons in the waning light were simply lifelike statues of the Emperor. He truly was everywhere, it seemed. They slipped between the tall villas toward the back of Vinicia's brother's home. Dodger knocked on the simple arched wooden door, the grander entryway at the front much too public for them. He waited, chin up and serene expression plastered on. A servant answered.

"Is Tiberius Nasennius Turibius home?" Dodger said stiffly.

The servant simply nodded and, after the briefest hesitation, allowed them entrance. The atrium was open to the sky with creeping vines and wildflowers reminiscent of the courtyard outside. The servant waved them to a bench on the side wall and strode off quicker than expected.

Before Fiona could dwell on the tension she had felt from the servant, Vinicia's brother entered. He was the spitting image of the painting in Vinicia's home: a tall cougar with reddish-brown fur and russet tunic loosely belted. He kept his arms behind his back, lingering on the edge of the atrium. "I am Tiberius. State your business."

Dodger stood swiftly. "We've come to inquire after your sister. I am Marcius Festinius Cervidus. I work with her at the Travel Guild. And this is my partner, Investigator Fiona Thorne."

Tiberius raised an eyebrow in acknowledgement but didn't move forward. "How do I know you work with my sister? Can you prove it?"

"Do we need to?" Fiona asked. Tiberius's movements said he was nervous about them, but Fiona couldn't tell why. She stood, trying to glance behind his back.

"Yes, otherwise I don't have time for company, and you'd best be on your way," he said sternly. His hand lowered slightly.

Dodger glanced at Fiona. She nodded slightly . Though they didn't know if they could trust him, he was clearly on edge. It was better to have him be sure of them than the other way around at the moment. In a home of this size, he probably had personal guards who would come at a sound.

"Vinicia is not a soft-spoken woman," Dodger said. "She's very upright in her ideologies and has a mind as clever as anyone I've known, making her slow to anger but like a scorpion on a mission. She's particularly interested in the Court of Copper as of late and has ensnared more than a few of us into the ideology of the faekin. If you've been around her in the last year, she'll have droned on about it to you too."

Tiberius tensed and said, "Travelers disguised with tomes—"

"Wandered the stolen road," Dodger whispered quickly.

Tiberius visibly relaxed.

Dodger did not.

Dropping his hands to reveal a brass bell, Tiberius set it on a bench quickly and motioned for them to follow him. Through a small wing they made their way deeper into the house to a sitting room of cushioned floor pillows and low tables. Two guards attired in more metal than cloth stood at attention.

"You are relieved," Tiberius said. They exited the room and Tiberius closed the door. "Is she okay?"

"Have you not seen her?" Fiona asked. "We heard she was in town recently and we're looking for her." She looked at Dodger with confusion as to what transpired.

Tiberius sank into a cushion. "I saw her a day ago. She said she wouldn't be coming back for at least a few weeks. Usually she tries to visit at least once a month. It was odd but she couldn't answer any of my questions. When you came...well, I was worried something had happened to her."

"Have you heard anything that would indicate that?" Dodger said in a tight voice.

Tiberius shook his head. "No, but I always know when Vinicia is doing something she shouldn't. She was so anxious about where she was going, but she couldn't tell me where. Normally I don't pry too much into that side of her life. I know a question just makes it harder for her, and who am I to ask? She's done so much for me and the family. She's amazing."

Dodger smiled faintly. "Yes, one of the best jackets we have, for sure."

Her brother grinned. "I'd love to hear about it. She's always so modest herself. If you have time?"

Fiona hated to interrupt but said, "May we stay here for the night? We've run into a bit of trouble and can't go back out into the city right now."

Tiberius clapped his hands together. "Of course, of course. Do you have transportation?"

"At the front gates. We left our chariot and horses," Fiona said.

"I'll have them brought here," Tiberius said graciously. "And food."

"Thank you," Dodger said. Hands behind his back, he glanced about the room. "Did Vinicia do anything while she was here? Anything strange or different than she might normally?"

"She made me promise not to open the door for anyone unless they knew the end to a sentence. She's never done that before. I thought it wouldn't be necessary, but I guess I should've kept my guard up." The tip of one of his ears turned down, and he rubbed his whiskers. "She also spent a good deal of time in her room. I always keep a place for her here, of course. We typically spend as much time as we can together. But she was in there for hours as soon as she got here."

Dodger stilled and said firmly. "It's good that we got here first then. Keep to your sister's instructions. Until she tells you herself, don't let any strangers enter your home without being able to complete that sentence. It's for your own safety. Post rotating guards around the villa and outside of your room."

Tiberius' eyes widened. "Of course. Right away." He left the room hurriedly.

Fiona closed the door behind him. "What is it?"

"There are only a few code phrases that signify trouble. That's one of them. I don't know whether she told her brother as a precaution or she wanted to make sure that if she didn't return, a jacket would take notice here. Vinicia is the attentive sort. But we need to know more."

Things were more intricately organized than she suspected at the Guild. Fiona began pacing the floor. "Perhaps she spent time in her room for anyone who may come along after her."

"Yes, if she failed to check in, then there would be a trail for the Guild to follow. She plants clues that a jacket can understand but that might fail for another person."

"Like the Painted Edge."

The door opened, startling them, but Tiberius seemed to take no notice as he strode in. "I've given instructions. Would you like me to show you to your room?"

"Actually, can we see your sister's first?" Dodger asked.

"Certainly." Tiberius led them through the halls and up the stairs.

Tucked away into a quiet corner of the villa, the room was larger than Fiona's home on Spine. The rumpled bed looked recently slept in. Tunics, dresses, and more covered cushions and spilled out of the wardrobe. Slippers and sturdy boots stood at attention against a wall. A few paintings were stacked against a closet door. Bookshelves lined one wall with many volumes stacked sideways or leaning on each other, though tidy in their own way. Here must've been where all of Vinicia's actual possessions lived to keep her Spine house neutral.

"Has anyone cleaned since she's been gone?" Fiona asked as she ventured down small steps into the spacious room.

Tiberius frowned. "No. But then they never do. She likes to tidy up her own things. Childhood habits die hard." He rubbed his chin. "She'll be alright, won't she?"

"Your sister is more formidable than a sandstorm and twice as loud. She'll be alright," Dodger said softly.

Tiberius gave a small smile and left them alone in the room.

Fiona gave Dodger a comforting smile. "That was kind of you."

Dodger turned away and began pawing through the paintings. "I wasn't trying to be kind. I was simply telling the truth."

"Still," Fiona said, pushing a cushion over with her foot, "if she's ensuring she can be followed by other jackets. then she's worried about not returning from whatever her mission is. Her brother may not understand what that means for a page turner, but we do." She shuddered to think about being trapped somewhere, unable to get back to Spine. Her recent bouts of nausea in Painted Edge manacles did not leave her desiring to feel the next effects of page turner sickness.

Dodger nodded curtly. "No one would reprimand her for turning back to Spine if she sensed that sort of danger, but she must just be cautious. The sooner we can find her message for the Guild, the quicker we'll continue on her trail."

"Last time she hid her message via a statue," Fiona said as she pulled up trinkets and small objects from a covered table.

"Yes, but last time she was making a show of hiding the Painted Edge instructions. While they may have questioned her not destroying them, they would admit anyone would have had a hard time finding them." Dodger lifted the covers gingerly on the bed. "This time we're looking for something obvious to the Guild that others will glance over. If we're lucky."

"You mean if the Painted Edge doesn't have Guild spies of their own." Fiona stood back toward the entrance, assessing the room as a whole.

"They'd have to. It wouldn't make sense how else they knew about all our people. We've been lucky with Vinicia but..."

She said nothing. Luck wasn't a token that could be counted on. Neither was coincidence. There were so many objects in the room it would be hard to know exactly where Vinicia might hide something without understanding her. "Dodger. Tell me more about her. Now that we're among her real belongings." She pointed to the portraits on the wall. "Family?"

He sighed. "And friends. Before she went undercover, she connected quite a few people at the Guild. It's no wonder those portraits would end up here. Safe."

Fiona knelt and ran her fingers around the frame of a picture. "What is she like?"

"Well, she's always kind. I guess—no, that's just what you say about people, isn't it? She's kind but she doesn't take any trouble. She has no problem standing up for herself."

"So she's aggressive? Sounds about right for the Travel Guild." Fiona smiled. She pulled the portrait that stood out the most, a scenic view of a snowy bright sky landscape and small hutches. It was different than all the other portraits, but there was nothing behind it or within its frame. She let her eyes roam around the room and she settled on the bookcases. There had to be hundreds of hardcover and leather-bound books there. An expensive collection. "Is there something she references often?"

He crawled from under the bed and dusted himself off. "She's particular about her reading material. Though she is always caught up on the latest research from Copper."

"Studious too?" Fiona bit her lip and inspected the titles of the books. Perhaps she put something in one of them that aligned with Copper or research. There were dozens of books that made her want to yawn simply by title alone that seemed to be in that category. She pulled one down and flipped through it.

"Wait, Fi," Dodger said, pointing to the book. "This bookcase is alphabetical."

"Yes, a good organization system that I quite admire."

Dodger pointed to the next shelf. "And the bookcase on the end is, too, but the three in the middle aren't."

She slid the book back into its place. "A bit weird. Who would go through the trouble of organizing two shelves but not the rest?"

"She could've simply started in earnest and then stopped, but that's not like Vinicia. She sees things through."

Fiona ran her fingers along the books of the second bookshelf. "No, these seem to be organized by genre rather than alphabetical. And are much more varied too. Research and romance and biographies. Why are there two different systems?" She picked up *The Embrace of Flyssa*. "I'm quite sure Mistress Humbledraft had me retrieve a copy of this for her. This sort of bodice ripper is all on its own though." Fiona took a step back, looking at the shelves. Was there something here?

"There are a few that seem out of place actually," Dodger said, tapping on another book.

"Hello, what if that's it? Perhaps she's telling us where to look." Fiona looked at the titles carefully. She tugged out the ones that looked odd or out of place but kept them on the shelf.

Dodger paced, staring at the books. "The titles together spell nothing. What about simply the beginning letters?"

Fiona shook her head. "They don't make any sense either. Perhaps if you translate it in into the smilodon language?"

"It would make even less sense. Besides, the Guild makes code in symbols." Dodger stopped and rubbed his face. "Too many languages to rely on words. Even our code phrases can be distilled into drawn symbols."

She bit her lip and walked from book to book again. She flipped the ones lying flat up on their edge, then triumphantly tapped the publisher symbol on the spine. "The emblems on the books, Dodger, what do they say?"

Dodger took a step back and rubbed his whiskers. "Look. Mine. Spine."

"The last one was published in Spine!" Fiona flipped open the book, but nothing came out.

Dodger grabbed the book from her and dug into the edge of the spine with his knife.

Fiona winced. "Why would you rip it?"

"Because she's saying it's in the spine of this particular book." He thumped the leather-bound book on the table.

Out poured sand and then a small folded piece of parchment. They opened it, but Fiona didn't understand a bit. It was simply more symbols.

"I assume you can read this," she said.

Dodger skimmed the symbols. "Flood of Painted Edge agents into Kerus. The group is scouting to uncover a key that will open the Book."

"What in the dark edge—a key?" And why would it open the Book? Taking down the Kerus page, she could understand. That was clearly part of the Painted Edge's agenda. But opening the Book as whole? This was new. "I find the Book bit odd. Does it say where the key is or the location of the scouting mission?"

"No. But if she knew, she would've included it. Perhaps the Painted Edge was keeping that beneath the sand."

"Well, we have one clue but not Vinicia herself." Fiona pinched the bridge of her nose. It wasn't exactly what she had hoped for. She had let herself believe in the back of her mind that Vinicia would be easy to get to.

"That Vinicia didn't bring this information back to Spine herself meant she thought continuing the mission was important." He sighed and stuffed the parchment into his satchel.

"I'm surprised she didn't mention a Guardian. Maybe that's just what they're calling it now." Though Fiona could see the light of the theory, it irked her. Why switch up the language now? It made no sense. She felt she was missing something rather obvious but on the edge of her mind.

"We have no leads from here. And it would be impossible to go back in town and ask questions until they've forgotten about us. For all we know, Vinicia and the other Painted Edge smilodons are long gone." Dodger put the book back on the shelf hard, rattling it. "I'm concerned that there's been an influx of Painted Edge into the page. Whatever they are bringing in people for, it must be something big and happening soon." He pulled the satchel on his back, his tail twitching. "But I'm worried Vinicia's in a vulnerable situation or, worse yet, compromised. What if she left this note thinking she'd continue spying but they've tricked her?"

Fiona stood and wiped her hands on her tunic. "Let's not handle this all on our own. You of all people know we can do more with support than by ourselves. We have to discover what the Painted Edge is up to and find her." They could even ask Soots or Richard if they knew what a key was—if he had regained his senses and ceased being ridiculous. The thought of the Guardians pushed the rather obvious to the forefront of her mind. "Hang on, there's always two parts."

"What do you mean?" Dodger said.

"Well, Soots was the Guardian, yes, but the Blackstone was their home. Their—oh, what's a good word for it—their vessel. And, well, Richard—" She stopped herself, remembering that Dodger wouldn't have a clue who that was, and said, "The Guardian of Rise's home was in an island."

"Hold on, you've met another Guardian?" Dodger exclaimed. "When you rescued the Queen?"

Fiona groaned at the amended memory. "Er, yes, but I'll tell you more later. The point is, each time these vessels were removed from the page, the entire page started to break down. It happened with Blaze and with Rise. I think this is what Vinicia is talking about. Has the Painted Edge been trying to open these pages?"

"That's more than I would've supposed. If that's true, then them finding something to open the entire Book will have dire consequences. We have the note. Let's get back to Spine."

THEY PARTED WAYS TO be as efficient as possible: Dodger to gather the Binder and Marcia at the Hinge, and Fiona to update her own circle. Though Fiona glossed over exactly what irons she had in the fire with her friends, Dodger knew her well enough to know involving them would be valuable in finding Vinicia and the Painted Edge or she wouldn't do it at all.

A quick carriage ride, the driver bribed with quite a sum of paper, and Fiona was back outside Thorne Investigations as the light of day began to dwindle. The familiar silhouette of Fali stood on her doorstep, and though surprised, she ushered him in quickly to the office. If he had traveled here, he must have some update on Priestess Raina to discuss with her.

At the sight of Fiona, Gaili and Matteo quickly closed out a client they had been managing. The client gave several glances to Fiona, who greeted them cordially before ushering them out the door. Unceremoniously, Fiona began her recount of what she had learned so far of the Painted Edge in Kerus. Though she would've told Gaili all, she kept the information on Vinicia to herself.

"Maybe these keys will allow the Painted Edge to return to their pages? Perhaps removing the key allows them back in permanently?" Gaili said.

"But why would a key that could open the entire Book be in Kerus? Of all places. No offense to the page, but it's no Spine. What's the significance to Larrakane?" Fiona said. And to the Leaves of Spine? Or the danger that Richard said was his brother? It wasn't all connecting.

"I don't know, but you're right. It doesn't make any sense," Gaili murmured.

"We have to operate under the assumption that the Painted Edge was feeding our spy false information," Fiona said. "But why tell the same to the rest of the group? I saw those two smilodon jubatas Painted Edge members. They are absolutely traveling somewhere in Kerus."

Matteo pulled out his maps, unrolling the painted parchment across a desk. "With that in mind, what or where could these keys be?"

"Key," Fiona said. "Singular. I truly believe each page only has one."

"How can we confirm that?" Fali piped in, moving closer to the maps.

"I'm working on that as we speak," she said, thinking of Dodger. Hopefully the Binder wouldn't push back and would acknowledge the urgency within her friend. One of the Leaves of Spine must know about the keys. Clearly this was news to Fali as well. But if they were each given a task, perhaps this was one. Could that be what Queen Eleanor meant about the abstracts in her memory? Or was there something else entirely? "Either way, I think it will take all of us to get ahead of the Painted Edge here. What are the most interesting points within the Kerus page?"

"Do you think that's a criteria?" Fali said.

"From what I've seen of the Guardians in Blaze and Rise, yes, their vessels were each in very unique places in the page. Far away from any pagemark actually."

Gaili's golden hand flew to her mouth. "Guardian of Rise? When did you come across a Guardian of Rise?"

Fiona huffed a sigh. She was never going to get used to that. "In my time last week. But let's not dwell on it."

"Not dwell on it? It's unlike you not to mention these things," Gaili said.

"Yes, well, sometimes secrets must." Fiona put up her hands, forestalling any more words on the matter. "I hate keeping anything from you all. I truly do."

Gaili's face softened. "We understand, Fi. Don't worry about it."

"I know better than anyone about the frustration with keeping certain facts that could be of great help from people who would do enormously wonderful things with the information." Fali coughed. "And I am here to say it gets easier."

Fiona nodded but kept her face a cool mask. If she had her way, she wouldn't be keeping secrets for long. She had every intention of getting her friends back up to speed once they could take a moment. It would take some time to explain, and unfortunately that was not on their or Vinicia's side. "Alright, based on my notion, what are the points of interest in Kerus? The Blackstone was in Obsidian's Tooth. But the Rise one was literally one of the many islands, albeit the smallest uninhabited one."

Matteo let out a small trill and pushed his hand through his perfectly coiffed hair. It fell back into place curled around his horns immediately. "Well, my friend, that is quite a tall tree to climb. Kerus is distinctly appealing because of the variety of pantheons they had before Larrakane showed up. In my time I've seen perhaps ten or fifteen unique areas. There's the pyramid on Siamor, and the stone face of Larrakane on Ozen. The giant abacus is but a new one found, though it's clearly old."

"There's the carved Great Stairs on Ozen," Fali said, "and then we elephas have the House of History with the three-hundred-foot painting on Disas. Not to mention the Oracle of Stars, our previous pantheon statues, in the Sea of Disas."

Fiona whistled. "Too many to investigate all at once. Not unless we involve as many regulation jackets as we can get."

"You could coordinate that with Dodger, couldn't you?" Gaili asked.

Fiona pursed her lips. "I can certainly try. While I'm gone, try to narrow it down please. And, Gaili, we may be traveling the rougher parts of Kerus for a bit."

The faun grimaced. "I'll start making provisions."

"Thank you. Without you it would be a hard road to travel, investigating as quickly as we are these days." She squeezed her friend on the shoulder and sighed. Truly without any of them she'd likely be walking from one end of the Book to the other, lost more than investigating. "Speaking of roads, where is Henrietta?"

"She's in Rise dealing with her new airship and taking your mother home," Gaili said, smiling.

"Yes, your mother wasn't thrilled you had run off without saying goodbye to her," Matteo said, wide eyed. "I thought she was going to commandeer the whole building and wait you out."

It was the first time she had ever seen the faun look somewhat terrified. "I intend to make amends as soon as Dodger and I find our spy. I'll send word as soon as I can when I have more news."

"Then before you go, let me look at your scarf," Gaili said and waved her hand to the kitchen.

Fiona followed, somewhat surprised. The camouflage on the scarf had done remarkably well. No one had commented on it once while in Kerus. Though she missed the bright coloring, she was prepared to begrudgingly admit it had helped her investigate more smoothly. But as soon as they were alone in the kitchen Gaili quickly made her forget about the scarf.

"I did some poking into the Binder and Dani," Gaili whispered.

"All in a day's work for you." Fiona grinned. "And what have you uncovered?"

"I've asked around, discreetly, and, well, I don't think you have much to worry about with Dani. I visited the farm district, and none of the workers had anything to say about her outside of her dedication to the area. She's not missed a day of being there, improving the aqueducts and the crops. But she's also struggled."

Fiona tilted her head. "How so?"

"Resources mainly. What provisions she needs to keep the district going come from outside Spine and are managed through the Travel Guild. If anything, the workers had a few unkind words to say about *that* organization before they had anything enlightening to say about Dani."

Fiona nodded. She could've guessed it was another place the Guild and the Binder had a heavy hand in. "But that does mean she has a reason to go against the Binder." Not that it seemed the Circle of Seasons needed a reason to argue with each other.

"Yes, but I can't see how she could make a prosperous district such as the farming one, manage Depth's Door, and raise a secret organization. She was quite pleasant."

"Did you talk to her?" Fiona said, surprised.

"I thought it best to interview her directly. It's what you always do," Gaili said with a half shrug and a grin.

Warmed at seeing Gaili so delighted, Fiona couldn't help but share her smile. "Direct is often best. Especially if you can get them speaking before they can think."

"That's not quite the direction I took." Gaili laughed. "But with the Binder, well, that was harder. I couldn't make more inroad than anyone not working directly with him could. I spoke to several people at the Hinge but I think it'll take more time to gather detail on him that may uncover anything of value."

Fiona thought getting any information about the Binder would be difficult, considering how secretive he was and how well powered he seemed to be. She sighed. "I appreciate what you've done. I can at least cross one person off my list."

Gaili clasped her hands in front of her. "I'm glad to help."

"You are more than a help, Gaili. You are a treasure." Fiona hugged her. "And I appreciate you. Oh, please don't work yourself too hard in my stead."

"I'll try," the faun said lightly. "But don't hurry on my account."

"Never." After swiping a hunk of hard cheese and bread from the table—one should always procure a snack when they have the chance—Fiona strode back to the office. Packing it away in her pack, she said her goodbyes to the others and invited Fali to ride with her to the Hinge and discuss why he had come to her home in the first place.

"Kerus, hmm?" Fali murmured once they were settled in the carriage. "I thought for sure the spy would be in Rise."

Fiona narrowed her eyes, slightly assessing the elephas. "What made you think that?"

He tilted his massive head, ears brushing the thinning red fabric of the carriage wall. "Raina made it seem as if you were there when I talked to her. Or perhaps I interpreted it wrong. She said you were just named baroness. Baroness Thornbeard. Is that your real name?"

"You've never investigated me to know that?" Fiona said. Fali really was the trusting sort.

"Didn't think I needed to. But Raina, she seemed very upset about the fact that you received this Forlorn Island from your Queen."

Fiona leaned in. "Upset? Crying upset or annoyed upset?"

"Annoyed." Fali raised a hairless eyebrow. "The last time I saw her get that frustrated was a month ago or so. I didn't inquire, mind you, but it had to do with another human."

"Was it Sir Henry Hawkport?" Did Hawkport go against her wishes with his plan? It would make sense if she was upset because Hawkport may have been messing up plans with the Painted Edge and she couldn't come to manage the situation herself.

Fali shook his head. "I didn't catch a name."

She rested her head against her hand and stared out into the darkened night sky. Only the light dangling from the carriage gave any illumination. They needed the letters to understand what Raina and Hawkport discussed. Or Vinicia to reveal the face of the leader. Richard was working on one... Well, he had been before their argument. Fiona rubbed the edges of her scarf, its true colors beginning to push through the gray. She could write to him. At the very least to see if he had made headway on getting the letters between Raina and Hawkport from Queen Brilliance. She pulled out the journal from her scarf and, keeping it close to her chest, opened it up, trying to steel herself from hope of an apology from him.

In stark contrast with the crisp beige page was written in dark ink: *"I'm sorry I'm not the man you thought I was."*

Fiona's throat closed up and a hardness settled in her chest. She pinched the bridge of her nose as hot tears threatened to spill over. How could one person be so obtuse? After what she had written, to come back with such a self-centered reply? It was worse than saying nothing back at all.

The carriage hit a bump, and she jumped, knocking the journal to the floor. She stared at it for a moment before picking it up as Fali reached for it. She tucked it back into her scarf. It was a distraction she didn't need. And a wrench in her heart she hadn't wanted. She tugged on her scarf, loosening it from suffocating her.

"Thank you for telling me, Fali. Raina's actions coincide with more than I would like." She quickly explained the connection to Hawkport and her thoughts on Raina possibly being a traitor.

The elephas wrapped his arms around himself. "I can't believe it. Priestess Raina? It seems so out of character."

"Do the other things you've mentioned also seem out of character?"

"I guess not," Fali said quietly. He looked down at the floor, trunk moving to rest on his lap.

Fiona pressed her lips together, watching the elephas take her thoughts about Raina to heart. He seemed to truly see the good in people. She had never thought of it before, but how young was Fali? She had a hard time telling age with anyone not human. She sighed and said, "Watch her, Fali. Perhaps I am wrong. But if I am, that means it's someone else."

Fali's head snapped up. "You have another suspect?"

"I have another who would make sense as the orchestrator, yes, but…" She hesitated. "Are you sure you want to hear?"

"I can't do my duty to Larrakane by keeping a closed ear and averted eyes, Fiona."

She nodded. "The Binder has all the means to spin up another organization. Most don't even know what the Binder looks like. It would be quite easy for him to manage both. Send jackets off on wild-goose chases while his Painted Edge members do their work."

"But the Binder cares for the Travel Guild. I truly think he would give his life for their work and the Book."

"That may be, but it doesn't escape my notice that he's angry at Larrakane." When he had come up the stairs and all the times Larrakane was mentioned, he tightened up. He lashed out. What was that if it wasn't anger? "Perhaps furious that she doesn't listen to him or that he can't control what she does. Maybe the Painted Edge is his alternate route?"

Fali tapped his trunk thoughtfully against the door. "I can see why you're holding these close to your chest. Either one would have the power to make these accusations go away quickly."

"And me with them to a jail cell or other." She sighed. "But I'll be watching, trying to draw them out."

"What about the others?" Fali said.

"I think everyone has their secrets. But I've known Mac since I was an upstart kid. She doesn't want more power and she doesn't want to leave Spine. Something I think the Painted Edge do want or have at least been promised. And Nic, well, they're just as worried about it being someone within. I've seen them beat themselves up about the Guardians and their need to be more proactive with them against this threat. No, I don't think it's them. And while I don't know Dani well, she's not given me any reason to look at her any differently than Nic does. Nor does she seem to have the resources to start an organization like that, according to recent investigations."

"I assume you've also ruled me out by how much you're telling me," Fali said. "I am thankful for that. I'm happy to be like shallow water if you want to dig more."

Fiona raised an eyebrow. "What makes you think I'm not already?"

Fali smiled. "Well said. So we meet with the other Leaves of Spine and you poke, is that it?"

She nodded. "I do want to keep you all on the same page with the same information. But this *is* another chance to see any breakage of the Binder and Priestess Raina. If either of them are hampering Vinicia or know where this key the Painted Edge are after is in Kerus, I want to see if I can trip them up into divulging it."

"I'll follow your lead," Fali said.

They arrived at the Hinge. The massive structure was dotted with small hanging lamps giving it a lurching silhouette in the darkness. The white marble steps were practically empty of jackets and Spine citizens having business at the building. As they rose to the top of the steps, they saw Dodger and Marcia standing off to the side of the wide entrance hall. Hushed, urgent tones told Fiona they were in the middle of an argument of some sort. Before she could listen to what exactly they were saying, Fali waved at them. They quickly jumped back from each other, Dodger nodding his hello while Marcia turned and walked away. Dodger looked torn for a moment before quickly walking after Marcia and leaving the vestibule empty.

Fiona shrugged at Fali. "Perhaps you should lead the way."

The Binder's office was tucked away among a myriad of empty corridors, sharp left turns, and a locked private hallway. Though the simple wooden door of his office was inconspicuous, there were faint lines within the wood reminiscent of Mac's personal wing in the Thread. Fiona peered at the pattern, trying to make sense of it, but Fali opened the door, breaking her view. It tugged on her memory, the pattern in Forest's Edge. Very much alike.

Inside were Priestess Raina, Mac, Dani, Nicolosia, and of course, the Binder himself. The big open room held large windows edged with frost in the manner of an early morning before the sun warmed the chill from the air. The windows looked out directly into Spine's forest, an interesting feat considering the Hinge was surrounded by other buildings. A large wooden desk took up one side of the room with the Binder occupying the chair behind it. Closed cabinets nestled underneath the window lining the back wall, holding who knew what. But Fiona's eyes immediately noticed that one was visibly locked while the others weren't.

Fali stomped in, the only way he could, and went directly toward Priestess Raina. Fiona shivered in the vacuum of his warmth and noticed that the room was much colder than the hallway—the Binder displaying the control of his domain quietly, perhaps.

She assessed each person as she moved around the spacious office toward the sideboard of cups and saucers. Nic and Dani sat at one end of the room, facing each other, talking quietly, and studiously ignoring the others. Priestess Raina inclined her head in greeting but smoothed out her gray dress and turned back toward the Binder and Mac, dismissing Fiona and Fali. Mac, golden skin radiant, sat upright in a stiff-backed chair with her tattooed arms crossed. If Fiona knew her less, she would think the tavern owner was angry, but no, this was Mac defensive. What had she done to look so chagrin?

The Binder looked calm, almost smug, sipping from a crisp blue porcelain cup. Though he didn't greet her, she noticed the lift of his eyes from under long lashes watching her. Fiona gave a pleasant, uncaring nod to him and turned toward the sideboard. If it wasn't for the tension in the air, it would've looked as if they were all having a pleasant evening coffee before supper. She went to pour herself a fortifying cup but found it to be the same sort of tea Dodger had brought over for her to try. She sniffed and turned her back on it. She'd rather deal with the Leaves head-on than with that drivel in hand.

"Well," the Binder said, setting down his cup, "what have you to report?"

"You didn't hear it from Marcius?" Fiona said, glancing around. Had he not reported before seeing Marcia?

"No," the Binder said curtly.

Shirking his duty was unlike him. Perhaps he was calming down beforehand? Or was the Binder pretending? Before Fiona could ask more directly, Priestess Raina spoke up.

"The Binder has made us wait so his *pupil* didn't have to hear more than he needed to," Raina said, leaning back in her chair. She brought her cup to her lips before saying, "I know you want to make him your protégé, Binder, but we can't keep breaking the rules."

"What rules have been broken?" Dani said with a toss of her copper hair. "Fiona isn't completely human anymore, so there's nothing wrong with her being bound to Nic."

"Dani," Nicolosia hissed. Their shoulders slumped. "That was for Mac to tell Fiona. Not you."

Dani dropped her head, staring at her hands. "Sorry, Nic. Sorry, Mac."

Focusing on the quick back-and-forth of the others was difficult. Fiona grasped the sideboard, steadying herself. "Hold on, I'm not *completely human*?" How in the dark edge could that be possible?

Mac froze at the comment before she took a deep breath. "I'm sorry, Fi. I didn't know. Apparently binding you to me had some...unintended side effects."

"Seasonal fae shouldn't use their powers on others outside of faekin. The consequences could be disastrous," the Binder said stiffly.

There had been an argument happening here, before she and Fali walked in. That was much clearer to Fiona now. All of her careful thoughts and pointed questions scattered with this new information. She wasn't completely human. Just what in the dark edge was she then? "Am I part fae?"

"Blessed Larrakane, no. Two percent faekin more like." Mac set her cup on the desk and rushed over to Fiona's side. "It's sort of how the different faekin were created in the first place."

"A history lesson for another time," the Binder said. He placed his tea down gently before standing up from the desk. "The good investigator didn't call this meeting to be sideswept by revelations." He looked pointedly at Dani. "Or to waste time."

Fiona took control of her emotions, inhaling shakily. She squeezed Mac's hand. Yes, she would talk to her afterward and clear this up, but there were more dangerous things to discuss. "Yes, well, we found the trail of the spy and it's clear to us she's in danger. She left several clues as precaution but then this coded message." She glanced around before producing the piece of parchment and handing it to Mac.

Mac pulled out her glasses from her ethereal robes and squinted at the paper of symbols.

"Who is this spy?" Priestess Raina said. "And where did you get this information?"

"Is that exactly relevant?" the Binder said. He strode to Mac and plucked the parchment from her hands.

"Yes, *Binder*, because once again you have more information than the rest of us. How do we know we can believe her?" Raina waved her hand at Fiona. "She's not unbreachable."

Raina had certainly turned on her quickly. Why had she come down so far in her estimation?

Fiona held up a hand. "If you'll let me finish, you'll know more, Priestess. In Kerus there's been a large increase of Painted Edge operatives coming to the page, according to her report." She kept her eyes moving around the room, watching Raina and the Binder. "And there's a mission to uncover a key that would open the Book. It could be a trap for our spy or half information, but we can't take that chance. Not with so many agents spilling in."

"Which means the Painted Edge is ahead once again," Dani whispered breathlessly.

"If they already know we know she knows their leader, then yes." Nicolosia pressed their lips together, disgruntled.

The Binder tapped his snowy-white fingers against the coded parchment. "It could simply be a trap for her because she works for the Travel Guild. Not because she knows who the leader is."

"That's splitting hairs." Raina crossed her arms. "And it doesn't solve our problems."

"Do we know what this key is?" Mac said. "Surely one of us must have some idea. Nic, is this a different type of Guardian?"

The fae druid shook their head, pine-green hair swaying. "Not that I know of. But if it's in the Kerus page, perhaps they're simply trying to use code words now after what happened in Rise." Nic glanced at the Binder before saying, "But that also makes little sense considering that the Kerus Guardian is indisposed."

Fiona raised an eyebrow. "What does that mean?"

"Perhaps that should be a private discussion with your protégé," the Binder said, striding into the center of the room. He held out his hands, commanding attention. "Nic, you should talk to someone who may know more."

"A Guardian?" Dani said excitedly. She looked over to Nic with wide eyes and a small smile.

Nic nodded and sprang from the chair. "I'll go now."

"I'll see you out," Dani said and with a small twirl was by Nic's side before Fiona could properly blink.

"Nothing more to offer, Dani?" the Binder said quietly. While it may have sounded sarcastic to others, Fiona noticed a slight grimace on his face. It was gone quickly, but what pained him here, in this moment?

"Gilded crowns grow heavy on the brow, Arc. Perhaps you should lighten yours." She flounced out of the room, the door settling and wafting the spiked scent of pine needles before anyone could move.

Nicolosia's mouth fell open and they glanced at the Binder and then Mac before throwing open the door and running after her. "Dani, wait."

The Seasons didn't bother showing restraint in warded spaces, it seemed. Fiona watched the Binder's frown deepen as they left. He seemed to feel her staring and whipped his head toward her.

Her scarf fluttered in the cold snap of air that accompanied his movement. Fiona raised her hand to stall his words. "I'll take my leave as well. I'm conducting a search based on my experience of possible locations in Kerus they could be holding our spy."

"I can help," Fali piped up, watching everyone with curious eyes. "As a recent Kerus native."

Fiona nodded. Though he had already promised the help at her house, she was glad he had the mind to call it out here. "Time and directness are of the essence. We need to work together."

"You'll get everything you need from the Guild. Marcius included. I'll make sure he's with you every step of the way," the Binder said. He left the room.

Marcius. The Binder had been distracted by the conversation here and forgotten to be formal. Fiona sighed.

It was easy to do. The revelation about her being likened to a faekin had distracted her as well. She needed to speak to Mac, but it felt selfish at a time like this.

Fali gently pressed her arm. "I'll wait for you at the carriage stand."

She nodded. "Thank you." Her neck prickled, and she turned to see Priestess Raina watching them closely. Before the woman could make excuses and leave, Fiona darted toward her. "Priestess, I know tension is high right now, but if I've caused you a reason to distrust me, well, I'd like to make amends."

"No, it's I who should apologize," the Priestess said. "Things are stressful, but that's no reason take it out on you." Her change in demeanor was alarming. The sudden turnabout was almost as chaotic as faekin.

"I know sometimes things beyond our control cause us doubt, but I only want to do what's best for the Book and the people in it," Fiona said cautiously.

Raina gave a small smile. "It's good to know that. But remember, Fiona, being a protégé isn't always about what's good for the Book. What's good for Larrakane is paramount. All else will flow."

"Do you mean if Larrakane is secure, then the Book will be as well?"

"Larrakane *is* the Book," Raina said. "They are one and the same. Always. And unfortunately."

It sounded exactly like something a Follower of Larrakane would say. Except the last bit. "Why unfortunately?"

"Things can't change without Larrakane changing. And she's in no position to do more than keep the Book going, I'm afraid." Raina frowned and glanced at the door. "Now I'm waxing theological when I should be making sure Followers are prepared to intervene as needed."

"Yes, I heard there were more Followers in Rise than usual," Fiona said brightly. If Raina acted defensive about the remark, it would tell her that the Priestess hoped they would go unnoticed. "Some even surrounding pagemarks."

"After what happened, we need to reinforce Larrakane's will and her guidance as much as possible. Having a strong foothold in each page is important to the goddess," Raina said, chin high. She didn't feel the need to hide it. Then perhaps it wasn't malicious. But that didn't mean it was beneficial to her in some way.

"And the church, I presume?" Fiona said.

"Of course. We only exist to serve her and protect her interests." Raina inclined her head. "And her interests go above page leaders."

Fiona raised an eyebrow at such a headstrong statement. It sounded too much like the Travel Guild's way of thinking for her liking. "So, what the Queen deems necessary or the Order of Seven has to match up to Larrakane's wishes or be overridden?"

"Not overridden. Simply redirected." Raina pushed her long sable hair behind an ear. "If you'll excuse me, I must set things in motion." She waved goodbye toward where Mac sat twisting the edges of her robe. "And I believe you have another appointment." She moved delicately past Fiona toward the door.

Well! She had been expertly dismissed. Though Raina had not hidden the increased Followers when confronted with the knowledge, she had never once brought it up in the previous meetings. She seemed to place everything she and the church did above all else. Zealous behavior to be sure, but what did that say about the possibility of her being the Painted Edge's leader? An open organization doing the work of Larrakane and a hidden one furthering her own agenda against the Book? It didn't connect. The only thing that might remove Raina from her list of suspects was understanding her connection with Hawkport. She sighed. She really was going to have to talk with Richard, wasn't she?

"I'm sorry," Mac said, breaking into Fiona's thoughts.

Fiona dropped down into the nearest chair. "Two percent faekin, Mac? Truly?"

Mac closed the distance between them. "If I had known... None of us have ever bonded with another kind before. I thought it would wear off once I released you."

"Is that how it works with faekin?"

"More or less. Our connections are spirit based. If someone's spirit is stronger, like the Circle of Seasons, then it's a dominant power, of course. But eventually the spirits either separate violently or are released." Mac hit the chair, fluffing it and looking away from Fiona. "We haven't done that for hundreds of years though. I should've made sure you would be safe."

"I asked to be bonded," Fiona said, grabbing Mac's hands and stilling them. "It was important to me, and for what it's worth, I don't regret it. It was quite the experience."

Mac took a deep breath before saying, "I want you to know I'd do anything in my power to make sure you are well."

Fiona squeezed Mac's hands. "I know, and I appreciate it. I would do the same for you. You've helped make me the somewhat nosy and confident person I am. I owe you."

"Oh, Fi, you owe me nothing." Mac shook her head, grinning down at her.

"Be that as it may, I want you to know you can count on me." When it was so hard to trust the powers around her, it lifted a heaviness from her to admit this to Mac so confidently.

In quick succession Mac gave her a swift warm hug, straightened up, towering over her, and whipped off her glasses, storing them securely back in her robe. She tugged the edges of the azure gauze and cleared her throat. "Well, I do have some information that I hope is helpful to us all in your hands. We were *discussing* it before you got here." Mac rolled her eyes, the wrinkles on the corners barely telling her age. "Going through my journals that you retrieved a few months ago, I was able to recall much quicker how exactly I built the crowns. I hate to say it, but after two hundred and forty five years you do tend to forget a thing or two."

Fiona squeaked but quickly tried to regain her composure. While she had ascertained that the Seasons existed before the Inking, she didn't realize it had been so much longer. Mac had been a Summer Monarch longer than Fiona had been alive. "Was it as easy for the others to leave the Court of Copper and ruling it behind them as it was for you?"

"No. No, not at all." Mac sighed and patted Fiona's hand. "Nic had a true affinity for the world in a way that's more dampened here. And Daniele—Dani, I mean, well, she barely got a chance to blossom before we were pulled away. Being the youngest, she had only been out of study for, my goodness, eight years or so."

A long-enough time for Fiona but what seemed a brief moment to the fae and faekin. She could hardly understand. Even at two percent fae, would her lifespan be expanded at all? Just her luck that she'd probably live two more years or something as slight as that. She tugged on her scarf, refocusing her attention on what Mac had been saying. There was a glaring omission. "And what about the Binder?"

Mac bit her lip and sighed. "Nothing could've been harder for him. Or easier after all was done. He's not one to stay in flux for long." Mac dropped her hands and shook her head. "Either way, once he made the decision, it was done. It's best not to poke at it too hard now. And with the crowns half here and half gone, well, it's bringing a lot of those decisions up again. Too much for my comfort," she muttered before pointing at Fiona. "And before you ask another question, yes, unfortunately all that research on the crowns came to show I perhaps did too good a job back then." She glanced at the door and then lowered her voice. "They each have a direct essence of us. Like a snippet of our being that powers them. The materials and other natural items from Copper I wove into them only enhance that, but they aren't meant to do more than allow us to use them instead of drawing from our own power reserves. Small acts when we were too overworked to do it ourselves. Arc would be furious if he knew I told you the truth." She shrugged. "But I think you should know what we're really up against. Unfortunately, with their use, they can impact all the pages."

While that hadn't exactly been Fiona's next question—she'd wanted to poke more about the Binder—she deferred to the conversation change, for it was an important answer. "So any faekin with the crowns could use them to interfere in the pages?"

"Influence their nature more like. The elemental pages are the ones to worry about the most with the Summer and Winter

Crowns still missing. The Painted Edge has already made a play for Blaze, so I'd watch out for Depths. They could do some serious damage there if they are trying to weaken the page with these keys. If they can get a new faekin to help them."

Fiona raised an eyebrow but said nothing. It seemed despite the Binder's assertion in the previous meeting that Stella had been human, Mac knew more than she let on. "This is good to know. Perhaps we can get the Binder to increase the jacket presence in Depths and be on the lookout."

Mac waved her hands. "He already has. I would've waited to tell everyone at once, but he can be so stubborn. The good news is, I can confidently say the Spring Crown is now in a safe place with Nicolosia." She glanced over her shoulder at the closed door. "Don't tell Arc that though."

"I feel much better about it being in the druid's hands than anywhere else." Especially if it was a place that could be gotten into anywhere. "Although why not put it in this storage the Binder spoke of?"

"Because Nic may need access to it in the days to come. And getting access to this office is rare." Mac let out a long exhale. "Come on, I'll walk you out."

Fiona took Mac's arm, patting the fae comfortingly, but her brain churned. Could she linger in the Binder's office? He wasn't here now, and this may be her only chance to find something telling. But before she could come up with an excuse even Mac would believe, her friend had tugged her outside and firmly closed the door.

"I just need to find Dodger before I go," Fiona said, extracting her arm delicately. "So we can get back to Kerus quickly."

"Oh, of course," Mac said. "If you need me, I'll be at the Thread. Miss the place already." She glanced around the marble stone hallway and tugged her robe tighter around her shoulders. "This place just lacks that cheery warmth, you know."

Fiona nodded and waved to Mac, heading in the opposite direction of her friend. She felt bad for lying to her, but when presented with an opportunity, one had to press advantages. Unfortunately, as she rounded the corner, she found Dodger and the Binder directly ahead. Marcia stood at a respectful distance as if waiting. Fiona quickly turned to go the other way, but their whispered conversation stilled her steps.

"Take care, Marcius," the Binder said softly. "I am not as disappointed as you would think. The key to the future is facing the past. Only then can you overcome its hurdles."

"I put our entire mission at risk," Dodger said, voice thick with remorse. "Vinicia, even Fiona. I can't go back to Kerus."

"I see there is more to do than just walk through the paths you have left behind." The Binder audibly tapped his cane on the marble floor. "We can reflect together on this. It is better to meet our trouble head-on, but no one says you have to do it alone. Walk with me?"

Their footsteps sounded down the hallway.

Although Fiona shouldn't have been, she was somewhat surprised at the familiarity between them. It was one thing for Dodger to say they were close and another to hear them interact. Though the Binder was no less formal, there was something there. It reminded her a little of herself with Mac.

Seeing them round the corner, Fiona doubled back. Since the Binder was preoccupied with Dodger, it was a great time to check out his empty office. A chance, she reasoned, she wouldn't get again.

Checking the hallway, she quickly opened the door and slipped into the office, closing it behind her. If he found her, she could always say she had been waiting for him. In fact, she just might. What better way to get answers than a direct conversation with the man himself?

However, it seemed Fiona wasn't the first to have the idea. Dani stared back at her from across the room, her hands deep within the Binder's desk. She straightened up and asked, "Did you forget something?"

"Only to wait for the Binder so I could have a word with him." Fiona smiled and strode to the desk. It was somewhat tidy with arranged papers, ink pots and quill sitting where they had last been. But the stack of books had been moved from one side of the desk to the other. Sloppy work on Dani's part. "I do think he'll notice the changes."

Dani closed the drawer of the desk, blinking. She shrugged and pulled open another drawer and began feeling alongside of it. "Arc makes up his mind whether are not there's proof. He's a touch quick to temper." Her poise was all gone and she was back to the cutting young woman of the Thread. Why did she toggle between the two so easily?

Fiona pulled herself away from curious thoughts. She didn't know how long she had until the Binder got back. If Dani was already snooping, perhaps she could learn from her work, as amateurish as it may seem. "Do you suspect him of something, or do you normally go through his things?"

"A bit of both." Dani straightened up. "How do I know you won't tell him you found me in here?"

"What could that possibly gain me?" Fiona said. Though she thought the Binder a traitor, she didn't think willingly giving up someone who could be an ally a smart move. "Whereas if I keep your secret, you may keep mine."

Dani raised an eyebrow but nodded. "Acceptable deal. I won't ask what you're looking for and you won't ask me."

"Agreed." Fiona moved the stack of books on the Binder's desk, reading over the spines of them, but found nothing to interest her. Out of the corner of her eye she watched Dani run her hands along the wall and then under the edge of the bureau. She was clearly looking for a switch or button of some sort. It was the most likely place for one. Was she looking for the Binder's storage room? Though there were plenty of papers on the desk that pertained to Travel Guild business, the fae had ignored all of them. Well, if she found it, it would save Fiona the trouble. She turned her attention to the desk.

Pulling the sheets of paper into a tidy stack, Fiona examined them one by one. Cargo shipments between pages, import and export contracts, and special licenses for an upcoming festival in the market were the lot of them. The Binder truly paid attention to the details to have these things land on his desk for signing off rather than his Gilded or Marbled jackets. But with so much time taken up here, could he really do the same with another organization?

Fiona scanned the bureau that Dani had so lazily searched and pulled out stacks of logs. Here were all the Travel Guild booth logs for the last few months. The number of names on the page made Fiona quickly overwhelmed. What was the point of keeping so much information? Could he truly be pouring over it? She shook her head. No, it had to be something else. Perhaps it was an easier way to hide activity that he wanted to blend in—if everyone logged in there would simply be too much to comb through and it would all end up being filed and forgotten. But then again rippers didn't quite log their comings and goings, did they? She sighed. It wasn't conclusive evidence at all. She pushed the stacks back into the drawer. There was a small thunk in the locked cabinet as she closed the doors, and she glanced around to see Dani running her hands across a decorated wall. The fae didn't turn to address her. Perhaps that hadn't been her at all.

Quickly reaching into her scarf of many pockets and thinking of her lock-picking tools, she made short work of the catch. Opening the doors, Fiona saw a small leather-bound notebook that had fallen from somewhere onto a stack of filed logs. She snapped it up quickly and locked the door back. Hidden books were her favorite finds. Peeling it open, she saw gently sloping handwriting throughout the pages. A familiar scent of enchanted paper and ink rose up, invading her nose. It was like her own notebook with Richard. She frowned. Had the Binder been writing someone in the same manner she did with Richard? She skimmed to the last few pages.

I have struggled enough with your choices. In vain I can struggle no more. I leave you to this alone. For the decisions you have made— You ask too much of me, Harmony. I beg you to ask of me no more. If you do what you must, then I, too, shall do my own. And may neither of us regret our actions.

"What have you found there?" Dani said over Fiona's shoulder.

Fiona jumped, dropping the book. The fae had been quieter than she expected. For a poor detective, she was quite stealthy. "I don't know, a journal perhaps?"

Dani's eyes lit up. "From Arc? More than interesting." She held out her hand.

Fiona hesitated. The Seasons fought constantly, but so far their encounters around her had been somewhat tame. Would this stoke the coals of a bigger fight? If the Binder was the Painted Edge leader, he had the power to hurt them all should he be pushed past his limits. She trusted herself to withhold this information until the right time, but would Dani? Gaili said no one had a bad word to say about the fae. Perhaps it was only in the presence of the Seasons she was her chaotic young self. Fiona handed the journal over, reasoning she could steal it back if she needed to.

The fae snatched it quickly and grinned. "I'm surprised someone as ridged as Arc even knows how to journal."

Fiona had once thought the same of Richard. The ease with which he spilled his thoughts on paper still surprised her. "Perhaps in talking to himself he has the ability to let his guard down."

"Perhaps." Dani tucked the journal into her dress. "Though I'm more interested in why he talks to himself."

"Wouldn't you, if you thought no one understood you?" Fiona got up and made a show of dusting off her tights as she watched the fae carefully. Did Dani want to taunt the Binder only because he was their leader?

"No. I'm lucky enough to have friends I can share my innermost thoughts with," Dani said quietly, "A seed beside itself cannot blossom alone."

The door of the office swung open, and the Binder strode in, a thunderous expression on his face. "I don't believe you were invited to wallow away your time in here."

Dani smiled and the subtle tattoos around her eyes glimmered. "I had hoped to be gone before you came back."

"What do you want?" he said, glancing between Dani and Fiona. "We don't have the leisure of time."

"Where have you moved the vault?" Dani said.

The Binder grabbed Dani's arm and pulled her away from Fiona. He began speaking rapidly in the faekin language. Clearly, he didn't want Fiona to know what he was saying. With as much grace as she could, she turned away from watching them but tried hard to pick out any words she understood. Something about the vault and moving it after recent thefts? Dani seemed to push back on being denied access, but the Binder wasn't budging. Soon Dani wrested her arm free and stalked toward the door. The items in the room trembled and swayed as a swift force of wind pushed through the room against the Binder.

"Dani," the Binder yelled, "do not use your powers when others could be harmed."

"Apologies, Fiona," Dani said through clenched teeth before walking out of the room.

The display was more than Fiona had expected. While she had seen her share of altercations, this felt deeply personal. She tried to push aside her feelings and focus on this chance alone with the Binder, but she found it hard. "Could you not think of a better way to handle that?"

The Binder's drawn form stretched taller and he eyed her with an unyielding stare. "How I handle my affairs is none of your business."

"She only wanted—"

"I know what Daniele wants. Far better than you do, Investigator. I suggest you leave yourself out of it unless you have something of worth to bring up."

Did he though? He did seem to take anger at her before he even entered the room. He was as chaotic as the rest of the fae. In that manner perhaps she could learn something of note by leaning into it. "Before I go, I wanted to speak with you about Stella."

His head snapped up. "Sadie. Her name was Sadie."

Fiona narrowed her eyes. "How long did you know her?"

"I didn't know her at all," the Binder said. He moved to his desk and sat down. He frowned at the papers and the books and then turned that frown to the door. He knew Dani had gone through his things. A keen eye, confirmed.

Fiona cleared her throat. "You seemed upset when I mentioned she had been lost to the dark edge."

"It's a tragedy that anyone should lose their life in such a way." He placed his hand on the stack of books, glancing at them and away from Fiona.

Though Fiona thought that point about the dark edge still debatable, she pushed on. He seemed upset at the mention of Stella. There was no doubt to Fiona that he had personal feelings in the matter. "Even one who has caused irreparable harm to the Book and your organization?"

"The Travel Guild is more than mine, Investigator. It would be good of you to remember that. The hard-working individuals who spend their time here day in and day out to keep the Book safe deserve your respect. Regardless of your personal feelings on authority or myself." He tidied his papers before clasping his hands together. "I think it's time you got on with the case, isn't it? Marcius is waiting for you at the entrance to the Hinge."

Fiona pursed her lips but nodded. What more could she get from the man directly? He clearly had a personal connection to Stella, but nothing conclusive could be wrangled. She cursed herself for not keeping the journal. It might have given her more information to properly link him to so many of her theories. Who was Harmony? Could she find out without asking the man himself?

She left the office and hurried quickly through the private hallway to the locked door and then through the bustling chambers of the Hinge. As she neared the front doors Nicolosia sprang up beside her like a blade of grass.

"You have to talk to your young man," Nic said, pulling Fiona away from the front door to a small alcove.

Fiona frowned momentarily, confused. Did the Elder mean Richard? "He's not my young man."

Nicolosia waved their hand dismissively. "Whoever he is, you must talk to him immediately."

Fiona placed her hand on Nicolosia's arm. "What happened?"

"I have a connection with the elemental Guardians," they whispered, "but the mortal ones are much more, well, mortal. I can't leave this place, and until he allows me, I can't reach out to him. You have to be the one to broker it. You're the only protégé and person who remembers him outside of the Leaves."

Was that true? Besides Hawkport, no one else but the Leaves of Spine did seem to remember Richard. Fiona rubbed her face. "You could send any number of druids, though, couldn't you? You could tell them, and they could go to him."

"I have, my dear," Nicolosia said, "and none have even gotten a glimpse of him. Which is why I need you to ask him what the keys could be."

Of course, the blasted man was probably barricading himself in with his books, eschewing the light of day for the security of his walls. He never let people simply help him. "Alright. If it will help us focus in on where we're going."

"It should. He has more information than any of us right now. He knew what the key to his page was and with him being mortal perhaps can help with Kerus. Even Glowkindle didn't realize that about their stone and the others..." Nic trailed off and rubbed the back of their neck.

"You've already talked to the other elemental Guardians?"

They nodded. "They are aware now that they have keys, but they are trying to determine where and what."

"What about the Kerus Guardian? Why aren't they available to help?"

Nicolosia grimaced. "He's been hibernating since the Inking. Recovering really. Nasty run-in with a Roma Emperor."

"So likely unaware this is all happening," Fiona murmured. From what she could ascertain, as long as no one attacked the actual page, he would go right on sleeping. That to her was the difference between what happened in Blaze and in Copper. "Shall I meet you at my office when I have information from the Rise Guardian?"

"Meet me at the Thread."

She frowned. "I have friends working on determining more on Kerus points of interest at Thorne Investigations. Why not there?"

The druid glanced around the vestibule and took a step closer. "The Thread is warded very well against those who might want this information or mean Larrakane harm. It's better to meet there. Even if one of the other Seasons meant to betray us, it would shield the city from that danger."

"Alright," Fiona said. "We'll be back as quickly as can be."

"Do you have any inkling yet as to the other question I put to you?" Nicolosia asked quietly.

"No, unfortunately. Suspicion but not enough to say it out loud. I am working on it as best I can though."

"I know you are, dear." Nicolosia squeezed her arm comfortingly. "Keep safe."

Fiona exited the Hinge, the visage of Larrakane in a snowy-white dress staring down at her. It had most definitely been blue. Perhaps, though, this was how the Binder saw the goddess: cold and distant.

Dodger waited outside, pacing, but nearly jumped toward Fiona when he saw her. "Well, what did you discover? Where in Kerus are we going?"

"Not Kerus, I'm afraid. Not yet. We have to make a small stop in Rise."

"Rise?" Dodger said as they hurried toward the carriage stands. "Why in the dark edge would we go there?"

"To see a stubborn man about his history." The one thing Richard always tried to avoid.

AFTER BRIEFLY REDIRECTING FALI back to her house to rally the others to the Thread (with a hearty please and thank-you), Fiona and Dodger made their way quickly to New Rise on Spine. From there they turned the page to a moonlit Rise.

Fiona was already looking at her pocket watch with a frown when they arrived. It was close to midnight in the page. They had no time to take a public airship. And with the Hawkport family in tatters, how were the airships even running? Richard said he was taking them over, but how much could he have truly done in two days?

"Excuse me. Are you Mistress Thornbeard?" a voice called out at the pagemark. It wasn't a Guild jacket but a young boy with a grubby face and clean brown clothes. Somewhat new, too, by the state of the round flat cap on his head. He held up a flicking candlelit lantern, peering into her face.

Fiona leaned down. "It depends on who wants to know."

He rubbed the back of his neck. "I've been waiting for a bit to give you this message."

She raised a weary eyebrow and held out her hand. "What is a bit?"

"Couple of days, but it was well worth it." He stopped rubbing his neck and straightened up as if remembering something. "Unless you want to gift me some more, that is. Then it wasn't worth it but could be made better." He held out his hand. This kid had more than a little flair.

"Let's see the message and find out if it's worth some paper," she said with a gentle smile.

The boy pointed down a path. "Follow me then."

Squinting, she tried to see if there was anyone waiting for her, but the torchlit path seemed empty. She waved over Dodger, who was filling out the logbook at the Travel Guild booth. "Looks like we have a message."

The kid frowned. "He only said it was for you. Not anyone else."

Fiona rubbed the edge of her scarf, throat warm at the young boy's words. "My friend has to come too."

"Alright, but I expect a bigger gift." The kid walked off down the path.

Dodger bounded beside her as they began to walk quickly following the youth. "What's all this about then?"

"I'm not quite sure," she drew out. She supposed it could be Richard, but then it could be anyone who knew of her. There was nothing to say that it was the stubborn man.

Following the young boy, they found themselves pulled away from the public docks toward a more private area. Newly built wooden airship platforms sat almost empty. Scant workers milled around in the dim lighting but tipped their hats to them as they went down to the bottom of the dock. The young boy pointed up. "He said you were to take that one to the palace."

She wrinkled her nose, a few emotions tumbling inside her all at once. "Well, that was forward-thinking of him. Although I suppose convenient for him too."

The boy shrugged. "Set us up at every pagemark. Seemed an easy enough job to wait for the woman with the pretty curly hair who matched the *Card*."

Fiona tilted her head, staring up at the ship. Who added the *pretty* part?

Dodger interjected, "How do we fly that?"

The boy smirked and waved up at the ship again. "Captain's waiting."

"Well, let's get to it shall we?" Fiona said, pulling herself back together. She deftly reached into her scarf, thought of a decent amount of money, and handed the boy the papers. "But spread that around to the others."

He grinned. "You're nice." He ran off.

Dodger shook his head. "Is this how it always works in Rise?"

"Not quite," Fiona said as she walked up the steps toward the airship. "Usually you have to wait for the public one to make rounds, but I suppose someone is making some adjustments."

"Someone? Do you know this person, Fi?"

"A little."

He glanced at her and raised his eyebrow but said nothing.

Her face warmed and she hurried along without saying anything further. She burst up the gangplank and onto the airship. It was smaller than the public vessel and unlike the ones usually parading around Rise.

A man with an elevated air—the captain, no doubt—gave her a once-over from the helm and then saluted to her. "Baroness Thornbeard, I presume. If you and your guest will take seats, we can lift off and be at the palace shortly."

"Yes," she said, unsure of what to say next. She wasn't quite used to people knowing what she needed before she needed it. Fiona led Dodger to a seat in the captain's room and took one herself.

The airship took off into the air at such speed Fiona found herself gripping the side of the chair. What was this thing—an airship or an air cannon?

The captain glanced back at her and grinned. "Wonderful, isn't it? Newest model meant to ferry a few people around quick as a whip."

"Quick may be an understatement," Fiona said. How was it working so? If Richard took back over the creation of these, then the answer had to be magic. The Word was the only thing that made sense, considering he couldn't let Hawkport remember exactly what he was doing when his family had control.

Dodger laughed. "Feels like I'm in a chariot again, though with more capable hands at the reins." He nodded toward the captain.

The captain smiled smugly and turned back to the darkened clear sky whipping around them. The moon seemed to join them on the fast-paced voyage as a tail.

Fiona turned to Dodger. "How is Marcia holding up?"

He pawed at his whiskers. "She's doing fine, which means she's not doing well at all."

"I can't even imagine." Knowing that one sister was actually alive only for her to be acting against your interests and then disappeared into the dark edge was more than a mouthful. She didn't think anyone could handle the highs and lows of such expedient revelations well. Especially not on their own. She squeezed his paw. "Do let her know I'm thinking of her. I may be the last person she wants to talk to, but I know what it's like to be somewhat overcome."

He grinned. "Going soft for the hard-nosed Gilded leader?"

"What can I say? She's grown on me." She smirked. "Like a book I thought I understood but when I read again it has many more layers to fully comprehend."

In less time than ever before, Fiona found herself deposited on the grounds of the palace docks. She couldn't quite believe her pocket watch, but the disarray of her coils and the ruffle of Dodger's fur was enough to tell her the trip had been very real. The captain explained that he would wait for them and ferry them where they needed to go.

Saying a small prayer for the forethought, she thanked him and hurried inside with Dodger. If she was being honest with herself, she was fairly upset with Richard but unsure of how to go about letting him know with Dodger around. Yes, it was nice of him to have thought of her needs with the airship. But that didn't excuse his previous behavior or the fact that he didn't respond to her frustration at him at all in any way that let them move forward. But the airship convenience did, however, deflate her plans to be professional and detached from him in her need to get information out of him. Curse him and his thoughtfulness.

Inside the grounds of the palace were numerous people milling about. While most were workers of the palace, some of them seemed out of place, and it wasn't long before Fiona realized they were druids. Though they changed their clothes to blend in, the interaction between them and other humans on Rise was awkward at best. Fiona hurried Dodger along to the palace entrance before his investigative mind started to notice.

Throughout the empty palace they walked with little reproach. Guards stopped them but, upon hearing Fiona's title and name, waved them through with a small bow. Though she was curious if the same empty halls were prevalent in the Great Hall or the Throne Room, she focused and led Dodger through the privy gardens to a flight of stairs. Down they went to the corner of the palace where the archives were set.

Fiona stopped at the bottom of the landing. There seemed to be more guards here than above. At least Richard was taking his safety seriously.

Dodger nudged her shoulder. "Fi, what are we doing here?"

"We need to speak to someone in order to more accurately theorize where this Kerus key may be. And this is where that someone lives."

"In the palace? Are they important? Should I address them in a certain way?" His tail twitched. "Should I be addressing you as Baroness Thornbeard as well now?"

She snorted, more from the idea of Richard being addressed than Dodger's suggestion. She shook her head. "Sorry, no. It's just..." Fiona pressed her lips together, thinking. How could she explain to Dodger quickly without him thinking her a bit ridiculous? "He doesn't take well to formalities. While he may be stiff, he'll be easier if you treat him no differently than you do another equal. Don't worry. I'll introduce you."

Dodger's cat eyes narrowed watching her. "Alright, but if I bow to your Queen all wrong and end up banished from the royal court, it won't be my fault."

"Oh, if only you could be so lucky to be banished from this court." Fiona sighed and strode forward to the protective wall of armed guards. After giving her name, they were allowed to pass to the archive's double doors. They were open. Surprised, she took a step back.

"Fi?" Dodger said, reaching out for her.

"He's changed too much. I'm not sure how to proceed."

Dodger stroked his whiskers and then took her arm. "As you normally do. Blusteringly confident and a bit controlling." He smiled. "In a good way."

Fiona wiped her face with her hand and stood up straighter. "I give you full leave to pester me with questions after we've recovered Vinicia."

"Oh, believe me, I am cataloguing them as we speak."

She sighed, squared her shoulders, and led him into the archives. The familiar wooden bookcases greeted her as old friends. Though there were plenty of candles to light the space, it was still hard to see past the shelves to the back of the grand archives. Surprised at the empty room, she called out, "Sir Mourninghide?"

There was a loud thump from the back of the chamber. She walked toward the alcoves where Richard's bedchamber and stored valuable texts lived side by side. Glancing off into the corner, she could see his printing press was once again covered up. Fiona looked quickly into his bedchamber, the flicker of flames in the fireplace pulling her attention, but it, too, was empty. In the last alcove she stopped. The door was closed but she could hear shuffling feet and rustling of paper. She brought up her hand to knock, but before she could Richard threw opened the door and collided into her as he rushed from the room.

"Oh!" He grabbed her shoulders before she could topple. "Apologies, I thought I heard you in the entry."

"I heard a noise." She waved toward the double doors. He still smelled of crisp paper and fresh ink. She took a step back, trying not to inhale his scent or notice the way his golden eyes held her own or his mussed curly hair as if he had been raking his hands through it more. Fiona preoccupied herself with dusting off her clothes, even though there was nothing to dust. "I should have waited."

"No." Richard shook his head. "I mean, no, I'm glad you've come back."

She paused before understanding his confusion. "I meant at the doorway."

"Oh." Richard tugged his growing reddish beard. "Well, it's good to see you."

"Is it?" Fiona raised an eyebrow. "Why?" If he was going to say things like that, then she was going to poke them.

He glanced around as if there was a way to escape. "Because I like seeing you."

"You have a great way of making that known." Fiona turned and marched back toward the entryway. She wasn't coming off as eloquent or as confident as she had hoped. She needed to regroup. Sighing and straightening her shoulders, she smiled at Dodger. "I found our host."

Richard came around the corner of a bookshelf and stopped, his eyes glancing at Dodger.

"Sir Mourninghide," Dodger said crisply, arms behind his back.

"This is my good friend Dodger. Dodger, this is the royal historian of Rise." She had wanted to goad Richard and say *Guardian*, but as upset as she was at him, it wouldn't do to betray his confidence or Nicolosia's. "Dodger is part of the Travel Guild. Marbled leader in fact."

Richard bowed. "Pleased to make your acquaintance. Any friend of Baroness Thornbeard is a friend of mine."

Fiona pursed her lips. What was he playing at? She tried to read his face, but he quickly walked around them to close the large archive doors.

"How can I help you two?" Richard said.

Dodger glanced at Fiona and took a step back. She nodded at his meaning and said, "We're on a case dealing with the Painted Edge. As the foremost expert of mortal page Guardians, we're hoping you can answer some questions."

Richard cleared his throat. His eyes briefly narrowed but he quickly said, "Of course. I'm always here. Ask away."

"We have found information that the Painted Edge are searching for a key in Kerus. While it could be another word for Guardian, I think it's specific to the vessel a Guardian could be in," Fiona said slowly. "Like Forlorn Tower."

Richard glanced at Dodger but then nodded. "Yes, quite right. Though I know them to be called keystones, they are items in the page that are linked to the Guardian. Often housing them, protecting them, etcetera."

"Keystones," Dodger repeated. "There was the Blackstone of Blaze. And this Forlorn Tower, Fi, isn't that the isle you're baroness of now?"

"You know quite a deal for being outside the page," Richard said gruffly. His cheeks reddened. "Though of course as a friend to Baroness Thornbeard, that makes sense."

He had righted himself before she even had the chance to say anything. She stepped closer to Richard. "Dodger is one of the few people who I hold in the strictest of confidences."

"Of course. You know your needs better than I."

He was trying hard to not be disagreeable. That much was becoming clear to Fiona. She disliked this new trait. How to get Richard to be Richard so she could have an honest conversation with him? Perhaps bringing Dodger had been a mistake, but it made no sense to separate, and she had hoped—she had wanted them to meet. But they needed to get to the point so she could talk to him one on one.

"Is the *stone* part of the word literal?" she asked.

"No, more a metaphor for the type of key. The keystone acts as an anchor or lock to the page."

"To keep page turners out," Dodger said.

Richard simply shrugged.

Fiona knew he would not mention his brother, but she supposed it was more to keep him out than page turners. That's what had bothered her about the theory. Spine was where page turners were bound to. Spine—or Larrakane, if you saw it the way Raina did—kept page turners locked there. Not blocked from the pages.

"I think it's more than that, Dodger," Fiona said. "But if this is what the Painted Edge is after and not the Guardian, then we're all laboring under the wrong impression. What if they've been looking for keystones this whole time?"

"You said they are linked to Guardians, correct?" Dodger said to Richard.

"Intricately. You can't have one without the other."

"You can," Fiona said. She wrinkled her nose and started to pace. "If you break one away from the other, you can. The Blackstone had a large chip in it. I thought it was an accident at the time. But that breakage allowed Soots to leave the page with me. And—" Fiona looked up at Richard, her shoulders slumped.

"Removing Forlorn Tower made it easier for this page's Guardian to leave Rise too," he said quietly. "I suppose they must've broken the tower at some point when they moved it."

"But with its size and its distance we didn't notice. Have you had a chance to look it over?"

He rubbed his chest. "It's there, so I didn't think I needed to."

Fiona fought the urge to comfort him and focused. "Stella said she had what she needed. Could she have a piece of the tower? Is that all that's needed to have the keystone?"

"That wouldn't make much sense. A piece is nothing," Richard said.

"A piece is everything when you're a page turner," Dodger interjected. "It's how bookmarks are made. While we can have something made from a place, of course, even just part of the native page can be used to find our way back."

"You use pieces of the page to travel to them?" Richard paced in the opposite direction of Fiona.

"Yes, all page turners do. Except for Spine of course." She watched him, gears turning. What was he trying to think through?

"We need to move on this information now. If we find the location of the keystone, we have a chance of picking up Vinicia's trail," Dodger said.

Fiona nodded. "But if she was being lied to, they could've led her anywhere."

"It's the only direction we have and a chance we have to take. It sounds like securing these keystones is the most important thing we can do to prevent the Painted Edge from breaking another page and taking control of the Book."

Dodger grimaced. "Even if it means it doesn't lead us directly to her."

"Do you know the Guardians of Kerus and Copper?" Fiona said to Richard.

He shook his head. "No, though that's my own fault. I didn't want to be more involved than I already was. But the keystone, it will be impossible to simply steal or access. It still took the Painted Edge countless attempts and intense planning to get that island, rooted as the tower is on it. And even then they needed help from outside the page."

Yes, without the crown, would they have been able to move it at all? She tucked that away in a compartment to discuss with the Leaves later. "What else do you think would help us narrow it down?"

Richard rubbed his hand and glanced at Dodger before saying, "It has to be made of something from the page. A natural material, so think stone, dirt, water. And it must have been constructed before the Inking, of course."

Dodger nodded, repeating his words without sound. "Well, that will narrow it down quite a bit."

"I'm glad I could help," Richard said earnestly. He smiled at Dodger and then at Fiona with a more relaxed air.

"We should get back to Spine and tell the others so we can plan," Dodger said. He bowed to Sir Mourninghide. "Thank you."

"Yes," Fiona said, pushing an errant curl from her face, "thank you."

"Of course." Richard took a step forward. He raised his hand but then dropped it. "I suppose you need to go right away."

She tugged at her scarf. "Well, I—"

"Fi, I need to stretch my legs before we get back on that racehorse of a ship. I'll meet you at the top of the stairs." Dodger nodded to Richard before leaving.

Fiona knew Dodger was being clever but couldn't help feeling the smallest bit appreciative. She sighed and turned back to Richard, but before she could say anything he said, "I dug more into Priestess Raina."

"Oh?" This was not where she thought they were headed.

"Yes." He paced away. "I tried several times to retrieve the letters, but they were burned."

"Burned! By who?"

Richard motioned away from the door and led Fiona farther into the archives near his rooms. "I'm not sure, though I suspect the principal secretary."

The principal secretary had not seemed the sort to deal with secrets other than the Queen's. Perhaps the letter had information that implicated her.

"So I suppose that line of inquiry is dead," Fiona guessed.

"On the contrary," Richard said quickly, "after finding the letters gone, I struck off with the servants of Hawkport House. I took over the houses and made it clear that they would continue on."

She was surprised he had thought of the servants now that the Hawkports were scattered. She warmed at the consideration. "And they told you about Hawkport's affairs?"

"After a little digging. Though they seemed to like the younger Hawkport, John, they weren't sad or surprised to see Henry Hawkport in shackles. Either way it seems she was trying to get Forlorn Tower."

Fiona took a step forward and said in a hushed tone, "Raina was working with Hawkport?"

"Perhaps, but she offered him money for it. Quite a lot of paper actually. Where she has the funds for that remain to be seen, unless you know?"

If it came from the Followers, that would be surprising indeed. Fiona had always taken them for a donation-supported organization, but perhaps that was the image Raina had wanted to give. She shook her head. "But if she was working with Hawkport, that surely proves she knew about him and his connection to the Painted Edge far longer than any of us did."

Richard tugged on his beard. "Well, it was no big secret among the nobles that Hawkport and Lionheart—I mean, well, Hawkport and I were in contest over the island. I'm sure they thought it was due to rank and all that. She could've learned it from that angle."

Though Fiona tried not to jump to conclusions, she was quite good at it, and it irked her that Richard wasn't jumping along with her. She considered his point. "If Raina was simply trying to secure the island by writing to Hawkport, why didn't she write to you?"

He glanced away and said with a lowered voice, "I made Baron Lionheart a bit hard to connect with on purpose. But I never saw a letter or even an invitation to visit her. Servants say Hawkport traveled to Spine a few times to meet with her."

"How do they know that?"

"The fool wrote it in Travel Guild records."

So they were useful to her for once. But just once. "Raina trying to get Forlorn Tower. I think she must've known what it was."

"As a leader of Spine, I wouldn't doubt it."

"They all have their secret tasks. Larrakane did not set up an alliance based on trust and openness, unfortunately." Fiona rubbed her temple. "Raina as the Painted Edge leader makes sense. She has enough knowledge, connections, and more to support the theory. Going after Forlorn Tower before anyone knew it was important is even more suspicious. But what is Raina's motivation for going against Larrakane in such a way? That's what I can't fathom. She's relatively short lived, being human." Fiona snorted, remembering her conversation with Mac. "A feat I can't even say of myself anymore."

"You're not human?" Richard raised an eyebrow. He seemed to start to say something but stopped himself. "If you want to tell me about it, feel free."

Fiona rounded on him. "Stop that."

"Stop what?"

"Being quiet. What did you just bite back?"

"Just an unhelpful thought."

"Yes, you seem to be doing a lot of thinking but no talking."

Richard frowned and tugged his beard. "I, er, can continue to dig into Raina if that is useful. Find her motivation against Larrakane or the Book. I didn't know if or when you might be in the page but can have the servants available to talk to if you want to investigate yourself."

He kept refusing to talk to her about what happened. He wasn't bringing it up or even trying to refute what she had written. He was just going on about these investigations as if they were the most important thing between them.

Her temper flared. "Did you know my friends can't remember you?"

"Pardon?"

Fiona pressed closer to him and said with a heavy chest, "My friends, the only ones I can trust and tell everything to, have no idea who you are."

Richard glanced away. "Well, yes, that's how my power works. Unfortunately."

"It's terrible." She didn't know what she expected him to say. Perhaps something, any pushback about what he had done. How he would change it if he could.

"I don't disagree." Richard clasped his hands behind his back. His eyes wide. "But you understand now, perhaps?"

"Oh, I understand alright." She marched to the doors. Throwing one open was made all the easier in her anger. Of course he wouldn't say he regretted it. That would be admitting his feelings or even fighting. Fiona turned to say something sharp and clever and make him feel as lonely as she felt at this moment. But when she looked back at him, his golden eyes were locked on hers, his shoulders slumped, defeated. She took a small breath. "You have to let the druids talk to you. They're outside. I know you're not letting others through, but you must let them. It's for the best. If you can trust me on that." She walked away before he could say anything more or fight less than he already was.

MATTEO'S MAPS SPREAD ACROSS a large carved wooden table in Mac's private meeting room. Though the room was one of several that Fiona had seen before, she had never felt so crowded in it nor with so many well-known faces. Gaili and Matteo sat uncharacteristically quiet at one end of the room with the Binder, Raina, and Mac focusing on Fiona, rather than each other, at the other end. Fali stood in between the two groups as if he hadn't been sure who to join, listening intently.

"We have our answers," Fiona said, "and think we can determine exactly which point of interest we should be heading for."

"The keystone must have been made from a natural source pre-Inking. It won't be a feature of the page like an island or mountain, however. But something nearly as impossible to misplace, displace, or remove," Dodger said. "Most of the monuments on the Roma-heavy continents were destroyed during the wars or stolen already, so that knocks down quite a few possibilities."

"That removes the Great Stairs and the House of History on Disas as well," Fali said eagerly.

"Yes, but the abacus could still be one. It's made of sandstone and pre-Inking, based on the study ongoing around it. It's a current archaeological site," Matteo said, waving at his map, "and so there will be other people around."

Fali motioned with his trunk across the other side of the map. "The Oracle of Stars statues set in the Sea of Disas are also pre-Inking. They were carved out of the island itself."

"Unfortunately, it could also be the pyramid on Siamor." Dodger pointed toward the southern tip of the continent. "Too close to Roma Valar for my comfort."

"It couldn't be the pyramid," the Binder interjected. "That was after the Inking."

Dodger frowned. "Not to disagree with you, Binder, but the old smilodon empire built it. Before the Inking."

The fae shook his silvery head and took a step toward them. "A story told for putting a shine on history perhaps, but no."

Fiona raised an eyebrow. "Are you sure?" For a fae from Copper who was rooted to Spine, he said it with as much confidence as anything. How could he possibly know?

"Yes. Quite." The Binder glared. "Let's focus on the other two places. They seem more in line with what you've found out."

She could've argued the point but thought better of it. There were other ways to uncover if he was lying. "How far is Spine to the Oracles and the abacus? And from each other?"

Matteo pulled out a silver triangular tool, its points dulled so as not to snag the maps. Thin pieces of blue and black material that looked like charcoal was adhered to one end. With a flourish he grabbed a ruler and set it beside it on the map. Where other cartographers would begin to make notes and plot, Matteo instead began dotting the map with miniscule black and blue beads for the possible keystone locations.

Mac pulled on her spectacles and moved closer, watching it in earnest. "Is that a walking compass?"

"Yes, with some modifications," Matteo said, grinning.

He pulled out a small stick that looked like a tiny bell hammer and hit the charcoal-like materials. As if it had woken up, the triangular tool began pulling from the set location, the pagemark in Spine, to the first beads, the ruler keeping a straight line. Distance notations appeared, marked by the different substances. From one side of the page to another the compass divided out the page into numbers.

"Steps and time," Matteo said, pointing to the black and blue beads.

Fiona shook her head at the way the elements interacted but was dismayed to see the marked distances grow and grow from each other. "We'll have to go to the abacus and the Oracles at the same time. We don't have time to lose."

"We should send in jackets," Mac said to the Binder.

"Too obvious. If this is where the Painted Edge are headed or with our spy, we need it to be a stealth mission." He sighed. "I can assign—"

"Let Fiona and me go," Dodger said. "We're already on the trail and we know exactly what is needed."

The Binder hesitated but nodded. "Of course."

Why the hesitation? Was it for care of Dodger or because he knew that was the right place to go? Fiona watched him as she said, "I don't want us to split between them, Dodger. Perhaps—"

"We can go to the abacus," Matteo said, motioning to Gaili. "I've been several times already and know the location and people running the dig site."

"It will make it much easier to blend in there and look around," Gaili said brightly.

Raina spoke up: "You two aren't trained for this sort of thing at all. I'll send Followers."

"With them, perhaps?" Fiona interjected. While her objection wasn't completely wrong, it was unlike Raina to volunteer. "Surely the Followers will be better equipped with Matteo and Gaili's knowledge."

The Priestess inclined her head in agreement but said nothing, pursing her lips.

"We are adjourned then," the Binder said, eyes trained on Fiona and Raina. He tapped his walking stick and then pulled Mac aside toward her office door.

Matteo whisked the tools off the table and rolled up the map. He handed it to Fiona. "Better for you, I think, than us."

"You two be safe." Fiona pointed at Gaili. "I mean it. If there seems to be a plot, please let the trained Followers handle it." She gave Gaili a hug, leaning in to whisper in her ear, "But if the Followers seem like the enemy, do run."

Gaili nodded. "Of course." She patted her satchel. "I'm prepared for any course." Matteo and Gaili left the room after a small goodbye to the others.

Seeing a window of opportunity she worried she wouldn't get again, Fiona pulled Raina aside. This was likely the only time to set up traps for Priestess Raina or the Binder and force one of them to reveal themselves as the leader of the Painted Edge. She would need to set the stage. What better way to do that than with the truth?

"The keystone in Kerus," Fiona started. "It would be in the best interests of Larrakane to protect it. But I worry one of us is not playing on the same side." She inclined her head subtly toward Mac's closed door on the other side of the room.

Raina faltered in her movements, then took a step toward Fiona. "Why did you not bring this up earlier?"

"I don't know who I can trust," Fiona said evasively.

"And what proof do you have?" Raina crossed her arms.

Fiona tugged her scarf. She would need to generalize the truth so as not to call out Raina as a suspect, but would Raina notice? "The incidents that have happened with the Painted Edge seem to be spurred on by someone clever with foreknowledge of our every move. And considerable organizational power." If she pushed her luck and blatantly implicated the Binder, perhaps she could lay one trap for both. She leaned in. "If you're sending the Followers to Kerus, then you should make sure they also go to the *pyramid*."

Raina raised an eyebrow and glanced at where the Binder had gone.

Fiona could practically see the wheels spinning in her head. She said nothing, not wanting to lean too hard on the leader.

Raina gave Fiona a once-over but inclined her head. "I'll make sure at once." She left the room without acknowledging Dodger and Fali.

Fiona quickly spoke to them about her trap for Raina.

"What do you think she'll do?" Fali said.

"If she's running the Painted Edge she'll make sure to find something at the pyramids to accuse the Binder with," Fiona said. She slipped Matteo's map into the new leaf pocket of her scarf.

"And if she's not?" Dodger said warily.

"Then actual Followers will go there. Either there's nothing, as the Binder suggested, or he's hiding something." Fiona ran a finger up and down her scarf. "Either way we'll know if Raina is the traitor or if the Binder is hiding something at the pyramids that could implicate him."

Fali rubbed his trunk across his large cheek. "It's a gamble."

"I'm not adept at cards but I know when someone is hiding something. And I'm quite good at getting it out." Though sometimes it was a bit more dangerously than she would like.

The Binder and Mac reentered the room with a chilly aura. Mac crossed her arms, turning her back on the Binder, and said, "All of you, be careful."

Concerned, Fiona moved closer to Mac. "We'll stay alert, I promise."

Mac looked at her for a long moment before whipping off her glasses. "The Thread needs tending," she said quietly and, with another glare at the Binder, left in a flounce of gossamer skirts.

Fiona watched her leave with eyebrows furrowing. What had the Binder said to frustrate Mac? She felt the Binder was staring at her, but his expression was one of annoyance more than anything. What in the dark edge could she have done—well, what had she done that he knew? The Binder and Fiona met in the middle of the room, coming toward each other surprisingly quick. Fiona stopped and said politely, "Where are Nic and Dani?" She used Nicolosia's shortened name not to irk him.

"Nic is still with the druids, working with the Guardians I suspect. And Dani declined to come to this meeting. Apparently, she has more important matters to attend to at the farms. Not that she's ever useful here."

Fiona frowned. Nic had told her precisely to meet at the Thread and that they had already talked to the Guardians. Perhaps they were busy with Richard now through the other druids.

"Why do you continue to doubt me?" the Binder said, looking at Fiona stiffly. He drew a breath before releasing it slowly, his shoulders lowering with it. "You have yet to take anything I've said at face value."

"You have yet to offer me anything that doesn't feel as if it'll put me in a bind," Fiona said. She glanced at Dodger, who was talking earnestly with Fali. "Or in the gutter."

"You know as well as I that Marcius would like us not to argue fruitlessly." The Binder pointed at her with his silver walking stick. "But perhaps you're not as good at reading people as others say."

He was baiting her, that was clear. She ignored it. "I'm not some unread turner. While I can see that the Travel Guild has had the Book's best interest in some affairs, I'm not positive that all extends to you."

He leaned away from Fiona. "Go on. I should truly like to know what you think of me then." His jaw clenched, in opposition to his confident demeanor. Nerves or restrained frustration, she wasn't quite sure. But if she could break his confidence and gain information, she had to try.

Fiona leaned in. "You are not as clever as you may think you are. I'm on to you."

He raised an eyebrow but said nothing.

"Tell me why you keep such powerful materials if you don't use them for the good of the Book."

He paused but said in a huff, "And what materials, Investigator Thorne, would that be?"

"You tell me. Wouldn't it be more beneficial to use what you have in your *vault* against the Painted Edge than to keep it locked up?" She quickly moved on to throw him off. "And I find it interesting we haven't recovered the rest of the crowns yet. Do you have jackets on it?"

He gave her a direct stare, answering swiftly, "Of course."

"It's your crown that's missing now. Presumably."

"Presumably?"

"You're quite good with your powers still. None of the other Seasons seem to use theirs." Though Nicolosia had used theirs to cover their tracks to the Thread, Mac and Dani didn't use their powers at all. Not on purpose at least.

He shrugged. "I've never lost my desire to have them. And they are useful."

"For what?"

"Everything." He smirked.

She barreled on, "Why do you serve Larrakane if you dislike her so much? It seems to me that a person with considerable influence tied to the goddess of everything might be more willing to give their life for hers. But perhaps she denied you something? It would make sense, based on how long you have lived, that you would have some regrets." She swallowed but forced herself to hint with what little information she had on the Binder: "Took away the *harmony* from your life when you were inked perhaps?"

His frozen demeanor cracked and his silver-white face flushed a dark purple. "Be careful what accusations you utter to me. I may allow you an inch out of others' care, but don't perceive that to mean you are safe to act as you please. Speak to me like that again and you *will* regret it." He stormed off out of the room without another word.

As far as reactions went, that was the most the Binder had ever given her. She had clearly hit the right note, but what did it mean? She didn't want to jump to conclusions, but unfortunately Dodger was already pouncing on her.

"What did you say to him?" Dodger scowled and crossed his arms.

"I just asked him some questions about the Guild and Larrakane," Fiona said, trying to keep her voice light.

"Fi!" He sighed and lowered his voice. "You need to be more careful."

"I know, I know. Don't accuse directly until you have evidence to support your case." She frowned at the door, wishing she had handled the ending of her interaction with the Binder a touch better. But it had confirmed that he was indeed sensitive about the deity. And that sensitivity made him quick to anger. A lost love was motivation for working against Larrakane if she ever saw one. "We should be getting on. It will take hours to get to Disas from the Mistral pagemark. Better we fly than walk. We'll have to rest in a hired cart when we get to Disas." The best way to get from one side of a page to another was through Mistral, where they could make somewhat of a direct beeline. Avoiding lightning of course.

Dodger shook his head. "Spotters have already found a way through Phyta that is faster. It's in hostile territory, but with the time difference it'll shave hours off our journey."

Surprised, she said, "To the plant page once again? I didn't think I'd get the chance."

"Finding pagemarks is a bit easier these days than when things opened up the first time. People are willing to trade with the Travel Guild in exchange for letting spotters sketch their land. The Binder has pushed forward quite a bit of innovation there along with some of his *friends*." Dodger inclined his head toward Mac's office.

Of course. It made sense why the Travel Guild always had the best gear. With Mac behind the eye scope of invention for the organization, Fiona shouldn't have been surprised. The Painted Edge also had gear, but it wasn't quite up to snuff. Their weapons, however, were more dangerous than the Travel Guild's. Who could be supplying them? "Besides the artisan district, where might one get weapons on Spine?"

Fali glanced up from the parchment he was studying. "That's about the only place. Why?"

"I was just remembering that the Painted Edge were quite outfitted last time I saw them."

"Could've come from Kerus, I suppose," Dodger said slowly, "or Travel Guild surplus. But we would've noticed them being stolen."

Fiona nodded but said nothing as they made their way out of the Thread. Could've noticed if they had wanted to be noticed. She wished Nicolosia had been at the meeting. She hated to move on without letting the druid know how she baited both Raina and the Binder. She supposed she could tell Spine, whatever that meant, but there was no time for it now.

A TRAVEL GUILD CHARIOT bore them quickly across the city and toward the new pagemark to Phyta. Fiona had to give credit where credit was due: the Guild worked splendidly fast to establish procedure for the new page, wresting control of the situation before there could even be a question of who or where this page was in the Book. Though the Leaves of Spine seemed as surprised about Phyta as the rest of them, Fiona wondered if any of them knew about it but kept it secret. It would make sense that the Binder had more than a notion as leader of the Travel Guild and first inked. Mistress Humbledraft, librarian Hanno, and Fiona herself couldn't be the only people in the Book with a fascination about possible hidden pages.

As the chariot came around the corner of the theater district, Fiona gasped at the sight before her in the darkened glow of the city. Mushrooms as tall and wide as houses stood in the distance. How did they get there so quickly, and who planted them?

"Is that what Phyta contains?" Dodger said wide eyed into the darkness.

"But larger even. I must admit I didn't think change would happen so rapidly in Spine to accommodate the new page."

Dodger murmured an agreement. "But that is what Spine is for. To house us and connect the pages. I wonder why the plant page didn't show itself before." He stepped down from the stopped chariot and held out his hand.

Fiona took it thankfully, getting out herself, and shrugged. "I think the Book does what it wants. There was no need to know about Phyta before it was opened to the rest of the Book."

"But didn't the Painted Edge find it before you did?"

Fiona frowned. "I don't know actually. In truth, Clara opened it up first using the Seasonal Crowns." She stopped. Had Dodger known that? She honestly was a bit too tired to remember who knew what anymore. "I'm going to assume you read that in the Travel Guild report."

"You would be surprised to find how little I know about the goings-on in the Book, Fi, especially when it deals with you."

She placed her hand on his shoulders. "Well, my friend, I will enlighten you more than you wish. I'm tired of keeping secrets. One can only hold so many."

"It is hard to continue holding them, feeling alone in the responsibility of them."

She nodded. "And as things get more and more dangerous with the Painted Edge, secrets aren't as helpful as they once were." She sighed. "Can I rely on you to find the gaps that I have missed?"

Dodger patted her back. "I will certainly try."

Fiona gave a half smile. "Alright then. First, let's see what Spine has cooked up with this Phyta pagemark. I wonder if any plantians have arrived."

They walked toward the mushrooms, their earthy scent growing stronger as they approached. Travel Guild jackets loosely guarded the area. All greeted Dodger respectfully as Marbled Cervidus. Many straightened shoulders, raised chins, and adjusted uniforms as he strode toward them. Dodger, hands clasped behind his back, nodded and talked to a few, greeting them by name. With prompt manners they acknowledged Fiona, gave her a pack of gear for their trip, and stood back waiting for orders. Fiona winked at Dodger. His tail twitched but he kept his professionalism as he marched toward the center of the district. A small cleared area was cordoned off with Travel Guild flags—a new pagemark.

Though Fiona had many questions she watched silently as a fairy, bald with thin translucent wings of shimmering green, flew to them. It was hard to tell among the layers of necklaces that draped down his chest, but the Travel Guild insignia did peek out from his infinitely more stylish uniform. A spotter perhaps?

As if answering her question, the fairy introduced themselves as the current mapper of pagemarks for Phyta and gave Dodger a bookmark to the new page. Rubbing the thick, rough-cut brown vine in his paw, Dodger focused on the faekin's clear instructions. Soon enough they were alone in the center.

The prickle of many eyes watching them made Fiona want to rub her neck, but she held off. Grabbing her hand in his, Dodger focused on the vine and started the page turn. Fiona tried to clear her mind so as not to upset the flow, but as soon as she did she found herself thinking of Richard. He held many secrets himself. Possibly more than she would ever know. Was he tired? Were all of the Leaves as well? It was a motive she hadn't considered before—simply being tired of holding the line.

The mushrooms and Guild banners folded away to reveal a sun rising in a world of stalks and vines. Morning, or something like it, beamed through the vignette, scattering light throughout the darkness of Spine. The sound of big, bold leaves scraping together in the wind rushed from page to page.

Dodger took a step forward and Fiona followed, thoroughly distracted now by the beauty of it. The pagemark was ground level, with recently cleared stumps dotting the area. Fiona was quite thankful they weren't simply falling from the sky for once. Surrounded by thick stalks and fragrant jungle, they took another step firmly into the page. With nary a sound, the world of Spine flipped closed behind them.

Two jackets, human and elephas, stood just outside the pagemark. The human's shoulders relaxed, seemingly relieved at seeing them. Just beyond them were three plantians, bronze weapons at their sides, watching with careful stillness. Fiona didn't recognize any of them but raised an eyebrow at the lack of Travel Guild structure on this side of the pagemark. Perhaps they hadn't been so quick after all.

The jackets seemed eager to talk to Dodger, and with furtive glances back at the plantians the human said, "Marbled Cervidus. They won't take you to the other Guild members."

"What do you mean?" Dodger said, leaning in.

The young elephas raised her trunk and pointed toward the ground. "The previous spotters, they led them underground. But now they say there are too many trespassing in."

Dodger grimaced. "I'm sorry, they didn't mention that there was friction here."

"I suppose the plantians are pushing back on the quickness of having an unknown group in their home," Fiona said quietly to Dodger. No surprise there, given what happened with the Painted Edge and her floating island. Two days was not enough time to broker complete peace and trust for anyone.

"Yes, until some of them become turners, why would they allow anyone to stake a claim on their land or near their home? Let me handle this," Dodger said to the jackets and Fiona.

"By all means, Marbled Cervidus." Fiona waved him ahead of her with a smile.

Dodger introduced himself to the small group of plant people, staying clear of their weapons. He stuck out his hand and, before Fiona could intervene, was pierced with a small thorn. It seemed Marcia had gotten him updated quite quickly on the plant people.

They turned toward Fiona, an unwrapped vine wavering in the air.

Fiona rubbed her face. "Is it possible to simply ingest spores again?"

They didn't seem to respond.

She warily placed out her hand and a thorny spike sunk deep into it. It didn't hurt, but she winced at the altercation all the same. How long would that stay in her hand?

"*We need to travel through your space to the other side of the water,*" Dodger thought to the group.

"*No. If too many know the way, then our enemies will surely find it,*" the smaller of the three responded. The vines of all three seemed to shift and move as they spoke.

"*You took two of our people already,*" Dodger thought.

"*We did not. Our leader, Caliope, did,*" the bulbous ones thought, "*and until she commands us, it is up to us to do what is right for the plantians.*"

"*Be that as it may, it's where we need to go,*" Fiona thought. She tried to control the frustration pounding through her head.

With an authoritative tone Dodger thought, *"We aren't asking you to accompany us, but it is imperative that you tell us the way. All of us are in danger and we have no time to wait."*

"And how do we know what you speak is true?" the smaller one responded.

Dodger looked at Fiona and sighed. "Do you think we need to get Caliope?"

"We don't have time. This pagemark is miles from their village." She poked his arm. "You know exactly how to handle this. You don't need me or anyone else interjecting and bungling it up."

"But you've dealt with these people before."

"Yes, when our common enemy was clear and ready to fight. Without that I don't think Henrietta and I would've fared so well." She patted Dodger on the shoulder. "You don't simply have the makings of a leader, Dodger, you already are one. And you've learned from the best. Remember, Caliope thought Marcia a proper leader."

He squared his shoulders. *"We would not lie in so early a relationship between our groups,"* Dodger said rationally.

The plantians looked at each other and the small one asked, *"So you would lie later on in our connection?"*

"If needed," Dodger said. *"To secure our pages, our worlds, we would push through any conflict. Wouldn't you?"*

Fiona grinned at Dodger's approach. A tad too riddlelike for her taste, but he was in love with a faekin. It couldn't be helped.

The others chattered without sharing their thoughts with Fiona and Dodger. Then the bulbous one said, *"You are honest. We will assist you."*

"Through?" Dodger asked.

The plant people nodded. With little ceremony they marched to a spot near the jungle's edge and rapidly opened up a hidden hole in the ground, lashing out with vines and stems. The bulbous one said, *"We will take you through the network. It is quicker and bypasses our enemies' lines."*

"Thank you for your trust in us."

The small one said, *"We trust in no one. We believe in you."*

Fiona smirked at the plantians' assessment of Dodger.

Dodger rubbed his whiskers, ducking his head away from her. He waved toward the other jackets, who quickly saluted Dodger as the plantians led them into the earthen tunnels. There was a somewhat steep decline of mounded earth to the bottom of the tunnel. Once they arrived at the bottom the plantians slung vines from their body, pulling in dirt and closing the hole, blocking out the sun.

A torch underground seemed a dangerous endeavor. With thanks to the fairy spotter, Fiona dug through the pack she was given to find small lanterns that reminded her of Gaili's creation back in Rise. Though they didn't burn as bright, they emitted no odor or heat. "What are these?" She watched the golden amber dance across the deep-brown walls.

"Endless flames. Uses some of the fire from Blaze but contained in copper from the faekin page." Dodger moved closer to her and whispered, "A Mac creation, I have no doubt."

Fiona shook her head, marveling at the ingenuity. They carried on through the tunnel for some time in relative silence except for the echo of their footsteps. The plantians didn't bother further communicating with them at all. The damp, compacted earth made for a more comfortable walking experience than Fiona expected. With the smell of leaves and plant coming only from their guides, it was clear that this tunnel was made long ago. How often was it used to get to the other side? For all the talk of the plantians' enemies, when was the last time they actually waged war? Though there wasn't much to see, Fiona did find a few pieces of forgotten root and rocks along the way. She pocketed a rough stone for herself as a bookmark, should she need it one day.

They stopped after what felt like hours. Unfortunately, her pocket watch agreed. Though it was faster than her previous plan, how close had they really gotten to Disas and the Oracle of Stars?

"We will not lead you farther or be threatened by our enemies. You will find a web of mycelium that will take you to the surface. Fight."

"Thank you," Dodger said to their retreating forms. He hefted his lantern higher to see that indeed a thick network of overlapping fungal roots led up toward the ceiling.

"Perhaps we should douse the lights before we run into *their enemies*," Fiona said. No doubt they would quickly become her enemies as well, coming from an invisible underground tunnel.

Dodger acquiesced and she began clumsily climbing the thick mycelium up toward the ceiling. Nimble Dodger quickly made it to the top. With some effort they pushed through the earth and exited the tunnel.

The sun bore down on them and the sound of lapping waves filled their ears and erased the noise of their boots tromping across the watery ground. Were they by the sea? There was no way they had crossed an ocean in such a short amount of time. But time did often work differently in the pages, and Phyta was already proving unpredictable.

Their shoes stuck in the muddy soil, making quickness difficult. Dodger weaved and moved stealthier across the area than she had expected. All those years running away from officials in Roma Mikar, no doubt. It reminded Fiona a little of investigating the Hawkport warehouse with Richard, and a pang rose in her chest at her desire that he be here with her. He would have plenty to say about this journey, she was sure. And he'd know how to have her back, though she wasn't really comparing him to Dodger in that way. It was unnerving how he would just pop into her head in quiet moments. Did she pop into his too? Was he thinking of her right now?

"Fi," Dodger whispered at the edge of the marshy land. He waved her over to a massive barrel-shaped dark-green fungus.

She hurried over, happy to be on slightly drier land, and shook the muck off her shoes. "Where is the pagemark?"

"You're standing by it." Dodger nodded to the fungus as he opened up his pack. He removed a thick woolen coat and began shrugging it on.

Fiona squinted at the barrel before noticing a small parchment stuck to the side with an open book symbol. "You can't be serious. There's not room enough."

"Spotters often make do in tight quarters. One of the dangers of the job. But the pagemark in Disas should already be cleared and safe enough."

"I'm not worried about getting to Disas. I'm worried about walking into one of these hunks on the way." She swatted the barrel with a dull thud. Definitely full of something, though her curiosity immediately desired to know what. She pulled away from it and began throwing on her own layered clothing. "If you trust the mark, then I'll trust you, but I'm going to have a long talk with Mistress Humbledraft about this. It sheds a whole new light on her title as best spotter in the Guild."

Dodger laughed and finished throwing on a heavy, scratchy-looking scarf that covered his ears. The sunlight broke through cover of other fungi, and he shook his head ruefully. "What a world to explore."

"Yes, when ours is a bit more secure." Fiona sighed and tucked in her precious multi-pocketed scarf, back to its vibrant colors, before pulling on a woolen hat. She grabbed Dodger's paw. "After you."

Dodger's whiskers twitched but he focused on a piece of dried pine cone before the cask-shaped fungus pulled away from them, the entire scene folding back to reveal an icy-cold clearing. The heat from the mycelium marsh clashed with the frosty wind.

Quickly they stepped from one page to another before anyone in Phyta could notice or surprise them. The page closed behind them, rippling out and cutting off the heavy plant scent. Fiona shivered in the lightly pouring snow and drew in tighter to herself. It was clear that this area was recently cleaned off from piled logs and debris pushed to the edges. In the distance soft amber lights twinkled, beckoning them through an early morning sunrise.

"Where are we exactly?" Fiona said, dropping his paw and pulling on thick gloves from the satchel.

"Nivalon nation," Dodger said.

"The ice ursidon?" Though Disas was heavily populated with elephas, that was farther north. Fiona knew of ice ursidon but had never seen one. It was rare enough to see one of the bearlike people in Spine as it was. Their people were rare page turners for some reason. "Will they be quite upset with the Guild for making a pagemark here?"

"Not if they don't know about it." Dodger's tail twitched and he patted his padded jacket. "At least for the time being, it's not public knowledge since one side is in hostile territory for our new allies and this side is in the dead of the frost. Our current procedure doesn't really have rules for this sort of thing. So there's room to wiggle, as you humans say."

Fiona raised an eyebrow at the assertation but moved past it. "How far?" She pointed toward the lights.

Dodger hesitated. "I'm not sure. The spotters returned to Spine to report as soon as they could clear this pagemark."

"Well then, I suppose we should get on." She rubbed her hands together as they began to walk on. She never experienced the cold with the places she traveled to. Always avoided Rise in winter after she was inked and had the choice. She preferred the warm sun on her face to cold frost slapping her cheeks.

Fiona huddled closer to Dodger and began recounting everything going on, from Soots's nature to apprehending and then losing the Seasonal Crowns, to Rise's near collapse into the ocean. She found that once she opened confidence to him, the walk passed by in a blur, each footstep lighter. Fiona hesitated when she brought up seeing Richard at the Painted Edge hideout, but Dodger interjected before she could say anything else.

"I already understand who he is, Fi." He nudged her shoulder with his own playfully.

Relief flooded through her. "You do?"

"Yes. I wouldn't be able to keep up with your talents if I couldn't read between the lines. And you're not going against any promises you made him by me acknowledging it."

She smiled underneath her scarf. Of course Dodger would see through to the heart of her issue. "I hate that I'm so transparent."

"Don't fret. If I wasn't in the same predicament myself, I don't know if I could read you so well about it."

"What do you mean?"

"Loving someone who is more powerful than you and trying to convince them that that's okay," he said quietly.

"I don't love Richard," Fiona said quickly. She didn't believe in instantly being attached to a person like that. The kind of love that her parents had took ages to ripen. It couldn't come to be between the alleyways and the secretive glances of a few meetings.

"Not yet, but if you let yourself, I'm sure you'll be right there with me. At the wall. Pounding your head against the stone over and over again."

"If that's what love feels like these days, then I suppose I'm a bit closer than I expected." Her stomach tightened and she began to fiddle with the fingertips of her gloves. "It *is* like talking to a wall at least. Imagine being one of the most powerful people in the Book and not taking charge to make things happen. Not fighting till your last for everyone you can. I don't understand."

Dodger put a hand on her shoulder, stopping her. "Fi. I saw a man who knew all about fighting. He fought against himself in every word he said to you. Every gesture he made." Dodger shook his head. "Perhaps because I've seen the same in the mirror, I could recognize it more."

"But I didn't ask for that!" She walked away from Dodger, her head down.

Dodger leapt and landed in front of her with grace. "I'm not here to argue with you." He stroked snowflakes off his whiskers. "But as your friend, let me give you some advice. When it comes to caring for someone who has outlived you quite a bit, remember that you are not the first they have loved. Or have the potential to lose. Loss will do strange things to people. And sometimes it's hard to live with the idea that you'll repeat the cycle again."

She glared at Dodger, though her fit of anger had already dissipated. If Richard thought he would lose her—he'd already lost so many, she knew—then it wasn't truly even about her. He was trying to be someone she wanted, but she just wanted him to be himself. And to let her have an active choice in the matter. Perhaps her being so involved, so tied to him through things he couldn't control made it harder. She had seen him as an avoidant person, but perhaps he was just trying to protect himself.

"I am considering your words," Fiona said stiffly. She sighed loudly, the ability to be upset without anxiety making her feel a bit better.

"Someone clever I know once said, 'Try simply being there for all the times you can. You don't need something formal to make it real.'"

She smiled within her scarf. "Thank you."

Dodger grinned, his whiskers twitching. "Any time." He turned and began trudging again in the snow toward the city lights.

Fiona would write to Richard when she could. Her life was fleeting, her time urgent. But he knew the weight of a long, empty life. Caution was understandable. At least in the way Dodger explained it. She could be clear with him and leave it at that. She rightly didn't know what it was like to have lost so much. He had watched his whole world fall apart, had lost his family, and had played a major part in making it happen. And then to still bear the brunt of it two hundred years later. So many people were bearing the problem from a time considered far behind. The Circle of Seasons. Fali and Raina with their handed-down memories. Marcia even, as a hag, had long been part of this. Had she always served the Binder? Had Stella always been around, a part of it too?

"Dodger, how long has the Binder known Marcia was a hag?" She walked faster, trying to catch up with him.

He wiped his face of fallen snow. "Since she was inked, I believe."

"Did he know about her sisters?"

He shook his head. "What are you getting at, Fi?"

"Hags always worked for the Seasons. They were right hands to them before they were banished. So it makes sense to me that the last remaining hags, once inked, would seek out the Seasons. Or vice versa."

"But Marcia was the only one inked. And she thought Stella dead these last few years."

"I know. But just because she thought Stella was gone didn't mean everyone did." Fiona rubbed her cold nose.

"The Binder didn't know about Stella until Marcia told him."

"How do you know?"

"Because I was there," Dodger said. "She told us both. She was so distraught, Fi."

Fiona rubbed his arm comfortingly. "I'm sorry, Dodger. I'm not trying to be insensitive."

He gave a heavy sigh. "You're convinced that the Binder is somehow in league with the Painted Edge. I thought we already agreed that the Travel Guild is not your enemy."

"We did. And I know they aren't!" Fiona said curtly before groaning out loud. "I'm not saying they are. It's just that someone with too much power and information is clearly working us all over here." She threw up her hands. "What would you do?"

"About?"

"About the Binder if he did turn out to be linked to the Painted Edge?"

Dodger stopped. "Do you have evidence he is?"

"No but I have set traps so it's only a matter of time to know for sure."

He crossed his arms. "What would his motive even be?"

"He's angry at Larrakane. I don't know why, but her name, me talking to her, everything makes him emotional. Even in the past he seemed at odds with her."

Dodger relaxed his arms but said nothing.

Fiona knew her friend well. "You've seen it before, too, haven't you?"

"He doesn't like to talk about her. Not even to Marcia."

"So he must have an issue with her." What was it between them? Was this the way the Binder showed he, too, cursed the Inking and his inability to stay with Harmony? It didn't sit right, but that was the only thing that made sense.

"But there's no evidence, Fi. If—and only if—we determine that the Binder is materially linked to the Painted Edge, I will do what needs to be done."

His words sounded final, but she asked anyways: "Which is?"

"Handle it. For the greater good of the Book." He shook his head. "Which is ironic because the only reason I even feel confident about that is because of the Binder's teachings."

The Binder had clearly done right by Dodger and Marcia, it seemed. They looked like a unit, each one more willing to take on danger for the other. Dodger didn't stand up to Fiona because he loved the Travel Guild. He did it because he cared and believed in the Binder. She rubbed her tired eyes. "Well, if it makes it any easier, I'm being so annoying because I do have my doubts. Neither the Binder nor Priestess Raina feel right here."

"Raina too? Who sent you down this trail?" Dodger said.

"The Elder druid."

"Are you sure it's not them?"

"Yes!" Her heart flipped. "Well, yes and no. My gut says I'm missing something, but I can't see one reason Nic would be the traitor. But I promise you, I won't accuse anyone until there's evidence. You can be sure I won't run afoul of you again."

"Fi, I know you're less short sighted than you used to be," Dodger said softly.

"Yes, well, I have tried," she grumbled.

He bumped his shoulder into hers. "Humble too."

She gave a small smile glad, that they weren't cross with each other. Bunching up her shoulders, she nodded toward the lights. "We won't get any closer if we don't hurry."

"I can still outrun you."

"Unlikely," Fiona said before breaking into a run toward the lights.

The thumps of sounds behind her said Dodger hadn't expected that. Always the one to beat in turner training, he quickly bounded in front of her. Fiona had never come close.

But still she put effort into it, glad for a moment to release all her pent-up frustration and confusion in a little exertion.

THE LIGHTS OF TORCHES dotting the perimeter of the city were fiery beacons against the pink-hued sky as they walked across the border from the snowy forest into the city. The snow-covered ground was devoid of foot tracks. The thin streets were quiet and empty. Dark-gray stone buildings stood at attention in neat rows crowding the roads and each other, as if they, too, wanted to share each other's warmth. Banners of green and gold hung from many of the buildings, depicting a symbol of intricate knotwork. It was much like the one Fiona recalled in the druids' encampment on Spine. Nature-loving folk seemed to carry it always, she had noticed.

"Welcome to the city of Nix Urbis," Dodger said, pointing at the banner. He grinned. "Come on."

Their feet crunched loudly through the snow down the main path. Past the perimeter of the city there was more life. Ursidons of all sorts milled around in the early morning, though the most common had white fur to match the snow falling around them. There were no more lit torches as they walked farther in, but many carried metal holders with small flames, like the lanterns of Copper though far more designed on the outside than the faekin's. A few people glanced at them but no one approached. It was rather peaceful, not being immediately accosted.

They turned and entered a small row of shops and tall buildings with overhanging roofs letting the snow fall off as quickly as it dropped. Flowing knotwork designs were centered on many doors, and Fiona quickly realized these signified homes of some sort. Perhaps a family crest?

Dodger stopped, glancing about the area.

"What are we looking for?" Fiona asked.

"That one." Dodger pointed to a shop. "After we got back to the Hinge and I spoke with the Binder, I looked up some of the people I knew in Kerus."

She smiled, glad that he had taken her advice. Fiona squinted at the shop sign. "A paper and quill shop?"

"Nicked was one of the best foragers around when we were kids. Not surprised she's set up here."

Surprised at the ease of his words, Fiona tilted her head. "And what are we going to do with Nicked?"

"*We* aren't going to do anything," Dodger said, pulling his cloak hood up higher. "You can go in, say you stumbled here from somewhere else. Mistral or even Copper will seem legitimate enough. You can't hide that you're human, but Nicked shouldn't give you any problems. We just need passage out of Nix Urbis to the coast."

"You're not even going to come in and talk to her?" Fiona frowned.

He shook his head. "I'm not one to repeat mistakes."

"Dodger, you're never going to get over things if you keep relegating yourself to the background. Absolutely not." She pushed him forward.

"Fi, stop. I know what I'm doing."

"So do I." She pushed him again, although without much luck. Dodger was stronger than she was and didn't budge.

But it was enough. He sighed "If this goes poorly again, I don't think I'll be able to live it down."

"You will. If no one in your previous life cares about you anymore, then I say to the pits of Cobbles with them. You have more than enough friends and people who respect you as you are now."

His tail twitched and he took another moment before raising his head up and moving toward the shop. He knocked lightly on the door.

The smell of inks and fresh paper wafted over Fiona as the door opened. It reminded her of Richard and she smiled despite herself.

A tall ursidon with thick brown fur stood in the entryway. It was clear she was just getting started for the day. Her apron was clean, and she held a large mug in her hand. Fiona had no incertitude that if the ursidon wanted, she could use it as a makeshift weapon in a moment. "Can I help you?"

"Nicked," Dodger said and pulled down the scarf covering his face.

The ursidon stopped, rubbing her eyes and squinted at him. "Marcius? Is that really you?"

Dodger nodded. "May we come inside?"

Nicked leaned back out of the doorway. "You may."

They stamped inside, wiping their feet on the entry rug politely. The interior room was small but cozy, a fire in one corner with large cushions seated in front of it. Wooden shelves held thick reams of paper, jars of ink, quills, and other tools of the trade. A large arched doorway, big enough to fit a bear, led to another room in the back.

"Sorry to drop in unannounced like this," Dodger said.

Nicked waved away the words and yawned. "Sorry. Where are my manners?" She nodded to Fiona. "Nicked Quills, scribe and presser at your service."

"Fiona Thorne." She smiled. "Did the name come with the job?"

"Other way around. Thought I would lean into it a bit, set myself apart. Figured no sense not using the nickname for something good, eh?" The ursidon laughed, a deep, vibrating sound. She quickly glanced back toward the open doorway and then lowered her voice. "Cubs are still sleeping."

"Cubs?" Dodger squeaked, seemingly shaken from his stupor. "You have kids?"

"Yes, and I'd appreciate you whispering if you can. Once they wake up they'll be nothing but questions and energy." Nicked grinned. "They are incorrigible. Sit, sit! Can I get you anything?"

Fiona shook her head. "We've come rather far rather quickly, actually. A minute by the fire is all I need." She bumped her shoulder into Dodger. "Marcius can explain."

"I'm just surprised," he said.

"Don't know why you should be. I'm not surprised you've turned up."

Dodger's brow wrinkled. "You're not?"

"Same old, same old. Right place, right time you are." Nicked sighed. "Well, with the Roma presence rising we figured the Travel Guild would get out here and make themselves known."

"There's more Roma?" Fiona asked from the fire. If they were increasing in this part of Kerus, there must be a reason for it, and it couldn't be good.

"On the northern edge near the port city, yes." Nicked frowned. "Isn't that why you're here? To push back against their forces around the new pagemark?"

Dodger glanced at Fiona, his demeanor changing. He clasped his hands behind his back. "Suppose you start from the beginning, Nicked."

She sat heavy on a cushion and took a drink from her mug. "There was rumor a pagemark was found, out off the coast. Near the Oracles. Travel Guild jackets arrived first, but then they got overrun by some of the Romas. Thought the Guild would come back, but it's been a couple of weeks and the Romas just keep increasing. Now they're patrolling the waters in a territory that isn't theirs." Nicked scratched her furry chin. "Too much like history repeating itself. They say they aren't looking toward Disas, but we know an oncoming invasion when we see one."

If they were near the Oracles, it could be that the Romas knew for certain the Oracles were important. But a pagemark wasn't what they expected. Nor had the Binder mentioned any Travel Guild activity. Fiona turned worried eyes on Dodger.

He seemed to understand her completely and said, "We need to get out to the Oracles immediately. But quietly. Can you help us?"

Nicked nodded. "Lucius thought you might ask for that. I can send word, but it'll get there the same time you will."

"Lucius?" Dodger asked. "But he's with the Empire. He ran me out of Nymar and Mikar."

"He's not." She put up her hands. "I know, I know what it looks like, but he's changed quite a bit, Marcius. Lucius and I are both part of a group keeping Disas safe from the Empire. If you can believe it from the little urchins we used to be." She chuckled. "Truly, ask him about it. He's been on the trail of the increased Romas activity. Had a lead in Mikar that went up in smoke, he told me."

Dodger's tail twitched and he sighed.

While Fiona was inclined to think Nicked didn't wish Dodger any ill will, she wasn't sure about her judgment on Lucius. The smilodon had fought Dodger and tried to stop them many times on Siamor. If he was working with some sort of resistance group, why the big act with Dodger? Didn't he know the Guild, via Dodger, could help? Or was he simply so stubborn against Dodger he refused to ask?

"Is that how you knew Dodger was with the Travel Guild?" Fiona asked.

"Nah, I kept up with all the goings-on of friends. You were the easiest, of course. Lucius was the hardest." She shrugged. "Knew you'd do something with yourself once you were inked. Just watched the headlines."

Dodger blinked. "What do you mean?"

"You were always someone to watch. I only got as far as I did because I followed you."

"I didn't do anything but get us into trouble," Dodger said, taking a step back.

"Not the way I saw it. Getting us fed, warmed, and housed was always your priority. Even when we made mistakes, you took it on." She stood and grasped his shoulders, pulling him several steps forward. "Only reason I got off Siamor was because of you. Didn't want to bother you in Spine with all the work I figured you were doing."

"You wouldn't have been a bother, Nicked," Dodger said, pulling his whiskers.

Nicked shrugged again and squeezed his arm comfortingly before releasing him. "Well, the cubs and I will come visit you then in that turner city. Heard you all have everything in the Book there. Maybe some of those inventive Copper contraptions."

Dodger smiled shyly. "That would be nice."

Nicked wrote delicately on a piece of parchment, large hand skilled with the ink and quill. She dusted it. "I'll send this now. If you're looking for a quiet ride out, the armorer has orders to send. I'll tell them to expect two riders."

"Thank you, Nicked," Dodger said. "I really appreciate your help here."

She patted him hard on the back and slipped out.

"I guess not everyone dislikes you," Fiona said, rubbing her hands in the heat of the fire.

"Nicked was always special."

"Did you ever think some people thought the same about you?"

Dodger lifted his scarf back up over his face and said a muffled, "Perhaps."

Fiona smiled. It was all he needed to say. They left the scribe's small shop and snoring children and headed out into the cold. The city had woken up a bit more by the time they reached the armorer and loaded into their laden cart. The journey started bumpy but quickly smoothed out. Dodger was quiet staring off into distance as they passed the city perimeter. Lost in thought, no doubt.

Her mind flicked to Richard as she stared off at the snowy landscape before her. Its untrodden banks and chilly atmosphere gave her a blank canvas with which to draw out all they had done and said between each other. She pulled out writing implements, and with a quick dip of the quill, recapping the ink lest it spill, she steadied the open journal with her knee and began writing, "I'm not sure when you'll see this, but I wanted to say, simply, I think I understand a little more than before. I know what it's like to lose someone you love. I lost my father long ago, and it still pains me to this day. But I don't know what it's like to lose everyone. I suspect that's a more unbearable pain, even as time goes on. I am here if you ever wish to talk about it. I am here if you want to argue about the merits of Larrakane's decisions or digest the idiocy of the court. I am here. Fighting in these frayed pages of the Book, yes, but for you as you are. Because if you can fight against those you loved and for those you have lost, Richard, well, I do believe I have enough strength for the both of us in this present struggle."

She put the quill down, the gentle rocking motion almost knocking it on the wooden slats. What would he say? Did she need to be more specific? She was so used to being direct, but with Richard directness and insistence seemed to be too much tied together.

Large sloping lines of text began scrawling beneath her words quickly. "I feel as if I've been bumbling around in the dark for years. Dark staircases. Dark archives. Dark rooms filled with quiet books that can't ask anything of me. That I don't have to disappoint or let down. That I don't have to lose." There was a pause as Richard's swirling thinking lines appeared on the page. "Queen Pompania was someone close to me. Someone who could give me orders from birth and loved me for me. In the formidable, unconditional way, if you understand what I'm saying."

Fiona's stomach knotted as she took in Richard's meaning: Eleanor was his mother. A flurry of thoughts and questions rose to the front of her mind and she tried to piece together what he was saying. She feared if she wrote directly about this family connection and the questions therein, the power of the Word would hurt her like it had with the mention of his brother, and she didn't want to encounter that pain again. But if Eleanor was his mother, the first human inked and crowned by his hand, that meant that Richard, poor Richard, had to put her in that position. And then they were separated, forever. Was this the choice he despaired having to make? No wonder he wanted to discuss Queen Eleanor in person. There was so much to say, and she suspected no one journal could contain it all.

She pressed her lips together and wrote back, "I understand and, though I know you can't go into detail like this, am here to talk about it next I see you. If you wish."

"I do," he wrote back hastily. "I've never talked to anyone about it before. And the darkness that I've been in for years seems to grow the more I dig into my regret and live in my past. It has, of late, been peeling back little by little since you've slipped into my life. The sun shines brighter, the day feels kinder, and for the first time I have happiness. I have hope. Truly it terrifies me." His words rushed together on the page as if he was writing as quickly as he could. "But I would gladly be terrified a little each day rather than not hear your voice or see your words. Can you forgive a foolish old man his overguarded heart?"

Fiona smiled broadly, a prickle behind her eyes she chose to ignore. She simply wrote back, "Yes."

"Blasted woman," came Richard's reply in sloping text.

"Blasted man," she wrote back.

Dots appeared and then a quick scrawl: "I'll never win another argument against you again, will I?"

"Perhaps." Stone walls didn't break overnight. She would look forward to hammering his down with him through many more ridiculous debates, she was sure. If he could share his regret and hope with her in writing, he'd get to it in words.

"I was going to write to you but then opened up to see this and almost forgot why I was here in the first place. I thought about what you said before and rather pressed Hawkport for a frank conversation. Hawkport had no more to add about Raina except that she simply wanted the island for the Followers. But a more valuable party made a better deal with him. When I pushed on that, telling Hawkport that I can simply wait out his short march to the gallows, that rat had the nerve to say he wasn't worried! No, indeed that he would be saved by an 'interested' party and that furthermore he was more than a man and more than I would ever be. In his blustering, though, it made me think: What if the thing you and Hawkport have in common *is* that you are more than a human? If you're even the smallest part of two different species, from two different pages. Well, you can see that's a variable even I hadn't thought to work against in using my powers."

"So either Hawkport is the union of two different species," Fiona wrote, "which doesn't seem likely given his family history, or he has to have been bound by a Seasonal fae." Which of them had given Hawkport a better deal? She chewed her lip. It had to be the Binder. Only he had the power and the incentive in commanding Hawkport. This way he would have control of Forlorn Tower instead of Raina. But that was only worked if he knew about Raina's desire for the island or anything like that. How were they even introduced?

"I take that to mean you know something," Richard wrote.

"I do, but unfortunately it only means I have to work that much harder to get evidence of my last remaining suspect. Otherwise, I'll be hard pressed to get people to agree with me." She glanced at Dodger, who had been lulled by the rocking into a quiet sleep.

"What can I do?" he wrote back quickly.

"Let the druids guard you and write to me," she scrawled back. "Be safe."

"As a button."

Fiona sighed and wafted the inked journal in the chilly air to dry before tucking it into her scarf. She had to use this time to think, to put all the pieces together. A sound conclusion and solid evidence were her only hope. But the ride was cold and long. Exhaustion overtook her eventually.

* * *

Too soon for a full rest, they were woken up by the driver. The crisp, cold wind of the salty sea wafted through the air. Gulls lifted wings over their heads as the Kerus sun rose high in the sky.

Beyond the vantage point of a beautiful morning was a bevy of workers—a mix of beastfolk, mostly snow-white ursidon, with a few humans scattered here or there. Longships with many oars floated restlessly in the sunlight-reflected water, the waves slapping against their hulls in a rhythmic thud.

Stretched and with a vibrating air of urgency, Fiona and Dodger made their way to a ship. They were unlike the airships of Rise, unable to be replicated. Or the crafted ships that sailed the hot, thick copper seas by the wind of fae inventions. These were longships, meant to hold many and fight against the Romas among the seas between Siamor and Disas. Trading between the continents was higher north where none but the elephas and ursidon held control of the waters.

Dodger tensed as they made their way down the dock toward all the longships waiting to set sail. Fiona scanned the workers, trying to find the source of his discomfort, and spotted a heavy-cloaked Lucius among the leather-bound ursidon. The sleek jubatas cheetah was towing rope into a boat as ursidon all around them took care of the ship. They gave orders, directed, and otherwise seemed in complete control of the situation.

Fiona tugged on Dodger's cloak. "You two are like peas in a pod."

He sighed. "We look almost nothing alike."

She would beg to differ but instead said lightly, "No, you're right. Shorter." And began moving toward the captain again. "Human eyes, you know. Misses all sorts of things."

"How I wish I had a scribe to hear that so they could make an official record for me."

They approached Lucius, who looked up at their arrival. He stood up taller, kept his head high. "Marcius."

"Lucius," Dodger said. He relaxed his shoulders, straightening himself. "Surprised to see you here like this."

"Like what?" Lucius said in a clipped tone. "Never seen someone work both sides of the same coin?" He shook his head. "Water's choppy and full of laurel wreaths, if you get my drift. Board now and get low. We'll talk inside."

Fiona looked around at the ursidon, who were giving them curious glances but none that seemed hostile. She lowered her voice. "No offense to you, but this feels a bit like a trap."

Lucius crossed his arms. "I could say the same for you two *Guild jackets*. But Nicked's note says you're our oasis in the desert. I'll believe her. So either get in or don't." He nodded to the longship and turned his back toward them. "We're leaving here in a few minutes all the same." Lucius moved into the crowd of workers bringing supplies onboard and began shouting orders again.

Fiona pulled Dodger closer. "Either I need more rest or Lucius openly admitted he's working two different factions."

Dodger frowned. "It falls in line with what Nicked said." He tugged at his whiskers. "But there's been so much inconsistency in his behavior. Nicked I can believe. She was always the reasonable, level-headed one of our group."

Fiona stared after Lucius. "He's not wearing Roma laurels under that cloak, that's certain. But can we trust him not to turn us over to the Romas if it would help his cause in Disas?"

"No one here loves the empire, and it would mean sinking others along with us. He wouldn't do that to the crew. Not the Lucius I knew." He almost sounded convinced.

Fiona shook her head but boarded the longship. She had been in tighter spots and the need to get to the Oracles and see what was happening there was more urgent than Lucius's possible betrayal.

Dodger walked the deck of the ship, glancing out into the sea. "The important thing is finding Vinicia and stopping the Painted Edge. It's been almost five days since she's been gone from Spine."

Fiona winced. "How read is she?"

"Better than most. But five days is still a lot to hold out from falling completely ill."

Page turner sickness was the reliable weakness in their ability. One Fiona never wanted to experience for too long. She rubbed her wrists, shuddering. "If she's in Painted Edge manacles, it'll be a lot worse."

He moved next to Fiona and hugged her shoulder. "You've been through a lot."

She snorted. "Understatement. But also I appreciate the acknowledgment." Fiona gave a small smile and moved below deck.

Through a narrow passage she walked through the large central space that housed many benches, quickly being filled by ursidon from up above. They grabbed oars, preparing to row out from the docks. Ropes slung out to skiffs being towed by the longship through open windows. Farther from the front of the ship were storage compartments with supplies, an assortment of swords and spears, and the only limited space not currently used by the leather-bound crew. It was small and cramped, but there were crates to sit on and for that Fiona was relieved.

The vessel soon got underway, with Dodger coming to join her below. The ship moved at a quick clip through the choppy water. They discussed their escape routes should they be needed, a turn to Spine the only sensible one without prior mapping or ornithopters. Dodger left the storage room occasionally to check on progress.

Before too long Lucius came down below, taking up what little room was left in the storage chamber. He swept back his cloak to hang a spyglass on his belt and said, "We're about half an hour away from the Oracles. Slower going because we're heading up the coast to avoid as much Roma activity as possible. There are still skimmers who brave the sea to visit the Oracles, so if we're stopped, that'll be our excuse." Lucius pointed at Dodger. "I trust it's easy for you to portray the skimmer life."

Dodger sighed. "What is that supposed to mean?"

"Flitting page to page." Lucius shrugged. "Seems the same as any tourist. Travel Guild or no."

Dodger took a breath and said calmly, "I can't keep apologizing for the past." He locked eyes with Lucius. "I didn't leave you or Nicked or even Kerus on purpose, and you know that. It was dumb luck that Larrakane inked me."

Lucius' eyes widened and he gave a sharp laugh. "I don't want an apology, you sunbaked swan. I want more from you." He bared his teeth with a low rumble. "You were the best of us. Still are, by the blessed tales I always hear from Nicked. But you're working for, nay *leading* people who are sitting back and letting the Empire repeat history all over again."

"The Guild isn't doing that." Dodger waved his paw dismissively.

Lucius poked Dodger in the shoulder. "No? Then where are they? Are you their one-smilodon army?"

Dodger got up slowly, standing square with Lucius. "What makes you think the Guild *isn't* working against the Empire? We've tried. I've tried countless times in countless ways, and even though we keep getting pushed out by this Emperor or that, we still push forward. You've seen the changes we've made where we can. You've seen the families who have a path now outside of Roma because of the work we do. Don't pretend because we haven't toppled the empire that it's not teetering with our help." He took another calming breath and said in measured tones, "The truth of the matter is you're mad at me, not the Guild. But I'm not your enemy, Lucius. I don't have to be your friend, but please, let go of your hate. We *can* achieve something working together if you can get that far."

Lucius frowned and swiped at his whiskers. He took a step back and leaned against the wall. "I don't hate you, Marcius. Oh, I've been furious at you. Especially when you didn't come back to retrieve my sorry behind away from Roma Valar." Lucius sighed. "But eventually I realized if you could, you would've."

"I regret that I couldn't. It took years to control my ability. But I showed up." Dodger gripped Lucius's shoulder and brought him closer. "I care about Kerus. I care about the people here and in Roma. With or without the Guild, I'll always fight for you."

Tilting his head side to side, Lucius eyed Dodger and then Fiona in equal measure. He relaxed back onto the wall. "I suppose that's sand in my eyes then."

Dodger smiled. "If you wagered coin with Nicked, then I'll cover the loss."

"Think she'll take apples like old times?" Lucius said, scratching the back of his head with his paw.

"More expensive ones, yes." Dodger nodded.

Fiona let loose a quiet sigh, watching the pair. If that's what went for apologies between them, she was happy to see it. Even if she didn't quite understand it.

The ship jerked and they all tumbled in the storage chamber, slamming into the wooden walls. A frantic shout from above made them scramble to regain balance and leave the hold. Through the rowing space and up the steps they ran until they were stomping the deck. On the horizon another longship sailed out of the light fog, moving straight for them with rust-and-corn-silk banners waving in the fast-increasing wind. Capped behind them like a choir of muses in the short distance loomed stone statues: the Oracles of the Stars. They blocked the sun, shadowing the cold seas and both ships. Fiona and Dodger were close to their destination, but the Romas were closer.

The sea churned violently, whipped into a frenzy by powerful winds. Unnatural dark storm clouds gathered overhead, occasionally pierced by forks of lightning that illuminated the waters and unveiled two more approaching Roma ships behind the front-runner.

The longship tried to pull up beside Lucius's ship, but he shouted commands to the crew. Before Fiona could understand, they had turned to skirt the first ship. She clung to the wooden rail, cold seawater spraying across her and soaking her from head to toe.

"They're going to come fighting," Lucius cried out.

I suppose our cover story wasn't going to work after all. Fiona fell hard on her back against the deck as the ship lurched, fighting against the sea. Pain blossomed quickly, but it had the helpful effect of making her ignore the increasing cold.

Dodger grabbed her by the arm and helped her right herself. "If we get caught by the Romas now, we'll never make it to the Oracles."

She suspected her slingshot wouldn't do much in the fight. "I doubt the Roma will listen to reason unfortunately." The front ship had gotten close to them again. The ships behind it had broken the line and were surrounding theirs.

"Get the skiff!" Lucius yelled to them. "Before they board."

"We can't just leave you," Dodger said. "We can at least be captured—"

"Don't be an idiot," Lucius said. "I expect you to find a way to retrieve us when you get back to that stately headquarters of yours. Now go!"

Lucius's crew steadied spears and weapons of their own. They had no illusions as to what was happening or how it could end. Across the narrowing gap between the ships, the Romas gripped their swords, adjusted helmets or shields. They waited, ready.

Fiona tugged on Dodger's arm. The island wasn't very far, but it wasn't the distance that worried her. It was the sea. Still, turners had been trained to survive in the Shimmering Depths. How bad could one suddenly angry sea be? "It's our only chance."

They ran toward the other side of the ship, where Dodger quickly helped her into one of the small tethered boats. He untied the rope and dove into the boat, landing on his feet. Fiona grabbed the oars and began rowing through the water. With the waves beating against them she thought it much quicker to go with the churning sea. Perhaps by its momentum and their oars they could thread themselves through the fighting. With Dodger adding his oar to the water, they picked up a small boost of speed.

Grappling hooks flew over them and landed on the longship. Fiona ducked so as not to be accidentally hit. With telling experience the Roma ship began to pull itself closer to the Lucius vessel. They rowed hard making their way unnoticed toward the edge of the fog. If they could get deeper into it, they would disappear while the others were fighting. The boat began to push into the opaque mist.

As if in answer to her thought, a grappling hook flew through the gray clouds and clattered into the skiff. It tightened and began pulling them out of the fog back toward one of the Roma ships. Dodger dropped his oar in the boat and with haste drew his dagger and sawed at the rope. Fiona tried to keep the boat moving away from the empire ships but it was as if she was pounding against a jammed stone door.

"What I wouldn't give for a little faekin ingenuity," she muttered.

Dodger tugged the cut rope, and it sailed into the water. "Gaili's spoiling you. A little knife work is all we needed." He grabbed his oar and began rowing again.

Red-plumed arrows shot through the fog toward them. The cover of the fog made it difficult to see the direction. They ducked and Fiona threw her heavy cloak hood up, its briny smell overwhelming her nostrils. Larrakane help her not be struck by a lucky arrow. The sounds of clashing metal grew distant as they rowed in the roiling sea toward land.

Hazy shapes growing closer told them they'd made it to the small island. They beached the skiff and dragged themselves out of the boat and onto the shores of the Oracles. They made a run directly to the base of the towering statues. Soaked and tired, Dodger flung himself toward a small stone door. It wouldn't open.

He pushed against it again with Fiona doing her best to help. It budged enough for Fiona to slip her thin body through. She tugged on Dodger's arm, helping him in, cloak scrunched around his body as it was. As soon as they made it inside, they pushed against the door, shutting it. Darkness with a side of damp silence muffled their senses, so different was it from the noises outside. There was room enough to stand, although not much more than that.

"What is this?" Fiona whispered.

"Entrance to the tombs," Dodger said. "Royalty used to be buried here."

Fiona shrugged off her soaked cloak. "Can we go farther in?" She retightened her scarf around her neck, thankful it was still there.

Dodger nodded and grabbed her hand, leading her from the small entrance into what felt like narrow carved tunnels. There was no light for Fiona, so she relied upon Dodger's eyes and the feel of the walls to keep her steps sure. They both silently agreed not to light a lantern and make themselves known.

"Why are the Roma so intent on this place?" Fiona whispered. "Either they're working with the Painted Edge or know something we don't."

"Nicked mentioned rumors about a pagemark here. Do you know where it might go?"

"I'm good with standard pagemarks but unfortunately terrible without a map. Nicked said there were Travel Guild jackets interested too though." But that made no sense. Why a heavy Roma presence and jackets? It still wasn't evidence against the Binder, but surely he had to have ordered the jackets here and then away to let the Romas in.

"The Guild jackets confuse me too," Dodger said quietly. "But we'll need to learn more. How do we know if this place *is* the keystone for Kerus?"

Fiona wrinkled her nose, the pervading dust making her want to sneeze. "If it is, the Guardian will be here. He's in hibernation, and based on experience, that likely means he's within the keystone. The others have been." Though Richard left his after a century, it was still under his control. "A worse way of telling would be Painted Edge agents."

Small scratching sounds echoed from the darkened corridor in front of them. They stopped and quieted down. Fiona strained to hear more, but it didn't repeat itself. Dodger tugged on her hand and took a few more steps, but the scratching noise came again. To Fiona it sounded distinctly like a small cry. She squeezed Dodger's hand and pushed him forward without words. He squeezed back and they went slowly and silently through the corridor.

At an unexpected arch in the passageway there was another corridor. Flickering amber torches dotting the walls lit this widened path. Dodger glanced back at Fiona, and she nodded, indicating they should take it. With light steps they walked, keeping eyes open and mouths shut. On the wall, etched carvings decorated the rough stone from floor to ceiling. Beastfolk of each type were depicted, one after another. The carvings repeated in various styles, some with smaller creatures looking up or surrounding larger robed beastfolk. It dawned on Fiona that these were the Oracles of the Stars. She faintly recognized Venus and Vixen as the celestial twins from Vinicia's apartment. But of all the previously worshipped deities, one seemed to be the most prominent: an ursidon. As they moved closer toward the end of the corridor, the bear grew in size, becoming the focus of the carving's stories.

The scratching sound interrupted Fiona's thoughts, closer now. Torches kept the area lit but gave off no heat. More modern implements then. Which meant that people had been within the statues recently. Dodger waved at her and motioned toward an upcoming branching path. He quickened his steps to the right and Fiona followed, the carved story quickly forgotten. They had encountered no one else so far. Luck or something else?

At the end of the short branch they entered a somewhat narrow room. Quickly they divided, backs against separate walls, and surveyed the area. Wooden chests with old metal fittings sat in one corner, but a large stone casket took up the focal point in the center of the room. The dusty floor was scattered with boot- and footprints alike. Fiona pointed to the floor and Dodger nodded with understanding. The scratching noise emanated again. This time it was clear it was coming from the casket.

Dodger held up a hand to Fiona and motioned to his eyes. She nodded and turned so she could watch the entrance and Dodger. Quickly he leapt toward the casket and tried to open the lid, but it didn't budge. It was clearly as heavy as it looked.

Fiona reached into the black leather pocket of her scarf, thought of her crowbar, and pulled it out once it appeared beneath her fingers. She tossed it to Dodger, who caught it deftly. With the extra leverage the lid raised a bit, and he shoved it farther ajar. He stilled, hands dropped to his side.

Fiona quickly came around to see what stunned Dodger so. Inside was Vinicia, shivering and in the throes of turner sickness. She was splotchy in color with bright-blue swirls dotting her furry reddish-brown face. Angry red swaths of skin, like blazing fire, covered her arms. Dark rocky patches covered her knuckles. She was bound in black manacles. Fiona blanched at the sight of them: Painted Edge turn stoppers.

"No. Run," Vinicia whispered.

Too late. Loud footsteps stormed down the corridor as if awaiting some silent command. Fiona frantically looked around for an escape, but there was only one way in or out of the room. Romas swarmed into the small space, swords gleaming in their hands. But at their back were official jacket-clad Guild agents. Fiona paused, trying to find a solution to the confusing scene.

Dodger shouted toward the jackets, "Hold them back."

The jackets grinned and pushed into the room, ignoring him. Dodger tried again to command his fellow agents, but it was rapidly apparent whosever orders they took, they weren't aligned with his. Without a way out and no time to turn the page, they were quickly apprehended and clasped in their own turn stoppers.

They dragged all three of them out of the room and through the tomb. The turn stoppers felt heavy on her wrists. Fiona gritted her teeth against the overwhelming power of the manacles. She couldn't feel the Book. Couldn't sense the thrum that kept her aligned to Spine. She was completely cut off once again. It seemed to sap her of her strength, but she pushed against the terribly familiar feeling to stay awake. To notice anything that would gain her insight into the trap they had walked into or where they were going.

Through a different corridor they took the opposite wider branch that could accommodate all of them and went straight into a spacious chamber. Its rounded ceiling reminded her of the temple to Larrakane on Spine. In the center of the room, surrounded by a smattering of benches and a shimmering translucent sapphire wall, was a sleeping bear on a pile of pillows, blankets, and rugs. Roma guards stood around the golden walls, looking outward on alert. As they were led through the room, Fiona realized the bear was the very depiction of the last oracle, brown furred and larger than any ursidon she had ever seen. Though he was swathed in robes and flat on his back, she was sure: he was the Kerus Guardian. The Oracle of Stars was the keystone, and they had gotten there but to their own detriment. They still weren't ahead of the Painted Edge.

Upset, Fiona pushed against her overly smug captor and made a direct line for the twinkling wall. Frosty glass met her pounding fists. She used the tattered remains of her strength striking the ice wall, yelling at the Guardian to wake up. To notice them. He didn't move. All her fight ended in dull silence through the barrier.

Rough hands grabbed her and dragged her away toward the exit. They scoffed at her, "He won't wake for a long while yet."

The Romas and jackets pulled their captives out of the tombs and loaded them onto separate longships. To go where, Fiona doubted even Larrakane knew.

FIONA TRIED TO STAY awake as the vessel sailed at breakneck speed across the water, but soon she succumbed to the nausea and drowsiness of feeling utterly cut off from the Book with the potent turn stoppers around her wrists.

Waking up on a cold stone floor, Fiona took a few minutes to adjust to the dim rocky-walled interior she was in. Metered light flickered from a small slit high in the wall. It was blocked on and off and on again. Someone was pacing in front of it. They could probably hear her if she yelled, but until she knew where she was, she threw away that idea. Any ally wouldn't have put her in a cell.

There was a solid door with an iron-barred window on one wall, but she couldn't see much outside of it from this angle. Simply more of the same rocky wall. Where was she? And the others?

There was a coldness about the place but not within the air. Her clothes were fairly dry, meaning she had been here for some hours.

Fiona rubbed her wrists where the heavy turn stoppers had chafed her brown skin an angry red. Thinner manacles kept her bound. Less potent, so that was encouraging at least. But something sharp within tugged at her skin when she moved.

She stumbled to the little light that poured into the chamber and peered at the turn stoppers. These were Travel Guild issued. She had seen them enough for a lifetime to recognize them even in dim light.

Fiona raised her hands above her head, looking at them from every angle possible. There was a small fastener that was bent at an odd angle. With enough pressure against the rocky wall, she could pop them open and be on her way. Her scarf was gone, so there was no getting anywhere besides Spine. Where she would end up, she hadn't the slightest clue. But there, in her home of homes, would be reinforcements. The room was snug but enough to turn the page in by herself if she wanted to live dangerously.

But why would they switch her manacles at all? Fiona bit her lip, moving away from the light. By switching manacles, they had allowed her to wake up, which didn't make sense to Fiona. She glanced at the cuffs. The Painted Edge had custom-made weapons and equipment. Surely someone would've noticed the bent fastener on such an important prisoner. Did they want her to wake up? To find the flaw in her bonds and flee?

She sighed and shook her head. No, there was no way they put that much effort into tricking her. Right? Fiona stayed very still, trying to listen to her surroundings. Small scratches lingered in the darkened corridor. Heavy footfalls stepped by high above. She picked up slippered feet, moving toward the cell door. There was no handle. How did they get her in? Cautiously she touched it, but it was solid and cold.

"Dodger," she whispered. "Vinicia."

No one replied. Where were Dodger and Vinicia housed? Wherever they were, she was apart from them. Well, if this was a trap to get her to escape without them, she wasn't falling for it. Better to stay and gather as much information as possible, find her friends, and then run. If things got too hot, she would break the turn stoppers then.

With a deep breath, she yelled loudly, "Hello. I'm quite ready to talk if you are."

Silence.

"You can keep me captive forever, clearly, but don't expect me to stay quiet."

No answer.

"At the very least let's discuss what you want so I can tell you no to your face."

A door clicked from farther down the passage and torchlight washed through from the outside. Similar iron-barred doors in the distance were grouped together. Hers seemed to be the only one in solitude.

A hulking elephas Roma guard came lumbering into the small corridor. "Good, you're awake."

Fiona raised an eyebrow. They had waited for her to wake up. That didn't bode well. "Where am I?" Disas wasn't known to have Roma holdings. And the middle continent was split between the two cultures. The doorway flickered with people moving back and forth in heavy armor. "Is this Roma Valar?" Had they really traveled back to Siamor already?

The Roma pulled out a crank wheel on the wall, ignoring her. The door began to rise.

Fiona took a step back. She had wanted an audience, yes, but if they we going to take her out of here, it probably wasn't to somewhere nicer. She had no blotter thoughts that she could take this Roma, or any of them for that matter. But perhaps she could reason. "Take me to your captain. I have valuable information to share."

The guard grabbed her arm, pulling her forward beyond the gate and into the corridor. Many heavy footsteps echoed as they strode past the doorway and into a larger chamber with cells lining each wall. Wooden doors with small barred windows capped each one. Fiona tried to peer into them as they passed, but she didn't see Dodger or Vinicia among the snowy-white ursidon. The crew of Lucius's ship filled the chambers. She glanced at Lucius in the last chamber. He gave her a curt nod, but no more could be said between them before she was pulled up a flight of short stone steps.

They passed through a narrow passage with a staffed guardroom. After a quick word, the heavy iron-banded door was opened and the guard dragged Fiona into a small strip of gardens. Though there seemed to be no one around, she felt seen as they stepped inside another building, this one decorated in rich, colorful mosaics: the palace proper.

Before Fiona could ascertain any escape routes, she was pulled into an enormous audience chamber. Marble pillars divided murmuring toga-clad citizens on tiered seating who watched the central floor from high above. At the head of the chamber, a raised dais held a large wooden settee, plump pillows, and silver trays on small wooden stools. Every corner, every wall held a Roma soldier. There was nowhere to run.

In front of the large dais, kneeling on the ground, were Dodger and Vinicia. Fiona sagged against the guard at the sight of them. Though they, too, were shackled, they seemed awake and tense—a good sign that they also had their turn stoppers switched.

The guard pulled Fiona to the front of the empty dais and pushed her down to the ground. "Kneel."

She bit back a retort of how thrilled she was to finally know he could speak. This was not the right crowd for that to go over well or gain her any edge. She quickly kneeled, dipping her head and whispering, "Are you two alright?"

"Yes," Dodger said, barely moving his lips. "Stay calm and as emotionless as possible."

She frowned. "What happens if I don't?"

"The Emperor will throw you in the pits." Vinicia shook involuntarily. Her patchy skin glistened with sweat, but she kept herself stiffly upright. "He's hated humans ever since the Val'ere romas were unable to capture Rise after the Inking."

They needed to get Vinicia back to Spine immediately. Bits of the Book were pressing in on her dearly. The rocky stone of Cobbles had covered both her hands now. There weren't many records about what happened to a page turner after the sickness grew to encompass the whole body and went from the elemental chapter to the mortal one. No one had ever survived that long.

Fiona's gaze darted quickly about the room. Attendants picked up the silver trays and idled near the dais but didn't move from it. Servants passed golden trays through the room. There was a waiting, bubbling atmosphere. It made Fiona's skin crawl at the thought that they were the center of attention. Or what would be done with them. "We have to get out of here. The Guardian. The Romas and the Painted Edge are holding them."

"And the Guild," Vinicia said darkly. "The jackets that have betrayed us don't do so on their own."

"Jackets don't betray each other," Dodger spit out.

"I saw *them*. And the cold they used," said Vinicia.

"The cold?" Fiona asked.

"There was frost on the boat. The water turned to ice, pushing us to Siamor," Vinicia said.

"It's how we got here so fast. I can't believe he would—" Dodger took a deep breath. "Perhaps you were right, Fi."

Thoughts tumbled in Fiona's mind and she said quickly, "Who is the leader of the Painted Edge?"

"I don't know," Vinicia whispered, voice choking. "I wish I did."

Fiona rocked back on her heels, dumbfounded. They'd had so much hope for confirmation from Vinicia. A definitive answer to the weaver of threads. How did she not know? With all the other evidence in play, it had to be the Binder. None of the other suspects fit. But still, a thought nipped at her. She glanced at Dodger's hardened face. "I—"

The sound of blasting trumpets erupted in the room. The murmuring of people watching the three prisoners rose into a shout of cheers as a tall, well-built smilodon panther with a laurel wreath circlet on his head emerged from the top of the stairs. He waved to the crowd with a beaming grin, holding his clean cream toga aloft. Several servants and attendants followed quickly after him and draped the bulk of his toga behind him as he lay to lounge on the dais. He ignored the prisoners and snapped his paws. A servant rushed forward with a large, unwieldly scroll.

Additional Roma guards filed into the chamber and took up stations near the exits. So this was to be a quick conversation then.

"Citizens of Roma Valar, I entreat thee," the Emperor started. He waved a hand toward the prisoners. "These page turner spies have come to steal our most sacred treasure. Our civility and our honor."

The crowd erupted in jeers and insults toward the group.

"Along with those acts of a most grievous nature, this group of spies has unlawfully seized property of dutiful citizens such as yourselves. They have coerced innocents, endangered and assaulted good citizens of Roma Mikar and Roma Nymar, and conspired against the empire. For this, we sentence them to trial by combat."

An explosion of cheers almost drowned out Dodger's cursed exclamation. He kept his head down, but Fiona felt and agreed with his anger. Ridiculous charges indeed. But how to get out of them?

Vinicia's head whipped up, her mottled cheeks puffed from exertion. "We have done nothing wrong. We are citizens of Spine and can't be held here."

Guards rushed toward them and pulled Vinicia to her feet. The Emperor raised his hand and tilted his head as if assessing her words. The guards seemed confused. Fiona noticed their hesitation. Would Vinicia's words really work?

"Are you suggesting you should be handed over to the Travel Guild for your crimes?" the Emperor said as if reading a line from a play. He chuckled.

"I am." Vinicia held her chin up high.

"Very well." He clapped his hands. The guards dropped Vinicia but didn't step back, looking at each other but quickly smoothing out their expressions into complacency.

Something was off. This was not how Fiona had heard the Emperor acted. Throwing them into the pits or forcing them into combat seemed more likely than a tête-à-tête. And to simply hand them over to the Travel Guild? The Empire for all intents hated the Travel Guild. Why would he do this?

Fiona's questions were soon answered as Guild jackets appeared. Two of them were the small jubatas smilodon from the House of Falchus. Oh, they were dressed in the right uniform but they were unmistakably the same smilodon women. They darted away from Vinicia, shielding their faces, to grab Fiona and Dodger. One jerked Fiona to her feet and pulled her away from the others. All three were separated quickly.

Fiona's legs locked up and she darted a glance at the quickly dispersing guards. They couldn't go with them. Couldn't be separated. These were Painted Edge through and through. This entire judgment was a farce. A show of the Emperor and a show from the Painted Edge that the Travel Guild was in alliance with the Empire. A show that was needed by them, but why?

If there was one thing Fiona understood, it was that a spectacle always made time stand still. She called out, "Emperor! I believe you have gotten it wrong."

The crowd stilled—Fiona was sure some in astonishment and some in anticipation. She would've certainly been the latter. She carried on before someone realized what she was saying: "We did not come to steal your most sacred treasure or what have you. We came to free it! Free it from the tyranny of the Travel Guild."

The Emperor scoffed. "What have the Travel Guild over us?"

"Even now you're ready to send us to the Guild to be dealt with rather than the combat ring. You would let them choose how Roma punishes spies?"

The room took a collective breath. Then the crowd began loudly talking among themselves. They were no longer leaving the chamber.

"Fiona, what are you doing?" Dodger whispered.

"Making a mess. Trust me."

The crowd began arguing and pointing at the prisoners.

The Emperor looked around and held up a hand for silence. He said loudly, "I fear not the Guild's overimposition."

"You should," Fiona said at a lower volume. She took a hesitant step forward. She wanted the Emperor to hear what she said as if it was just for him. "For the Binder sees you as a loose end that must be snipped to achieve his goals. Why else would they send us? A Gilded leader, a jacket spy, and their consulting investigator? Naught but to free this nation of Roma for themselves. But if you release us, we can make him pay."

The Emperor raised an eyebrow and smirked. "Do your best."

It was not the reaction Fiona expected. Most leaders saw the Guild and the Binder as a threat to their power. The Emperor not so much. Either he was foolhardy and thought himself more powerful than the hidden leader, or he was sure of something else.

"He's already done it," Fiona continued. "Or have you not heard about Rise being subjugated by him? Even now Travel Guild jackets flock from pagemark to pagemark and run the palace." Half truth, half lie, but gossip spread quickly enough that even the Emperor must've heard about the increased measure of jackets by now. "A pity you could not do it first."

His eyes grew wide. "See here, human, I don't need the pittance of your page any longer." He marched down from the dais and stood next to the guard holding Fiona. "For soon I shall have my choice of pages. And I will see yours subjugated to a lower status. The rose of opportunity blooms but once, and I will seize it here and now." Looking out to the crowd, he raised his voice again: "For Roma!"

"For Roma," the crowd shouted.

The guards tugged on the captives as the Emperor marched out of the room. Dodger and Vinicia struggled, but Fiona didn't fight back. The Emperor was sure of himself, despite what she had said and what could be proven about the Binder. Why? Her thoughts churned like sunbeams, trying to coalesce into a ray. She squinted at a half-torn memory. This was wrong. What she thought was wrong. She needed a moment of focus and lapsed into silence as the Painted Edge member disguised as a jacket led them from the chamber.

"Fi," Dodger said.

She shook her head and slid a glance at their captors. Dodger quieted as they were taken into a surprising room. It was a small but formal library. A large stone table resided in the middle with a stone bench on one side. Shelves lined the walls except where the doors stood, one they entered and the other opposite them. There were scant books on the shelves but some scrolls stacked up. This was more for greeting guests than lounging. Odd that they weren't taken to a holding station. The jubatas closed them into the room before leaving a couple of guards at the arched wooden door. Where would they be taking them after this?

"It's not right," Fiona whispered quickly. "What he said. *The rose of opportunity.*" That wasn't the first time she had heard those words. Nor poetic phrases in general. The messages of the Painted Edge followed the same flow as well. "Was there a second message, in Mikar?"

Vinicia took a small breath and nodded. "It was waiting for us at the trading site. *Seek out fellow kin who still in the bright of the day and hold the key to our relief. Make haste. Our journey's end awaits.*"

Fiona wrinkled her nose. It sounded like the Oracle of Stars monument alright. "But you thought it was suspicious?"

"Yes, the Painted Edge members didn't seem confused at the message. Normally when there's a notice, the group spends time working on deciphering it. But they all seemed to know. I didn't want to let them know I didn't, so I played along. As soon as I could, I snuck away with the help of an informant and went to my brothers. But I knew if I could convince the Painted Edge well enough, I'd get more information, so I returned. Is my brother safe?"

"He's alright," Dodger said, "on guard and protected."

Vinicia's shoulders relaxed a bit. "That's good."

"But you don't know who the leader is? We were told you had gotten closer to valuable information. What was it?" Dodger said.

Vinicia frowned. "I don't know. I didn't know anything of value until I got to Roma Mikar. Shortly after I returned from my brother's, they trapped me with turn stoppers."

Had the Binder set this all up? Why? He couldn't have known Vinicia was compromised, but perhaps it was never truly about getting information from the smilodon. Perhaps he wanted to get them out of Spine. Or to ensnare someone he thought would leap at an information leak within the Painted Edge. That had to be it. "I think we've all been bait. Good bait at that." Fiona shook her head.

"What do you mean?" Dodger said.

"I mean the Binder wanted to let the other leaders think the Painted Edge was about to be unmasked. To lure the real culprit into the light." It was not him. She tugged her manacled hands, wishing she could rip them apart. "Going after Vinicia was a clear goal for that person. If Vinicia had valuable information, confirmation about who they were, they couldn't let that get back to the Travel Guild. Unfortunately, they played their hand too far this time. The ice, the wall around the Guardian, everything had to have been from the Winter Crown. Displays for us, Dodger, so we would think it was the Binder. Because we're the only ones who know who he truly is." Only someone with a monumental grudge against the Binder would try the same trick twice. Someone who knew Stella. A page turner who hated being one. Who couldn't even enjoy the impact they were having because they were bound to stay in Spine. Of all the Leaves of Spine, only one came to mind. "It was Dani. The ochre fae."

His whiskers twitched. "You're positive?"

"Yes." Dani first told Fiona about the rose of opportunity. Her lyrical nature seeped out when she was acting with a clear mind. Fiona had suspected that the young chaotic persona and the poised woman she switched between were a ruse. It was clear she hated the Binder with every action she made. But did she curse him because of their lives in Copper or because of the Inking? Was it the past of the Seasons coming to play in the present or something more? There was only one person in this palace who might actually have valuable information to use against her. "We need to make things right. Quickly." She looked at Vinicia. "And get you back to Spine."

Dodger leaned closer. "What's your plan?"

"Think you can take them?" Fiona mouthed and inclined her head at the two guards outside the door.

He raised an eyebrow but nodded.

Vinicia bared her teeth in agreement.

Fiona pressed her turn stoppers into the hard stone bench. She tried to push down to snap the small fastener that was bent at an odd angle. Moving to the edge of the bench, she wedged the corner of it against the fastener. It popped, releasing the cuffs on her wrist. She caught them before they clattered to the floor. Her skin tingled where they had lain, her full connection to the Book restored. Odd how the Guild turn stoppers barely subdued her abilities. Another thing to think about later. She pushed the thought away and approached the door.

"Get on the ground," Fiona whispered to Vinicia.

Without question Vinicia slumped to the floor, eyes closed.

Fiona put as much overwrought emotion as she could into her voice and shouted through the bars, "Please, help. She's fallen unconscious."

Heads swiveled and looked through the grate. One of the guards cursed and opened the door.

Fiona turned away from the guards toward Dodger and Vinicia with expectation. The guard didn't disappoint, walking past Fiona to kneel and check Vinicia's neck.

Dodger jumped up and threw his manacled arms around the guard, toppling him with the unexpected attack. Vinicia quickly pulled off the guard's helmet and hit him square in the jaw, her rocky hands resounding with the impact of a stone wall.

The other Roma guard tramped into the room at the noise. He tried to pull out his sword, but Fiona grabbed the hilt as well. Surprised by her unbounded reach, the guard faltered for a second, which was enough for her to distract him as Dodger kicked at his leg, which buckled.

Fiona fell back out of the way of the guard as he withdrew his sword fully. He swung it and his body around to slice deftly at Dodger, but Dodger fell prone to the floor, out of the way. With a pained grunt Vinicia slammed into the guard, knocking him down. Fiona kicked at his hand, forcing him to release the sword, which clattered to the stone. Shooting pain ricocheted up her foot and leg and she hobbled back.

With quickness Dodger removed the guard's helmet and knocked him out with it. He huffed, catching his breath. "That could've gone easier."

Closing the door, Fiona leaned against it, flexing her pained foot. "Hurry, Dodger, you change into their outer armor. We need to get back to the Emperor." He was sure to know what was going on. She picked up the keys from one of the guards and unlocked Dodger's manacles.

"How are we going to do that?" Vinicia's chest rose and fell heavily.

Fiona unclasped Vinicia's cuffs. "Not we. Us. You need to turn the page back to Spine."

The cougar shook her head. "No, you can't get past the Painted Edge without me. I will not leave. I just need a moment." She turned away and began putting on the outer armor of one of the guards.

"There's no way we're getting in front of the Emperor again. Too many soldiers," Dodger said, doing the same.

"Then we'll have to make a bigger distraction to take them away," Fiona said. She helped Vinicia dress, using the guard's tunic to cover her burning arms. She didn't say anything more about her leaving. The smilodon was bound to see things through. Fiona couldn't fault her for that.

Manacling the unconscious guards and taking their swords, Fiona put her broken cuffs back on her wrists and close to her chest. Though they touched her, without completing the clasps she remained tethered to her page turning ability. A small relief.

THEY HURRIED FROM THE room, closing the door behind them. With whispered conversation, Fiona suggesting their new plan, they walked down the passageway back toward the dungeon cells. They had all been pulled from the same area and, with a confident Dodger in the lead, found their way back to the strip of garden. As they reached the iron-banded entrance to the dungeons, two familiar smilodons ran up behind them: the Painted Edge jubatas.

"Where are you taking her?" one said in a lilting tone.

Dodger deepened his voice. "Emperor wants her back in the prison. He said you should take the other two with you."

They glanced at each other before the tall cougar stepped forward imposingly. "We don't answer to the Emperor." She held out her hand. "Give her to us. Now."

Vinicia spoke up, her voice smooth and confidant. "Seek only the end, not the peril."

The cougar squinted, but after a moment dropped her hands. "Always sending backup," she muttered. With a sigh she fell back and waved them on. "Right then."

As soon as they were out of sight of the steps, the trio picked up their pace.

"They are going to find us gone as soon as they get to the room," Dodger said.

"Yes, but their confusion will buy us some time. Those two never were easy." Vinicia coughed but said, "Feels good to pull one over on them."

With their Roma disguises, Vinicia and Dodger walked through the doorway and down the passage into the main prison without a question from the few other guards around. Fiona whispered directions to Dodger, and soon they were in front of Lucius's cell. Dodger pulled the keys from his tunic and unlocked the cell. Vinicia cranked it open with the lever. Without a change of stance Dodger slid the keys to Fiona as she walked in.

Lucius looked up, eyes wide at Fiona. "Got yourself right back here, did you?"

"Only with a little help." Fiona smiled. The door shut behind her but without the telltale click of being locked again. She moved away from it and lowered her voice. "Do you think you can handle a jailbreak?" She showed him the keys before putting them in to his hands.

"Always could. Easier with the help though." Lucius grinned. "What are you planning?"

"Those two *guards* and I are going to find the Emperor. Talk to him about what's going on."

Lucius looked over her shoulder and raised an eyebrow at Dodger's disguise. "I'm never going to let him live that one down." He stood up taller. "Right. And you need a distraction." He wiped his whiskers. "Leave it to me. Besides my crew, there are a lot of folks here itching to return home. Don't think it'll be much of an issue to convince them they can leave with me."

"Alright then." Fiona traipsed back to the door and began beating on it. "Let me out of here. I know my rights as a member of the Guild."

Vinicia and Dodger strode to the other guards and pointed toward her cell as planned. They waved them up the stone stairs, momentarily removing them from the chamber.

Fiona opened the cell door, and an unbound Lucius sprang out toward the next cell, unlocking it. He quickly began to crank it open as Fiona mirrored him at another door with another set of keys. Within moments they had a few open, Lucius's crew free and making short work of the remaining cells. Others went straight for the chests at the back of the room to retrieve their weapons and gear. Fiona darted back and dug through the chests to find her own equipment. Finding her bright scarf, she wrapped it comfortingly around her waist and tied it tightly. Fiona slipped her slingshot in hand in case it was necessary. She hoped to Larrakane it wasn't.

Minutes passed in a flurry of activity. As the Roma guards tramped back into the room with Dodger and Vinicia successfully unmasked and momentarily captured, they stopped upon seeing so many open doors and free prisoners.

Like cascading waves, the two groups crashed against one another. The ursidon raised spears and makeshift shields, pushing at the guards as Fiona skirted the fight to join Dodger and Vinicia. With unmatched momentum the guards were pushed into cells, doors pulled down and locked.

"We'll get the other dungeons open and swarm through the palace." Lucius threw keys to one of the ursidon, who strode away.

"Out of it," Dodger said shortly.

"Sand in your ears?" Lucius said. "Of course. We'll hold the door open as long as we can, but the crew comes first."

"Understood," Dodger said.

With a rallying yell, Lucius commanded his crew toward the oncoming guards. Shouting and the clang of metal grew louder as the trio ran in the opposite direction. Dodger led through passageways of gawking servants and running soldiers. When a guard tried to stop them, he convincingly ordered them to subdue the riot without breaking stride. He seemed to know exactly where he was going. How often did Dodger pour over insider information about the palace and the Empire? Enough for Fiona to understand while he had not planned this moment, he may have thought about confronting emperors many times in his life.

Dodger pulled them toward a bedroom that could fit half a dozen or so of Vinicia's apartments within. It was deserted save for one guard, whom Dodger commanded to the dungeons, stating he would take over watch of the Emperor. As the guard darted off, Fiona rounded the corner and entered after Vinicia.

Boisterous singing wove toward them from a deeper chamber. Humidity clung to the air as they strode purposefully, entering the bath of the Emperor. Unrobed and lathered in soap, he was far from the smilodon who had just put on quite a performance. In a bronze basin large enough to fit three of him, he lounged, singing loudly and off key. The steam from the water rising up made the room hazy.

Fiona cleared her throat.

The singing cut off abruptly. "What are you two doing here? And with that human?" His eyes widened. "Guards!"

Vinicia jumped forward as if waiting for the moment. A quick flash of a dagger pressed to his throat, and she growled, "Don't say another word or one of your least favorite generals will be taking your seat in no time."

Dodger said quietly, "No one will be coming to help you for a while."

The panther's eyes darted to each of them, and without any theatrics he shrank, cowering in the tub. "Here, I can give you gold. Will that be enough?"

Fiona reasoned the only way she was going to get answers was to play into knowing what Daniele wanted. She leaned in and said, "It will not be enough. You know what *she* wants."

The Emperor fumbled with his scrubbing stick. "B-but I've already done what she asked."

"Yes, and perfectly adequately." She needed something to get the Emperor saying more than he should. But how? What? "Except for me, of course. You were supposed to keep me separate."

"But that's not what the instructions said! I was supposed to keep you until you thought it was the Binder, and then let you escape."

Of course, so they could rush to the Binder and confront him. What did that buy Dani? Fiona raised an eyebrow. "Are you sure you interpreted them correctly?"

He raised his chin. "Of course."

"If so, then how would I know about our fae acquaintance?"

He wavered but then a knowing look covered his face. "I thought when her usual messenger didn't appear something was amiss, but"—he squinted—"is that you, Seia?"

Who was Seia? Who would be Dani's usual messenger? Thinking quickly, Fiona sniffed, buying herself some time. She tilted her head suggestively. "Wouldn't you like to know."

He grinned. "This form I wouldn't have expected. It's so…pedestrian. Impersonating the investigator?"

Of course, Dani would've sent her right hand: Stella.

Dodger gave her a quizzical look from behind the Emperor, but she ignored it to keep the Emperor focused on her. Fiona adopted a smirk. This was one persona she could certainly lean in to. "I am here to make sure of your loyalty."

"Why is it being called into question?" the Emperor demanded, more assured now that he seemed to know to whom he was speaking.

Vinicia tightened her claws on his shoulders, and he winced.

Fiona tutted. "The closer we get to our goals, the tighter the circle. Now, recite her message to me."

He lowered his voice. "You can find it in my drawers."

"You kept it!" Fiona scowled in a show of mock anger. While relatively stupid on his part, she was glad not to have to interpret his words. "Did you think to use it against her?"

"No, of course not." He bowed his head. "I would never go against her, Seia. You know that."

He was quite scared of Daniele, by the speed at which he relented. What sort of power did she hold over him? Retrieving the message he had tucked so neatly away from the adjoining private study, Fiona read it quickly. It was much less like the ones that she and the others had found. The orders had been meant to confuse those not used to reading such things. Without Stella to deliver messages or command the factions, it seemed Dani needed to be a little more direct.

Those who seek the key come

Stay your eyes on the prophets and capture strays from their robes

When you find the thorn, catch and release only after a captive reunion

Once the tree has fallen, Spine will give way

And the Binder will be too accused to find us

How had she not seen it before? So lyrical a message copied out by multiple hands still came from the same person. What was the tree? How would felling it make Spine give way? Whatever it meant they had to stop it. Spine wouldn't be broken like the other pages. Not if she could help it.

Fiona nodded to Dodger and Vinicia. "We're done here."

Vinicia knocked the Emperor on the head, making him pass out, slumped outside the basin. "I've always wanted to do that," she said and she sheathed her dagger but winced, hand flying to her eye. A rosette of copper encircled it, pushing through the other patches of off coloring.

"Let's hurry," Fiona said quietly.

Dodger led them on a direct run toward the closest exit from the palace he knew of: through the audience chambers. They burst from behind the dais and ran along the high seating until they entered a walled-off open-air garden. Exotic plants and statues of emperors past were surrounded by rows of columns that encircled the garden and directed away from the chamber. Geese squawked loudly among the green at the trio's arrival.

"There's a pagemark outside of the palace, deeper into edges of the city. But there's only one way out from here," Dodger yelled over the noise. He waved them on through the columns, geese sounding the alarm and following on their tail.

A Roma guard appeared on the fringes of their run, as if called, but before he could reach them, he was shoved unmercifully to the ground by Lucius. Surprised, the guard reached for his sword, but Lucius swung his out quicker. Another smilodon jumped from the shadows onto the guard and subdued him.

"You should be long gone from here," Lucius said. He nodded to the smilodon, who began stripping the guard.

"We need to get to the pagemark," Dodger huffed.

Lucius shook his head. "It's going to be crawling with soldiers at this point. The whole city is, normally."

"Escaping out into the streets isn't impossible, right?" Fiona said.

"Depends on your definition but if you can leave right here, right now, it would be the smarter move." He waved his hand, beckoning approaching prisoners.

"Any place in the palace we can turn from?" Fiona looked at Dodger.

He shook his head. "Nothing official. While the open air is good, we need a spot where we won't be interrupted for a few minutes."

Fiona pursed her lips, thinking. "The formal library. It was large enough and I suspect will be closer to the city than anywhere else."

"Why do you think that?" Vinicia asked.

"She wanted us to escape with knowledge of the Binder. What better way than to leave us alone in a big enough space to turn the page back to Spine?" Fiona said. Dani wouldn't think that instead of coming directly back home they'd go after the Emperor for information. She always seemed to think people might look out for themselves first. "It would waste time and keep him in the spotlight if we went directly to confront him." Perhaps she needed time without him in the way. What would she be doing that would turn his gaze on her? "Her directions said something about a tree falling and Spine giving way."

"There are more trees than people in Spine," Dodger said.

"How are we supposed to know which one, or even if it's a real tree?" Fiona said.

"Well, you believe this is a fae, right?" Vinicia said. "In their philosophy a tree is more than simply a tree. It is a spirit or being from their reincarnation cycle."

Fiona gasped. A fae spirit, one specifically connected to trees, could only mean one thing. One person. Nicolosia. "The Elder druid is in danger."

"We'll cover you." Lucius took a stolen helmet from one of his crew and settled it on his head.

"You don't have to do that," Dodger said.

Lucius shrugged. "You can owe me."

With Lucius at the head and some of his crew at the rear of their small party, they made their way back inside toward the front of the palace. The far-off sounds of clanging metal grew closer as they approached the vestibule. Fiona shut the door while Dodger ran to close the other. Vinicia slumped heavily against the stone table, energy seemingly spent.

Lucius and his group surrounded the trio, facing off against the doors with weapons poised.

Dodger grabbed hands with Vinicia and Fiona. "I'll lead."

Fiona squeezed Dodger's hand and stared out toward a shelf, trying not to flinch from the sound of fighting. They needed a few minutes. Dodger just needed to keep focus.

With a shaking hand, Dodger took a step forward as the room around them began to fold away. Trees pushed into the room, obscuring the shelves and stone table. As Spine began to solidify the door to the room burst open. Dozens of people fighting and pushing together, guards and prisoners alike, spilled into the library. Lucius and his group stood their ground toward the oncoming Romas.

Fiona fell into Dodger, smacked hard by the shoulder of a soldier. The vignette shimmered, unstable. Dodger gripped her hand tighter. They didn't have minutes.

"Everyone, focus on Spine together. Now," Fiona commanded. Too many leading a page turn was never a safe bet, but it was all they had to center the connection.

With intensity she thought her previous teachers would be quite proud of her as she gritted her teeth against the rough hands that tried to grasp her and thought of the Thread. The comforting light, the warm atmosphere, and its place in her world. She took a step forward, walking with Vinicia and Dodger toward home.

WITH AN ARCHED CRY in the distance, the grasping hands fell away from her. The trees of Spine encompassed her but not as she had hoped—she was tangled among the limb. Sharp edges of wood dug into her at odd angles. But she was intact. Thank Larrakane for that. She took a shaky breath and called out, "Dodger. Vinicia."

"I'm alright," Dodger called from somewhere far below. There was no sound of Vinicia. The telling sounds of the page snapping closed were also missing. The turn had not gone as expected, but at least it had gone.

Fiona gingerly picked her way out of the branches, the heavy pine scent like a coat covering her hands and arms. She would smell of nothing else for some time. But where was Vinicia? Why wasn't she answering? With careful movements Fiona climbed down from the tree to find the unconscious cougar on the ground. Her breathing was shallow but her reddish fur had already reclaimed much of her face. The page turner sickness was fading. They had gotten her to Spine in time. Fiona sighed with deep relief as if she had been holding her breath for a long time.

Dodger joined Fiona and bent down to gently wake Vinicia. She didn't budge. "She'll need time in the infirmary to recover."

"You need to warn the Binder," Fiona said, wiping her hands. She glanced around, hoping for a sign that they were close to the city. "Gather him, Marcia, and Mac. They'll know what to do."

"What are you going to do?" Dodger carefully hefted a limp Vinicia onto his back.

"Find the Elder druid. If I can get to them before she does, then we may have a chance."

"And if not?"

"Then I'll stop her." *We all have our duties. For better or worse.* That's what Nicolosia had said to her. Her duty was to her friends and the people who couldn't help themselves. The Painted Edge put all of them in danger with their actions. She would see the trouble ended by blocking Daniele.

But it would take hours and hours on foot to get to the druid camp. They weren't close enough to the city to shave off time for her trek. And there was little to waste. She wasn't a druid, but perhaps she could figure out a way to get through the trees as the Elder did. Marcia had even communicated with them once. Maybe they listened to reason?

She jogged toward the edge of the forest, looking for a suitably large tree as she had seen the Elder and Marcia do. Finding one not too far from where they had landed, she placed her hand on its warm, rough exterior. She felt a little foolish but still closed her eyes and concentrated. Inhaling the heady pine scent, she tried to relax and connect. But the sounds of the forest filled her ears, and she took a step back, frustrated. She wasn't one to commune with nature or understand exactly how these things worked. Had the Elder said anything when touching the tree? Had Marcia? She racked her brain trying to remember. *Tell it to Spine.* That's all

Nicolosia had said. Well, she needed Spine now. She placed her hand back on the tree. "I need to find the Elder druid. Please, take me to them."

A bird chirped near her shoulder. Fiona opened her eyes. Another chirped farther off from her. She looked for it and saw it flapping its wings at her. She took a step forward and the birds flew off chirping. With some caution she followed as more birds joined the other. Like a siren in Depths, they led her on and on through the forest. She ran around the bend of a tree but stopped, her mouth dropping open at the sight of a massive evergreen with an open door in it. It was three times the size of the one she had chosen and could possibly fit a small army. Hopefully not at this very moment.

The birds hovered in the doorway and chirped before flying away in different directions. With hesitant steps that quickly turned into an eager stride, Fiona walked into the tree. Two passages branched off, and if she wasn't mistaken, both were tree lined, with leafy canopies for roofs. She glanced around. "Hello?" Her voice echoed before dying away into the passageways. Warm earth and musk were all she smelled. Like an animal who had run around for a bit and was now lying down. It had been one moment and then the next before when traveling with the druid through the tree. She bit her lip and decided the sensible thing to do was try both pathways a little.

She started off in the right passageway, feeling the trees and counting her steps. While there was some flickering light, perhaps the waning sun peeking through the gaps of the trees, it was disappearing rapidly. Was she getting closer to the druid camp or farther away? She should've been more specific. There was no telling what Dani or the Painted Edge were doing.

She blinked and suddenly found herself at a vined wall. That hadn't been there before. She tried to press on it, but it was unmoving.

She turned around, counting her steps hurriedly back to the branching point. It took fewer steps than it should've. How odd. It was as if the passageway had tightened up around her. Was her indecision of where to go what changed the tree? Or was it her thoughts of the Painted Edge?

Fiona ran her hands along the wall, trying to find the doorway. The stacked vines that made up the interior were warm to the touch. Small flowers bloomed on the rough bark walls. Vines wrapped the edges of the floor, rapidly bordering the pathways. As she touched, a feeling of absolute suspicion emanated from the surroundings. It surprised Fiona and yet was vaguely familiar. Her senses tingled with an unasked question: What did she want?

She knew names were powerful and hesitated before saying, "Nicolosia?"

The walls tightened around her. The vines beneath her feet shifted. The flowers bloomed bigger.

She thrust out her hands on the closing walls. "They're in danger. I need to find them and help."

Confusion emanated from within the inner chamber. It was much like Soots when they got emotional, Fiona realized. That inability to hold in their emotions and let it wash over everything in their path. Was this tree, the forest, a Guardian like Soots and Nicolosia? It stood to reason that if Spine was the Elder druid's duty, then this forest-walled city could be more much than simply land.

She called out, "Spine, I am a friend of Nicolosia. I am their protégé. I will not harm them, I promise. But you must allow me passage to them." She rubbed the walls as if soothing the forest. "Please."

The walls quivered, a tense uncertainty. How could Fiona prove it so that Spine would take her quickly? She pulled off her scarf to quickly go through the contents of it, but as she did the circle tattoo on her chest peeked out from her pulled doublet. Perhaps if everything was Larrakane, as the goddess and Raina had said, then her symbol would be proof enough. She pressed opened her doublet and pulled her undershirt to the side. "I am bound to Larrakane under Nicolosia. I wish them no harm." She pressed her circle to the vine. It warmed, not like the pain from writing to Richard, but like an old ache of a past injury.

The vines rapidly receded from her, and the path cleared. Flowers shrunk, and at the edge of her vision Fiona saw light.

"Thank you, Spine," Fiona said, patting the wall.

A feeling of surety emanated from them along with a thread of tiredness. Fiona yawned despite herself—she always seemed to do that in the trees—and walked toward the open door and through it.

Trees edged a line around a plowed field. In the distance a windmill spun as the wind whistled swiftly through the air. Loud crashing of waves from the waterfall to the aqueducts below met the whistle, and together they spun a tune of a soft, bright evening song. The air was cold and crisp, and Fiona shivered as she buttoned up her doublet hastily. It had been so long since she had been up here: a seat above the city of Spine—the Rocky Bluff.

If this was where Spine knew Nicolosia to be, then they were either already with Dani or waiting for her. Fiona hoped desperately it was the latter.

The cold wind pushed against Fiona, and she dug her heels into the ground to keep balance. Was this natural, or was Dani already playing with her? How best to handle this? She was alone, for the moment at least. Strangely, no one seemed to be working the land or milling about, though there should've been dozens of people here.

Dragging out the time would give the other Seasons a chance to get here after learning who had orchestrated everything. Fiona knew she was no match for the Autumn fae, but Mac and the Binder surely had to be. She would not raise suspicions. She had come here to find Nicolosia and so that was what she would do.

Fiona trudged out across the damp field toward the only structure she could see—the windmill. Stalks of wheat lined her path and seemed to overshadow her. It was only her imagination, yes? She hurried through the muddy fields but tripped, falling into the wet mud. It clung to her, and she found she couldn't pull herself out.

"Fiona, I didn't realize you'd be visiting so soon," Dani's strong, poised voice rang out from the windmill. "Pity. I wanted to spare you, but I suppose that was much too hopeful."

The earth of the mud hardened, and Fiona found herself being propelled up by the stalks of wheat until she was facing the windmill, her arms shackled by earth and legs wrapped by food. If it wasn't shocking, she'd be impressed. Fiona struggled against the binds. All in all, she was quite sick of being bound and called out, "Is this how you treat all visitors to the Bluffs? It's a wonder I didn't come up here sooner."

"Only the ones who would try my patience at a time like this," Dani said. "I suppose you came here to try and stop me."

"I came here to find Nicolosia."

"Oh?" Dani said, a bright lilt to her voice. She strode across the field, the ground surging her forward so she was in front of Fiona in a moment. Her hunter-green cloak with a wide cream lace and bronze collar around the neck billowed out behind her. A thin bronze bracelet dangled around her wrist as she flipped her copper hair back over her shoulder. She leaned in. "I don't believe I've seen them yet. They must've gotten tied up somewhere."

A sweet, sickly smell of overripe fruit wafted from Daniele. It was almost intoxicating. "Must have," Fiona said tartly. What in Larrakane's name was she to do? Dani wasn't wearing a crown and still seemed to have more power than Fiona had expected. She needed to monopolize her time until the more powerful Seasons got there. She didn't think there was much point in hiding her thoughts however. "That's quite impressive. I didn't realize you had abilities such as this."

"No one ever does," Dani said quietly, "but through the years this land has become my domain. I keep to the Bluff, the farm, and Depth's Door the same way Arc keeps to his Hinge or Mac to her Thread."

"And Nic to their Forest's Edge," Fiona added.

Dani flinched almost imperceptibly. "Nic was always one to commune with nature. And I to command the crops and change of harvest's bounty to nature's decay."

"Very poetically put," Fiona said.

"Yes, well, I do like words." Dani smiled, and the earth receded as she began to walk away from Fiona.

Fiona needed to keep her in sight. She blurted out, "If it's not too much to ask, I'd love a tour of the Bluff while I'm held captive here."

Dani laughed, tossing her copper hair. "I'm afraid not. I'm in the middle of a hefty undertaking. It takes considerable concentration." Dani waved her hand, forcing the stalks of wheat to propel Fiona higher up in the air. "And you're an unnecessary distraction."

What would make her stop? Her chest tightened, but Fiona pulled on the one name she thought would distract her. "Stella always gave me the time to cause chaos," she said as she rose through the air.

The Autumn fae's smile dropped and she shook her head. "No. *You* don't get to speak her name to me."

"She threw herself into the dark edge. I didn't force her," Fiona shouted.

"She wouldn't have if it wasn't for you and your intrusion into everything!" Dani paced the small dirt path beneath her and muttered, "We are so close and you had to interfere. And for what?" She swallowed and stared at Fiona. "She had such high hope for you. The clever investigator."

"You like clever, don't you?" Fiona baited her. It seemed hard for Daniele to keep up her careful demeanor when passion got in the way.

Dani didn't answer. She turned away, stomping across the sodden field to the open doorway of the windmill. She smoothed her hair down and took a small breath. "I appreciate a good means to an end like any other dedicated individual. But don't be discouraged. You still can be."

The earth and wheat binding Fiona pushed her closer to the windmill. Fiona gritted her teeth and tried to pull out of her bonds as the slowly spinning blades came closer. One hit and she would certainly be knocked out, if not seriously injured. "What are you doing?"

"Simply putting you somewhere safe."

The blades kept spinning, but like a thread through a needle, Dani's power directed her through the window. It was short-lived relief for Fiona. Bare pale tree branches encased her in an odd cage. She stooped in the cramped interior. Pushing on the branches, she expected them to be as weak as they looked, but they held strong.

There was not much in the tower of the windmill besides a large round wooden table in the center of the room. Fiona couldn't see the top of it, but by straining against the ceiling of her cage, she spied Nicolosia in their own cage across the room. It seemed more fortified with black metal bars all around. Could she find a chance to free them before Dani made it up here?

"Nicolosia!" Fiona whispered urgently.

The Elder druid didn't respond.

"They can't speak right now," Dani said, coming up the stairs into the room. Cracking red and golden yellow leaves swept around her feet and laid a carpeted path for her. As she stopped near the round table, the leaves swept up and settled around her body, attaching themselves to the lace collar of her cloak. She looked as if she was heading out for an evening show in the colors of her nature. "They didn't quite agree with my plan in the end. I thought it would go another way, but"—she sighed and glanced at Nicolosia—"they always put duty before love."

"That *is* love. For more than simply you. The safety of the Book is much more important than all of us. This is our home."

Daniele pursed her lips at Fiona but turned away, ignoring her and focusing on the hidden contents of the table. Fiona pushed against the branches again, trying to see what the fae was doing. If Daniele thought she could still be useful to her, then it meant she had a plan for her and Nicolosia. A scheme to open the Book by breaking Spine, going by the message to the Emperor.

Fiona called out, "What is your plan exactly? If you don't mind my asking, since I'm rather at your mercy. I am interested in just what you and Stella were trying to accomplish."

"We work to free us all, of course." She ripped something on the table, like tearing parchment, though there was nothing in her hands. The leaves on her body quivered and then settled. Dani slipped on a silver bracelet and then moved to the other side of the table and picked up a quill.

"Destroying so many people's lives in the process. Who gave you the right to make that choice for everyone?"

"Who gave *her* the right?" Dani spat out. "I can't leave." She motioned out the window. "They can't stay. We shouldn't have to be subjugated to live our lives as that 'deity' wants."

There was a dot of understanding that hit home for Fiona. "But you and I both know forcing others into your plot isn't the right way to change Larrakane's claim on us." Raina's words echoed back to Fiona and she grasped at the bars, pressing closer. "If we want change, we should be working to fight whoever Larrakane is defending against. When she can change, the Book can change. Our situation as page turners can change." If it was Richard's brother who brought the danger, then they should be fighting him. Not each other.

Daniele threw her quill down and snorted loudly. "Don't be naive, Fiona. She'll never allow us to be free of her needs. We are her creation." She picked up a small copper bracelet from the table and slid it onto her wrist. "No, we must make other avenues, other allies, if we're to choose our own fate."

Fiona's eyes crinkled as she watched Daniele. The fae wanted out of being a Leaf—of being a page turner altogether. If Larrakane couldn't or wouldn't give it to her, was there someone who could? Did she have access to knowledge that could let her change? She seemed so confident. But who would have that kind of power? A tightness crossed over Fiona's chest as she realized. "Is that what he told you?"

Dani's head snapped toward Fiona. "What did you say?"

She didn't know that Fiona had inside knowledge. She didn't know about Richard. Fiona could use this to her advantage. "How did he get to you?"

Dani's face flushed as she took a step closer. "Have you heard him too?"

Fiona wet her lips, trying to recall what scant information Richard had given and what she'd gleaned from Queen Eleanor's memory to piece together a response. Perhaps if she could get Daniele to believe she had heard of this person, it would draw more time until the Seasons arrived. "Through words."

The fae knelt gingerly beside Fiona's cage. She swallowed and tilted her head, watching her. "If you can hear him, why do you fight for her?"

"I don't fight for Larrakane." Fiona leaned in. "I work for all of us. So that we can have a life of freedom to do the things we desire."

A slow smile spread on Dani's face. "Then we're on the same side."

"We want the same things. Through creative means we can solve this." Fiona stretched out her hand to the fae through the branches.

Dani bit her lip, frowning. Then she shook her head and leaned back from the cage. "No. Only through her destruction can this end." She rose to her feet, standing over Fiona.

Her throat tightening, Fiona fell back against the bars. "But why?" Why did it have to be Larrakane's ruin, other people's misery, to solve this? There had to be another way, but perhaps Dani was too far down the road to hear her out.

Dani sagged against the table. "Because we deserve more than to be bound here in Larrakane's domain for her needs, under *her* choice of leadership. Destroying the Book frees us."

"And that puts us where, Daniele?" the Binder's voice boomed out of the horizon. Gusts of aching-cold wind burst through the window, and on it rode the snow-colored fae. "I can't believe it. I had earnestly hoped it wasn't you." He dropped to the floor and grabbed Daniele by the shoulder. "Where could you possibly go that she would not be? She is all."

Dani tore herself away from him and leapt back toward Fiona's cage. "Soon enough she will be nothing. The pages will part and us along with them. We will go to our homes and live out the lives we want."

In the distance there was a spark of shimmery gold light flitting toward them. If it was Mac, then perhaps they had a plan to deal with Dani.

Fiona shouted to distract the Autumn fae, "What could you possibly have in Copper that would be better than Spine?"

"The life I was born to," Dani said.

"Selfish," the Binder said. Ice crystals whipped out from him toward Dani, encasing her. "You haven't changed."

There was a cracking sound and then the ice broke apart. Fiona closed her eyes as small shards showered her. How had Dani broken the Binder's encasing just like that?

Dani didn't move or even acknowledge the ice. "Selfish? I'm not the one who turned his back on the very people he was supposed to protect. All for the love of someone who just uses you for her own ends."

The Binder shook his head, spiked white hair quivering violently. "You know nothing. You would bring in another who would rule us all for your life back."

"He is better than Larrakane. He has promised to release us from this prison," Dani said. "Or has *Harmony* told you differently? You barely know her, and yet you choose her over us!"

A beam of warm light moved through the window and encased Daniele. But then ash-gray flames licked at it and it evaporated into nothingness.

Dani crossed her arms. "Glad to see you could join us, Mac."

"Dani, stop." Mac wringed her hands, glancing between the two. As if making up her mind, she nodded to herself and stepped between them. "We weren't meant to use our power against each other."

"No, *you* weren't meant to. I am the change of seasons. I embrace them all."

"Enough," the Binder said. He raised his hands as if to attack Dani but stopped. He seemed somewhat frozen in place.

"I dissolved the wards of this place when I brought in Nic. As soon as you used your power on me, Arc, you lost. Or did you forget how the crowns were created?" Dani held out her hand with the stacked bracelets dangling from her arm. "I bind you, Archae Albergotti Fiaschi, first." Branching vines with lush verdant leaves spun quickly from the bracelets, and with a flick of her wrist she encased the form of the Binder from head to toe. He swayed but then toppled to the ground, the vegetation of his wrapped body softening his thudding fall.

The bracelets, of course. She had transformed the crowns into easier tools. But there were only three. Where was the fourth? Better yet, perhaps without all three, Mac could overpower her. If Dani moved closer, Fiona could grab them.

"You didn't take the crowns to break the Book," Fiona said loudly, trying to draw attention from the fae. "Was it just to go against the Seasons?" She reached slowly through the bars.

"If they could all stand against me, I would lose. Even a solid strategy needs a backup." Dani dropped her hands. "I'm sorry, Marcela. You should go."

Mac glanced at Fiona but then back to Dani. "Dani, please. Don't do this." Mac took a step toward her from the windowsill, ethereal blue robes flowing in the wind. "We can make it right."

Dani shook her head, holding her place against the bars. She said quietly, "We weren't meant to stand still. Let me go."

Mac pressed in. "Please, I don't want to hurt you."

"And I don't want to hurt you." Dani's voice was thick with emotion.

Fiona grabbed the bracelets through the bars, yanking hard trying to remove them.

Dani struggled but Mac wrapped her arms around her, pulling her away. Fiona managed to grab two of the bracelets off her arm. She held them tight. There. Without them Mac could overpower her.

The ochre fae broke out of Mac's grasp. "You won't stop me. I'm going home."

With a quickness that seemed like a hazy blur, Mac raised her arms and a cascade of warmth and golden light emanated from her. She reached out to Dani. "Please."

With only the silver bracelet left, Dani hurriedly flung up a wall of ice between her and Mac, but it melted just as fast.

The rays increased, amber light cascading through the small room. Hot, hazy humidity had sweat dripping down Fiona's neck. It made her want to stretch out and laze around, too hot to contemplate doing anything.

Dani took a step back, scrubbing a hand over her face. She squeezed her eyes shut. "Marcela Aurica Caragiale, I bind you." The bronze and lace collar on her cloak tightened around her own neck. Red and gold leaves swirled from Dani's dress toward the Summer fae. As they passed Mac, they began to crack and fade.

Mac clutched her throat, and the warm amber light abruptly cut off as she fell to her knees gasping.

Fiona had been wrong. Dani had kept the most important crown with her the whole time. She reached out toward Mac's unconscious form. "Stop it!" Fiona shouted. "You're hurting her."

"I know." Dani fell back against the window and dropped her face into her hands. "But what's done is done."

Fiona pushed against the bars. She had the bracelets still clutched in her hands, but that didn't seem to matter. They felt like nothing. "They're your friends."

"No. They're my family." Dani waved her hands, and the bars of Fiona's cage decayed into ash on the ground. "And my home. But setting us all free is more important than anything. I know you agree."

"Why are you letting me go?" Fiona stayed still, wary of Dani's change in demeanor.

"I'm giving you a choice. With the Seasons here I have more than I need to move on. And the crowns, well, they were never meant to be weapons." She slid off the silver cuff and tossed it on the ground. It shattered. She bent toward the unconscious Mac and placed a hand on her chest. She grimaced but a large gust of wind pushed Mac from the ground toward the cage of Nicolosia. "The city will be destroyed soon. Regardless of what you think of me, I do care about the people of Spine. Page turners and non-turners alike. You can either warn everyone and begin evacuating, or you can stay here and try to stop me from going. You can't do both."

Fiona glanced out the window toward the buildings in the far horizon. The other pages had come apart in a few days. How long would Spine last? Larrakane had built it to hold the Book together, but that didn't make the place invincible. She swallowed hard, heartbeat racing at Daniele's chilly confidence. With a tentative step backward, Fiona kept her eyes on the fae as she trudged toward the top of the stairs. "This isn't over. You know that."

Dani carefully opened Nic's black metal cage and ushered the vine-wrapped Arc inside, barely glancing at Fiona. "Perhaps, but it will take awhile for you to amass an army who can outnumber the Painted Edge. You'll find the Followers and the Travel Guild jackets indisposed."

Images of Fali and Dodger flashed through her mind, and Fiona gripped the wall, steadying herself. "What did you do to them?"

Dani patted the bars of the Seasons' cage. "A little bit of this goes a long way. Just enough in the aqueducts and a fashionable new drink to temporarily block the page turning *curse* in most people." She summoned another gust of wind that encased the cage, floating it aloft. Dani threw open her cloak and pressed her hand on a vivid blue bar tattoo that materialized across the gray circle of Larrakane on her chest. "Goodbye, Fiona. May we never have to meet again."

Pain blossomed in Fiona's chest over her own mark of Larrakane. She groaned, stumbling toward the door as a whirlwind began to take shape around Dani. The fingers of wind crooked toward Fiona, trying to pull her in, but she clung to the wall and pushed herself through the archway onto the stairs. She ran dizzyingly down them away from the increasing hollow sound of the unnatural gale. As she burst through the bottom door, a wrenching cracking like a massive tree falling pierced her ears. The top of the windmill tore off, sucked into the whirlwind. Gold and russet leaves, yellow stalks of corn, and brown roots ripped into the air from the surrounding land. Head covered, Fiona dashed through the storm until she broke free from its pull.

Arms outstretched to the sky, Dani stood at the top of the rubble of the windmill. The freezing-cold whirlwind circled around until daggers of ice rippled out of the maelstrom and flung in all directions. A bright light pulsed into the storm, eclipsing Dani and the rest of the caged Seasons. Sweet floral notes of jasmine and honeysuckle perfumed the area, permeating the nightmare in a clashing wave.

Fiona held her breath and stumbled back on the dirt path. She had to give it one more try. She needed to get through to her. "Dani, please! I can help you."

Dani stared down at Fiona and then past her, dismissively. With a jerk the fae pulled the sky toward her ripping the world like a thin page. Mountainous shards of stone and immense crusts of ice jutted out from the ragged sides of this new torn doorway.

Fiona couldn't see Dani anymore. Nor the Seasons or anything beyond the chaos of the shifting weather and the utter size of the world now imposing itself in Spine.

But Dani's whispered voice trailed into her ear as if she was right beside her: "I suggest you run."

The impossibility of the situation finally broke through to Fiona. There was no time to ponder or sate her curiosity about the how or whys of the situation. Spine only had a short time before breaking down just like the other pages. She had to gather those who could follow her and stop Dani. Her and the one who commanded her. Fiona swallowed and rushed through what was left of the farm fields toward the path that would lead into the city.

Sounds from the torn page trailed after her, causing her to cover her ears. Loud roaring, like an untamed beast being prodded, overwhelmed her. Fiona bolted, stumbling over rocks, an innate sense of fear dripping into her from the primal bellows. She had to be faster if she was to outrun the destruction Dani had so confidently promised.

With a snap the sound vanished. Leaves fell around her as the wind abruptly died too. Fiona dropped her hands from her ears but kept moving through the still, quiet world, not turning back. She didn't need to. The page had been turned and Dani had left, taking most of the Leaves of Spine with her. That was always the choice she was going to make, wasn't it? With a heavy chest and unabashed tears, Fiona ran.

If you enjoyed *Frayed Edges*, spread the word by writing a review! Reviews really help my books get into the right hands, so I'm super grateful for every single one.

Not only will you get me in your inbox with news and giveaways, you'll also receive The Planar Pages prequel HIDDEN WORDS

About *HIDDEN WORDS*

Life flourishes in the Book, a world of stacked realms spanning the ages. Those who can travel between them are page turners, blessed with the power to go from one page to the next.

For investigator Fiona Thorne, turning the page is normal life. Solving mysteries is where the excitement lives. No case is too small to ignite her curiosity, no page too familiar to explore.

Hired by her charming, gossipy neighbor to track down a shipment of rare books, Fiona thinks it'll be easy. She'll search for clues, sort out the issue, and be back in time for her nightly cup of coffee. And her reward? An introduction to one of the most reclusive leaders in Spine, the Druid Elder.

But that dream slips through her fingers as she realizes there's little evidence. She'll have to kick this investigation into high gear if she wants to impress her neighbor and earn her way into a privileged connection.

You can only read HIDDEN WORDS by signing up online for my newsletter at www.dhalerambo.com/newsletter/

Glossary of The Planar Pages series

Find expanded lore, world information and more at
https://go.dhalerambo.com/tpp

Spine: A realm connected to every page in the Book. All page turners live here and can suffer ill effects for being gone too long. Split into over a dozen districts.

Eight Known Pages (as stacked in the Book)

Elemental Chapter

Blaze: page of fire, contains salamanders, flarions, ragnis, and other fire elementals

Depths: page of water, contains water elementals, merfolk, turtles, and more

Mistral: page of air, contains sylphs and other air elementals

Cobbles: page of earth, contains gnomes and other earth elementals

Mortal Chapter

Restless Rise (Rise): page of humans, contains a central mountain with floating islands all round it

Kerus: page of smilodon, elephas, and ursidon

Court of Copper (Court): page of faekin: fairies, fae, fauns, centaurs, and nymphs
Phyta: page of plant and fungi creatures

<u>Terms</u>

Aer: language from page of air, Mistral
Aguan: language from the Depths

the Binder: leader of the Guild

the Book of Larrakane (the Book): all the known pages of the universe

bookmark: token from a page, used to travel there by a page turner

the Card: a free leaflet by the Travel Guild

the Church of Larrakane: organization devoted to worship of Larrakane

Claire: a language from page of fire, Blaze

Depth's Door: a lake in Spine

diamonnette paper (papers): universal currency

dusty: used to described a page turner who's ready to retire

elephas: like elephants standing on their hind legs, from Kerus

faekin: fauns, fairies, pixies, centaurs, all from the Court of Copper

flarion(s): fire elementals who live in pools of magma from page of fire, Blaze

the Followers: a subset of the Church of Larrakane

format: slang for rumor

the Gilded: six leaders in the Travel Guild

the Hinge: Travel Guild headquarters

inked: blessed by Larrakane with the ability to turn pages

the Inking: historic event that created page turners

jacket(s): slang for officers of the Guild

Kerus: one pages in the mortal chapter, home of the smilodon

>**Disas:** a continent containing:
>>**Nix Urbis**
>
>**Ozen:** a continent containing:
>>**Roma Tykar**

Siamor: a continent containing:

> **Roma Mikar:** desert city between Nymar and Valar, home of the Mei'kar

> **Roma Nymar:** pagemark to the Caseo district, sea town, home of the Nyx'mir people

> **Roma Valar:** Roma capital

Kerusian: someone from Kerus

Larrakane (she/her): bestows the ability to turn pages and creator of the Book

the Leaves of Spine (a Leaf): group of protectors/leaders

Marbled: a title at the Travel Guild

Mikar: nation in Kerus

Nivalon: nation of ice ursidon in Kerus

Nymar: nation in Kerus on Siamor

Nyx'mir: people from Nymar

pagemark(s): safe places where turners can move between pages

page turners (turners): people who can move between pages

the Painted Edge: a group of rippers marked by blue tattoos

Pestles and Mortar: smithy in the Spine

pulp: slang for creatures from various pages who are not page turners

ripper(s): slang for thieves and smugglers across pages

Roma Empire, Empire: smilodon war culture

Romas: people from the Empire

Schiflan: a language spoken from page of humans, Restless Rise

skimmer(s): slang for tourists visiting other pages

skips: slang for criminals on the run

smilodon(s): catlike people, from Kerus

Sod: language from page of earth, Cobbles

spotter(s): explorers and cartographers

sylph: stark white air creatures from page of air, Mistral

the Travel Guild, the Guild: organization that regulates all the comings and goings of page turners in the Book

Valar: Roma capital

Val'ere: people from Valar

Valerian: language of the Roma Empire (origin Valar)

unread turner: slang for someone new to being a page turner

ursidon: bearlike people, from Kerus

About the Author

D. HALE RAMBO IS a fantasy author whose books transport readers to wondrous worlds filled with magic, mystery, and humor. With compelling and memorable characters at the heart of her stories, Hale Rambo weaves tales to entertain and enthrall.

A lifelong storyteller, she's been writing and creating other worlds since she was old enough to mark them on her bedroom wall.

When she's not writing, you can find her enjoying a stiff cosmopolitan while reading mysteries alongside her favorite pet companion.

Discover more about her wondrous worlds, the versatility of gnomes, and fun fae cocktails at www.dhalerambo.com

Also by D. Hale Rambo

A SERIES OF DECISIONS ON KAIRAS

A completed cozy high fantasy trilogy set in the world of Kairas where the deities may be sealed away but their troubles are not.

Book 1, TOOLS OF A THIEF

How do you stop being a thief? Zizy Zakar assumed quitting her job, stealing from her boss, and teleporting hundreds of miles away was one way to give it a go.

Buy it now: teleport yourself to books2read.com/toat

Book 2, COMPONENTS OF A CASTER

Laysa has always vowed to do whatever it took to learn magic. Can Laysa keep her friends alive and survive uncovering the depths of the unknown? Does she have what it takes to be a Caster?

Buy it now: cast your coins at books2read.com/coac

Book 3, ROUTES OF A RANGER

A family under threat. A perilous journey home. Skinny has spent her life running from her past. Now she must achieve the destiny she was denied before she can defeat the enemy at her doorstep.

Buy it now: steer yourself towards go.dhalerambo.com/roar

THE PLANAR PAGES

A historical fantasy mystery series with investigator Fiona Thorne and her motley crew of friends.

Life flourishes in the Book, a world of stacked realms spanning the ages, like the pages of an epic chronicle. Those who can travel through them are page turners; blessed with the power to go from one page to the next. For investigator Fiona Thorne, being a Turner is normal life. Solving mysteries is where the excitement lives.

Book 0, HIDDEN WORDS (newsletter exclusive prequel)

Cases are ramping up in the Spine and Fiona is in the middle of the action. Hired by her charming, gossipy neighbor to track down a shipment of rare books, Fiona thinks it'll be a piece of work.

Read it for FREE by signing up for my newsletterat go.dhalerambo.com/freestory

Book 1, BETWEEN THE LINES

Blaze, the page of fire, is wasting away. Fire elementals are being smuggled out in waves, but by whom? Fiona is on the job and nothing will hold her, not even the overbearing Travel Guild.

Read BETWEEN THE LINES and buy it now at: go.dhalerambo.com/tppbtl

Book 2, HARD BOUND

Someone has stolen from the Court of Copper, the illustrious fae page nestled within the Book. Is it a member of the fractured counsel, the fabled Order of Seven, or could the thief be much closer to Fiona than she realizes?

The fae realm is only a step away. BUY HARD BOUND at: go.dhalerambo.com/tpphb

Book 3, PRESSED

Between the tangled politics of home and facing her overbearing mother, Fiona counts herself lucky the yearly attendance with Queen Brilliance is only for a few days. But this year, the Queen presses Fiona with an unexpected request—find the mythical Guardian of Restless Rise. Amid schemes and betrayals, Fiona must piece together palace intrigues and myths to discover if the Guardian truly exists.

Join the investigation. BUY PRESSED at go.dhalerambo.com/tpppressed